Seeking Father Khaliq

Seeking Father Khaliq

by
William Peace

Strategic Book Publishing and Rights Co.

Strategic Book Publishing and Rights Co., LLC
USA | Singapore
www.sbpra.com

For information about special discounts for bulk purchases please contact Strategic Book Publishing and Rights Co. Special Sales at bookorder@sbpra.net.

ISBN: 978-1-68181-800-9

Table of Contents

Chapter 1

Princess Basheera

"May I ask you, honored Professor al-Busiri, if you will go to meet Princess Basheera?"

I looked up reluctantly from the student essay I was reading and considered the bearing of the woman who had entered my office unannounced. She was tall and slender, graceful; she was motionless, but there was a suggestion of incipient mobility. She was dressed in a black naqib and a jilbab so that I could see only her dark eyes. Her voice, however, had an optimistic lilt to it. She must be about thirty, I thought.

Deliberately, I pushed the essay to one side. "Who, may I ask, is Princess Basheera?"

"She is my employer, sir."

"And what does this Princess Basheera want with me?"

"She has an assignment that only you can fulfill, Professor."

This is very strange. A young woman comes into my office at (I glanced at my watch) two thirty-six in the afternoon and asks me to meet with a Princess Basheera (glad tidings), about whom I know nothing, to undertake an assignment, about which I also know nothing, but which, it is said, only I can undertake.

I closed my fountain pen, thinking for a moment. "Can you give me a reason, madam, why I should say 'yes' to your request? I have a full afternoon of work ahead of me, and I cannot afford the time to discuss university business. That should be pursued through the office of administration."

1

The woman nodded. "I can assure you, Professor al-Busiri, this has nothing to do with university business. Nor does Princess Basheera wish to sell you any product or service. The assignment is related to your status as a renowned professor of philosophy."

This sounds like an approach for a consultancy assignment, but when was the last time, Kareem, that you were given a paid assignment in philosophy?

"Where am I to meet with this Princess Basheera?"

"Sir, you may inquire for her at the Kempinski Nile Hotel."

The Kempinski Nile is a five-star hotel. She must be a person of importance. "What, may I ask, is her family name?"

"Her family name is Chagma (wisdom), but she is well known at the Kempinski."

"And at what time will she be expecting me?"

"If you will kindly tell me, Professor al-Busiri, when it is convenient for you, I will inform Princess Basheera, and she will know to expect you."

I consulted my watch again, and opened my leather-bound diary. I have no classes until 8:30 in the morning. However, I must see Hadad about this unfortunate essay at 3, and then at 4 I have sophomore student Quraishi, who wants to study the great philosopher Ibn Rushd.

I leaned back in my creaking, antique chair and considered the slowly-turning paddles on the ceiling fan. Well, I am curious. Who is this Princess Basheera, and what does she want with me? A 'yes' will satisfy my curiosity and may bring an unknown reward. A 'no' avoids the risk. What risk? Perhaps I can spare a couple of hours. "I could be at the Kempinski at about six – depending on the traffic."

"Very good, Professor, I will inform Princess Basheera."

The woman bowed and disappeared.

* * *

Anpu Hadad rose from his seat opposite my desk. He was a slim, clean-shaven youth dressed in jeans and a red and blue-striped Barcelona football shirt: across the front it said 'Qatar Airways'. "I am sorry, Professor, I will try to do better." His hangdog manner was in stark contrast to that of his hero, Lionel Messi.

"Hadad, I have told you many times that philosophy is not about being hafiz (learning the Qur'an by heart) in some madrassah. It involves independent, critical thought. It is about challenging what you have been told, what you understand, and what you see. You cannot present me with an essay in which you merely quote the positions of various thinkers on a topic! You must take a position of your own! You must employ logic in your commentaries. You must think; you must reason!"

"Yes, I understand, Professor."

"Sit down, Hadad!" I pointed at a page in the open essay on my desk. "Here, you say that Socrates and Plato believed that a democracy will degenerate into tyranny."

"Yes. It is in the Republic. They say that tensions within the social and political structure will lead the common people to seek the protection of a demagogue whose eventual corruption by power will lead to tyranny."

"You have been reading the Republic as a political essay. It might also have been written as an allegory, or as a model of philosophical inquiry." I considered the demeanor of my crestfallen student. "Tell me, Hadad, how much of your thinking about the philosophy of politics is influenced by what you have seen here in Cairo of the so-called 'Arab Spring'?"

"Well, Professor, I am concerned that such a demagogue may arise from the Muslim Brotherhood, and Egypt will slide into tyranny."

"And so you see your essay as a kind of warning against the slide into tyranny?"

Hadad gave a slight concessionary nod. "I hadn't thought of it that way, Professor, but I suppose so."

3

"I am concerned that your essay is more in the realm of political science than philosophy. Do you wish to change departments within the university?"

"No. No, Professor, I like philosophy. It makes me think, and I am greatly impressed by the philosophers we have studied." He paused, looking down at his leather sandals. "And I have learned a lot . . . listening to you."

I considered my student for several moments. "Hadad, I suggest that you select a different topic for your dissertation – something more abstract than politics – something like free will, or the nature of the human soul. Pick a philosopher whose thinking on the topic you select attracts you. Then, using your own analytical thinking, move the topic forward." Hadad nodded and gave an awkward involuntary bow. "When you have selected your new topic, come back and see me."

I believed that Anpu Hadad was capable of independent thought, but like so many young people today, he was caught up in immediacy and perceived wisdom. I must teach him how to ask the awkward questions and how to seek uncomfortable answers!

Mairisha Quraishi was not really – as I sometimes thought – scatter-brained; it was more that she gave the impression of being disorganized. She dropped the olive drab backpack which had been slung over one shoulder on the floor beside her chair. She began to rummage through the various compartments. "Sorry, Professor, I just want to find this book by Ibn Rushd."

I glanced at my watch and leaned forward, as if my familiarity with Ibn Rushd would help me spot the book.

"I'm sure I have it here somewhere." She looked up apologetically and brushed a wayward wisp of brown hair behind her dark blue hijab (head scarf). Her face had even, pleasing features; her lips shone with pink gloss. Frustrated, she picked up the satchel, set it on her knees, and began to search more diligently.

"Never mind, Quraishi, let's just talk about Ibn Rushd."

"Oh. Yes, Professor." She dumped the backpack onto the floor, brushed some imaginary dust off her jeans, and took a deep breath to compose her thoughts. "I think Ibn Rushd was wrong."

"In which of his works do you think he was mistaken, Quraishi?"

"The Decisive Treatise, Professor.

"And in what do you find him mistaken?"

"He says that philosophy contains nothing which is opposed to Islam."

I smiled. "Tell me more."

"Well, some of the German philosophers, for example, Schopenhauer and Nietzsche, were very critical of religion. Nietzsche said 'God is dead' and Schopenhauer said that philosophy is a science and has no articles of faith."

I was amused. "So you're thinking of refuting a twelfth century Islamic philosopher – Ibn Rushd – with the work of eighteenth philosophers who were critical of Christianity?"

For a moment, she chewed the inside of her cheek. "I wasn't thinking of refuting." Her dark eyes were full of concern. "Well, Professor, it's just that I think it is possible for philosophy to contain something which is opposed to Islam."

"Can you give me an example, Quraishi?"

"The Qur'an says, 'Man is truly created anxious: he is fretful when misfortune touches him.'"

"Yes, it is in The Ways of Ascent."

She nodded. "But I think it is possible for a philosopher to assert that the anxieties of man are learned, not created; the anxieties are the result of nurture, not nature."

I smiled. "And are your anxieties learned rather than created?"

She shifted in her chair. "I'm not sure about me, but I have observed my sister's children from the time they were born, and none of them was born with any anxieties."

"Were they not anxious about being fed?"

"When they were hungry, they were uncomfortable. They weren't fearful or doubtful about being fed. That would come much later – when, for example, they were on a long trip."

"So you think that our anxieties are learned – not part of our nature."

"Yes. We learn to be anxious about important events which are in doubt. But it takes some logical processing to recognize – from prior experience – that the event may or may not happen."

"Could that recognition not be instinctive, and therefore part of our nature?"

"But Professor, instinct, by definition, involves no logic, whereas assessing the probability of a particular outcome requires thought."

"Tell me, Quraishi, how did Ibn Rushd come to the conclusion that philosophy contains nothing that is contrary to Islam?"

"He said that two truths cannot contradict one another. One kind of truth is scriptural and the other is demonstrative, by which I suppose he meant the application of pure logic."

I nodded. "Did Ibn Rushd mention any exceptions to his assertion that two truths cannot contradict?"

"Yes, he said that if the apparent meaning of scripture conflicts with demonstrated conclusions, the scripture should be interpreted metaphorically."

"Isn't that possible in this case?"

"No. I don't think so."

"Perhaps a metaphorical interpretation is that man is an anxious creature."

"But that isn't what the scripture says, Professor. It says 'truly created'. To me, this implies that God created us to be anxious. I don't believe He did. I believe He created an uncertain world, which causes us to be anxious."

"You have other examples of philosophy which is opposed to Islam?" She nodded.

For some moments I considered the paddles of the ceiling fan. "You know, Quraishi, if you proceed with this dissertation and it falls into the public domain – as inevitably it will – you will be accused of attacking a central belief of Islam: that the Qur'an is the word of God. Goodness knows what that would lead to."

She nodded. "There are at least two possibilities. First, philosophy is an assertion of truth; it is not necessarily truth itself. For example, I can't prove that anxiety is not an original part of human nature. It's just that I've seen evidence that it's not what we're born with. Therefore, my philosophy is that anxiety is learned, not created. Second, God did not actually write the Qur'an. He had the archangel Gabriel pass the words to the Prophet. And we know that the Prophet did not immediately write the words. In fact, we don't know who did write the words, except that they were recited by the Prophet, and . . ."

I held up my hand. "I know where you're going on your second point, Quraishi, and I wouldn't go there. It could be very dangerous!"

Mairisha Quraishi gave a concessionary shrug. "I am a good Muslim, Professor. I believe in Allah and the Prophet. I live by the Five Pillars of Islam, and the Qur'an is my guide. I just don't believe that the Qur'an is exactly the words of God."

After a moment, I said, "I think it would be better not to announce the last bit publicly, in writing. You may find yourself the subject of an unpleasant fatwa." She nodded. I leaned back in my chair and studied the ceiling fan for a long moment. "I think your suggested topic is suitable for a dissertation as long as you stay on the philosophical, rather than the spiritual, side of the fence. I would like to see your outline. . ." I consulted my diary. "…this time next week."

She reached down to pick up her knapsack. As she lifted it awkwardly, several books fell out, including a collection of the

7

writings of Ibn Rushd. "I knew it was here somewhere. Thank you, Professor." She gave a slight bow. "Next week then."

I spent several moments gazing at the door through which she departed. She is certainly not a stupid girl. She's capable of original thinking, although perhaps she doesn't follow her thoughts to their logical conclusion. And it has to be said that she's not always well prepared. But she has courage – perhaps a little too much courage. What I must do is teach her to be more mindful of risk – intellectual risk – and how it can arise when we don't anticipate it. How does she manage risk in her daily life? I shrugged. But these are mostly obvious risks. She is a rather beautiful girl. Actually, by the shape of her she's a woman. . . . I wonder how she and Shakil (handsome), my brother's oldest son, would get along. Certainly, he would find her attractive, but would her independent mind scare him off? Maybe she's not prepared to think of marriage – or maybe she's already betrothed. . . . Marriage is not high on his agenda – though it's time it should be. . . . Maybe I'll make quiet inquiries into her family.

* * *

Just after 5, I got into my three-year-old Honda Civic and drove west off the new campus of the American University in Cairo toward central Cairo. I don't particularly like the new campus, built on what had been desert and opened in 2008. Yes, it has a collection of modern stone buildings, its gardens give the feeling of a welcome oasis, and the students are very fond of 'New Cairo'. But for me, the old, crowded Tahrir Square campus at the heart of Cairo is more expressive of what AUC is: an excellent liberal institution in a non-Western setting.

But I had no choice: the entire philosophy department was moved from Tahrir Square to the new Liberal Arts complex in 2009.

I don't really have much to complain about. I'm a ten-ured, full professor with the best university in Egypt. Some would say that Cairo University is more authentic. Maybe. But it has a quarter of a million students. How can one teach and learn in a place like that? It's like feeding pigeons. Cairo is a public university. Pay is lower; facilities are out of date. Worst of all: they have no philosophy department! And then there's al-Azhar University, the second oldest in the world and the leading institution for Islamic thought. But it is riven with political and religious tug-of-wars. I'm better off where I am.

* * *

I did not park in the Kempinski garage. I am – among other things – a frugal man. I parked in the public garage on Ahmed Raghab Street. There! I've saved at least ten pounds (Egyptian = $1.50). Outside the garage, a small, dirty child was sitting in her mother's lap on the sidewalk. I do not usually respond to street beggars. I feel that too often they become dependent on addic-tive, misused gifts rather seeking honest pay. But there was a look of genuine pathos in that child's eyes and I dropped a one pound coin into her outstretched palm.

* * *

At the concierge's desk, I stated, "I believe I have an appoint-ment with Princess Basheera Chagma."

The concierge was wearing a dark jacket, grey vest and striped cravat; he seemed like a fugitive from a film set. He frowned doubtfully. "Your name, sir?"

"I am Professor Kareem al-Busiri."

The concierge picked up his telephone and turned away, as if his attention had been diverted elsewhere. But the effect was that what he said on the telephone was inaudible. I waited; the concierge listened and spoke.

"Miss Basheera will meet you over there." He gestured toward the carpeted lounge area in earth colors with its scattering of low tables and comfortable sofas. "Please be good enough to take a seat."

"I'm afraid I have never met Princess Basheera."

"I'm sure she'll introduce herself, sir."

I reached into the breast pocket of my grey suit. "Thank you very much. Can you tell me . . ." There was a five pound note in my hand. "Is Miss Basheera a Saudi princess?"

The concierge whisked the note away as if it were an annoying insect. "Perhaps, or perhaps Jordanian or Lebanese, and, as I'm sure you know, Professor, we had our own royalty here some years ago."

"Yes. Yes, of course. So you can't be more specific?"

"I have not had sight of the lady's passport, sir."

I took a seat at one end of a couch upholstered in a desert tapestry. Here, I could observe much of the traffic through the lobby. The guests were diverse, but universally wealthy. Men, many with brief cases, moving purposefully in suits and open-necked shirts in recognition of the heat and humidity. Women, at a more leisurely pace, conscious of their surroundings and their own expensive (or shrouded) attire. I watched and waited. How will she know me? Will she inquire at the concierge?

But from the direction of the elevators, a figure was striding purposefully toward me. It was a woman. She was wearing long, black voluminous trousers, a knee-length, black silk jacket and a midnight blue niqab which covered all but her eyes. She was tall – perhaps 1.8 meters, and she moved fluidly, with assurance. "Thank you, Professor al-Busiri, for coming to meet with me." She did not offer her hand; instead, she sat at the far end of the couch, obliquely facing me. I noticed that two other people – apparently un-introduced associates of this woman –

sat in chairs opposite. There was a young man in a dark suit and an open white shirt, a notebook in his lap and a pen in his hand. There was also a woman, all in black with only her brown eyes visible.

"It is a pleasure to meet you, Princess Basheera."

"Would you like tea or coffee, Professor?"

"I prefer tea at this hour."

Princess Basheera glanced at the man in the dark suit, who gestured for a waiter.

"Thank you again, Professor." She turned slightly toward me. I could see her eyes now that they were fixed on me; they were large, cocoa-colored, with a glistening central light. She spoke Classic Arabic, softly, deliberately. It's as if she grew up in a family of language purists; I can't hear a regional accent or trace of dialect. "You are, I believe, quite a distinguished professor of philosophy," she continued, "and you have a broad understanding of the topic."

"Yes, I teach a course in ancient Greek philosophy, and two courses each in Western and Arabic philosophy. I am familiar with the writings of the principal oriental philosophers, but as yet, we have no demand for a class in eastern thinking."

"Excellent! And the university is about to begin the summer holiday?"

"Yes, the summer solstice will soon be upon us."

"Forgive me, Professor, but do you have plans for your holiday?"

"I have a small flat near the beach in Al Jamiah – west of Alexandria. I go there to read and to consider."

She nodded. "To consider . . ." It was almost a question.

"As you say, Princess, I am a philosopher."

"Ah, yes." She leaned toward me slightly. "And I understand the beach at Al Jamiah is very popular."

"Perhaps so, but I go there only in the early morning or late afternoon, when it is less crowded."

She nodded and brushed the sleeve of her jacket. "Professor, there is an important task for which I believe you are extremely well suited by your intellect, your knowledge, your experience and your character."

I paused for a moment. How can a task about which I know nothing suit me so well?

"What is this task, Princess?"

"Professor, do you know Father Khaliq?"

"No, I know no one by that name. Tell me: who is he?"

"His origins are somewhat uncertain, but he is someone dear to me."

"Is he your father then, Princess?"

"Yes, I believe he is."

"And what is it that you would like me to do with this Father Khaliq, Princess?"

"I would like you to find him."

A white-jacketed waiter set a silver tray with a porcelain tea service on the table. Basheera poured tea into a cup and handed it to me. "Do you take milk, Professor?"

"No thank you, but may I have some sweetener?"

She offered me a bowl filled with sachets.

"You mention my experience, Princess, but I have no experience finding people who are lost."

"When I speak of experience, Professor, I was not referring to any experience you may have as a detective. Rather, I was referring to your life experience: to what one might call 'wisdom'."

"Oh, I see." (I didn't at all, so I cast about for a clarifying question.) "Yes. So you want me to find this Father Khaliq, who has, more or less, gone missing?"

"In a general sense, that is true."

"Where is he then?"

"This is the problem. It isn't exactly clear."

"If it isn't clear to me, how I can help you?"

The corners of her eyes creased with her invisible smile. "I think you are a man of great wisdom and intuition. I feel certain that you can find Father Khaliq."

"Perhaps so, but I have no idea where to start looking."

"Professor, have you ever taken the Hajj?"

"No, but I intend to do so. Perhaps next year."

"I think that the Hajj is an excellent place to start."

"So you think that Father Khaliq will be on the Hajj?"

"Yes, I feel sure he will be."

"But Princess, there are more than three million people on the Hajj. How can one possibly find an unknown person?"

"Do you believe in being open to possibilities, Professor?"

"Yes, of course."

"I believe this openness, your wisdom and intuition will yield the clues you are seeking."

"But can you tell me what Father Khaliq looks like?"

"I have never seen him."

"And about how old he is?"

"He is said to be very old."

I leaned back on the couch and sipped my tea thoughtfully. "Forgive me, Princess, but am I wrong to consider that there is reward of some sort attached to this search?"

"There is indeed reward, Professor."

I opened my wallet and withdrew a personal check. Tearing it in half I handed it to the princess. She made a chucking sound with her tongue. "Shame on you, Professor! I have neither the inclination nor the skill to forge your signature!"

I felt embarrassed. "Sorry. I thought I was just being prudent, and I thought you would like to know my bank details in the event my search is successful."

"Prudent perhaps, but what is missing is trust. You must trust me, Professor, if you are to find Father Khaliq."

"Yes, I apologize, Princess. How can I contact you if I find Father Khaliq?"

She turned toward the man in the grey suit, who gave her a business card which she passed to me. I looked at the card: 'Princess Basheera Chagma +20 109 643 0712'-- nothing more. "This is an Egyptian mobile number."

"Yes. That is my Egyptian contact number." She rose from the sofa and bowed slightly. "It was a pleasure to meet you Professor al-Busiri, and I wish you success in your search."

She turned and strode away, the man and woman following her.

For a moment, I considered going to the registration desk to make inquiries about Princess Basheera Chagma. But I shook my head. If this were a two star hotel, a little baksheesh (bribe) might do it, but in the five star Kempinski Nile, there is not a chance.

* * *

I am, intrinsically, a curious individual, particularly when I am placed in front of a mysterious situation: for me it becomes irresistible. In this regard, I remember my grandparents' house particularly. It was an imposing three-story building, of brown and tan brick, with cream castings of lion heads in what we used to call the 'Farouk Style'. My father's father, 'Papa Grand', was an enigmatic figure with white hair and an impressive matching moustache. Sometimes, he would sit my brother and me on either side and tell us fascinating but improbable stories about "Cairo long ago, when I was a boy". At other times he would be remote and taciturn. There was a room under the eaves on the third floor of that house, the door of which was always closed and locked. When I asked my father about it, he said, "That's none of your business, Kareem. That's Papa Grand's special room."

"What does he use it for?" I asked.

"That, also, is not your business."

Whenever I had an unobserved opportunity, I went up to see if the room might be unlocked. No. It was locked. This served to make me more determined to discover what was inside. Where would he keep the key? I wondered, and I decided that it would be in his bedroom dresser. One Saturday afternoon when we had finished the mid-day meal and the adults were still at the table, my brother and I were sitting in the living area reading our Black Scorpion action magazines. I put my copy down, gave notice of my need to use the toilet, and went upstairs. In my grandfather's room, I quietly slid open the drawers of his dresser and peered inside. In the second drawer, toward the back, there was a black leather box. I took it out and opened it. There, inside it, was a tarnished brass key. I put the box back and scurried up the back stairs to the mysterious door. My hand was trembling but I managed to turn the key, and the door swung open silently. Stepping inside, I closed the door behind me. Within the tiny room were a comfortable reclining chair, an antique wooden table, a wall cabinet and an argilah (hookah pipe). The argilah was tall, with an elaborate brass mid-section and a cloudy glass base; the pipe was resting on the table. I knew – even at the age of ten – that the argilah was used to smoke tobacco, but the pervasive odor in the room was stronger and sweeter than tobacco. On the table was a fragment like a piece of chocolate. When I picked it up, the smell was more intense. I opened the wall cabinet. On the shelves were small, rectangular packages wrapped in brown paper. I picked one up; on it, handwritten in pencil, it said hashish, and it gave the weight at eighty-four grams. So this was my grandfather's secret! He came up here to smoke hashish! I understood that he had to keep it a secret: all Muslims are forbidden to use any intoxicating substance. As I replaced the key in the box in Papa Grand's dresser, I felt considerable satisfaction in having solved the mystery. And until now, I have told no one of my discovery.

My attraction to the mystery that Princess Basheera presented felt similarly compelling: who was Father Khaliq, and why was I asked to find him? Then, too, there was the mystery of the Princess herself: who was she and what motivated her?

As I think about it now, I suppose my curiosity is what steered me into philosophy. For me it is the science of answering fundamental questions and solving life's mysteries.

* * *

I have a four-bedroom apartment in a residential section of New Cairo. As a traditionalist, I am not entirely at home there: it is too quiet and too modern. I much prefer the chaotic bustle of central Cairo, where I grew up: noisy, with the call of street vendors, and traffic horns, the air pungent with spices, and people: some drab, some colorful, in constant motion. There, too, was the old house with thick walls and high ceilings, pleasant in summer and cool in winter, where I lived with Elizabeth, my late American wife, for nearly twenty years. It was there that my two sons and a daughter had been born, and where I slept so many nights with Elizabeth. Elizabeth: may she rest with Allah. A reflex thought. I am mindful that she had not called Him 'Allah'; she had called Him 'God'. Whatever He is – if He is.

Elizabeth had come to Cairo as a Peace Corps volunteer – from Chicago – an idealist in love with humanity. She had stayed; she had learned Arabic; she went to work for the Red Crescent; she had taken a beginning-level course in Arabic philosophy at the American University. I was a doctoral student then, her instructor, and I had never met a student with such intellectual intensity – particularly a woman. What did she see in me then? My style was more cautious, more deliberate, more reliant on precedent. Hers was creative, chaotic, and fascinating. We spent hours in a coffee shop just off Tahrir Square jousting, debating, thinking. Then, one evening she asked me to come and appraise her skill in cooking Ful Medames (a national favorite bean dish). I protested that I couldn't possibly come to her apartment: what would people say? Her reputation would be ruined. She had shrugged. "Don't be silly." After dinner – she was a very good cook – she seduced me. At least I think the seduction was her plan: how could I – an ordinary-looking young Egyptian man – have thought to seduce a lovely, blonde American woman? She took me to Chicago, where she married me in a Methodist church. Before returning to Cairo, Elizabeth made sure I had an American passport. For 20 years we lived on Al Kobidan Street from which I could walk the half kilometer to the university.

I was amused when Elizabeth joined the Coptic Church. "Well," she said, "there is no Methodist church. I live in Egypt. There is a Coptic Christian Church nearby. I will become a Copt."

When Elizabeth died, there was a celebratory outpouring of grief and thanksgiving for her life at the small Coptic Church. I, who had never previously accompanied Elizabeth to the church, was very touched that she was so honored by people who were strangers to me, and I was startled by the naked religious fervor of the ceremony.

I am, I confess, an ambivalent Muslim. Frequently, I miss the morning prayer, or attend to it later in abbreviated fashion. When I am tired, the evening prayer might be short and early. I know there had been a Prophet Muhammad, and there might be an Allah – somewhere. During Ramadan, I keep a small, surreptitious bottle of water behind the files in my desk, and I am entirely observant of the prohibition of sexual intercourse during the day. I give to charity. Why, just that day, I gave to a beggar child near the Kempinski.

But I have never been on the Hajj, though I would plan to take the pilgrimage some time. Perhaps, when I'm a bit older. . . But now there is this assignment from Princess Basheera. . . It

will be bloody hot this time of year. . . . I don't want to go alone. . .
Perhaps someone will accompany me.

* * *

The ceiling fan in the living room was turning lazily when I
got home. There was a faint smell of garlic and coriander coming from the kitchen. I went to investigate and raised the lid on a
deep pan on the stove. Ah! It's that potato-lamb stew that Nane
has made for me, Wahida and Kalifa.

Nane is my housekeeper. She comes twice a week to clean,
do the laundry, and prepare some meals. Wahida is my daughter;
she is twenty-two and should be married by now: no boyfriend,
but a herd of friends – male and female. I say to her, "Wahida,
there is a certain student of mine who is from a good family. He
is going to join the family firm. You should meet him."

She says to me, "Papa, I am too young to get married. Mama
was twenty-three when she got married. There is time for that later!"

"But Wahida, you must not wait too long, or the men will
consider you past your sell-by date!"

"Did you consider Mama to be past her sell-by date?"

"No, but she was American, and this is Egypt."

"Phaaa! Egypt is changing, Papa, and you are not up to date!"

That may be true. I follow the trends in politics and econom-
ics, but for me, sociology is a bore.

Kalifa is my younger son, a traditionalist, much like me. He
is about to get his degree in physical science from American University, and his present ambition is to join the Egyptian Army.
Kalifa does not get along well with his older brother, Naqib,
who is an aspiring lawyer and politician, a secret member of the
Muslim Brotherhood. I also worry about Naqib: he is headstrong
and impatient; he lives with his wife, Anisa, who is six years
older and has two children of her own. I understand, though, that
Anisa is expecting again. (Hopefully, my son is the father.)

There was a gentle hum of the air conditioning from my bedroom. Wahida's bed had been made and her scattered clothing put away. There was that large poster of the Egyptian national football team in place of pride on Kalifa's wall: six red-shirted players behind five crouching colleagues, their green-shirted goal-tender in the center.

I like my home office, which used to be Wahida's bedroom, before Naqib left and bequeathed his room to her. Three walls are nearly packed, floor to ceiling, with books – mostly philosophical books in Arabic and English – a few in French or German, which I read with difficulty. There are assorted texts used by the university, reference books, some history, biographies, and psychological works. The only novels in my collection are from Elizabeth. Why would I want to read about something that isn't true?

The mahogany leather recliner chair and the antique walnut partner's desk provide all the comfort I need. And if I want to distract myself, I can watch the comings and goings of my neighbors outside the window.

I opted, as ever, for the stuffed armchair in the living room, from which I could greet my children on their return. I picked up a copy of the Al-Ahram (The Pyramids) newspaper, turned to the editorial and letters pages, and began to read.

I woke with a start when the front door closed noisily. There was a thump: Kalifa's backpack slid from his shoulder to the floor. "What's for dinner?"

"Nane made a potato-lamb stew."

Kalifa was a tall, slender young man; he has his mother's blue eyes and an almost feminine face. He flopped down onto the old leather sofa.

I said, "Tell me about your day."

"It was OK. We won the football game."

"What was the score?"

"Three – two."

"Did you play the whole game?"

"Yeah, but we should have just tied. The ref made a mistake."

"What mistake did he make?"

"He said that we scored a goal. I was right there, but the ball never crossed the line."

"The other team must have been annoyed."

"Yeah. One of the guys from Cairo U called the ref a 'blind mole'."

"That wasn't very clever. What happened then?"

"He got red carded."

"And what happened after he was sent off?"

"We scored another goal." Kalifa gave me an ironic look.

I thought for a moment. "Are you thinking you should have protested to the ref, too?"

"I don't know, Papa. What do you think?"

"I wasn't there. It was your decision." He gave a nod and a shrug. "Why didn't you protest?"

"The rest of the team wouldn't have liked it."

"Did any of them see what happened?"

"No, not really. I was the only one with a view of the ball and the goal line."

"What happened at the end of the game?"

"I told the guys we didn't really win."

"And what did they say?"

"After they understood what I was saying, they said, 'It serves them right for calling us rich kids.'"

"Do you agree with that?" I asked.

"No."

I smiled. "Did you score the third goal?"

"Yeah, but it was easy, Papa. We were three on two."

"How do you feel about it now?"

"Not very good."

"What do you make of this experience?"

"Right and wrong get very mixed up," he said. "The trouble is, every time we play Cairo, it gets really emotional."

"Yes, and you have to live with yourself afterwards." I thought for a moment. "Maybe, Kalifa, if you had protested, too, the other team would not have called the ref a blind mole. Nobody would have been sent off, and the game would have ended in a tie."

He made a sour face. "That assumes that the ref would still have allowed the goal, and everybody would know that really Cairo won."

"It depends on what's important to you, Kalifa: winning or playing fair."

"I guess that's why I'm bothered by what happened today, Papa. What's important to me is playing fair, and I get frustrated when other people just want to win."

* * *

I find it difficult to be father and mother to that boy. When Elizabeth was alive she would attend to his emotions while I tried to teach him logical behavior and discipline. But the priority he places on the feelings of others over natural justice seems inverted to me. I mean: empathy is all well and good, but isn't fairness more important than the love of others? Elizabeth did not agree. She would say: if I love a person, I will treat him fairly, but if I treat a person fairly, I may not love him. I suppose this was a reflection of the Christian teaching to 'love your neighbor' (meaning 'everyone', as I understand it). There is no such teaching in Islam, where the emphasis is on charity and honesty. This, it seems to me, is difficult enough to put into practice without trying to love everyone.

But I was encouraged that tonight, for the first time, Kalifa seemed to be coming around to my way of thinking: he put justice ahead of the feelings of others.

* * *

Perhaps you have already understood that Elizabeth and I are very different people. (I find it difficult to use the past tense when thinking about her: to me, her spirit and her influence are very much alive.) Elizabeth is that very rare idealist, who understands the world with all its faults, refuses to be put off by them, and works with a tireless smile to improve what she can. For my part, I am a dedicated realist, who sees the world for what it is: an unpredictable tableau of chaos with occasional moments of blissful calm. Our charge, I believe, is to use reason as the oil to pour on the troubled waters. In this sense, Elizabeth and I shared an objective: creating peace and calm.

In spite of our differences, we almost never argued. Each of us understood and accepted – even respected – the framework of the other. We would sometimes laugh and tease each other; then, in those cases where joint action was necessary, we would negotiate a compromise, which often involved a two-pronged approach. In those rare cases where we could not agree, Elizabeth would give me her look of sultry intensity which invariably led us to the bedroom. She was a glorious, uninhibited lover, such as I, of a repressive Arab culture, could never have imagined. When we lay spent, looking into each other's faces, smiles would creep over us and the joint plan of action would emerge.

* * *

This time the door opened and closed quietly. "Good evening, Papa. How was today?"

"It was . . ." I sought a description. "It was normal . . . and interesting, Wahida."

She sat on the adjacent couch and removed the dark blue headscarf; the cascade of dark hair flowed over her shoulders. Her voluminous grey shalwar covered her knees where her hands rested. "What was interesting, Papa?" She cocked her head to one side.

"I'll tell you and Kalifa over dinner. How is your work at the Red Crescent?"

"There is talk about opening a new center in Al Marj."

"Oh?"

"It is an area of great need, Papa. There is the un-permitted area east of El Souk."

"The un-permitted area is also the un-policed area. You're not thinking of transferring there, are you?"

"I might." She has a way of lifting her head to indicate her resolve.

I scowled and picked up the newspaper.

"Papa, don't you care about those poor squatters? They have no other place to live!" A frown emphasized her black eyebrows, set above hazel eyes.

"I care about them enough to contribute to your employer but not enough to entrust the safety of my daughter to squatters."

"I'll be all right . . . if I decide to go." The last phrase was almost a question.

"Wahida, I know you don't like to hear me say this, but if you were male, I could not object, but . . ."

She interrupted, "Oh, Papa!"

"Wahida, hear me out! I am very proud of you. You have followed your mother's example of working for the Red Crescent. You dress plainly – not with the many clinking bracelets of some of your friends. So you do not attract thieves. But Wahida, you are obviously an attractive young woman. Nothing short of a niqab (face veil) and jilbab (long, dark garment) can hide that fact. And there are men, Wahida, who . . ."

"I know, Papa, I know," she interrupted. "But it doesn't seem fair."

"It isn't fair."

"I mean, after all, I would be there to help them."

"The difficulty is that some men could conjure up a perverted meaning of 'help'".

She sighed morosely. "What's for dinner, Papa?"

"Nane made a potato-lamb stew."

* * *

"Papa," Wahida prompted, "You said something interesting happened today."

We were seated at the old, round table with the yellow cloth. Chairs for five were arranged around the table, but the three of us sat together.

I put down my fork. "Yes. I have been asked to go on the Hajj."

Wahida looked up. "Who asked you, Papa?"

"Quite an important person – I believe from Saudi Arabia."

"Who is this person?" Kalifa asked, "Someone connected to the royal family?"

"Yes, I think so, but I am still thinking about it."

"So you haven't decided yet?"

"No, but I have to go sometime, and I thought I might as well go sooner rather than later."

"Who would go with you, Papa?"

I shrugged. "I was thinking that you might like to go with me, Kalifa."

"When is it?"

"It starts on the twenty-eighth of June."

Kalifa shook his head. "Classes will just be over then, and I may have some army interviews. Besides, it's awfully hot then. If I had some spare time, I'd rather go to Al Jamiah and relax on the beach."

I asked, "What army interviews might you have?"

"They said that once I have my degree, I can apply for an army commission, and once my application is in, I expect they'll want to talk to me."

I nodded.

"You're not thinking of going alone, are you, Papa?" Wahida asked.

"No, no," I said dismissively, "there's always a contingent going from the university."

"What about the fellow from Saudi?" Kalifa inquired, "Would he be meeting you there?"

"No, I don't think so."

Wahida was puzzled. "Well, why did he even mention the Hajj to you? Is he selling arrangements?"

"No, no, nothing like that. I think it was mentioned because there was a thought that I might meet a Father Khaliq."

"Is he the Saudi guy's father, or is he one of the Saudi royalty?"

"No, no, he is the father."

"But Papa, there are a couple of million people on the Hajj. How can you find someone you've never met in a crowd with that many people?"

"I asked about that, too. I think the answer is that I'll have to make inquiries. I know a little bit about him."

"The thing I don't understand," Kalifa offered, "is why the Saudi guy doesn't go on the Hajj himself and look for his father."

"Well, I think you have to bear in mind, Kalifa, that there are some very complex relationships in the Saudi royal family. Sometimes families are not as close as we are, and if that's the case, my Saudi contact may have good reasons for wanting to involve a very neutral third party."

"OK, but I hope you have a nice contract with this guy."

"I am assured of a reward. Besides, it's my obligation to go on the Hajj."

Chapter 2

Naqib & Anisa

"Hafez," I said on the telephone, "have you got a few minutes?"

"Yes, of course, Professor. You want to come here?"

I was irritated at his expectation that I might walk down the hall to his office. After all, he may be a professor of philosophy, but he is seven years my junior and does not have tenure. I said, "My office is not busy, Hafez You can come here."

About ten minutes later, there was a knock on my office door, but before I could look up and respond, Hafez opened the door, entered, and closed the door behind him. "What can I do for you, Professor?" he asked solicitously.

I gestured toward the old-fashioned, straight-backed oak chairs in front of my desk, but as usual, he seated himself in the upholstered armchair to my right. Leaning forward, he surveyed me. "Everything all right, Professor?"

"Yes, of course, Hafez." I eyed my colleague for a moment. He was a small man in a rumpled beige linen suit. His black beard was trimmed to a fashionable centimeter; he had a habit of tilting his head back so his eyes could examine the world down his bony nose. I leaned back in my chair, composing my thoughts with the help of the ceiling fan.

"Hafez, I have a proposition for you."

His back straightened. "Ah, and what would that be, Professor?"

"Hafez, would I be correct in the assumption that you have never undertaken the holy pilgrimage?"

"If you refer to the Hajj, Professor, that is correct."

"Well, I myself am thinking of taking the Hajj this year."

Hafez frowned. "Last month was Ramadan. That means that Dhu al-Hijjah – the month of the Hajj – occurs in two months' time."

I nodded.

"But Professor," he objected, "that means you are considering undertaking the Hajj in the midst of the summer heat – in Saudi Arabia – in the desert – and you are thinking that I might come with you!" He shook his head in disbelief.

"Well," I spread my hands in soothing counter-argument, "Mecca is hardly the desert and we are in good health. One must not forget that Cairo, and indeed Al Jamiah, gets quite hot in summer."

"But you – as far as I know – are not a religious man. What prompts this sudden interest in the Hajj?"

"It is true," I said, "that neither of us might be called 'devout', but we are Muslims nonetheless, and as such we have an obligation to undertake the Hajj."

"On that point, I agree, Professor, but consider: in five or six years, the Hajj will fall at this time of year, when the heat is more tolerable."

I searched my memory for an ayah (verse) from the Qur'an that might convince him. "Do you remember the sura (chapter) Daybreak, Hafez?"

He shook his head.

"Well, as you know, my father sent me to a traditional school, where one was expected to memorize the holy book. And I remember now that in Daybreak, the disobedient man says, 'Would that I had provided for this life to come!' and the obedient man is told, 'But you, soul at peace, return to your Lord, well pleased and well pleasing; go among My servants and into My garden.'"

"And you believe that, Kareem?"

"I think that it contains some practical advice that one should not put off the important things."

Hafez gave a shrug of resignation. "Go, then, with my blessing! But for me, I prefer not to sleep in a tent, on sandy ground, surrounded by a horde of unwashed Pakistanis."

I shot him a glance of condemnation. "One should not say such things, Hafez!" I changed course. "However, my view is that at this point in our lives, having reached a certain status, we are entitled – actually, I think we are expected – to select a first class accommodation package. I understand that there are such options."

"What is this first class accommodation package?"

"I shall be discussing this with a travel agency shortly, but I believe it includes excellent accommodation, comfortable transportation, good meals and a dedicated tour guide."

He scratched the back of his neck. "All the same, I prefer to spend my money on a trip to Paris or London."

At that point I decided to play my winning card. "Have you met the new Regent of Studies, Hafez?"

"No, I haven't. Have you?"

"Yes. He had a meeting with all of the tenured faculty last Thursday."

"Oh? Anything interesting?" he asked warily.

"Well, the main new item was a system he has in mind for evaluating the faculty."

"Yes?"

"Of course, there is the usual stuff about published books and papers, feedback from students, demand for courses, etc. But there was one new thing . . ."

"Which was?"

"Well, it's a little vague, but it seems to be about the extent to which a member of the faculty contributes to the overall ethos of American University."

"What does that mean?"

"As I say, he was a bit vague, but he mentioned that we should not be misled by our name; that we are an Egyptian university, in a country which is largely Islamic; that our student body is mostly Muslim; under the jurisdiction of a conservative government which rewards traditional Islamic values, and . . ."

"So," he interrupted, "you're saying that we're going to be evaluated for tenure on our apparent dedication to the Five Pillars of Islam."

"Apparently, it could be something like that."

"In that case, you can put the word out that we're going on the Hajj this year. I don't think it needs mentioning that we will be going on a VIP package."

* * *

I have to confess that I did feel a trace of guilt for being unusually manipulative with Hafez. The truth is that I don't know what the new Regent of Studies has in mind, but it is quite possible that the government wants to see traditional Islamic behavior as opposed to the more radical approach taken by the Brotherhood. Certainly, they don't want any more anti-government demonstrations. But I would like to see Hafez eventually get his tenure, and going on the Hajj surely won't damage his prospects. In fact, it may open a whole new theological dimension in his lectures on philosophy.

* * *

A day or two later, at lunch time, I decided to see Adeeba, my colleague at the university. She is a professor of Egyptian History, who at the age of fifty-one was tenured last year. She has distinguished herself as a world-renowned scholar of the ancient Egyptian Copts. She understands the Coptic script, the various Coptic languages, and has written a number of books about the evolution of the Copts from the first to the tenth centuries.

Adeeba was a close friend of Elizabeth's, having met my late wife many years ago at a university function. In fact, the two of them attended the same church. Adeeba's husband, Soliman, died of a heart attack two years ago; theirs was an arranged marriage that produced two daughters, one of whom has entered into her own arranged marriage; the younger one is still single. Soliman was at least fifteen years Adeeba's senior.

Adeeba is a strikingly handsome woman with dark green eyes, strong eyebrows and clear, tanned skin. Unlike many of her colleagues who wear loose-fitting trousers and a jacket, Adeeba can be spotted by her colorful headscarf, voluminous, ankle-length skirt and pastel, long-sleeved shirt.

It was perhaps six months after Elizabeth died that I saw Adeeba across the room at a regent's meeting. There is a real woman!

As couples, several times a year we would exchange dinner visits. But now, we were a single man and a single woman in our fifties, with grown-up children – at least in my case, they were partially grown-up. And in Egypt, a woman in an important position in society must be careful to avoid any hint of impropriety. I knew, for example, that it would be considered unwise for me to go and see her in her office – even with the door open. Our two departments had nothing in common; we were not related; so what was I doing in her office? I suppose that in other circumstances, un-related, single men and women can meet publicly without generating disagreeable rumors.

In any case, I liked Adeeba; I even had fantasies about her, but I could only guess that she considered me an old friend and respected colleague at the university.

* * *

There are several dining rooms at the university: most cater to students, but one is particularly for the faculty, though students can be invited for a meal-time conference with a member of the faculty. The large faculty dining room is informally divided into two sections. I say informally because while there is a low screen dividing male from female sections, the screen is often ignored for conferences.

Adeeba was sitting with her tray at a table with two students. I gave her a friendly nod and sat at the other end of the table. I devoted my initial attention to a torli, an open pie with potatoes, squash, onions, vegetables and tomato sauce. I was able to make out that the students wanted advice from Adeeba about joining an archaeological project.

After a few minutes, the two students departed, and Adeeba glanced up at me. "How are you, Kareem?" she asked.

We exchanged small talk about our respective children for a few minutes, but owing to the background rattling of dishes and the hubbub of voices, it was sometimes difficult to hear. Adeeba made a gesture of annoyance at the noise, and offered, "If you move a little closer, I think we could hear each other better, Kareem."

I pushed my tray down the table and followed it to a seat diagonally across from Adeeba. "So, you were saying that Nakia, your older daughter, is expecting again?"

There was a look of frustration on her face. "Yes, but it's to be another girl."

"You are very fortunate, Adeeba, to be so young with three grandchildren."

She smiled. "I am not so young, Kareem. Besides, I am only one grandchild ahead of you."

I shook my head regretfully. "I cannot count Anisa's two children as my real grandchildren, but she is expecting in a few months."

"All right. That puts you in the running! And you have Wahida and Kalifa to look forward to."

I shifted the conversation to her work.

"Yes," she said, "this summer I am going to participate in the exploration of a new site near Oxyrhynchus. As you know, the

Oxyrhynchus site is of tremendous importance for Egyptian history. It has yielded an enormous collection of papyrus texts dating from the Ptolemaic, Roman and Christian periods." She paused. "Are you going to be spending some time at Al Jamiah, Kareem?"

"Probably, but my main project this summer is to go on the Hajj."

"My goodness, Kareem. I didn't know you took the Five Pillars seriously."

"Well, perhaps I am motivated more by curiosity than religious fervor, and Hafez is going with me."

"It's good that you have a friend to go with you. Does Hafez share your curiosity?"

"I think so, Adeeba. We both want to experience the holy sites and performing the rituals with so many people."

"I can't imagine what it would be like to be with two million people in the al-Haram mosque in Mecca. My preference would be to watch the videos on YouTube and pray in the solitude of my bedroom at home."

I acknowledged her comments with a nod. Then I thought, *Tell her!* "Actually, I'm curious about another point, Adeeba: someone has asked me to locate a Father Khaliq while I'm on the Hajj."

"And you know where to find this Father Khaliq in the midst of two million people?"

"Well, this is what is interesting. She implied that I would be provided with clues on the Hajj."

"She?"

"As it happens 'she' is a Princess Basheera."

"Oh my goodness! How did you meet her?"

"A woman I've never met before asked me to meet the Princess at the Kempinski Hotel."

She gave me a suspicious look. "And what happened at the hotel?"

"Nothing! We met in the lobby. There were two colleagues with her, and she asked me to locate Father Khaliq during the Hajj."

"What did she tell you about this Father Khaliq?"

"Not a great deal. She said he was her father, quite old. I gather that he is quite prominent, and she didn't say that I would recognize him, but that was implied."

"Did she explain why she couldn't find her own father?"

"No, but I believe there are some complications."

"Did she offer you money if you find him?"

"She said there would be a reward."

"Did this princess appear to be a substantial person?"

"Yes. She and her colleagues were very well dressed – polite – spoke classic Arabic."

"I don't suppose the Kempinski was any help, but have you tried to Google her?"

"You're right about the Kempinski, and there is absolutely nothing on Google."

"How odd! Have you scheduled another meeting with her?"

"No, but I have her Egyptian mobile number."

"And no address, apart from the Kempinski." I nodded. She gazed into the distance. "How old was this woman?"

"She was wearing a niqab, but I would guess twenty-five to thirty-five."

Adeeba reached her verdict. "It's a mystery. I don't suppose there's any actual harm in it. You're going on the Hajj anyway, and you haven't promised to give her any money or marry her." She paused for a moment. "My work often involves solving puzzles and mysteries. I really enjoy them. I look forward to hearing a report of your trip, Kareem."

* * *

I was very pleased by my meeting with Adeeba. Clearly, she was interested in my mystery, but also – Allah be praised – reading between the lines, interested in me as a friend. Best of all, she asked me to keep her informed. She would therefore welcome periodic updates from me. Where could this lead? Only time would tell.

* * *

I knocked on the door of apartment J on the third floor of 71 Sayed Mahran in Al Moatamadeyah, which is outside the ring road, about four kilometers west of central Cairo. It is a neighborhood crowded with a jumble of huge, beige boxes of buildings: here ten, there four, there eight stories high, pushing and crowding out the light from one another. There was no lift; neither the stairway nor the street outside had been swept in weeks. I knocked again; then I heard my son's voice within. The door opened wide. "Come in, Papa!" My son, Naqib, embraced me, kissing both my cheeks through his great bush of beard. He led me to the small salon, where I was seated in what was undoubtedly the armchair of prominence. We spoke about his siblings and my work at the university.

A small head with a great mass of dark curls peeked at me surreptitiously around the door frame. I opted into the cat and mouse game.

"Basima, come here, my little cherub! This is your grand-father." A girl of about four appeared in the doorway. She was wearing a long denim skirt and a blue T-shirt with tomato stains; she paused, head to one side, considering her stepfather.

"Come here, Basima," Naqib spread his arms open. "Where is your sister?"

The child stood next to Naqib while appraising me with her dark eyes. "She is with Mama."

"I brought you a present, Basima," I said, reaching into the bag by my feet. "Do you want to guess what it is?"

The little girl came two steps closer. "Is it for me?"

"Yes, it's for you."

She reached out, took the prettily-wrapped object, and hugged it to her, still gazing at me.

Naqib said, "Basima, can you say thank you to Grandfather?"
Her eyes never left me. "Thank you."

My daughter-in-law, Anisa, came into the room with a tea tray. She was wearing a shapeless, long-sleeved abaya, (casual, floor-length dress) dark blue, with green trim at the cuffs and high neck. Her black hair fell in a single cascade to her waist. *Her pregnancy is not disclosed,* I thought. Having set the tray down, she gave me a slight bow. "Good afternoon, Professor." Turning toward her daughter, she asked, "What do you have, Basima? Is it a present?" The child nodded. "Let's open it!"

"I have something for her sister, as well."

"Husna, come here, please!"

A smaller version of Basima, dressed identically, but with more generous stains, stood in the doorway, sucking her thumb.

I took the second present from the bag and held it out to her. "This is for you, Husna."

There was a shriek of delight as the toddler snatched the present from my hand. Anisa drew her younger daughter to herself with murmurings of love and chastisement.

My step-granddaughters occupied themselves with their dolls, Anisa poured the tea, and I looked around the room. As I say, it was small: two chairs, a well-worn couch, a table, thin geometric carpet, and three large reproductions of French impressionists.

Naqib intercepted my appraisal. "It's not much, Papa, but we have two bedrooms, the rent is good, and there's a bus line to central Cairo. This makes it easy for Anisa to get to work."

I nodded. "What is your work, Anisa?"

"I am a teller at the Pyramids of Islam Bank."

"That seems a very good position, but I guess you must arrange for child care."

Her face was serene and confident, except when she revealed bad teeth. (I admit to prejudices against tattoos and bad teeth.) "My working hours are nine to three, Saturday through Thursday. So Naqib takes care of the girls from when I leave at eight until I get home at four. He goes to class from five until ten."

I said, "That makes for a long day for you, Naqib." But I also thought, *and it makes life easier for you, Anisa.*

Perhaps reading my thoughts, Naqib said, "Ours is a modern marriage, Papa. Anisa is the wage-earner, while I am the child-carer, but I am also able to carry a heavy course load."

"How are your studies for the legal profession progressing?"

"I expect to take my qualifying examinations within the next two months."

"Remind me, Naqib, in what field will you practice?"

"Most likely human rights law."

"That will put you on a collision course with the government, will it not?"

"Are you suggesting, Papa, that government policy has priority over human rights?"

"No, not at all. I am merely suggesting that in life one has to choose one's battles with care, weighing up the possible consequences."

Anisa intervened, "The battle for individual freedom of Egyptians must eventually be won, don't you agree, Professor?"

I said, "Much depends of one's definition of 'freedom', Anisa. If one is using 'democracy' as another term for individual freedom, Plato argued that a bad democracy is worse than a bad tyranny, because the mistakes made by many in a bad democracy are worse than the mistakes made by a single individual. He also argued that individual freedom in a democracy can bring harm to many, and that in a democracy, political power may not be shared equally."

"But Professor, surely you are not arguing for a dictatorship?" Anisa persisted.

"No, I agree with Plato that the best form of government is what he called an Aristocracy, where the rulers were very wise men – or should I say people – who are Philosopher Kings."

"What my father is saying," Naqib interjected, "is that Egypt should be ruled by himself and the rest of the department at the University."

"Really?" Anisa turned in surprise toward her husband.

Naqib held up a hand. "It's just a family joke, Anisa."

"Actually," I put in, "while the concept of an Aristocracy has much to recommend it, it does not fit the human mold, and, as far as I know there has never been one."

Anisa nodded. "Is that because human beings insist on accumulating personal power?"

"I have the impression that the Greek philosophers would have considered you a promising student, Anisa."

She blushed. "Well, I . . . I don't know anything about philosophy, but I think that dictatorships are wrong." She rose and left the room in response to a call: "Mama, potty!"

Naqib put down his tea cup. "OK, Papa, how do you define democracy?"

"Well, if one thinks of the natural rights of the individual, the United States Declaration of Independence puts them quite succinctly: Life, Liberty and the Pursuit of Happiness."

"That's fine as far as it goes," Naqib responded, "but it doesn't define the relationship between a free people and their government. That relationship is defined by the constitution of a country." I nodded. "And in the case of Egypt," he continued, "the constitution defines a flawed relationship."

"Go on," I said, knowing that he would, in any case.

"There are many problems with the new constitution, but the principle one is the outlawing of political parties based on religion."

"That excludes the Muslim Brotherhood."

"Not only the Muslim Brotherhood, but a number of small Islamist and even Christian parties."

"If we look to the United States as an example," I offered, "there is a requirement that church and state be separated."

"But Egypt is not the United States. Our constitution says that Islam is the state religion. Why, then, are political parties based on the state religion forbidden?"

I said, rather softly, "I think that the US took its approach because of experience with the intermingling of church and state in Europe. The Spanish Inquisition comes to mind."

Naqib was stunned by my reference to the Spanish Inquisition, which severely repressed the Jewish and Muslim faiths. For a moment, he didn't know what to say; then, "Surely, Papa, you are not suggesting that Morsi (the deposed Egyptian President) would have persecuted the Copts!"

"No, not at all. But I think that the majority of the Egyptian people felt that Morsi was too focused on the agenda of the Muslim Brotherhood, giving too little attention to the dire needs of the economy."

"Papa," Naqib whispered between his teeth, "you know I am a member of the Brotherhood!"

"Yes," I said softly, "I gathered as much, but given the attitude of the current government, I hope you'll not speak or act in a way that your membership becomes general knowledge."

"Papa, you would say, 'it's a binary choice': either one is a member, or one isn't!"

"Be careful, Naqib," I cautioned. "I don't want to see you taken off to prison!"

He gave a shrug. "I believe in the agenda of the Muslim Brotherhood!"

I felt an acute need to change the subject and the venue. "This is not the time or the place to argue about the agenda of the Muslim Brotherhood. May I suggest, Naqib, that I take you and your family out to dinner?"

"But Papa," he objected, "Anisa has spent all morning preparing our meal!"

"I'm sure it is a delicious meal, but you can keep it for your family. Let's go to your favorite restaurant!"

"Our favorite restaurant is quite expensive, and at the moment, we can't afford it."

"I think I probably can. Get Anisa and the girls; let's go!"

* * *

At the restaurant, which specialized in tender lamb, pepper and onion kababs with a tomato and cucumber salad, the atmosphere was more relaxed, and the little girls became the center of attention.

As I thought about it afterwards, I have to admit that my view of Anisa changed. Before they were married two months ago, I had met her only once, briefly. My impression then was of a woman, recently divorced, who was desperate for a man, and who would use her sexuality to get one – before it was too late. This image wasn't helped when I met her family. Her father is a taxi driver – a smoker – and her mother is a seamstress. She is the oldest of eight children. And my mental picture seemed confirmed when Naqib told me a month after the marriage that he was going to be a father. I thought, Well, just as I thought! She used her big gun to hunt him down! She got pregnant!

As we walked to the restaurant, I was able to see her in profile. She was certainly advanced in her pregnancy. But then, I thought: What else could she do? A single mother in her late twenties with two little kids. Living with her parents would be a nightmare. She has a job, so she'd need child care. There was one grandmother at the wedding, but she seemed in need of care herself. Along comes Naqib and she reels him in, having satisfied herself that he's willing and able to take care of her little ones.

From Naqib's point of view, the marriage made sense. He got room, board and sex (apart from her teeth, Anisa was not a bad-looking woman). His only responsibilities were to look after the little girls and to keep the small flat in order. He was free to pursue his law degree with evening classes and daytime reading. I'm sure he had some sort of a scholarship – maybe even a full scholarship.

My older son is stubborn. He certainly could have continued his studies at American University – tuition free – but he would have had to continue living at home. (I wasn't about to pay for his room and board when it was available at home.) He told me that it was time he got his own apartment. Looking back on it, he probably felt that living at home would be inconvenient in terms of his social life, and, more importantly, for his meetings with the Muslim Brotherhood. He knows I do not approve of his membership, so better to avoid my possible harassment!

I remembered that Naqib had not mentioned the Muslim Brotherhood or his radical views in Anisa's presence. Probably Anisa had reservations about the Brotherhood, in spite of the fact that her family seemed to fit the profile of Brotherhood supporters. Her reservations may have been more practical than ideological: she certainly didn't want to see her new husband locked up in prison. Therefore, I sensed that she would apply a brake to Naqib's radical idealism.

The relationship between Naqib and Anisa seemed to have moved beyond a marriage of convenience. Naqib's obvious fondness for Basima and Husna certainly endeared him to Anisa and seemed to cement the four of them together as a family. I thought, Better than I expected. Now, if Naqib would just get qualified, and find a job with a mainstream law firm!

* * *

I remember, when the boys were about ten and fourteen, an event which says much about Naqib. When I returned to the house that day, Elizabeth had been dealing with the trauma since the school day finished at three-thirty. Kalifa had come home with a swollen upper lip, a large purple bruise on his left cheek, and assorted cuts on his hands and knees. Knowing that he had been playing football in the early afternoon, Elizabeth assumed that Kalifa had experienced a rough tackle. The pitch available to fifth year students had no grass and was littered with sharp pebbles. As she cleaned and plastered the cuts, he was evasive about what had happened, said he had homework to do, and went to his room.

Naqib arrived home half an hour later. His shirt was torn and he had wrapped a handkerchief around his right hand. He avoided his mother and went straight to Kalifa's room, where Elizabeth could hear them talking. She joined them in the room and insisted on knowing what had happened. Reluctantly, it emerged that Kalifa had scored a goal, and was celebrating when one of the boys on the opposing team had called him an "asshole rich kid". Kalifa retorted something equally offensive. This was just the excuse the opposing player – who was in seventh year – needed. He attacked Kalifa and beat him up before the referee could intervene. When Kalifa went back to school to change and collect his books, he met his brother. Naqib wanted to know what had happened and who had attacked his brother. He told Elizabeth, "I fixed that slum kid."

At about that time, there was a knock at the door. It was the seventh year student, considerably bandaged on his face, and his irate father, who was seeking compensation for his son's injuries. Elizabeth produced Kalifa, also bandaged, who argued that the older boy had started it. Eventually the visitors went home without either apology or compensation. I think Elizabeth was sufficiently unsettled by the angry father that she went on the offensive with Naqib, asking him why he had taken it on himself to attack the seventh-year boy.

"Because he hurt my brother!" was the reply.

"I think it would have been better if you had helped Kalifa report it to the sports instructor," Elizabeth replied. "That way the only one who was wrong was the older boy and the school authorities could deal with his bullying."

"I don't agree, Mama! That scum had it coming to him!"

Naqib has a stubborn disposition and an ingrained bias for the underdog.

* * *

"Please take a seat, Professor." The young man gestured toward a seat opposite his in the small cubicle. Faded travel posters were taped to the glass partitions which surrounded us on three sides. There was a computer monitor on the desk to his right and a disorderly jumble of manila files to his left. A buzz of conversation rose from the beehive of cubicles around us. "Now then: you are interested in making arrangements for the Hajj. My name, by the way, is Mahdi. Please tell me what you have in mind."

"Well," I said, "I have not been on the Hajj before, so I am unsure of the choices one can make, but I am interested in comfortable accommodation."

"A VIP package?"

"I don't consider myself to be a VIP."

The young man nodded without conviction. "As to the religious ceremonies themselves, there is nothing to choose. It is not, shall we say, like a restaurant menu." He noticed my frown at what I thought was an inappropriate analogy and hurried on. "But there are many possible choices regarding accommodation, travel and meals."

"Perhaps you would refresh my memory regarding the religious ceremonies."

"Certainly, Professor. Most pilgrims from Egypt fly from Cairo to Jeddah, which, as you know, is not far from Mecca. Near Jeddah, one enters into ihram (a state of holiness) by putting on plain white clothing. On arrival at the holy mosque in Mecca, one performs the tawaf (seven circuits around the Ka'aba – the holiest building in Islam), one offers prayers and one completes the sa'i (walking or running between the nearby hills of Safa and Marwah). Then on the first day of the Hajj, which is the eighth of the month, one travels to Mina, where the day is spent in prayer. On the second day one travels to Arafat, where one prays and listens to sermons by Islamic scholars. After sunset one leaves for Muzdalifah, where one says prayers and sleeps under the open sky. On the third day, one returns to Mina for the several stonings of the devil, the sacrifice of an animal and the cutting of hair. One remains in Mina until the fifth day when one travels to Mecca where one performs a final tawaf before departure."

"Yes. Yes, I had forgotten that there was so much stoning of the devil and so many tawafs."

"As you know, Professor, the devil does not give up easily!"

"Yes," I murmured, "I suppose not. Tell me, Mahdi, have you yourself ever taken the Hajj?

"Yes, of course, many times. I am one of the guides. In fact, all of the employees here at the agency are required to take the Hajj before the completion of the first year of employment."

"That's commendable." I was beginning to believe that this young man might be very knowledgeable. "And can you tell me the distance between the various locations?"

"Yes. All the sites are within ten kilometers of Mecca. The hills of Safa and Marwah have been enclosed within a long gallery of the great mosque.

"That's very convenient."

"Yes. The Saudis have spent over one hundred billion dollars in upgrading facilities to make them safer, more comfortable and better able to handle the very large number of pilgrims."

This comment brought a memory to mind. I said, "My father told me that when he went on the Hajj – I believe it was in the nineteen fifties – he said that it was quite rustic, and that while it was uncomfortable, it made him think back to the times of the Prophet and Abraham."

"I'm sure that's right," Mahdi said, "But one has to remember that in those days there were always a considerable number of injuries: people falling, getting sick or even being trampled!"

"I suppose that some pilgrims travel from Mecca to Mina to Arafat on foot."

He shrugged. "Yes, some do. But it is important to remember that this year it will be very hot, and walking in large crowds can be extremely slow. Most of our clients opt for travel on our air conditioned busses, which are more convenient and comfortable, and avoid any risk of a client being trampled.

So, he is quite concerned about the safety of pilgrims. I certainly don't want to be trampled. "Mahdi, can you tell me about the choices regarding accommodation, travel and meals?"

Mahdi proceeded to tell me that there were three packages: gold, silver and bronze, with varying levels of luxury, all based on a two-week tour that included a four-day visit to the Prophet's Mosque in Medina.

I said, "But the Hajj itself does not require a visit to the Tomb of the Prophet."

"Most people like to include it since it is not far from Mecca."

"I think we will save it for a separate visit. What we would like is a package which puts us in Jeddah on the sixth of Dhu al-Hijjah, and has us departing for Cairo on the thirteenth."

We had a rather lengthy discussion about transportation. Walking could take five or six hours to go from place to place, while private busses took only about half an hour. Government-sponsored air travel was not guaranteed to arrive or depart on the assigned day, so I opted for commercial air travel. "But," I said, "the flight from Cairo to Jeddah can't take longer than two hours. We don't need to travel first class."

He made a reluctant note of this.

"How does one get a package where you, Mahdi, are the guide?"

"Well, sir, I generally take care of our gold customers on the Hajj."

I want him! "Might we come under your care if we opted for first class travel?"

"Possibly, Professor. There are two of you?"

"Yes. See what you can do and call me tomorrow with the prices, will you?" I left him my card.

"Certainly, Professor."

* * *

Late the following afternoon I called my colleague. "Hafez, when you have a chance, could you stop by? I have spoken to an agency about arrangements for the Hajj."

Moments later he was seated in my armchair. "What have you learned, Kareem?"

"I have learned," I said, "that the Hajj is quite repetitive: plenty of circling the Kabaa, and much throwing of stones at the devil."

"Can it not be shortened to, say two or three passes around the Kabaa, and one session of accurate stone throwing?"

I looked at Hafez to see whether he was making a joke. Judging by his serious face and his history of – dare I say – agnosticism, he was not.

"Hafez! A Muslim – no matter his religious commitment – cannot permit himself to even think what you have just said!"

"Sorry, Kareem! I suppose that I have just demonstrated the need for my eternal soul to go on the Hajj and take it seriously."

"Probably so, Hafez!"

"And then there is also the not inconsiderable benefit of my tenure."

He is incorrigible! I thought. "Now, Hafez, I have proposed to the travel agency a trip beginning on the sixth of the month and concluding on the fourteenth."

"So long?"

"You have something better to do?" I snapped.

"No, but . . ."

I interrupted: "There is a very knowledgeable young guide – his wisdom may provide particular enlightenment to you, Hafez

– who will lead us through the Hajj if we select the agency's gold package."

"How much is it?"

"The all-inclusive gold package for eight days is nine thousand, nine hundred and fifty pounds ($1250)."

"Great Allah! That is a lot of money!"

"Not when you consider what we get for it: first class airfare, private busses, VIP tent at Mina, a room for the entire time in a five star hotel in Mecca, and a sacrificial animal. Plus a full-time guide."

There was a look of alarm on Hafez' face. "We have to sacrifice an animal?"

"No. It will be done for us and the meat distributed to the poor."

"Why do we need a tent at Mina and a hotel room in Mecca?"

"It was explained to me that this is a standard feature of gold packages. Many pilgrims find it reassuring to know that they can retreat to their hotel room in Mecca if they become indisposed or ill."

For a moment, Hafez gazed out the window of my office. "It makes me wonder how our old janitor ever managed to go on the Hajj."

"I can tell you, Hafez. He took a crowded, unscheduled flight provided by the Egyptian government. He slept in teeming barracks in Mecca and tents in Mina, provided by the Saudi government. He shuffled along in dense crowds and extreme heat at one kilometer per hour, and he paid next to nothing for his beans and rice."

"And he had to slaughter his own goat."

"Yes, I suppose so, but you can ask him."

"All right. Go ahead and book it."

* * *

During this time, I kept wondering, What about Father Khaliq?

I had spent a considerable time in my home office examining the results of a Google search for 'Father Khaliq'. It seemed that most of the results involved someone's father whose given name was Khaliq. For example there was a Kashmiri poet named Samad Mir who came from a Sufi family. His father, Khaliq Mir, was also a Sufi poet. But I could find no connection with Princess Basheera. If, I reasoned, the Princess is of Saudi origin, Father Khaliq must also be Saudi. On this basis, before going to Saudi on the Hajj where Father Khaliq would be in attendance, I should see what I could learn from the Saudi embassy.

I tried to make an appointment with the cultural attaché, but when I told his secretary that it was in connection with some research I was doing about genealogy in Saudi Arabia, I was referred to Abdul Al Musaed, the deputy attaché. Mr. Al Musaed was about my age; his clean-shaven face was dark-tanned and leathery; he wore a starched white thawb (full-length shirt), white ghutra (head covering), and a braided black and white igal (head band). His desk was devoid of paperwork. We drank very strong coffee and spoke about the weather as his king smiled down benevolently on him from a portrait.

"Mr. Al Musaed," I asked, "what can you tell me about the use of the given name 'Khaliq' in the royal family?"

"Ah, yes," he said, "You had a question about genealogy." He paused to consider, taking a sip from his porcelain demitasse. "The Saudi royal family is quite large, Professor al-Busiri, comprising some fifteen thousand individuals, and I can't say that I know more than about a thousand of them." (This with a modest smile.) "However, I cannot think of anyone who has been given that name."

"But can you recall a prominent Saudi person with the name 'Khaliq'?"

"No, I cannot, Professor."

"May I ask you, Mr. Al Musaed, whether you have access to the Saudi passport system?"

He glanced at his sleeping monitor. "Yes, I do."

"Is the system searchable by name?"

"Yes, of course, but I can't provide you with any individual information."

"Can you tell me how many Saudi citizens have the given name 'Khaliq'?"

For about five minutes he was busy at his keyboard, glancing up at the screen. "There are fifty-four Khaliq's in Saudi Arabia, Professor!" he announced proudly.

"And how many are fifty or older?"

There was a pause.

"This is interesting. The name seems to have been more popular in our parents' time. There are forty-three."

I shook my head. "Can you tell me: is there a Basheera Chagma in the database?"

"I am sorry, Professor, but I can't answer questions about individuals."

I nodded. "Can you comment on the prevalence of the surname 'Chagma'?"

Another pause.

"There are twenty-seven Chagmas with Saudi passports, Professor."

"Would any of them be royal family?"

Mr. Al Musaed ran his finger down the screen. He shrugged. "There's no one that I recognize, but, as I say, I only know about seven percent of the royal family."

I thanked Mr. Al Musaed and left him a signed copy of my book Concepts of the Soul in Classical Arabic Philosophy.

* * *

The meeting with Mr. Al Musaed was certainly frustrating. But I consoled myself with the thought that Father Khaliq was probably among the forty-three and Princess Basheera was likely to be found in the twenty-seven.

Was I deluding myself?

I could not have dreamt my encounter with the princess. She seemed real enough.

Was she trying to mislead me or involve me in some sort of scam? If so, what could her motive be: Money? Power? Sex? I dismissed the latter two immediately: my power was confined to the classroom. And sex? Well, she would be better off with an attempt on Khaled Naga (Egyptian actor), though, of course, I would be willing to try.

Money? Not enough bait in the trap. Why make it so hard for me to fall for her scam, if that's what it was? Besides, my intuition – on which I usually rely – told me that she was to be trusted.

Was she really a Saudi princess? That was my assumption. With fifteen thousand members, the royal family of Saudi Arabia seemed the obvious choice. Besides, she asked me to find Father Khaliq on the Hajj, which is in Saudi Arabia.

Could she be of another nationality? Possibly. There were royal families in Jordan, Lebanon, Egypt, Iran, and pretenders in Turkey and Iraq. It seemed unlikely that Basheera could be connected to a past or present European royal family.

But most of all, I was convinced that Basheera was serious: she believed that I (and she?) would benefit from discovering Father Khaliq. I was curious! And at this point in my life I welcomed the intrusion of a mystery.

Chapter 3

The Hajj

There were thirty-six passengers on the bus. Mahdi, sitting opposite the driver in the front seat, was continuing his announcements. "We will shortly arrive at a Station of Ihram. There you will undress, wash your body in the shower, and put on the two-piece garment of ihram. The garments will be given to you as you enter. When that is completed, you should recite the prayer of intention, which is in the guide book. Are there any questions?"

From the back of the bus came a question: "What about footwear?"

"You should put on the clean sandals which are in your overnight bag. Your street clothes can go in your laundry bag. Both your overnight bag and laundry bags will be taken to your room in the hotel."

*　*　*

The bus stopped at a modern cluster of single-story buildings. Inside, as he was undressing, Hafez offered, "I think it would be nice if there were some women in our group."

I thought this was a rather gratuitous comment. "There is another bus with a different guide for the women."

"I know, but whenever I get naked, I tend to think about women."

"Hafez, you need to change your habits during this week."

"Don't you think about women, Kareem?"

"Yes, but not during this week."

After the shower, I was wondering whether my underpants should go back on. I looked in the overnight bag. There were none. I looked around at the other men. No. I tied the closure strings of the bottom garment. (It was a rectangular piece of white cotton fabric.) I wrapped the bottom garment around me and tucked it in at my waist. The similar upper garment I wrapped over my left shoulder, as others were doing, and tied it on my right.

* * *

The bus was traveling on a modern, eight-lane highway toward Mecca. The central reservation was planted with oleanders. To the right was a semi-barren expanse of ochre sand, broken here and there by dark grey splintered rock. As we came into Mecca, the streets on our left were packed with high-rise residential towers, and on our right there was what appeared to be derelict ground, with less affluent residential buildings in the distance.

* * *

Hafez and I took the elevator up to the sixteenth floor of the Dar Al Tawhid InterContinental Hotel. Our room faced east. When the porter opened the curtains, there below us was the colossal white Masjid al-Haram Mosque. The open circular plaza immediately caught our eyes, and at the plaza's center, the black Ka'aba. Already, we could make out multitudes of white figures moving slowly, counter-clockwise. I was overwhelmed with unexpected elation. "We are actually here, Hafez!"

He was consulting the guide book and looking at the scene below. "Yes, and you see those copper domes at the ends of that long building, there, Kareem?" I nodded. "Those are the hills of Safa and Marwah. They are enclosed within the long building. We have to walk seven times between the hills tonight!" He sat down on a bed and continued reading. "The guide book says that Abraham tested the faith of his wife and son by leaving them in the desert between Safa and Marwah. Hagar ran from one hill to the other seven times in the scorching sun to look for help or water. When she returned to Ishmael, her infant son, she found that a spring had broken forth between the baby's feet. The spring was named the Zamzam Well."

* * *

At the reception desk, I made my inquiry, but I hadn't noticed that Hafez was crowding close behind me. "Who is Father Khaliq? He's not your father."

Irritated, I turned on Hafez. "I think it's quite enough that we're sharing a hotel room, Hafez. Am I to be allowed no privacy?" Hafez was indignant. "What could be private about a question to reception? You asked me to accompany you on this trip and we are friends. Perhaps I could help you. You need only tell me who Father Khaliq is!"

I relented. "I don't know exactly who Father Khaliq is. A Saudi acquaintance asked me to look him up while I'm on the Hajj. Apparently, he is someone important."

"Did they say why you should look him up?"

"No, but the implication was that I would benefit from meeting him."

"What did they say at reception?"

"That there is no one registered at the hotel using the name Khaliq."

Hafez looked around the busy lobby. "Well, if he's important, somebody must know him." He gazed thoughtfully at the tide of white-clad bodies. "I'll tell you what we can do, Kareem. We can make a large sign." He spread his hands half a meter apart. "And we can write on it 'Father Khaliq' in large letters." He drew a question mark in the air.

"No! No, Kareem, that will never do! Have you noticed the level of security they have here? We'd be arrested within two minutes; we'd be questioned for hours and then deported as nut cases or terrorist conspirators."

He shrugged. "We'll just ask important people whether they have seen Father Khaliq."

"Hafez, how in the world can you tell who is an important person when everyone here is wrapped in white bed sheets?"

He tapped the side of his temple. "Don't worry, Kareem. Hafez can tell!"

"All right, Hafez. Let's go and perform the tawaf."

"Just a minute. Let me see what the guide book says."

"We know what it says: seven circuits, counter-clockwise, around the Ka'aba."

"Yes, but let me read about the Ka'aba." He steered me toward a seating area and began to summarize. "The Ka'aba is the world's oldest temple to the one god, Allah. It was built originally by Abraham and his son Ishmael near the Zamzam Well in about 2860 BH (2130 BC). (BH = before Hijra; Hijra is the year Muhammad left Mecca.) It is cubic in shape, about twelve meters on a side. It is made of brick, but the interior walls and floor are lined with marble. Inside the Ka'aba are three columns and a stairway to the roof. At the bottom of the eastern corner is the Black Stone, which was brought to earth by the angel Gabriel. It was originally white, but it has turned black from the sins of the world. It is the only stone remaining of Abraham's original building. The Ka'aba was a heathen place of worship for many years until Muhammad restored it as a temple to Allah and replaced the Black Stone. Outside the door of the Ka'aba is the station of

Abraham: a glass and metal enclosure within which is the footprint of Abraham."

* * *

I will always remember my first tawaf. The heat was inescapable, even at four o'clock in the afternoon. I was surrounded by
white-covered shuffling bodies: moving, always moving, with a
slight deviation to the left. There was the constant hiss of sandals
sliding across the marble pavement, and the indecipherable murmuring of a million prayers. At first, I was afraid I would faint,
falling under two million feet. But then I knew that I would be
floated along by my fellow pilgrims, unable to reach the ground.
At the beginning of each new circuit, left arms, all around me,
would be stretched out in the direction of the Black Stone, and
the intensity of the prayers would be amplified. Light-headed, I
felt the perspiration trickling down my cheeks and sliding down
my back. But I felt no discomfort. It was as if I had left my
body behind, and I was in state of peaceful awareness, riding on
the crest of a wave of humanity, but alone as a seabird. Hours
seemed to float by.

"Kareem! Kareem, are you all right?" It was the insistent
voice of Hafez.

Surprisingly, he was right behind me.

"Yes. Yes, of course."

"How many circuits are you going to do? There are eight
already!"

"Oh, I wasn't counting. It's time for us to complete the sa'i."

* * *

We allowed ourselves to drift out, centrifugally, from the
tawaf and into the sa'i. There were three wide marble-clad parallel galleries: one going in the direction of Mount Safa, one

going in the direction of Mount Marwah, and a central gallery, for infirm pilgrims, which was divided lengthwise in two. Here, it was not so crowded, and as I walked along, I could take in the other pilgrims. Some, indeed, were women. Most of them were dressed in black, and I had expected that their faces would be uncovered – based on what the guide book had said. But many women allowed only their eyes to show. As I scanned the faces of the other men, I thought I could make out a range of emotions: from simple pre-occupation with the task of walking to powerful feelings of religious fervor. Some men, lost in their own identity, were praying aloud as they walked. What are they praying about? I tried to walk close to one man with a grey beard reaching to the middle of his chest. I could make out an occasional 'Allah', but I soon realized that he was speaking a remote tribal dialect, or a language other than Arabic. Walking near other pilgrims was equally unsuccessful: their utterings seemed to have no orderly sentence structure. Rather, it sounded like the murmurings of disjointed thoughts and feelings.

Was this prayer? Elizabeth had said that for her, prayer was the expression of her love for God, a plea for forgiveness of errors, and a request for God's guidance in the future.

I asked her, "Don't you ever pray that something good will happen to you?"

"No," she said, "that isn't necessary. God knows what I need, and it is presumptuous for me to ask."

"Well, do you ever pray that something good will happen to someone else?"

"No, but I sometimes pray that God will help someone who is in difficulty."

I have often wondered since: in what context did I feature in Elizabeth's prayers?

As a child, I was never taught extemporaneous prayer. I suppose my father never thought it was necessary. Rather, in the mosque I recited the Qur'anic prayers, and other memorized invocations and responses. That was all I needed.

Now, I wondered, *What should I be thinking about as I walk along this beautiful corridor? Hagar? Ishmael? Abraham? The Zamzam Well? Or should I be thinking about Allah's gracious gift of the Zamzam Well to Hagar and Ishmael? But I couldn't help thinking, Why did Abraham put Hagar and Ishmael to the test? Perhaps it was Allah's instruction. If so, was it not Allah's intention to demonstrate his care for those who have faith in him?* I didn't know. Perhaps more importantly, I found myself unable to connect at a spiritual level with Hagar and Ishmael. I liked the story, but I didn't feel the personal connection with it that others around me apparently felt.

* * *

When we started the sa'i, Hafez had said, "Kareem, I will meet you back here when I've completed the seven transits."

As we were standing near Mount Safa at the time, I said, "That means you'll complete eight transits, Hafez."

He thought for a moment. "Yes, you're right. But that seems permissible. The main thing is to complete seven. I'm going to run between the green markers. The guide book recommends it. I'll walk the rest of the way."

I slowly ambled back to the starting point, having covered nearly two and a half kilometers.

When Hafez saw me, he rushed over. "I think I have found Father Khaliq!"

"Where?"

"There was a man sitting down there," he gestured to along the gallery toward Mount Marwah. "He looked like a tribal elder."

I frowned, not being clear what a tribal elder looked like.

"You know, Kareem," he said with exasperation. "He looked old, and wise and distinguished."

"OK," I conceded.

"So I went up to him, and I asked him if he knew of a Father Khaliq."

I nodded.

"He looked me up and down for a moment. Then he asked, 'Who wants to know?' And I said, 'My colleague, Professor Kareem al-Busiri, the distinguished professor of philosophy at American University in Cairo.' He nodded wisely for a moment, and then he said, 'Bring him to me.'"

"OK. Let's go."

We walked to Mount Marwah and back toward Mount Safa, as it was forbidden to climb over the barriers between galleries.

Hafez suddenly stopped at a niche in the dark marble wall. He gave an elaborate bow, and I saw that in front of him was an old man sitting cross-legged on the white marble floor. He was balding, his face deeply tanned and creased, and he appeared to be sleeping: his head was slumped to his chest. His white irham clothing formed a kind of tent around him.

"Honored sir!" Hafez began. There was no response. Hafez looked back at me in alarm. I gestured for him to continue.

Hafez moved closer. He boomed, "Honored sir!"

Slowly, the man raised his head; his attention began to focus on Hafez. As the man reached up to stroke his sparse grey beard, I could see that he was indeed old. His nose was running and his eyes were rheumy. "Yes, what is it pilgrim?"

"Honored sir, we spoke not long ago about Father Khaliq. I have brought with me my colleague who is trying to find him."

The old man began to focus his attention on me. "So, you are Professor al-Busiri."

"Yes, sir. May I ask your name?"

"I am Alim of Medina." He paused, considering me. "You are seeking Father Khaliq?"

"Yes, sir, I am."

"Why do you seek Father Khaliq?"

"Well," I said, "it was Princess Basheera who asked me to find him. I am doing it as a favor to her."

"Hmmm. Did Princess Basheera promise you some reward if you found him?"

"No, sir. No specific reward, but I believe she said I would be rewarded for finding him."

"Yes, quite so."

"Sheikh Alim – may I call you 'sheikh' (ruler)?" I began.

"No," he said, "I am only Hakim (wise man)."

I nodded. "Do you know Princess Basheera, Hakim?"

"No, I have only heard of her."

"Can you tell me where I might find Father Khaliq?"

"Have you not encountered him, pilgrim?"

"It is possible that I saw him, but how can I pick him out among all these people?"

"Have you followed the prescribed rituals for the Hajj? I see that you are in irham. Have you said the prayer of intention?"

I didn't see the point of this question, but I said, "Yes, Hakim, and we have completed the tawah and the sa'i."

He shrugged. "I believe that you will find him . . . if you are diligent."

I found his confidence reassuring, but his evasiveness was frustrating. I decided to be more specific. "Have you, yourself, encountered Father Khaliq today?"

He stroked his beard for a moment. "Yes."

"Where was it?"

He thought for a moment. "It was over by the Ka'baa."

"And what time would that have been?"

"I don't measure the minutes and hours, pilgrim."

That was probably true, I thought. "And do you have an idea where he went after you last saw him, Hakim?"

"No, but I am sure he is still here somewhere."

"Thank you, Hakim!" I bowed and stepped back. The old man closed his eyes, lowered his chin to his chest and seemed to fall asleep.

As we walked away, Hafez grabbed my arm forcefully. "Kareem, you didn't tell me about this Princess Basheera! Where did you meet her?"

I told him briefly about the encounter at the Kempinski. "Was she good looking, Kareem?"

I gave him an impatient look. "How would I know, Hafez?"

Lamely, he said, "I thought you might have . . ."

"There's no point in guessing, Hafez."

Glumly, he said, "I suppose you're right."

We walked on for several minutes.

"Still," he said, brightly, "I think this Princess Basheera is probably quite good looking and very wealthy. Have you ever thought of marrying a younger woman, Kareem?

"No."

"Well, I suggest you give it some thought!" He gave me a meaningful look. "Because I'm going to help you find Father Khaliq, and when we do, Princess Basheera is going to be so grateful she'll take off her niqab and kiss you, and then . . ."

"Hafez!" I interrupted. "You've been reading too many fairy tales!"

"Well, Professor, you just wait and see. Hafez is going to make it happen!"

And I couldn't escape the cynical thought: And Kareem will be so grateful to Hafez that Kareem gives Hafez the boost he needs for tenure.

* * *

"Have you had some of this water, Kareem?" Hafez was gesturing toward the side of the gallery where there was a table covered with a white cloth. I took in the large transparent bottles, the sides of which were streaming with condensation. The water must be cold, I thought. I was suddenly thirsty.

"No. Is it good?"

"It is excellent! It's Zamzam Well water." Hafez accepted a plastic cup from an attendant and handed it to me. To me it tasted like perfectly normal cold mineral water.

Hafez thought otherwise. "Have you ever tasted such soft, sweet water? Most unusual! Delicious!"

Hafez is really enjoying this experience! But what is it about the Hajj that he finds so exciting? Somehow I don't think it's the spiritual dimension.

* * *

That night at dinner, I asked Hafez what he thought was motivating most of the pilgrims on the Hajj.

"Well," he said, "the main motivation is that it is one of the Five Pillars of Islam: one is expected to complete the Hajj sometime in one's lifetime."

"All right, but once the pilgrim is here, what does he or she find most rewarding?"

"It could be any one of a number of pleasing aspects."

"How about for you, Hafez? What do you find most pleasing?"

"For me, it is a great experience of the senses!" He was looking at me for affirmation, but when I frowned in puzzlement, he continued, "Have you ever seen a spectacle like this? Two million people here in this mosque! Moving as a tide of white! Have you ever heard so many prayers uttered at the same time? Have you ever tasted water as pure and refreshing as that from Zamzam Well? And the scents? Hundreds of perfumes of women from all over the world! Have you ever rubbed shoulders with so many nationalities, so many races, so many occupations, from the very richest to the very poorest! I will remember it to my dying day!"

I nodded, but my affirmation was unconvincing. "Is it the same for you, Kareem?"

"I see what you mean, Hafez, and I share your assessment, but for me the most memorable aspect is the mystery."

It was Hafez's turn to be perplexed. "What mystery? Are you referring to the whereabouts of Father Khaliq?"

"No, it's not about Father Khaliq. I am speaking about the mystery of these ceremonies. Why are we here? Why these particular ceremonies? What do they mean? What should I pray and why?"

"With great respect, Kareem, the answers to those questions are printed in the guide book."

He doesn't get it. How can I get him to understand? "The mysteries involve me as a person, Hafez. If one looks at my questions from the point of view of the general public, and one discusses them socially, historically, anthropologically, the mysteries disappear. But what do these mysteries mean to me, as an individual person? That is my question."

He shook his head gently. "I think you're trying to read too much into it, Kareem."

"Perhaps so. In any case, you enjoyed today."

"Yes, very much so."

* * *

The following morning, our group of thirty-six was herded together by Mahdi in one corner of the lobby. "In a few moments, we will be boarding our private coach to Mina. We will be spending the next several nights in Mina, so I want to be sure everyone has his overnight bag." He scanned the group for a possible problem. None was presented. "In the Valley of Mina, Abraham stoned the devil, who was standing in the way of fulfilling a command Allah gave to Abraham. It is also the place where Abraham sacrificed his camels. There are over one hundred thousand air-conditioned tents in Mina. We have three adjacent tents for our group. There are toilet facilities nearby. We are in an executive area, but may I suggest that you avoid being 'nosey,' as this invariably leads to security investigations. Our buffet meals will be served in the tents. There are franchised take-aways operating in Mina; we recommend that you try to avoid these. We have made arrangements for a lecture by a knowledgeable Qur'anic scholar at four this afternoon. This will take place in the middle tent. We recommend that you try to attend this lecture. Otherwise, today is a day of prayer and rest. Please make a note of the number and location of your tent. We don't want anyone to get lost! I will be in the middle tent, if anyone has any questions."

"Excuse me, Mahdi," someone spoke up, "Is it possible for us to walk to Mina? I understand that there is a tunnel. Somehow, walking seems more authentic."

"There is a tunnel, part way. It tends to get very crowded and quite hot this time of year. The distance is about four kilometers, and it will take around two hours. There is also the problem of locating our tents on arrival. I think you will be better off taking the bus."

* * *

Mina was an incredible sight! A seemingly endless vista, reaching in every direction, of white tents, each with its conical cap. Our tent, like most, was about four meters square, with at least a meter of head room. The walls were insulating block and there was carpeting over the sandy floor. Inside, there was no ornamentation, but it was a welcome 25 degrees (77° F) and the air-conditioning unit was humming.

I didn't plan to pray all day. Some of my fellow pilgrims settled themselves with pillows and blankets and slept. Knowing that I would neither sleep nor pray, I reached into my overnight bag and brought out two books, one of which was the Qur'an. From a stack in a corner, I released a white plastic chair and seated myself by a polystyrene window.

"You going to read, Kareem?" Hafez inquired.

"Yes, for a while."

"I think I'm going to take a look around."

"You have your mobile phone with you?"

"I'm not going to get lost," he replied; he stepped outside the door flap and disappeared.

* * *

For a time I perused my copy of the Qur'an, looking up occasionally to see what other pilgrims were doing. Only eight of us were left in the tent, and four were asleep. One was praying, facing away from me toward Mecca, and the other two, unlike me, were absorbed in their reading. I drew out the other book: St. Augustine of Hippo, Life and Controversies, by G. Bonner. Here was a philosopher about whom I knew next to nothing – for two reasons: he was a Christian, and he lived in the second century BH (4th century AD). But I knew that he was reputedly a wise philosopher – one with some interesting ideas about man and his relationship with the Almighty. What better time to explore his ideas?

I skipped over his early, immoral life and adherence to paganism, as well as his conversion to Christianity and the positions he held in the church.

Augustine described the human being as an entity originally in perfect harmony: a marriage between the body and soul, but since the fall of humanity, the body and soul are in conflict. This is interesting! He is saying that the body tempts the soul into sin, and it has been doing so since Adam and Eve! He said that the soul has no spatial dimension, while the body is three dimensional, and he classified the soul as superior on the basis of three categories of existence: those that merely exist, those that exist and live, and those that exist and live and have intelligence.

Shortly after lunch, I went outside the tent to see what was to be seen. Immediately, I was subsumed in the intense heat: with no head covering, the sun's heat was fierce, and the ambient temperature – I learned that it was 42 degrees (108° F) – made it inescapable.

I looked down the pathway to the west, and there was an extraordinary sight! At the base of a hillside were the exits of two huge tunnels. And from the tunnels flowed a dense stream of people. It was as if the tunnels were vomiting humanity. The stream flowed down the roads and dispersed into Mina's capillaries of roads and pathways en route to its cellular tents.

* * *

Augustine argued in his 'doctrine of inner illumination' that the Almighty plays a part in human perception and understanding by illuminating the mind so that humans can recognize the intelligible realities that God presents. According to Augustine, illumination is obtainable to all rational minds and is different from other forms of sense perception. I'm not sure about this. It seems to me that some rational minds – mine included, perhaps? – don't 'recognize the intelligible realities that God presents'. But maybe the operative word in that sentence is 'obtainable', meaning that it is possible. If that is the case, what is it that makes that special sense obtainable? This, he has not disclosed!

Augustine's philosophy includes the claim that the Almighty created humans as rational beings, possessing free will. Free will, Augustine thought, was not intended for a sinful world, so that free will is not equally predisposed to good and evil. A will that has been defiled by sin is not considered to be "free" as it once was, because it is bound by material things, things that can be lost and difficult to part with, thus resulting in unhappiness.

Sin impairs free will, but it is restored by grace. Only a will that was once free can be subjected to the corruption of sin. All this makes sense to me! But what is 'grace'? He does not say.

* * *

"Kareem, come with me! I think I've found a lead!" An excited Hafez burst into the tent.

"A lead to what?" I enquired.

"To Father Khaliq, of course! Come with me!"

I followed him along a zigzag route among the tents, along pathways, down streets and under overpasses. We finally came to a large tent with an open flap through which a stream of people were entering and leaving. Inside, was a long table which had been divided into eight or ten stations. Behind the table, at each station, was a seated man wearing the typical Saudi head covering: ghutra (a piece of fabric) and igal (headband). At each station, there was a monitor and keyboard.

"Let's get in this queue!" Hafez commanded, pushing me toward a station.

"Hafez, what is this place?"

"This is where you can find out whether the old friend you haven't seen for twenty years is here on the Hajj and what tent he's been assigned to."

"So they check some sort of a database?"

"Exactly! And it's only 50 Saudi Riyals ($13)."

"But Hafez, this isn't going to work. You're assuming that somebody has registered for the Hajj under the name 'Father Khaliq'."

"Well, perhaps he did. Here's your chance to find him!"

As we approached the front of the queue, I could observe other pilgrims completing their transactions. The operator would ask for the name and would type it on the keyboard. More often than not, the operator would nod, hand the pilgrim a slip of paper, and collect 50 SR. Apparently, some names were blocked. I heard one pilgrim ask for a name which I recognized as the Saudi oil minister. The operator shook his finger at the pilgrim. Occasionally, a match could not be found and the operator shook his head.

We were next in the queue. "Name, please?" the operator prompted.

"Basheera Chagma," I responded.

I felt Hafez elbow my ribs. "What are you doing, Kareem?"

"Be patient, Hafez."

The operator nodded, tore a strip from his printer, and handed it to me. "Fifty riyals, please."

I handed him fifty riyals from my purse and asked, "I have another name, if you don't mind."

"What is it?"

"Father Khaliq."

He typed the name and perused his monitor. "Nothing. Sorry."

Outside the tent, Hafez was shaking his head in disappointment.

"Excuse me, sir, unable to find someone you were expecting?" A man in an unblemished white thawb (knee-length shirt) and carrying a briefcase approached. "Ah," the man offered in a sympathetic tone, "he's probably on the blocked list."

Hafez looked at me. "You said he's a prominent person, Kareem. He probably is on the blocked list."

"As it happens," the man said, "I may be able to help you."

"How can you help?" Hafez asked.

"Well, sir, I have certain connections to the interior ministry which allow me access to blocked names on the database."

"So you think you can find Father Khaliq?"

"Undoubtedly, sir, if his name is blocked, I will be able to get you his tent number."

I didn't like the man's confident unctuousness. "How much is your service?"

"It is only five hundred riyals, sir, and in terms of the value of reaching an important friend, it is only a small gratuity."

I decided to make things difficult for this man. "We will come with you then."

"Sir, that's not necessary. You only need wait for me here."

"All right, then."

"The money, sir?"

"We'll pay you when you return."

"No, sir. You will understand that I have certain expenses to meet in the interior ministry."

"Thank you for your offer," I said and turned away. The man began to remonstrate, catching at the sleeve of my ihram. I stopped and faced him, making eye contact. "No, thank you."

The man bowed and disappeared.

"Do you think it was a scam, Kareem?"

"Yes, Hafez, it was certainly a scam."

"Well, what about the ticket you have for the princess?"

I looked at the slip of paper, which read: 'Basheera Chagma Female Area 746 Section G4 Row 17 Tent R.'

I shook my head. "I don't think she's here."

"Then why did you pay for the search?"

"I was just curious, I guess."

"Well, if you're curious, let's go check!"

He can't wait to meet Princess Basheera! "Where is Area 746?" I asked.

"Let me have the ticket. I'll find her."

We set off, Hafez leading and holding a map in one hand, the ticket in the other.

"OK," he said, "This is Area 746. Now Section G4 is over this way. OK. Here is Row 17. And Tent R is this one!"

We were standing outside a tent, the flap of which was closed. Hafez put an index finger to his lips and we listened. There was the low murmur of female voices within. My colleague gestured for me to continue. I cleared my throat. "Ahem! Is there a Basheera Chagma in this tent?"

The murmuring stopped. I repeated my question. "Who is inquiring?"

"Professor Kareem al-Busiri of Cairo University."

Silence within. Then, "What is it that the professor wants with Basheera Chagma?"

"I only wish to speak briefly with the lady."

Murmuring from within. The tent flap opened and a woman in black, holding a piece of black fabric over her nose and mouth, appeared

"Excuse me. I am seeking Basheera Chagma."

"I am she."

The voice was half an octave lower than I remembered. The pronunciation was imperfect and slower. I could see crow's feet at the corners of the eyes.

"Excuse me, madam, but did we meet about six weeks ago in the Kempinski hotel in Cairo?"

"No," she said coldly. "You are mistaken. I have never been to Cairo."

"I am indeed mistaken. My apologies, madam." I turned away, but when Hafez and I were about to turn a corner, I looked back. The woman was still standing at the tent flap. She's probably wondering what I wanted with the other Basheera Chagma and whether it was wise to say 'no' so quickly.

* * *

Hafez was thoroughly disappointed with our failure to find a clear path to Father Khaliq. When we had returned to our tent, he was casting about for alternative paths. "Maybe, if we . . ."

"We have a guest speaker who's going to address us shortly, Hafez. I think we should listen to what he has to say."

Mahdi announced, "Our guest speaker this afternoon is Imam al-Shahab from the central mosque in Tunis. He has studied the Jinn, and he has personal experience in dealing with the Jinn. I know you will welcome the imam and his talk on this fascinating topic."

The imam began his talk by asking, by show of hands, how many of us had experienced the Jinn. Five or six people raised their hands with conviction, and about another ten responded tentatively. I knew that Jinn are mentioned in the Qur'an, but I had only a foggy notion of what they are, and I certainly had no experience in dealing with them.

"Let me explain," the imam began, "that the Jinn are like human beings, but they are invisible. In the Qur'an, sura 15, ayahs 26 and 27 say: 'We created man out of dried clay formed from dark mud – the Jinn we created before, from the fire of scorching wind.'" The imam continued, "The Jinn are mentioned many times in the Qur'an; they are beings created with free will, living on earth in a world parallel to mankind. The word 'Jinn' is from the verb 'Janna' which means to hide or conceal. Thus, they are physically invisible to man. This invisibility is one of the reasons some people have denied the existence of the Jinn. However the effects which the Jinn have upon our world are enough to confirm their reality."

The imam went on to say that sura 55 of the Qur'an divides mankind and the Jinn into three categories: disbelievers, best of believers and ordinary believers. Jinn are like humans in many respects: they have children and they die; their social organization is similar; they have kings, courts of law, weddings, and mourning rituals. They, like humans, will be judged by almighty Allah. Qur'an 37:158 says: '. . . Jinn themselves know that they will be brought before Him'. They will be judged on the Day of Judgment and will be sent to Paradise or Hell according to their deeds.

Jinn can adopt animal forms, and can see humans clearly, even taking possession of them sometimes.

The imam said that each human is assigned a jinni or qarin, who may be good or evil. If the qarin is evil, it will whisper to the human soul and persuade it to submit to evil desires. Apart from the qarin, Shaytan whispers into each human mind. Shaytan was an ordinary Jinn who refused Allah's command to bow down to Adam after Adam's creation. For this disobedience, Shaytan was banished from Paradise.

"The Qur'an 16:98-99 says: 'Prophet, when you recite the Qur'an, seek Allah's protection from the outcast, Shaytan. He has no power over those who believe and trust in their Lord'."

Imam al-Shabab went on at considerable length to give examples of the prayers which will afford protection from Shaytan and the evil Jinn. As, for example, before engaging in sexual intercourse.

For me, this was quite interesting. I can believe I have a qarin, because sometimes I have a thought – seemingly independent of my own mind – which urges me to take a particular course of action. I'm not entirely sure, however, whether my qarin is good or evil. Sometimes the 'voice' urges what seems on the face of it to be a good action which turns out to be bad. At other times – not very often, I have to say – I find myself succumbing to wicked advice which turns out to be quite good for all concerned. I suppose what I should do is have a little prayer handy that I can use to ward off the wicked advice! But that assumes I have the willpower to say, and, if necessary, repeat the prayer before seizing upon the wicked advice!

* * *

Early the next morning, we were awakened by Mahdi. "We are going now to Mount Arafat. This is the place where the Prophet gave his last speech in which he asked Allah to forgive all those who were with him. In fact, Arafat is known as the Mount of Mercy, because Allah granted the wish of the Prophet.

We will spend the day on the Plain of Arafat; you can climb the hill if you wish. It is only seventy meters high, but it will be quite crowded, and very hot. Be sure to bring plenty of water with you. Our group has an awning that will provide some shade, but it is not air conditioned and has no side flaps. Pilgrims who come to Arafat spend the day in prayer seeking the forgiveness of their sins and resolving to lead a new, sinless life."

Once again, we boarded the bus for a short, slow trip. From the windows of the bus, we could see great rivers of white-clad pilgrims creeping toward the Plain of Arafat.

Hafez, sitting next to me, whispered, "Kareem, I am very glad that you booked us on the VIP package. Can you imagine walking hours in that sun with no head covering?"

I said, "But they are not foolish, Hafez. They know the sun is hot, and they will be in pain. Nonetheless, they persevere, and they believe."

Hafez shrugged. "They believe in Allah."

"Yes, but that isn't what motivates them to spend a day on foot, in intense heat, praying incessantly."

Hafez shook his head; I could see he didn't get it.

I whispered, "What motivates them is the blessing of forgiveness, and the knowledge that they have not lived in vain."

Hafez frowned. "I don't think I've lived in vain."

"I know you don't."

Hafez gave me an indignant stare. "Do you think I've lived in vain, Kareem?"

"No, I wouldn't say that, but do you ever regret your sins?"

"What sins?"

"Well, there was that married student you mentioned."

"Oh, come on, Kareem, it was private and we both enjoyed it."

"How many of those pilgrims out there," I said, gesturing out the window, "do you think are putting themselves through extreme discomfort for exactly the same private enjoyment?"

"Too many!"

There was no point in giving Hafez a lecture.

I lapsed into pensiveness. It isn't just that Hafez has a higher threshold of pain for his sins than that fellow there, I thought with a glance at a pilgrim in the dense crowd whose perspiring face was turned up to heaven. Nor is it that Hafez's sins are lighter than that fellow's – though they may well be. And I don't think the difference is accounted for by their relative faiths in Allah. I think the difference in their behavior is attributable to the way each of them experiences repentance. Hafez doesn't want to be bothered with repentance. For that man with the sunburned, sweating face, the physical and mental anguish of repentance yields – somehow – a joyful catharsis, a new and welcome identity.

Where am I on the spectrum between Hafez and That Man?

I am much closer to Hafez than to That Man.

And it's not because I have no sins. For a second, the image of Nane, my servant, bent over the table, her back to me and her skirts piled on her back, flashed through my mind. It is not that she is unwilling. She is glad of the one hundred extra pounds (£15), but she is married with a family. Does it matter how it started? No. What matters is that I want no one to know. I have a secret; Hafez has an open secret. He can just shrug; I am obsessed with secrecy, and the search for rationalization.

I spent most of that day under the blue awning, which became too hot to touch. There was not the slightest draft of air. One had to loosen the ihram and mop away the perspiration. Sleep was impossible: the ground was uneven and rocky; no mattresses, only plastic chairs were provided. Most of the pilgrims in our group sat, moaning what sounded like prayers. I prayed silently that the day would be over, opening my Qur'an, turning the pages slowly, and comprehending almost nothing. For his part, Hafez talked with whomever would listen, and, when he ran out of listeners, he borrowed my book on Augustine of Hippo.

* * *

At noon there was a call to prayer which came over the loudspeakers. An imam led us through the noon and afternoon prayers together. Then he summarized the instructions which Muhammad gave to his audience. He abolished blood feuds and said that the color of a man's skin was not to be used to judge superiority. He said, "Be good to women, for they are powerless captives in your households. You took them in God's trust, and legitimated your sexual relations with the Word of God, so come to your senses, people, and hear my words ..." He forbade certain devious practices in inheritance. And finally, he said, "Today I have perfected your religion, and completed my favors for you and chosen Islam as a religion for you."

* * *

At about two in the afternoon, I felt an urge to climb Mount Arafat. I had come within half a kilometer of the icon; how could I not say I had climbed it? I made my way through the crowds of pilgrims standing or sitting in small groups in the blazing sun – many with their upper ihram converted into a kind of awning. When I arrived at the base of the hill, I looked up, hoping to see a pathway to the summit. Instead, all I could see was white clusters of pilgrims amidst brown boulders. There were paths, but each path was jammed completely with pilgrims – in fact, there was at least one pilgrim sitting on each rock and boulder, from the base to the summit. At the summit itself, there was a huge white concrete obelisk, and from that point one third of the way down, the hill was packed solid with white-clad human beings. Well, I guess I'm not going to make it to the summit. I can't say that I was disappointed. In fact, I don't even think I want to climb up five meters. What would be the point?

I stood and gazed at Mount Arafat. Then I turned and looked two hundred and seventy degrees around the Plains of Arafat with their rivers of pilgrims, millions of individuals covering the scorching ochre earth. Why? There is mystery here, was all I could conclude. I knew that there was a commandment to fulfill, a once-in-a-lifetime experience, perhaps an element of faith, but I sensed that this was not enough to account for the spectacle before me.

A mystery.

* * *

I was beginning to pick my way back to our awning when I heard shouts from people approaching me. There was always the buzzing murmur of the pilgrims, and, if you were near their moving river, the shuffling sound of their feet. But never shouting. Here was a group of five men running through the crowds and shouting, "Make way! Medical emergency!" They rushed past me to the base of the hill. There were answering shouts from the hill: "He is here!" The medics began shouting at the pilgrims to clear a path, and they hurried upward, bearing a stretcher. There was a kerfuffle involving medics and pilgrims about a third of the way up the hill. I couldn't see what was happening, except that there was some disagreement. The scrum of medics and pilgrims was surrounded by a press of pilgrims, three or four deep, who were trying to make out what was going on. The kerfuffle subsided and the medics began picking their way down the hill: one in front, shooing people out of the way, four carrying the stretcher, and a group of pilgrims immediately behind. When they reached level ground, the medics set the stretcher down. When I moved closer to see what was going on, it became apparent that the disagreement had resumed. Lying on the stretcher was an emaciated, white-haired pilgrim, motionless, mouth open.

"You can't just leave him here!" one of the pilgrims protested.

"We are not the mortuary service!" the lead medic responded. "You can call General Security Services on four one one. They will send someone."

"But can't you just carry him to a tent? We can't just leave him here in the sun!"

The lead medic shook his head vehemently. "The tents are all private. We can't go invading them. You'll have to cover him and await Mortuary Service." He gestured for his colleagues to remove the man from the stretcher. "Sorry, we have to respond to another call."

The body was removed from the stretcher and the medics hurried off. The friends or relatives of the dead pilgrim stood around him, trying to decide what to do. They were speaking a tribal language I didn't understand, but from their body language they seemed somewhat remote from the deceased. Not family, maybe not even friends; just acquaintances? I moved closer, as all but the most curious drifted away.

"May I help you?" I asked in Arabic.

Their conversation stopped and they turned to face me. One of the men said, "This man has died. We're not sure who he is. He was assigned to our tent in Mina."

"Where are you from?" I asked.

"From Algeria."

"I think he was also from Algeria," another pilgrim volunteered, "but not from our village." He paused. "We want to get him to a tent. Then call Mortuary Services."

Without even thinking, I said, "You can bring him to my tent."

One of the men took off his upper body ihram. The deceased was laid in it and four men lifted the corners. "He is very light," one of them reported.

As we approached the awning, I began to worry that Mahdi would object to sharing the shade with a corpse. I explained the situation while the cortege stood outside in the sun. But Mahdi was immediately sympathetic, inviting them in and calling Mortuary Services, giving them the location of our awning. He also found spare ihrams to cover the deceased.

"But sir," one of the Algerians lamented, "we don't know who this man is."

"The officials will find out. One of you may have to go back to your tent with an official."

"You mean they're going to take him back to the tent?"

"No, they will take him to the mortuary. But if one of you can go to your tent with an official, they will be able to identify the man and collect his personal effects."

"Will the man be buried here?"

"No, his body will be sent back to Algeria."

"We are poor people, sir, will we have to pay something on his behalf?"

"No. His repatriation will be paid by Saudi, Algeria and his travel company."

Later, I said to Mahdi, "Thank you for being such a help to those poor Algerians."

"Thank you, Professor, for bringing them here so I could help."

"You seem to be quite familiar with death during the Hajj."

He shrugged. "It happens all too frequently. You have two million pilgrims exposed to intense heat in the summer or bitter cold during winter nights. The majority of pilgrims are getting on in age: they are preoccupied with the need to complete the Hajj during their lifetime and may not be in the best of health to begin with. Then, too, there are man-made disasters: falls, accidents and so on."

I couldn't resist. "Have you lost one of your clients, Mahdi?"

He nodded. "A few years ago, I had an elderly client who was quite overweight. He felt the need to imitate Hagar by running the full length of the seven transitions of the sai. He had a heart attack and died." There was a pause. "But you know, Professor, I was with that man just before he died, and he said something like, 'I've done it! Just as Hagar did! Now Allah is going to take me!' It was as if he felt that his last act justified his entire life. And I've heard other tour guides say the same thing: generally, people are happy to die on the Hajj!"

At sunset the temperature started to moderate. We boarded our bus for Muzdalifa, which is midway between Arafat and Mina. Here, we would spend the night on the open, sandy ground, but unlike the barren Plain of Arafat, there was a scattering of deciduous trees. Mahdi led us to an area between four trees which had been fenced off. We each selected a spot which would be our bed for the night. Loudspeakers boomed out the call to the evening prayer, which was immediately followed by the isha prayer, the last of the five daily prayers.

Grateful for the blanket I had been given by Mahdi, I lay on my back looking up at the stars, which were quite clear. I felt peaceful, but very much alone in spite of Hafez's presence a few meters away. *I wonder what my children are doing. . . . I wonder if Elizabeth is aware of me. . . . I'm often aware of her.*

I heard Hafez ask Mahdi, "When do we have to collect the stones?"

"You don't have to look for them, Professor, we will give you a bag of stones in the morning."

In the morning we moved back to Mina, and from our tent we walked to the Jamaraat Bridge for the Stoning of the Devil. This stoning takes place on three successive days during the Hajj. It is a re-enactment of Abraham's stoning of the devil on three occasions under the direction of the Angel Gabriel.

"It is intended to remind us that we must put aside our own temptations," Mahdi explained, "and be closer to Allah."

More than any other aspect of the Hajj, the Stoning of the Devil brought home to me the scale of the Hajj in the twenty-first century. In my father's time, there were only three jamarat (pillars) which pilgrims would stone seven times, each in sequence, at ground level. But now, there were three jamarat walls, each nearly the length of a football pitch, and accessible to pilgrims on the four-level Jamaraat Bridge. It is now possible for pilgrims on each side of the three jamarat on four levels to throw stones. In this configuration, thousands of pilgrims can simultaneously stone the devil without overcrowding and without hitting each other with stones.

Mahdi told us that the Stoning of the Devil has been the most dangerous event of the Hajj: in recent years, hundreds of pilgrims have been killed in stampedes. But now, with the huge, new multi-level bridge, the new jamarat walls, and with a fatwa permitting the stoning to take place between the noon and evening prayers (rather than immediately after the noon prayer) the event is considered quite safe.

Hafez and I, each with a sack of large pebbles, followed our group to the second level of the bridge. There was no artificial light; the air was filled with dust and the drone of murmurings of thousands of pilgrims. At a higher pitch came the constant crackle of stones against cement. As I threw each stone, I tried to focus on the symbolic meaning: I am stoning the devil. I am renouncing my own temptations. I want to be closer to Allah.

But my intentions – weak as they may have been – were drowned out by my consciousness of the press of bodies around me, and my awareness of being crushed if there were to be a sudden panic.

As we walked back to our tent, I asked Hafez, "What was that experience like for you, Hafez?"

He gave a brief shrug. "All right. Nothing particularly exciting. I noticed some people who seemed to take a lot of time between each stone throw. I just fired away at the old bastard."

"Probably they were praying between throws."

Another shrug. "Probably. . . . We have to get our hair cut now, Kareem."

"That comes after the sacrifice," I reminded him.

"We've already done that."

"Yes, we've paid for it to be done on our behalf, but I think Mahdi expects us to attend one."

"I don't need to attend one to remember the story of Abraham being ready to sacrifice his son at the request of Allah."

Nonetheless, we went to an open area among the tents where there was a paddock filled with young sheep and goats. Under foot, the sand was almost black and sticky. The animals were making anxious bleating noises. A group of men dressed in stained coveralls were selling the animals, assisting with the slaughter, and piling the carcasses into a truck. I watched one pilgrim dressed in his white ihram take a terrified, bleating goat from a seller and struggle to keep the animal quiet while he said his prayer. Then, brandishing a knife provided by the seller, he slit the animal's throat. In its death throes, the animal sprayed the pilgrim with blood.

I nudged Hafez, and we went back to our tent.

I had not seen an animal slaughtered since I was a child and I had accompanied my father to buy an Eid al-Adha (Feast of the Sacrifice) lamb at the market in Cairo. The lamb was dispatched very quickly by a professional, but I remember being sick and distressed – unable to eat much of the lamb. I remember when I told Elizabeth about that childhood experience, she said, "You pretend to logical and indifferent to emotion, but you are sometimes quite illogical and vulnerable. Besides, you are entirely happy to eat the lamb I cook."

"Yes, but I don't have to watch it die."

"Neither do I. That's why I buy a whole leg of lamb from the butcher."

* * *

Hafez was having difficulty making up his mind. He understood that on the Hajj, on 10th of Dhu al-Hijjah, men could either shave their heads or cut their hair. Shaving his head was, I suppose like me, out of the question for reasons of vanity. I had decided that Hafez was to cut the top knot at the back of my head with the electric clippers which Mahdi was passing around. This would leave me with a rather obvious bald spot, but I thought, I can cover it with a Taqiyah (prayer cap). Left to decide for himself, Hafez would have carefully trimmed his beard, but Mahdi ruled this out. "Professor, you can trim your beard any day. On the Hajj, you must do something memorable!"

Finally, Hafez handed the clippers to me. "Do the same for me."

* * *

On the next two days at Mina, in addition to more Stoning of the Devil and prayer, we listened to lectures from prominent imams. The first of these was from Muscat, Oman, and he spoke about The Life History of Our Prophet. He started out by telling a story of how Muhammad, as an orphan child, was accompanying a caravan bound from Mecca to Syria, loaded with frankincense, spices and silks. The caravan stopped at the cave of a Christian hermit named Bahira, who became supernaturally aware that there was a person of great importance in the caravan. Bahira insisted that the boy, who had been left to watch the camels, should be brought to him. The hermit examined the boy and spoke with him. He recognized a mark between the boy's shoulders as the seal of prophethood. As the caravan was about to depart, Bahira said to the boy's uncle, "Go back home with your nephew and keep an eye on him. If the Jews see him and get to know what I know about him, they will certainly do him harm, for he is going to be a very big man."

The imam went on to explain that it was very difficult for an orphan growing up in Mecca in the first century BH (600 AD). The Meccans were traders, and without the financial resources and strong family/tribal connections, it was difficult for Muhammad to make his mark in society unless he found a rich woman to marry. At the age of about twenty-five he married Khadijah, a wealthy, independent woman with property, probably in her late thirties, who already had two husbands. With Khadijah, he had four daughters and two sons, although the latter died in infancy. He was modestly successful in commerce with the nephew of Khadijah's second husband as his partner. Muhammad was a talented administrator, and, although he could have succeeded in the largest trading operations in Mecca, the great merchants excluded him from their inner circle. This exclusion weighed heavily on Muhammad and caused him to seek solitude in the barren, rocky hills outside of Mecca. There was a particular cave where he went for several nights at a time to pray and meditate in solitude. On several occasions he had vivid dreams or visions in which a glorious Being approached him. The Being communicated a revelation to him. The Qur'an 53:4-11 says, "The Qur'an is nothing less than a revelation that was sent to him. It was taught to him by an angel with mighty powers and great strength, who stood on the highest horizon and then approached – coming down until he was two bow-lengths away, or even closer – and revealed to Allah's servant what He revealed." At first, Muhammad thought this was Allah himself, but later, he identified it as the angel Gabriel.

Apparently, Muhammad, in moods of despair, would walk along the rocky hills and think of throwing himself down a cliff. At these times an angel would remind him, "Thou art the messenger of Allah."

I found it surprising that the great Prophet and Messenger of Allah would be subject to fits of depression. I imagined him striding down the streets of Mecca, nodding with just a hint of condescension to his new converts and turning away disdainfully from the polytheists. I visualized him speaking thunderously in the mosque after a momentous hill-top discussion with

Gabriel. But here was this outcast orphan boy who, through his own credibility and commitment, founded the great Islamic religion. I wonder why Allah chose him to be his Messenger.

The mention of Muhammad's dreams and visions brought to mind a tendency of my own. When I was a child, alone in a quiet space and feeling tired, I reported to my mother that her sister had come to see me and had asked me to bring her a small bouquet of flowers.

"But Kareem, you know that my sister lives in Paris," Mama protested.

"Yes, I know, but I saw her, and she wants me to bring her some flowers. She didn't mention what kind of flowers."

"I will speak to her about it."

Sometime later Mama mentioned to me, "Auntie said she would like you to bring her some nice white Nile lilies when you come to Paris for a visit."

And with Elizabeth, I remember telling her that her father had asked for help. He was leading a project to replace the plain glass windows down the nave of the church in Chicago with a stained glass depictions of Old Testament scenes.

"What kind of help did he ask for?" asked my doubtful wife.

"He wasn't very clear, but I think we wants us to propose something for one window."

"But I'm sure he knows that Islam has no images of Old Testament figures," Elizabeth protested. She found out that what he wanted to know was whether we would contribute to a group which was commissioning a window on Abraham and the Burning Bush.

* * *

A breathless Hafez came and shook me while I was listening to the Oman imam. "Come outside! I have a new lead!"

I bowed to the imam and made my way out of the tent. "What is it, Hafez?"

82

"I've been listening to this speaker in the tent over there, and he mentioned Father Khaliq."

"Which tent?"

"This tent . . . right here," Hafez announced, steering me forcibly to the entrance of a tent.

Inside the tent the pilgrims were all on their feet, talking. Accosting one of the pilgrims, Hafez asked, "Where is the speaker?"

"I think he left."

"Where did he go?" Hafez had a hold on the pilgrim's arm.

The pilgrim frowned and pushed Hafez's hand away. "How should I know?"

"Well, he did mention Father Khaliq, didn't he?"

"I don't remember."

"Well, it's very important. My colleague is trying to find Father Khaliq."

Hafez animation and sense of urgency was attracting the attention of bystanders, one of whom offered, "I think he did say something about Father Khaliq, but I don't remember what it was."

Hafez looked around. "Does anyone know where he went?"

For the next hour and a half, we followed the suggestions we were given, but we were unable to locate the missing speaker. No one could remember his name. Several pilgrims, however, thought he was an imam from Amman, Jordan.

* * *

On the 12th of Dhu al-Hijjah, Hafez and I returned with our group to Mecca, where we performed the Tawaf al-Wida, our seven farewell circuits around the Ka'aba. More than before, I felt the mystery of this ritual, but it was beyond a mystery. I felt that I had been spiritually cleansed and renewed. It was not that I felt a new dedication to Islam, or that I intended to be more committed to prayer. I just felt that I had become a better person.

"You know," Hafez said while we were waiting at the airport, "that we can now use the title 'Al-Hajji'.

"No, I didn't know that."

"I am now Professor Al-Hajji Hafez Al-Khadri, and you are Professor Al-Hajji Kareem al-Busiri."

"Hmmm."

I didn't see any point in telling Hafez that the extra title was pretentious, but I understood why he would want to use it around the university.

Chapter 4

Kalifa & Wahida

When I got home from the airport, Wahida had already set the table for three, and she was reheating a chicken dish which Nane had made earlier. She gave me an embrace. An embrace from my adult daughter always lifted my spirits, particularly because it was not the norm in Egyptian society. It was part of Wahida's inheritance from Elizabeth.

"How was the pilgrimage, Papa?"

"It was very . . ." I tried to think of the right adjective. "It was a very unique experience." She gave me a skeptical look. I continued: "Uniquely positive and uniquely negative."

"What was positive about it?"

"Wahida, you can't begin to imagine the number of people: rivers of people, hills covered with people, almost all dressed in white. Great seas of tents. One had a feeling of participating in something very historic."

"I've seen pictures, Papa."

"I have, too, Wahida, but . . ." I paused to consider. "It's a little bit like sitting in the best seats at a football match instead of watching it on television." Wahida smiled. "I mean, one gets caught up in all the emotion and being bombarded by the sounds, the physical contact the smells, the raw emotion, the . . ."

"What was all the emotion about? The Hajj has been the same for thirteen hundred years."

I could see that she didn't understand. Then I remembered something. "A few years ago, your mother wanted to watch a program about Italy. It was in the springtime, and it showed those men slashing themselves until they were all bloody and they carried a cross through the town. I don't know whether you saw it."

She nodded. "The flagellation of Christ."

"Well, it was a little like that. I mean, nobody actually hurt himself – I did see someone die – but there was this powerful sense of commitment to Allah."

"You saw someone die?"

"Yes, an old pilgrim from Algeria died at Mount Arafat, probably of a heart attack."

Wahida sat down at the table. "So Papa, you have a new commitment to Allah?"

"No, not exactly, but I was very impressed with what I saw and felt all around me. It was mysterious."

She tugged at her earlobe. I knew she was thinking. "Papa, you're not like all those men you saw in Saudi Arabia. You're a Muslim, you acknowledge the Prophet and Allah, you're been on the Hajj, you give to charity and you go to prayers – sometimes – so you uphold the five pillars of Islam. But you're not what one might call a devout or a committed Muslim."

"I suppose not." I felt uncertain about this aspect of my relationship with my daughter, having never discussed religious matters with her. I knew that she, like her mother, was a Copt, that she went regularly to the Coptic Church, and that she and her mother had shared the same values and beliefs.

"I'm not being critical, Papa." I must have looked doubtful. "Honestly, I'm not, Papa. I was only trying to tell you what I perceive. Am I wrong?"

"No, I think it's probably about right. But . . ."

"But what, Papa?"

"But you think I should be a little more committed. Maybe become a Christian?"

She shook her head vehemently. "No! You were born a Muslim, you were brought up a Muslim – as a child you had to memorize the Qur'an. Let's leave out the fact that you would be considered a heretic if you converted. If you want to do something, it's better to build on what you have!"

There was a question I had always wanted to ask. "Didn't your mother believe that Christianity is the true religion?"

"I don't think she was that narrow-minded. She certainly wasn't a proselytizer."

"OK, but don't Christians feel that because they've got Christ, their religion is better?"

She gave a sigh. "Yeah, there are some people who think that, and there are some white people who think they're better because their skin isn't yellow or black. Mom didn't believe any of that; neither do I." She paused for a moment. "I'll tell you one thing that bothers me about Muslims."

"What is it?"

"I think that too many Muslims have an inferiority complex about their faith."

"An inferiority complex?"

"Yes.

"Can you give me some examples?"

"First of all, I'm not talking about you, Papa. You may have doubts about your own faith, but that's not the same as feeling that your religion may not be 'the best'." She made quotation marks in the air. "I'm talking about Muslims who feel resentment about their lot in the world, and who feel that something in 'the system' must be to blame. They tend to be poor, uneducated, or see themselves and others like them as victims. They are angry: angry at their poverty, angry at their social or political oppression. They look for a scapegoat. They look at Europe and America, where the streets of their cities are paved in gold, and they hear about democracy. They may hear of Westerners who are critical of the Muslim world, and they become defensive.

They begin to think: It's western Christians who are oppressing us; they think their religion is superior to ours. And they may begin to feel – but not think: maybe they're right. They become more defensive and protective of Islam, to the point where they offer interpretations of Islam that the Prophet never intended: holy wars against infidels. Infidels being anyone who is seen to be or who could be an oppressor."

"You're painting a picture of radical Islam, Wahida."

"Yes, but not just radical Islam, Papa. It's also many discontents who are resentful but unprepared to take action. And the irony is that all these discontents feel inferior but act superior."

"So what is the solution to this problem, Wahida?" I felt that as a father and a teacher I should hold her accountable for thinking in terms of solutions, not just problems.

"In my opinion, it is for educated, rational and caring Muslims – people like you, Papa – to recognize the psychology at work here, and to demonstrate, through their own example and their own faith, that Islam is truly a great religion."

I was amazed! "You really think it's a great religion?"

"Yes, of course."

I could not resist. "Then why aren't you a Muslim?"

"Because of Mama. I was impressed by her great faith and the person it made her. I wanted to be like her."

I bit my lip.

She shook her head. "No regrets, Papa. I have none; you should have none." She stood, embraced me and looked into my face. "I am what I am because of you, as well. I love you, Papa."

I hugged her fiercely, gratefully. "So . . . well . . . I . . . So you think I ought to try to be a little more committed as a Muslim."

She sat down again, an amused look on her face. "It's not what I think, it's what you feel that matters."

"Hmmm."

"You've heard that American expression 'go with the flow', Papa?"

"Yes."

"Well, that's how it is."

I felt the need to challenge this glib assertion. "How do I know that the flow is taking me in the right direction?"

"You'll know, Papa. There's absolutely nothing wrong with your direction finder."

"Sometimes I wonder."

She shrugged. "That's good."

"What do you mean 'that's good?'" I demanded.

"I think the people who get into trouble are the ones who never question their direction finder." I had to admit that this was probably true. "Papa, you said there were some negative things about the Hajj. What were they?"

"I didn't find Father Khaliq, although several times Hafez is convinced we almost did. But then, how does one find one person among two million? It was very hot and pretty uncomfortable sometimes. That was to be expected. I suppose the aspect that bothered me most was all the time allocated for praying. On average, it must have been about four hours per day."

"What did you do during those long hours, Papa?"

"I brought along a book about the life of Augustine of Hippo."

"Oh, Saint Augustine." I nodded. "That must have been interesting."

"Yes. I read through the parts about his later life several times, and then, out of sheer boredom, I read the first part about his early, dissolute life, which I had skipped over."

"Anything you feel you've missed out on?"

"What are you talking about?" But I should have guessed from her mischievous grin.

"I was referring to the early, dissolute life."

"Oh, for goodness sake, Wahida.

* * *

When Kalifa arrived, the three of us sat down to dinner. At my son's insistence I gave an abbreviated report on the Hajj, but then the discussion shifted to his joining the army. "Where do things stand?" I asked

"I've put my application in for officer's school. They've checked my academic records and I've had an interview. The interviewer seemed to be more interested in my football than in my studies. I've had a physical exam: no problem. I think it's just a matter of waiting for the call-up and seeing when it will be."

Wahida asked, "When do you get a chance to decide which branch you want to join? You know: there's infantry or armor."

"I think that will come toward the end of my training. Everyone in a training class gets ranked, and number one ranked gets first choice."

"And the bottom of the class gets sent to guard the border (with Libya) at El Salloum," Wahida suggested.

"Probably." Kalifa's grin confirmed his expectation of avoiding such an assignment. Nonetheless, I knew that Kalifa would be joining the brightest and best of his age group on the eight-month officer training course. Most of the Egyptian army officers are graduates of the Military Academy, where they complete four years of study for a Bachelor's degree before they earn a commission. They enter the Academy as top-ranked high school graduates, but this path did not suit Kalifa and many of his peers, who prefer to select their own university and their own course of study. But the risk was that they could be drafted as enlisted troops if, at the end of their university deferment, they failed to win admission to officer training.

I had some doubts about the value to the individual of Egyptian army training, having served two years after high school in an infantry battalion in Suez. It was mind-numbingly boring: four hours of guard duty, two hours of platoon drill, and two hours of preparation for inspection every day except Friday. What did I learn? Well, I learned how to march in close order, how to shoot a rifle, how to make a pair of boots shine, and how not to be selected for a special detail.

Naqib has avoided military service altogether. I think he managed to string out his educational deferment, and by now he probably has a fatherhood waiver. Kalifa says that being an officer is far better than enlisted service. Apart from superior pay and accommodation, one acquires some technical skills: communications technology and mathematics, for example. Leadership and people-management skills are also drilled into young officers, so that they have an advantage in winning desirable civilian jobs. It's not that I worry about Kalifa being in the army: Egypt is not at war. I just hope that his two years on active duty will be time well invested.

"Where is your training going to take place, Kalifa?" Wahida asked.

"It's at the army base at Heliopolis (Cairo)."

"Isn't that where the Military Academy is?"

"Yes, but we won't be part of the Military Academy. We have our own barracks, canteen, lecture halls and gym. The only thing we share is the parade ground."

"And probably some of the instructors."

"Yeah, probably."

"I know you have to decide later," Wahida asked, "but if you had your choice and you had to decide now, what branch would you want to join?"

"I've thought about the Sa'ka (special forces), but that requires thirty-four extra weeks of training, and I've heard it's very tough. Maybe the airborne. The engineers are also a possibility, because I could learn something useful."

"What about the Republican Guard?"

"I don't think so, Wahida. The trouble with the Guard is that you don't really do anything. You just hang out in Cairo and guard the politicians."

I had heard that Republican Guard officers often move into politics because of the connections they have made, and I was pleased that Kalifa apparently chose not to consider this 'opportunity'. As far as I'm concerned, to be a successful politician in Egypt, one must be either amoral or a narcissist (or both).

* * *

I had been debating whether to contact Princess Basheera. Did I not owe her a report on the assignment she had given me? Might she have further advice on how I could contact Father Kahliq? But at the same time, I did not want to appear too anxious, and for this reason, I ruled out another face-to-face meeting. I decided that a brief telephone report would be best, as this would give her the opportunity to provide further guidance if she wished.

From my office, late in the afternoon, I called the number she had left me; I used my mobile phone to avoid the rumor-mongers on the university switchboard.

"Hello, this is Basheera Chagma. I'm sorry that I am unavailable at present. Please leave your name, telephone number and a brief message. I will return your call as soon as possible."

"Hello, Princess Basheera, this is Professor al-Busiri. I thought I might give you a brief report on the Hajj from which I have just returned, and on my search for Father Kahliq. If you have time, you can call me on +20 109 579 0814."

That evening, as I was beginning to peruse the local news, my cell phone rang. Neither Wahida nor Kalifa had come home yet. I pride myself on keeping my contacts up to date (as a university professor, one has to, as every student has his or her own mobile telephone). The screen said 'Princess Basheera', but I decided on formality: "Hello, this is Professor al-Busiri."

"Hello, Professor. Thank you for your message. Yes, I would like to hear about your experiences on the Hajj."

"Well, Princess, it was very interesting. I actually went with my colleague, Professor Hafez, and I believe he also found the pilgrimage very worthwhile. We . . ."

"Excuse me, Professor, but are you free tomorrow afternoon at about three? I would very much like to hear about your experiences in person."

"Oh, I see. That's very kind of you. Just a moment. . . I have a class that finishes at three, and a conference with a student at four-thirty."

"I could come to your office at about three-fifteen, Professor."

For a moment, I didn't know what to say. "Well, I don't want to trouble . . . that is . . . I could meet you at the Kempinski at about six-thirty."

"It's no trouble at all, Professor. I'll see you at your office at about three-fifteen."

"Yes, Princess."

Great Allah! What have I got myself into! A Saudi princess in brocaded silk and her entourage come sweeping into the Liberal Arts Building at three-fifteen! They make themselves known to the staff and ask directions to my office! Up the stairs they come, down the hall, checking names on doors until they find mine. They knock, enter and close the door behind them. In this process, they will have passed two dozen students, four instructors and two professors, all of whom will be overcome with curiosity, and each one of whom will try to find out what is going on! Then the process will be repeated as they leave! I can surely expect to be called to the Chancellor's Office for an explanation!

I thought about calling the Princess again to arrange an off-site meeting. But I had already done that: she had turned down a meeting at the Kempinski.

Surely, she must know what she's doing, coming onto a university campus to meet with a professor. She knows she attracts attention when she moves about. She's been a princess for some time and she knows how to handle the attention. OK. So she doesn't mind. What about me? Well, I won't exactly be hurt by the publicity. I can say to the Chancellor something like: 'Yes. You see she's been reading several of my books, and seems to have quite an interest in a couple of my ideas. She just came along to have a brief chat.' There will be the inevitable questions about 'Let's think how your relationship with this Saudi princess can benefit American University, shall we?' I'll have to play down the hoped-for opportunities with the disclaimer that the 'relationship is entirely casual, intellectual and transitory'.

Nonetheless, I had to admit that if American University is a fantasy bourse and if professors represent traded securities, the value of my shares will have risen appreciably.

* * *

I confess that I was more than a little apprehensive as the appointed hour drew closer. Perhaps I should call and say that an emergency has arisen, repeating my offer to meet at the Kempinski, but I felt sure that she would see through such a communication to the cowardice which lay behind it. I also surfaced the idea of telling Hafez about the meeting, but dismissed it immediately. He would want to be present, and he would certainly try to conflate what I hoped would be a casual meeting into the romantic event of the century.

I had just returned to my office and was putting my files away, when there was a knock at the door. I hurried over to open it. There in the hallway stood a woman with a partial face veil, who was wearing a Cambridge University sweatshirt, a pair of jeans and brown trainers. I must have looked confused, because her eyes, eyebrows and forehead crinkled into a smile. (The Emirates-style blue face veil she wore exposed her large dark eyes and brow almost completely.)

"Oh, Princess, it's you! Sorry, I almost didn't recognize you. Please come in."

There was a soft laugh. "Thank you, Professor."

I noticed that there was no one accompanying her; I left the door slightly ajar.

"Princess, I can make you some tea, if you like."

"Thank you, Professor, but I'd like a just glass of water."

She walked over to my bookshelves, glanced at the titles and occasionally reached out to touch a volume.

"You've read all of these, Professor." It was more statement than question. "What is this one?" She had selected a slender, leather-bound treatise with red Arabic inscriptions.

I glanced at the work she was holding and could not resist a smile. "That is On the Harmony of Religion and Philosophy by Ibn Rushd. He was an Iberian philosopher of the sixth century After Hijra (12th century AD)."

Her attentive eyes met mine. "There is something about this work which amuses you?"

"It's just that one of my students does not agree with the great Ibn Rushd. She is writing her thesis on the disharmony between religion and philosophy."

I could see in her eyes that Basheera was also amused. "And what is your position on this matter, Professor?"

"For me, religion and philosophy are two separate human activities. Religion is about belief; philosophy employs logic. They therefore use entirely different capabilities. Sometimes they are in harmony; sometimes not."

"But don't theologians sometimes present logical arguments, and philosophers begin their theories with their beliefs?"

"Yes, that is often the case, but such an approach is usually subject to attack and ultimate failure."

"So how did Ibn Rushd conclude that religion and philosophy are in harmony?"

"He started from the premise that religion – Islam – is true, at least allegorically. And that, therefore, any conflicting philosophical premises are false."

"So your student plans to show that Islam is mistaken on some points?"

"No. I have advised her to present an entirely philosophical thesis." Basheera nodded. "Please take a seat, Princess."

She sat facing me for several moments. "What are your thoughts about your search for Father Kahliq, Professor?"

I had not expected this question, having prepared myself for a discussion about the Hajj itself. "Well, I made several attempts to contact Father Kahliq, Princess, but I always seemed to just miss him."

She nodded. "Are you thinking to give up the search, Professor?"

"Well, I thought you just wanted me to look for him on the Hajj."

"And if you didn't make contact, the search would be over?"

"Did I misunderstand, Princess?"

"It all depends on you, Professor."

"In what way?"

"It depends on how much one desires to make contact with Father Kahliq."

I suddenly felt that I had let Princess Basheera down. "Well, I don't know. You asked me to find him, so I . . . I decided to go and look."

She looked at me steadily, appraisingly; her dark eyes seemed to be reading my newly-formed thoughts. "So you didn't believe that there was much chance of finding Father Kahliq, but you took an interest in the Hajj, which surprised you."

I nodded. "Sorry, Princess."

"Don't be sorry, Professor. I think you made a very good start."

"A good start? You want me to continue?"

She made a noncommittal gesture. "What was most interesting about the Hajj?"

"The mystery of it. There were many dimensions of mystery."

"Do you think that Father Kahliq is also somewhat mysterious?"

"Yes, I know so little about him."

"I've told you all I can."

"Yes, I believe you, Princess, but how can I find him if we both know so little about him?"

"Professor, you are a man of good character; you are wise and intuitive. I believe you will find him if you wish to."

I wanted to ask, Why would I wish to? But she said, "You have already found some value in the search." I must have looked ceptical. She continued, "You found mystery."

"And mystery is value?"

"Yes. Particularly to a good philosopher. A mystery – particularly an existential one – is the best point of departure for a philosopher, is it not, Professor?"

She has a point! "Yes, you are right, Princess. But where should I resume the search?"

"Wherever you wish, Professor, but I don't believe you went to Medina during the Hajj. Is that right?"

"No, we didn't go to Medina."

"It is another mysterious place and I believe Father Kahliq will likely be in the area. But may I suggest that you go alone? Hafez is not the best influence on you."

How does she know anything about Hafez? I never mentioned him! I wanted to ask her about Hafez, but a glance told me she was waiting for my response. "I can certainly take a few days to go to Medina. Is it best to start at the Al-Masjid al-Nabawī (The Prophet's Mosque)?"

"Yes, that is a good place to start, but I'm sure you'll find other mysterious places in Medina, and I'm sure you'll find traces of Father Kahliq."

She stood, gave me a slow, deferential nod, and left my office.

I remained at my desk and tried to make sense of it. She seems to know more about me than I can explain; in fact, she seems to be able to read my mind! Is she real? Perhaps I dozed off here in my office, and dreamt that she came to see me. That could explain her insight. But I distinctly remember making a call to her from this office. Was that another dream? Well, what about the first meeting I had with her? Was that also a dream? If so, the young woman who came to my office with the summons to Princess Basheera must also have been a dream. Here's the test: I'll see if the reception desk has a record of her arrival or departure!

I called reception. "Good afternoon, this is Professor al-Busiri. Do you have a record of the name of the person who just visited me? Oh, I see. You have no record of a visitor to my office. Is that right?" I hung up. But that doesn't prove that she's not real. She could have been mistaken for a student and slipped by reception. But how would she have found my office? Actually, I had to admit it would not be difficult. There are departmental direction signs all over the place.

What about the Cambridge University sweatshirt? If she wanted a disguise, that would certainly be a good one! Of course, she could have simply bought the sweatshirt. But what if she actually went to Cambridge? That would at least prove she is real!

I decided to place a query through official channels about whether a Basheera Chagma had ever studied at Cambridge. For a bright woman from an important and wealthy Saudi family, it certainly wasn't out of the question.

Two days later, the reply from Cambridge was relayed to me. "We have no record of a Basheera Chagma, but there was a Bushra Chagma, a citizen of Saudi Arabia, who graduated from Magdelene College in 2006."

That must be her! She's just changed her first name as part of her disguise! But that doesn't explain how she knows so much about me. Then I remembered her three associates: the young woman who came to my office to summon me and the man and the woman who were with Basheera at our first meeting. They could be Basheera's researchers, and essentially everything personal that Basheera mentioned about me is pretty much public knowledge.

OK. But why is this woman so intent on motivating me to find Father Kahliq? What's in it for her? That is the mystery! In fact, what's in it for me?

But I had to admit that I was extremely curious, and as she said: a good philosopher loves an existential mystery!

* * *

A couple of days later, I had just sat down to dinner with Wahida and Kalifa when the telephone rang. Wahida answered. She passed the phone to me with a puzzled frown. "It's Anisa for you."

"Anisa?" (It would be the first time my daughter-in-law ever called me.)

"Yes, Anisa."

"Hello, Anisa. How are you?"

"I am concerned, honored Professor."

"What is concerning you, Anisa?" I braced myself for the news that Naqib had left her.

"Naqib has gone to a meeting at the mosque."

"Well, I'm sure he'll be home before long."

"Sorry, Professor, I haven't explained the situation. It is a meeting between the Brotherhood and Al-Gama'a al-Islamiyya."

I was shocked. "Why would he go to such a meeting?"

"I don't know, Professor, but Naqib is very ambitious. Perhaps he sees the connection between the Brotherhood and the terrorists as a stepping stone in his career."

"But if the police learn of this, Naqib will certainly be jailed."

"Exactly, Professor! He must be stopped!"

"Have you tried to persuade him not to attend such a meeting?"

"Yes, of course. He brushes me aside. He says, 'I know what I'm doing!'"

"I'm not sure I can be any more successful."

"Please, Professor, you have to try! But don't tell him that I called you. He will be very angry."

I tried to think. "Where is this mosque, Anisa?"

"It is not far from our apartment. It is the El Nasr Mosque, just off Sixth October Street in Nahia."

"I'll see what I can do, Anisa."

"Please be careful, Professor!"

I hung up and explained the situation to my two younger children.

Wahida was furious. "How can he be so stupid? He will soon have responsibility for three children!"

Kalifa said, "I think Anisa is right."

"What do you mean, Kalifa?" I asked.

"Well, Al-Gama'a al-Islamiyya have been operating almost exclusively in the Sinai – killing hundreds of people, mostly police and soldiers, but women and children, as well. The theory has been that they don't have the infrastructure – the people – to start a campaign of terror in Cairo. They need people in Cairo who know the city, share their hatred of the government and are willing to take risks. Naqib meets those requirements. He's also ambitious. He can win recognition and eventually some kind of command position."

Wahida was horrified. "Kalifa, how can you even think that Naqib could become a terrorist?"

"Am I wrong about his ambition and his hatred of the government?"

"No, but that doesn't make him a terrorist."

"Let's hope not."

Wahida turned to me. "Papa, what are you going to do?"

"I thought I might go to the mosque and see if there really is a meeting."

100

"But, Papa, if the police are already there, they'll arrest you, too."

"So I'll need another good reason to be there." I thought for a moment. "Wahida, look on the Internet. See if there is anything special about the El Nasr Mosque."

Wahida consulted her iPhone for some moments. She announced, "The El Nasr claims to have several pages of the original, handwritten Qur'an. It says they were written by Abu Bakr."

Kalifa gave a derisive snort. "Yes, and I invented Bluetooth!"

"OK, but that's probably a good enough cover. I'm going there to see, firsthand, whether the original Qur'an makes a vital philosophical point."

Kalifa was ceptical. "But Papa, why would you go at nine o'clock at night?"

"Because I have classes during the day, and I'm trying to avoid the crowds that have to be expected during the day."

* * *

The mosque was sandwiched between shabby apartment buildings in a run-down area. There was no evidence of any surveillance in the littered street outside. The mosque had no minaret – only four loudspeakers mounted on a mast. The blue paint was peeling from the dome. The front doors of weathered wood were closed, and when I tried to open them, they were locked. I rang the doorbell and waited.

Eventually, the right hand door was opened by a small old man with very bright eyes. "Yes?"

"Good evening. I am Professor al-Bushiri from American University. I am here to look at the Qur'an manuscript."

"Come back tomorrow." He moved to close the door.

My foot impeded this process. "I am sorry for the hour, but it can't be helped, and I have been given assurances by a senior imam that I would be welcomed here. What is your name, sir?"

The man relented, the door swung open and he stepped aside. Inside, the mosque was very dark. I could barely make out the minbar (raised pulpit) at the far end of the prayer hall, the floor of which was covered in worn carpets.

"Where is the manuscript, sir?"

"It is in the small room at the end on the right."

I sauntered along the right hand wall of the mosque, looking about me as an interested visitor might. There were three doors in the wall, the first of which was open. It was dark inside. The second door was closed and I could hear voices inside. I stepped up to the door and opened it slightly.

"No, sir! It's the next door down!" the porter called.

I hurriedly closed the door and mumbled an apology, but not before recognizing the back of my son seated at a long table with other men.

I turned on the lights in the small room at the end. In the center of the room was a display case, and under the glass was a long piece of papyrus parchment. The parchment had darkened so that it was difficult to distinguish the Arabic in handwritten, faded ink. I pulled over a chair and began to read. There was a passage from sura 5, The Feast:

> The Jews and Christians say, 'We are the children of God and His beloved ones.' Say, 'Then why does He punish you for your sins? You are merely human beings, part of His creation. He forgives whoever He will and punishes who-ever He will. Control of the heavens and earth and all that is in between belongs to Him: all journeys lead to Him.'

I wondered whether Abu Bakr, a colleague and confident of the Prophet, could have written these very words as they were spoken by the Prophet. Possibly so.

I became aware that there was someone standing behind me. I turned and saw a large man whose face was shrouded in a black beard. He wore a black shirt and jeans. "What are you doing?" he demanded.

"I am studying this manuscript by Abu Bakr."

"Why are you studying it now?" His voice was impatient.

"I am studying it now because I teach classes during the day. Besides, in the evening I can avoid the crowds."

"There are no crowds here."

I feigned surprise. "Well, there certainly should be! This is a very precious document!"

He shrugged dismissively. "Why did you come into our meeting room?" His tone was distinctly hostile.

"I am sorry for the interruption. I misunderstood the porter's directions."

"You will leave now." There was finality in his statement.

"But I just got started."

"You will leave now!"

"But the senior imam told me I would be welcome here."

The man stepped close to me, seized my arm and lifted me bodily to my feet. "Leave!" he shouted.

I left, somewhat shaken.

* * *

The next day, at one in the afternoon, I knocked on the door of apartment J on the third floor of 71 Sayed Mahran. My son's voice answered, "Who is it?"

"Papa."

Naqib opened the door, and uplifted hands conveyed his surprise. "Papa?"

"May I come in?"

"Yes, of course. I hadn't expected you."

"The world is full of surprises."

"Can I get you a tea?"

"No thanks, Naqib. I just want to have a chat."

"About what, Papa?"

"About the meeting you attended last night."

"Come and sit down, Papa." He led the way into the living area where the two little girls were playing. Occasionally, one or the other would come to Naqib or me to ask for help in buttoning a doll's dress, or to show us something.

"Did Anisa tell you?"

I had decided that an outright lie was the best approach. I shook my head. "I was contacted by a friend in the GID (Egyptian General Intelligence Directorate). He told me that Al-Gama'a al-Islamiyya was planning a meeting with the Brotherhood, and that your name was on a list of Brotherhood attendees. He called me again to tell me that the meeting was scheduled for last night."

"Was it you who opened the door during the meeting?"

"Yes. I wanted to see if it was true."

"Papa, that was dangerous!"

"Look at who's talking about dangerous! You could end up in prison for quite a long time!"

"And you could end up . . ." He didn't finish the sentence.

"I won't go to any more meetings with Al-Gama'a al-Islami-yya if you don't."

"We both need to be more careful."

"What are you talking about, Naqib? 'Be more careful!' Are you thinking of becoming a terrorist?"

"No, Papa. The meeting last night was just for liaison."

"Liaison? Liaison for what? How to plant a bomb in Tahrir Square?"

"No, Papa. Nothing like that. The meeting last night was just about politics."

"Since when is Al-Gama'a al-Islamiyya interested in politics?"

"They really are, Papa; they want to understand how the Brotherhood got Morsi elected."

"A lot of good it did them! They're now a banned terrorist organization!"

"Papa, you know that's not true! The Brotherhood is not a terrorist organization!"

"I'd like to believe that."

"Papa, you really have to be more careful. It's lucky that last night the porter couldn't remember your name."

"And if he had remembered it?"

He gave a slight shrug. "There would have been a little trouble for you."

"Only a little? You mean like having my life threatened?"

"They wouldn't do that Papa," he said without conviction.

I continued to stare critically at my older son. He gave another shrug. "Have you talked to your friend in the GID today?"

"No."

"I think he might tell you there's nothing to worry about."

"The only thing I'm worried about is that my son is meeting with what is definitely a terrorist organization. I want that to stop, Naqib: for the sake of your family and mine."

"OK."

* * *

As I thought about the meeting later, I was pretty sure the concessionary "OK" did not represent a commitment. Rather, it was an appeasement. It was: 'I hear you; now leave me alone'. What more could I have done? My son is almost thirty, well beyond the reach of any sanctions. I had made it clear that he was taking a personal risk, a risk for his family and mine. I had also implied that he was under the scrutiny of Egyptian intelligence.

I called the bank where Anisa worked and left a message when she could reach me. She returned the call a couple of hours later and asked if I had spoken to Naqib.

"First, I went to the mosque and verified that he was actually in the meeting."

"Oh! You shouldn't have done that, Professor! That could be very dangerous!"

"It's all right. I wasn't identified."

"Did you speak to him afterwards?"

"Yes, I told him that I had been tipped off by a friend in Egyptian intelligence."

"Were you?"

"No."

"Thank you, Professor! What did he say?"

"He said it was a harmless liaison meeting."

"Do you think it really was?"

"No."

"What was it, then?"

"I don't know and I suspect that he doesn't actually know either."

There was a moment of silence. "What should I do, Professor?"

This was the question I had been dreading. "Anisa, don't forget that your first priority is your own safety and the safety of your children." There was another gap of silence. "Whenever you have a chance, you should make it clear to him that you are completely and fundamentally opposed to any dealings of any kind with an organization like Al-Gama'a al-Islamiyya. I suggest that you avoid emotion: he will see it as blackmail. But he understands steely determination."

There was an amused expulsion of breath. "And what about . . ." She paused. ". . . conjugal relations?"

"I'm unable to advise you there, Anisa. But, speaking generally, I will do the best I can to back you up on any action you decide to take."

"Thank you, Professor! Thank you very much!"

* * *

106

That evening, I was able to give Wahida and Kalifa the details of my trip to the mosque, my meeting with Naqib and my subsequent conversation with Anisa. Kalifa expressed the opinion that Anisa "is afraid of Naqib, and she may love him, but she is right to be concerned."

Wahida shook her head. "Kalifa, how is it possible to love somebody you're afraid of?"

Kalifa regarded his sister thoughtfully. "It may not be exactly the kind of love you have in mind, Wahida. But, Anisa isn't a free and independent spirit like you are. For example, a slave can love his master for his benevolence and fear his power to punish."

"Oh, come on, Kalifa! Anisa isn't a slave!"

"I didn't say she is. What I'm saying that love is a matter of perspective."

Wahida was amused. "OK, Philosopher, what kind of love will you be looking for?"

"Probably the same kind you'll find – like Mama and Papa had: two equals, with shared values, who are different, and who find their differences intoxicating." He paused. "It's just that in the case of Naqib and Anisa, they are not equal. But they are different and they find their differences interesting – even necessary."

Wahida nodded. "And I don't think they share the same values."

"That's true," Kalifa said. "Politically they're at opposite ends of the spectrum, and in both cases, they're at the ends opposite to what you'd expect."

"You mean because you'd expect Anisa – from her background – to be a flaming liberal."

"Yes, and you'd expect Naqib to be a staunch conservative. But I think the reason it's turned out as it has is that one's identity is the main determinant of one's values."

"You're saying that because Anisa has a trusted position in a large bank, has managed to distance herself from her parents, has a husband and child care, she wants to conserve all that."

Kalifa smiled. "Exactly, and Naqib has always styled himself as a rebel – someone who takes advantage of change – someone who is always looking for faults in the 'system'."

Wahida was pensive. "But I think that you and I are pretty conservative, aren't we?"

Kalifa's smile burst into a grin. "That's partly because we both went to American University, but mostly because our father is a strict disciplinarian."

"Hogwash to both points!" I said.

"But seriously, Kalifa," Wahida continued, "how was it that you and Naqib always seemed to be the best of buddies?"

"Because he taught me to play football and beat up my enemies."

"Come on! Answer my question!" Wahida demanded.

Kalifa looked at the ceiling and sighed. "Well, it wasn't always easy. Sometimes I felt like the slave I mentioned earlier. But he's smart, and I respected him."

* * *

I usually expect Nane to go to the market, but on this particular Thursday, I decided to see if I could find some good seafood that Wahida and Kalifa had asked me to grill at home. When we are staying at the beach, I often grill local seafood – a real treat! Nane is very good at vegetable and meat dishes, but like most lower class Cairenes knows nothing about good quality seafood. There is a modern shopping center on the west side of New Cairo which has a new Carrefour. I don't like the Western feel of the place with its trolleys, bright lighting, extraordinary cleanliness, and neatness. To me, it seems artificial, and I think maybe the food is artificial, too!

But I know that Elizabeth liked American-style supermarkets and the food she served at home was always excellent. Maybe Carrefour will have some good fish!

I went straight to the fish counter. Yes! They had plenty: tilapia, perch, mullet, mussels and crabs, but more importantly, they had octopus and fresh shrimp! There is nothing we like better than a plate of grilled octopus and shrimp! I bought some extra for the freezer.

As I was walking to the checkout, somebody called, "Kareem!"

I turned. There was Adeeba with her younger daughter, Sagira. We stopped and chatted for a moment.

"Is that all you're buying, Kareem? One small package?"

"Yes. It's octopus and shrimp. Wahida and Kalifa are very fond of it, so I'll be using the grill tonight. We often have it at when we're at Al Jamiah."

"Al Jamiah is very nice! Do you remember, Kareem, we joined you and Elizabeth when you had first bought your place? We remember it well." Mother and daughter exchanged glances.

There's an opportunity, Kareem! "Well, I wonder whether you and the girls would like to come for a visit – for the day, I mean."

"Yes, of course! We would like that very much. When would be convenient for you?"

"Most any time. This Saturday?"

"Yes, that would be fine. I don't think Nakia (the older daughter) can make it. What about you, Sagira?"

"Yes, I would love to. Will Kalifa be there?"

"Yes, I expect so. He's just waiting to hear from the army, and Wahida would spend every weekend there if she could."

Adeeba's face was lit with enthusiasm. "Do you suppose, Kareem, that you might be willing to do some more grilling on Saturday?"

"Yes, I should think so. What would you like?"

"Octopus and shrimp! We'll bring enough for everybody."

"We look forward to it. Will you need directions? It takes a little over two hours."

"No, I remember the way, Kareem. We'll see you before noon on Saturday. Is that OK?"

"Yes, that's wonderful, Adeeba."

In fact, I thought, it's truly wonderful. For the first time as two single adults, Adeeba and I will be together! OK, we'll have three of our children as chaperones, but that doesn't matter: we'll have a chance to establish a new relationship without adult, third-party interference. Not that anything will happen. I wouldn't even dare to hold her hand, but that's not the point. We'll begin to see whether we can become good friends, independent of our late spouses. I think Adeeba feels something similar. After all, it was she who 'fished' for the invitation. It was interesting also that Sagira wanted to establish whether Kalifa will be there. They've known each other since they were quite small.

* * *

To make my arrangements for the trip to Medina, I felt I should make use of the university's in-house travel service. The Head of University Services had sent around a note requesting that all staff make use of in-house travel, where possible. He conceded that there had been complaints about the service in the past (without mentioning specifics), but he said that a new manager, Mr. Adel Mansour, had been appointed, and he was confident that the service would improve. "I'm sure you'll agree that we don't want to go back to the bad old days of everyone making his own arrangements."

Actually, I wasn't sure I agreed with the Head of Services. I was rather comfortable in the bad old days making my own arrangements. But I recognized there was little to gain in presenting him with an overt disagreement at the out-set. Besides, I wanted to see what the 'newly-restructured' service was like.

When I walked into the university travel office, which occu-pied a dungeon-like space in the basement of the Administra-tion Building, I was pleasantly surprised. The brown brick walls had been plastered with colorful travel posters, and the old blue fluorescent lighting had been replaced with warm, white incan-descents.

A man wearing a dark green tie and an almost iridescent blue vest (I had never seen anything like it in Cairo, let alone the Uni-versity offices) leapt to his feet and came forward. "I am Adel Mansour, Manager of Travel. How may I help you, sir?"

"I am Professor al-Busiri, and I wondered whether you might help me with a trip to Medina."

"Yes, of course, Professor. Will this be on a credit card or your university account?"

"As this is a personal trip I should put it on my credit card."

"If it's more convenient, Professor, we can put it on your university account and that can be settled later." Obviously his preference. He is able to report an increase in university busi-ness under his new regime.

Mr. Mansour invited me and a young employee to sit by his desk while arrangements were made. The young (female) employee must have been a trainee, because as he worked at his computer, he provided her with a running commen-tary. She didn't appear to fit the mold of university staff. While she was wearing a dark headscarf, in other respects, she seemed to be a daughter some American tourists had left behind: she took no notes, her amply-filled sweater was too tight, her bright lipstick was brazen, and she was chewing gum.

We selected an Egyptair flight, two hours nonstop from Cairo to Medina – economy in this case – and a four-star hotel in Medina that had good Trip Advisor results, and a special rate for half board.

I went on to my senior class in Western philosophy. When I returned to my office, it was immediately apparent that my secretary, Miss Aboul-Nour, was irritated. She is in her early sixties, and as she has been my secretary for about sixteen years, we know each other's habits.

"What happened?" I asked.

She swivelled her chair to face me and folded her hands in her lap. "Well, some girl from travel came up here and wanted to put your travel documents on your desk. I explained to her that I am the one who puts things on your desk. She said, 'All right, then' and handed me the envelope. I could see that she was wearing cheap bracelets, had nicotine stains on her fingers and chipped scarlet nail varnish!" She shook her head as if she was trying to banish the memory.

"I see," I said.

"And not only that: she was chewing gum, and she was listening to headphones while she was talking to me!"

"How could you tell she was wearing headphones? Wasn't she wearing a head scarf?"

"Yes, but when she turned around to leave, there was a wire running down her back to a phone in her back pocket. And her jeans were too tight! I don't know where they get these stupid girls!"

"I'm sure I don't either, Miss Aboul-Nour, but I'm sure that if one looks in the right places, one can find plenty of them."

Chapter 5

The Prophet's Tomb

"This is much more impressive than the Masjid al-Haram in Mecca!" I said, as we approached the colossal Al-Masjid al-Nabawī (Prophet's Mosque) across the sunlit expanse of white marble square.

My local guide, Ibrahim, gave me a teasing smile. "You should have seen it in the year one! It was 30 by 35 meters, open air, supported by palm trees, and the roof was palm fronds. It was built next to Aisha's (Muhammad's second wife) house, and the Prophet used to preach standing on the ground, but in the year six, a wooden platform was added. Since then, every ruler who has had responsibility for the mosque has added to or modernized it. Now, it is a hundred times the size of the original mosque, and the main prayer hall in the ground floor can hold one million worshipers. King Fahd (of Saudi Arabia) has also added air conditioning, and the roof of the mosque now has twenty-seven moveable domes."

"Is everyone happy with these changes?" I asked.

He glanced briefly around him, and then stepped closer. "With the building additions, air conditioning, ventilation, and the beauty of the building: yes." He turned to face me. "But in 2007, the Saudi Ministry of Islamic Affairs announced that the green dome is to be demolished and the three tombs flattened."

"Isn't the green dome over Muhammad's tomb?"

"Yes, and it had been there for about seven centuries, since Sultan Al Mansur Qalawun had it built."

"Why is it to be destroyed?"

"You are perhaps forgetting, Professor, that in Saudi Arabia, the dominant, ultra-conservative version of Sunni Islam is Wahhabism. The Wahhabis believe that tombs or mausoleums are a form of idolatry, and when bin Saud took over Medina one hundred and fifty years ago, the Wahhabis had nearly every domed tomb in Medina destroyed – except the one over the Prophet's tomb."

As we approached the great mosque, I looked up at the ten minarets, their elaborate confectionary seeming to pierce the sky. Inside the mosque, there was a vista of red carpets, white columns, gold ceiling arches and row upon row of lights. Solitary figures prostrate on the floor in prayer were scattered about, and there were groups of awestruck pilgrims huddled together.

We walked to the far corner of the mosque – to what was once Aisha's house. (But there was no hint of a residence.) This small section of the mosque was quite different: the oranges, yellows and green carpet – the hand-painted Arabic calligraphy – the huge brass screens gave it a feeling of antique mystery.

"Behind this screen here," Ibrahim whispered, "is the tomb of the Prophet."

"These two are also tombs?" I asked, gesturing toward the two screened rooms to the left.

"Yes. Those are the tombs of the early Caliphs, Abu Bakr and Umar ibn al-Khattab. Aisha was to have been buried next to Muhammad, but she gave up her place to Abu Bakr. This space here to the right of the Prophet is reserved for Jesus."

"For Jesus?"

"Yes. Some scholars of the Qur'an say that Jesus will return to kill the Antichrist, rule for forty years, and then be buried next to Muhammad."

It didn't make sense to me. I thought, somebody is trying to conflate Christianity with Islam, but I nodded.

"It is said," Ibrahim continued, "that if one offers a prayer here, in this holy place, it will surely be answered."

"You have been here many times," I remarked. "It is true?"

"I am very happy in my life."

I looked at the huge brass screen with its curving Arabic script 'Muhammad' covering the black curtain, and I thought about Ibrahim's comment. If I offered a prayer, might it come true? There was only one way to find out. I looked for the qiblah which indicated the direction of Mecca. "This way," Ibrahim gestured. I knelt beside one of the pillars, bowed my head to the carpet and began the al-Fatiha: "In the name of God, the Lord of Mercy, the Giver of Mercy!" . . . What do I want to pray for? "Almighty Allah, protect my son, Naqib, from the temptations of evil people. Help him to obey the law and to be a loyal husband and good father." What else? There's Adeeba. No. Let that be. Well, Wahida and Adeeba say I should strengthen my faith. "I confess, Almighty Allah, that I am not a man of great faith. If it please You, help me to grow my faith." There! That's done!

* * *

On the edge of the square, there was a simple restaurant with a green awning. It was crowded, but in the back, there was a small table. "The mutabbaq is good here," Ibrahim announced. When our plates and steaming mugs of tea arrived, he poured a flood of gravy over his pastry. I did likewise and began to attack what appeared to be fried, stuffed bread. Inside, it was filled with chicken, onions, peppers and spices. Delicious, but in spite of the air conditioning, I found myself sweating from the tea and the hot, spicy mutabbaq.

"When the Prophet came here in the year one," Ibrahim began, "he attracted many followers, but there were some who resisted his teaching. There were many Jews here in Medina, and there were a number of rival Arab clans devoted to their traditional idols."

I interrupted, "Why did he decide to come to Medina, in particular, apart from the hostility he faced in Mecca?"

"The political situation in Medina was not stable. The Arab clans did not get along, and there was friction between the Jews, who were the principal political force, and the Arabs. Muhammad was recognized as someone of importance – as a leader. Moreover, because of his semi-ostracism in Mecca, it was understood that he would not join forces with the Meccans in a feared conquest of Medina. The Arabs were aware of the Jews' belief in the coming of a messiah, so there was an acceptance of the religious credentials of this new Prophet. As a result, there were two pledges made to Muhammad by the key figures of Medina. The first was to accept him as a prophet, to obey him and to avoid certain sins. The second was to fight on behalf of Allah and His Messenger. The people of Medina knew that Muhammad's relocation would cause trouble with Mecca."

"But they didn't know how much trouble was coming."

Ibrahim nodded. "You're right. There were five years of raids and open warfare between Medina and Mecca, but before we come to that, I should mention the Constitution of Medina."

"That was the contract which formed a community of the various tribes in Medina."

"Yes, and it is unique in several respects. It was the first time that the leader of a federation was not a military figure, but a religious one. The Constitution implies that all the tribes are 'believers' – suggesting acceptance of Muhammad as Prophet. In addition, it provides that any differences between tribes should be referred to 'Allah and Muhammad'."

"But," I asked, "was Muhammad universally accepted as prophet?"

"No. Some of the Jews called attention to certain differences between the Qur'an and the Torah regarding historic events, and they argued that the Qur'an was not the speech of Allah, and that therefore Muhammad was not a prophet."

"There were some Jews executed, were there not?"

"Yes. After the Siege of Medina, which ended in complete failure for the Meccans, all of the men of the Jewish tribe of Qurayzah – about six hundred – were executed for the tribe's treachery in supporting the Meccans in contravention of the Constitution."

"That was a severe punishment; it effectively wiped out that tribe."

"Yes, but it was pretty much the norm at the time, and Muhammad may have felt it necessary to uphold his authority."

"And after that?"

"After that, Muhammad tolerated the Jewish presence so long as they did not criticize the Qur'anic revelations or side with his political opponents. But eventually, there was no escaping the Jewish denial of the historical accuracy of the Qur'an, and their conclusion that Muhammad was not a prophet. There is also the Islamic denial of Jesus' resurrection after his death on the cross. This denial may have been motivated by preventing the Jews from claiming that Jesus' death on the cross was a victory for them."

I shook my head. "I'm not so interested in these religious claims and counter-claims. The facts are obscure in any case. But is it not true that one man founded one of the world's great religions more or less single-handedly?"

Ibrahim shrugged. "One can say the same about the man Ibrahim, for whom I am named, and Jesus. But we Muslims – and the rest of the world, for that matter – forget that Muhammad was more than a religious figure. He was a visionary leader, a very skilled diplomat, and a successful general. By the time of his death, ten years after his move to Medina, he had not only gained control of Mecca, but of most of the tribes in what is now Saudi Arabia. His concept of a federation of Arab tribes, joined by religion, social and economic convergence, and devoid of external influence, was the unique platform which facilitated the spread of Islam."

For a moment, I sipped my tea. This man Ibrahim is very knowledgeable about the Prophet. What other questions do I have? "Ibrahim, Muhammad's Night Journey is mentioned briefly in sura 17 of the Qur'an, but what are the facts about this journey?"

"Professor, the details of the Night Journey are contained in several hadiths (compilations of oral reports about Muhammad, his teaching and his actions). The gist of the story is that a year or two before Muhammad left Mecca, he was dozing and a white steed was brought to him. He flew on the white steed with the angel Jibreel (Gabriel) to the farthest mosque, which is thought to be the Al-Aqsa Mosque in Jerusalem. From there they ascended into heaven. Muhammad spoke to Adam, Moses, Ibrahim, Jesus and others as he ascended from the first level of heaven to the seventh. In the seventh heaven, he received instructions from Allah to pray fifty times a day. Moses, however, advised Muhammad that fifty prayers per day was too much for the people to bear, and eventually the requirement was reduced to five prayers per day."

I shook my head. "With great respect, Ibrahim, this sounds to me like a fairy tale. First of all, the Al-Aqsa Mosque was not even built in Muhammad's lifetime. And why would Muhammad go to heaven a dozen years before he died? And does it make sense that mighty Allah would negotiate a requirement for fifty prayers down to five?"

Ibrahim was amused. "You are right, the Al-Aqsa Mosque did not exist in Muhammad's time, but the hadith does not refer to it by name. It refers to the 'farthest mosque', and that was thought to be Al-Aqsa. Another interpretation is that the original word, which has been translated as 'mosque,' could also mean a place of 'religious significance'. In any case, does it matter if is a fairy tale?"

"Of course it matters!" I replied with some vehemence. "When one is trying to verify the claims of religion, and one is presented with a fairy tale about the Prophet, how can one have faith?"

"Professor, you are a professor of philosophy; am I correct?"

"Yes, that is correct."

"As I understand it, philosophy is a logical science in which theories are accepted based on evidence or argument."

"It is also," I replied, "an art in the sense that one can imagine untested theories or propose various forms of evidence."

"OK, Professor, but you must know that theology is a very different field. It may sometimes involve philosophical approaches, but it also calls on cultural, historical, and spiritual methods, some of which are not based on logic. For example, do I think that Muhammad really had a Night Journey as the hadith describes? No, I don't. But for me, there are many aspects of the story which I like and that have meaning for me. I like the idea of ascending to heaven on a white steed. What better way to get there? And being accompanied by the great archangel Jibreel, who introduced Muhammad at every level of heaven. Pretty good guide! And Muhammad gets to talk to all the key people in heaven. Why make the trip without seeing the right people? I like the bit where Moses says, 'In my experience, you'll never get people to pray fifty times a day'. He was right! And I don't see Allah's reducing the prayers from fifty to five as an indication of weakness or being out of touch. To me, it demonstrates His almost infinite flexibility. So, for me, the Night Journey is one brick in my personal connection with Allah. There are lots of other bricks—some large, some small—and they are held together by the mortar of faith."

For a long moment, I sat thinking. I liked Ibrahim's analogy of a bridge made of bricks and mortar. "Tell me, Ibrahim, what is this mortar 'faith' in your construction?"

"For me, faith is active acceptance which sets aside doubts. It is active, not passive, acceptance which is constantly subject to refinement."

"What do you accept?" I asked.

"Let's start with the first pillar of Islam: there is no god but Allah and Muhammad is his Messenger."

"OK, and what doubts arise for you?"

"I have had various doubts about the meaning of 'Messenger'. I have listened to what imams say; I've read what Qur'anic scholars believe; I've even listened to the atheists. Gradually, over time I have developed my personal understanding and acceptance of 'Messenger'. For me, this sort of process keeps my mortar strong and all my bricks together."

"It may be a good process."

I commend it to you, Professor."

* * *

The next morning, as I was leaving my hotel, a clerk in reception caught my eye. "Professor!" he called.

I went over to the desk. "Yes?"

"You are Professor Mansour, are you not?"

"No, I am Professor al-Busiri."

"Oh, my apologies, Professor."

I was to meet Ibrahim at ten o'clock at the Quba Mosque, the oldest mosque in Islam, but in the meantime, I thought I would explore the Dates Market, which was only a few hundred meters from the Aramas Hotel.

In Muhammad's time, Medina was an oasis, consisting of agricultural settlements, and one of the products for which it is famous was dates. As an Egyptian, I am quite familiar with our native Zaghloul dates which are very sweet and crunchy (they are served fresh), but I wanted to try some of the Saudi varieties, particularly the Ajwah, a sweet, black date that is supposed to have been a favorite of the Prophet.

I was walking down a darkened alley which would open into the market. There was shouting, angry unintelligible shouting, from one voice in the square ahead. There was a bright flash and a boom which shook the walls. Dust, then smoke, boiled into the end of the alley. There has been an explosion in the market! Terrified, I pressed myself against the wall; there was an urge to flee in the direction from which I had come. Several seconds of silence, then screams of mindless agony. I cannot run away! People need help! But suppose . . . I forced myself to edge forward and look into the square. It was shrouded in a grey smog. I could see buildings to either side, and passageways disappearing in the center. Then I could make out people: lying on the ground, or sitting or standing, dazed – some were moaning. There was the acrid smell of burnt wood and fabric. I heard shouts of men running through the passageways, calling for help or shouting instructions.

I moved forward. "Was it a bomb?" I called to a man who had appeared.

"Yes! It was over there!" he said, pointing to the left. "Suicide bomber! Come and help!"

The grey shroud and dust were dissipating. I could begin to make out the wreckage which was strewn everywhere. Stalls ripped apart, carts and bicycles flattened, a car burning and on its side to the left in the worst of the damage, debris everywhere.

"Father Khaliq, help us!" It was an old woman bending over another figure. "Father Khaliq, help us!"

Perhaps he is a famous aid worker. I tried to block out the carnage and human misery that surrounded me as I went over to the woman. She was leaning over another woman, shrouded in black, whose leg was awry. "She's bleeding very badly!" I saw then that the prone woman's abaya was shiny and wet at the bottom.

"We must make her a tourniquet!"

The older woman looked at me, uncomprehending. "Father Khaliq!" she called again.

"We must make her a tourniquet!" The older woman stood erect now, ignoring me.

I've just got to get on and do it! I knelt by the prostrate woman and began to rip open the bottom of her abaya. The woman did not move. Must be unconscious. She was wearing brown trousers underneath; the left leg was soaked with blood. Where is the wound? I didn't dare to tear open her trousers. Must be above her knee with all this blood. I pressed my hand against her thigh. The middle of her thigh, left side, was soaked. I tore the abaya again, removing a long strip. "Help me!" I shouted to the woman who stood above me. There was no response. "Help me, damn you!" I shouted again; I slapped her leg. The old woman knelt. I passed the strip of fabric under the injured woman's thigh, put in half a knot and pulled it as tight as I could. I looked at the old woman for acceptance of what I had done.

"My daughter," she murmured.

"You have to keep this tight."

"Father Khaliq."

"I am not Father Khaliq."

"I know."

"Is she injured?" It was a loud voice above and to my right. I looked up. Two bearded workmen with a stretcher, wearing dirty jeans and sweatshirts.

"Yes. She has a bad wound in her left thigh. I have put a tourniquet on it." I looked at the woman. "I don't think she's conscious. She's lost a lot of blood." The woman raised her head slightly and moaned.

"Here!" one of the workmen announced, setting down the stretcher. "We'll put her on this and take her to the hospital." The

122

men manhandled the woman onto the stretcher. "You with her?" I shook my head.

"You?" he demanded of the old woman. She nodded. "Come on then!" They disappeared.

I sat on the ground for some time, unable to process what had happened. There were shouts and moans all around, wisps of acrid smoke, a dewfall of ash. My hands and one leg of my trousers, where I had wiped them, were bloody. Several people asked if I was injured. I shook my head and stood up. The devastation was hard to comprehend. The only stalls recognizable as such were off to my right. Most of the area to my left had been flattened into splintered piles of wood and fabric. There were deformed metal and plastic containers strewn about, and the ground was littered with dates in every color, from black to yellow. Here and there were human bodies, like broken mannequins, bloodstains, shoes, items of clothing, an arm, a foot. Sickened, I started back to the hotel. As I reached the safety of the alley, I paused for a moment. I was right here when the bomb exploded. If I had been ten seconds earlier, I would have been in the midst of it. Perhaps on the way to the morgue right now. There, but for the grace of Allah . . . Then I remembered the mistaken interruption at the hotel desk. Was that mistake the grace of Allah?

* * *

When I met with Ibrahim, I told him what had happened at the Date Market – leaving out the part about my being interrupted on the way.

"Probably a Shiite," was his comment.

"I know that you have a large population of Shiites in the east of the country, and I know they feel oppressed by the Saudi government, but why choose the Date Market in Medina for a suicide bomb attack?"

"The short answer is 'I don't know', but I suspect that the attack was not motivated by the Shiites' feelings of oppression, although that induces a hostile climate. Medina is the burial site of the Prophet. His first caliph, Abu Bakr, is buried beside him. The Shia claim that Muhammad designated Ali, his son-in-law, to be his successor, but after Muhammad's death, Ali was passed over by the leaders of Islam in avour of Abu Bakr. As you know, Ali became fourth caliph, but his son, Husayn, was killed in the Battle of Karbala in the year sixty-one (680AD), which marks the split of Shia from Sunni. I would guess that the shouting you heard was the suicide bomber taking revenge for the killing of Husayn."

"But why in the Date Market?"

"The security at the Al-Masjid al-Nabawī (The Prophet's Mosque) makes any attempt at bombing there pretty much impossible. The Medina Date Market is famous and any atrocity there would attract attention."

"Will it be on television this evening?"

"I doubt it very much. The government does not wish to give oxygen to terrorists."

"You mention security. How would the bomber have gotten his suicide vest?"

Ibrahim shrugged. "Most likely provided by the Quds Force." (special forces unit of Iran's Revolutionary Guard, with external responsibility and reporting directly to the Supreme Leader).

* * *

The Quba Mosque was a disappointment. As the oldest mosque in Islam, and one whose stones had been laid by the Prophet himself when he first arrived on the outskirts of Medina, I expected to see at least a remnant of a very old building. Instead, we toured a white mosque in the Medina architectural style with Arabesque latticework, black and red marble flooring. It had been built in 1986 when the original building was torn down.

"Why was the original mosque destroyed?" I asked Ibrahim.

"There was some work done on the original structure two or three hundred years ago, but it had fallen into a poor state of repair."

"With all due respect, Ibrahim, I think you Saudis have a fetish for grand, modern buildings, and you have little appreciation for the authentic grubbiness of historic structures."

He smiled. "You are not the first person to say so, Professor."

Masjid al-Qiblatain (Mosque of the two Qiblas) similarly fell short of expectations. One of the three oldest mosques, and reportedly constructed in the year two, it was rebuilt in the Medina style, in a north-south layout, to reflect the point for which it is famous. Muhammad received a revelation from Allah that the direction for prayer (quibla) should be changed from facing Jerusalem in the north to facing Mecca in the south. Prayers were underway when the imam of the mosque heard of the change. He announced the change, faced the opposite direction, and those praying behind him did likewise.

* * *

It was a particularly warm day with no sea breeze at Al Jamiah. I had just finished lunch and there was a glass of American iced tea on the table beside me. Kalifa was at army training; Wahida was at work in Cairo (it was a Thursday); I was reviewing my lecture notes for my autumn introductory course on classical Arabic philosophy. So I had not only my notes but several dozen books piled beside me. The notes were very familiar – too familiar. The comfort of a deck chair beckoned. It's an introductory course. Why bother? Besides, I tend to ad lib the lecture anyway. No, Kareem! You have to look at these notes critically. Do they fully represent the arguments about the eternity of the world? Reluctantly, I picked up The Incoherence of Philosophers.

There was a knock at the front door. Who could that be? Maybe one of the neighbors. I slid aside the screen door. A woman dressed in a loose-fitting grey track suit with blue stripes down the arms and legs stood on the front path. Incongruously, she had a dark cotton scarf wrapped around her head. At the beach, the few women who wanted to cover their faces wore a traditional niqab.

"Yes?" I said.

She turned to face me. "May I come in, Professor?"

The large dark eyes, the lilting perfect diction. "Yes, of course, Princess. I'm sorry I . . ."

"That's all right, Professor. I happened to be in the area, and I thought, 'I wonder if Professor al-Busiri is out at the beach.'"

"Yes, well, I am here, and I'm preparing for the autumn semester. Come in. Can I get you something to drink – an iced tea, perhaps?"

"An iced tea sounds lovely."

She sat at the other end of the table, her iced tea in front of her. "I seem to have interrupted quite a large project." She gestured toward the piles of books.

"The interruption is very welcome. I am required to review each course I teach based on feedback from students. Some of the comments are quite stimulating, intellectually. Others are just a nuisance."

Her eyes sparkled with mirth. "And my visit interrupted your consideration of a nuisance comment."

"Yes." I picked up a grey manila file. "This one says, 'It is not clear why we should study Al-Ghazali. He lived one thousand years ago, and he never liked philosophers.'"

"To which the answer is . . .?"

"The answer is: first of all, time is unimportant. If it were important, we would not study the Qur'an, let along Aristotle. And second, to fully understand an idea or concept, one must listen to the critics of that concept."

126

She nodded. "And what did Al-Ghazali have against philosophers?"

"His education was focused on Islam and Islamic law. He was openly hostile to philosophical theses which he thought contradicted Islamic teaching. He opposed them as heresy and 'bad philosophy'. But at the same time, he was aware of the value of philosophical concepts and reasoning, using them in his own writing."

"Can you give me an example of a thesis to which he was hostile?"

"He did not agree with philosophers who claimed that the world is eternal. He said – in effect – that if someone proposes that the world was created by an eternal God for His reasons at a certain point in time, there is nothing illogical about such a proposal. Therefore, the world may not be eternal."

There was a soft chuckle. "And you agree with Al-Ghazali?"

"Yes, of course."

"Was he not also a theologian?"

I offered a nod in acknowledgement of this unexpected information. "Yes. In his autobiography, he says that he became too attached to worldly success and sought deeper spirituality which he found in Sufi mysticism. He then spent eleven years writing The Revivification of the Religious Sciences, which argues that Sufism is the personal and mystical dimension of Islam."

"In that it focuses on the heart to achieve a deep love of and connection to Allah."

"Exactly." For a moment we sat in silent contemplation and understanding. This person, this Princess Basheera, is quite extraordinary in the working of her mind! What does she not know? What does she not understand? Perhaps she is really a hundred years old!

She studied the full glass in her hand. "This tea is American: light with lemon, mint and sugar. And cold. Not at all like Egyptian tea. It must be your late wife's recipe."

"Yes, it is. One of several things she bequeathed to us."

There was a nod. "She gave you many gifts."

I wanted to ask her what she meant: 'many gifts'. How did she know? Why would she say that? But I couldn't summon the temerity.

"Tell me about Medina, Professor."

I began by describing the Prophet's Mosque and the tomb of Muhammad. But then I tried to get a defensive response from her by criticizing the Saudi approach to replacing ancient buildings with palatial marble structures. "The Quba Mosque was a great disappointment. It is a shame that the Saudis have destroyed the modest mosque which was built by the Prophet's own hands." I expected her to come to the Saudi's defense. Instead, she said, "There are many pilgrims who feel as you do: wanting to have the actual evidence of a connection to the Prophet. But the faith of others is stimulated by costly, grand and beautiful buildings which serve as evidence of the power of Islam."

"Is it not possible to provide both kinds of evidence?"

"You make an excellent point, Professor, and this is what has been done successfully in Mecca, where the Ka'aba – an ancient, authentic structure, is at the heart of the world's largest mosque. But it is important to avoid confusing the two kinds of evidence: each needs to stand on its own, and it is necessary to prevent the destruction of the ancient and authentic by millions of touching hands."

I nodded. One has to admire her wisdom.

"Tell me, Professor, were you in Medina at the time of the attack on the Date Market?"

I was stunned. "How did you learn of the attack, Princess? Even the Medina newspapers made no mention of it."

There was a soft chuckle. "Let's just say that I subscribe to a particularly good news service. It alerts me to items in which I have an interest."

128

"Oh, I see," I said, torn between my curiosity and my politeness. As usual, politeness won. "Yes, I was there. In fact, I was only a few steps from entering the market when the bomb went off."

"That must have been very frightening!"

"I suppose my initial instinct was to flee, but once I entered the market, any fear I had gave way to shock. The devastation was unspeakable."

"And many people were injured. What did you do?"

"There was one old woman who kept calling out, 'Help us, Father Khaliq!' and I thought perhaps he is someone famous in the emergency services."

"Perhaps. And what did you do?"

"Well, I went over to the woman, and I found that her daughter had been wounded. So I put a tourniquet on her leg, and some volunteers carried her away on a stretcher."

"Did you meet Father Khaliq?"

"No. But the old woman mentioned Father Khaliq's name again. She seemed to think that I am Father Khaliq, but I told her that I am not. She said she knew that. Strange."

"Perhaps not. And after that you went back to your hotel?"

"Yes, but I've been thinking about how lucky I was not to have walked into the market just as the bomb went off. You see, I was delayed by a desk clerk for just a moment at the hotel."

"Yes, in a way, it was quite lucky."

"I've been wondering if it was something more than just luck. I mean . . . Well, you know, Princess, that I'm not particularly religious."

"Yes, you told me."

Did I? "Well, anyway, it crossed my mind that perhaps Allah caused the desk clerk to mistake me for someone else."

"Oh, I see. Do you think that's possible?"

"I just don't know."

She nodded. "What other thoughts have you had, Professor, about the bombing?"

I shook my head in disbelief. "For the life of me, Princess, I can't understand why someone would want to kill and maim innocent people – women and children – just to make a statement."

"I see what you mean. What reason could there be?"

"Well, my colleagues at the university say that it's because individuals have been radicalized. They've been told they'll go straight to heaven and be among Allah's favorites."

"Do you believe that?"

"No, of course not! It's a terrible lie!"

"What then? How can ordinary people, who are friends and neighbors, be persuaded that it's a good idea to kill innocent people?"

"For me, it's beyond understanding." I raised my hands in frustration. "May I ask you, Princess Basheera, what is your view?"

She stood up and looked out the window toward the sea. "I have heard it said that it is the work of Satan."

"The work of Satan?"

"Yes. I suppose that for one to hold that view, one must believe in Satan."

"As one believes in Allah?" I could not disguise my surprise.

"No. Not exactly."

"How then?"

"One can love Allah and hate Satan and believe in them both."

I thought for a moment. "But I have read that many of these terrorists profess strong Islamic faith. How can they be devout Muslims doing Satan's work?"

"That is exactly the question, Professor." She picked up her glass of tea, and turning away from me, partially unwound her head scarf. She raised the glass, re-wound the scarf, turned back to me and set the half-empty glass on the table. "The tea is delicious! Thank you very much, Professor."

"Please sit down, Princess. Would you like some more tea?"

"No, thank you. I have to go."

I stood up. She's going to leave. I must ask! "Where would you have me go next, Princess?"

"Ah, so you are still keen to find Father Khaliq?"

"Well . . ." I paused for a moment to think. "I know I have very little to show for it, but I feel that the search you have sent me on has been very beneficial."

"In what way, Professor?"

"I have learned something about myself." Her nod urged me to continue. "I have found that there is a kind of emptiness within me. It isn't just the loss of my wife, or that my children have less need of me, or that I am growing older and sometimes lonely. It is something about who and why I am." She nodded again. "I feel that in some peripheral way, the trips you have sent me on have helped me understand that I am missing something."

She sat down again. "Professor, are you familiar with Shia Islam?"

The question took me by surprise. "Well, I am more familiar with the history of Shia Islam than I am with the theology."

"Well, you may have assumed that Father Khaliq is Sunni, but his religious preference isn't clear to me." She paused. "Perhaps you would consider attending Arba'een."

I said: "That is the Shia pilgrimage in honor of Husayn, the grandson of the Prophet (whose death at the Battle of Karbala initiated the Sunni-Shia schism)."

"Yes. The date this year may correspond with your half-term break."

I thought for a moment. "Isn't the pilgrimage to Iraq?"

"Yes. To Karbala, southwest of Bagdad."

"But is that part of Iraq safe?"

"It is outside the territory of ISIL, and last year, there were no significant attacks on pilgrims."

"But as a Sunni, would I be welcome on the pilgrimage?"

"Sunnis, Christians, Jews and non-believers participate every year."

"I will consider your suggestion, Princess."

She nodded. "Thank you, Professor." And she was gone.

* * *

I woke with a crick in my neck. I had fallen asleep with my head on The Revivification of the Religious Sciences, which was lying open on the table. I rubbed my neck, gyrating my head slowly. Was Princess Basheera here? There was no sign of her, except the empty glass on the table.

* * *

Having my entire family at the beach with me was, simultaneously, something to look forward to and something to dread. Until Kalifa went to army officer training, I had his and Wahida's company most evenings, but now with Naqib, Anisa and the two young girls coming for the weekend, as well, it would be a genuine family reunion. It was not the accommodation that worried me. The house had only three bedrooms, but I had a plan that everyone said was all right. Kalifa would join me in the master bedroom that I used to share with Elizabeth. He said he would nudge me if I snored too much. Naqib and Anisa would have the boys' room, and Wahida would be in her room with the two little girls on porta-cots. The table in the main room was for five originally, so it could accommodate five adults again. Basima and Husna would be fed earlier. Wahida, Anisa and I would do the cooking. Fair weather was promised and we all looked forward to time on the beach. No, that was all fine. What worried me was potential conflict between my older son, the not-so-secret member of the Muslim Brotherhood, and my two younger, traditionalist children. In particular, Kalifa, the army officer in training, represented conservative Egyptian values, while Naqib was attached to radical, socialist, insurrectionist views. I could not even count on Wahida and Anisa to intervene: Wahida would side immediately with her younger brother, while Anisa would (reluctantly, I hoped) take her husband's side. I had therefore set out one rule: there was to be no discussion of politics at any time during the weekend!

* * *

Taking my rule perhaps too literally, Wahida and Kalifa spread out their towels on the beach and promptly closed their eyes to their brother and his family. Naqib sat nearby reading what was probably a law journal. Anisa accompanied her daughters to the water's edge, where I joined them, intending to pass on my skills at building sand castles.

"You see," I said to Basima, "you let the wet sand dribble out of your hand and it will make a nice minaret."

"Thank you for inviting us, Professor."

"I'm sorry, Anisa, I should have thought of it earlier. You're welcome here any time."

"That's very kind, but we always seem to be busy on Friday and Saturday."

"How is your job, Anisa?"

"Oh, it's all right." She gave a slight shrug. "Don't put that in your mouth, Husna!" She looked up the beach to where her husband was sitting. "Naqib has just started a new job."

"Has he? I'll have to ask him about it."

Anisa pulled her younger daughter into her lap; she said softly, "My father is not very happy about it."

"What are your father's concerns?"

"He says that the law firm is affiliated with the Brotherhood. Naqib says that they have plenty of other clients."

"Does this law firm specialize in its practice?"

"My father says that their specialty is human rights. Naqib says that their main practice is personal and commercial law."

"How is this new job affecting you and the children, Anisa?"

"Well, we have more money, but I don't know where the money comes from."

"What do you mean, Anisa?"

She gave another shrug. "Naqib went to Riyadh for a couple of days a few weeks ago. But he said he was going to see a client in Aswan."

"How do you know he went to Riyadh?"

"I found the stamps in his passport."

"What does Riyadh have to do with money?" I asked.

She glanced at me and said quietly, "People say that it's Saudi money that keeps the Brotherhood going."

I nodded. "And I suppose he's working longer hours."

"He's been admitted to the bar, so all the studying is done, but he's working more than full time now."

"So who takes care of the children?"

"They go to a nursery from eight until one. My mother picks them up and stays until I get home."

"And what are Naqib's hours now?"

"He drops the girls off at the nursery and gets home at eight or nine."

"That's a long day."

"We don't see much of each other."

* * *

Friday evening: the two little girls had gone to bed; Wahida and Anisa were sitting by the television. There was a popular romantic comedy on, but they were talking and only half watching. Naqib, Kalifa and I were still sitting at the table, drinking coffee.

Naqib asked, "So, how is the army training going, Kalifa?"

Kalifa gave a gesture of indifference. "It's all right. Three months down, five months to go."

Naqib nodded. "Any thoughts on which branch you want to join?"

"I'm not sure. At the moment, I'm leaning toward the infantry."

"Why the infantry? Why not a technical branch like Signals or Engineering?"

"The technical branches require additional training. Besides, I like the idea of leading my own platoon."

"As an officer, you would have enlisted men assigned to you in Signals or Engineering."

Kalifa glanced at me. I thought, He doesn't like it that his brother – whom he thinks of as a conscription dodger – makes recommendations about military service.

"There's something special about serving as an infantry officer. The lives of your men – and your own life – can be on the line. It takes a special kind of leadership."

Naqib nodded sagely. "Any thoughts on where you'd want to be posted?"

"Well, Sinai is where the action is these days."

Naqib was visibly stunned. "But . . . but, the army is taking a beating there. Haven't you read about it in the papers?"

"Of course." Kalifa looked directly at his brother. "Terrorists are also being rooted out and killed. The army is learning how to fight a stealth war."

"But for every one . . ." Naqib did not use the word 'terrorist'. ". . . killed, two more take his place."

Kalifa leaned forward, toward his brother. "So, are you saying that we should give in to terror?"

"No. No, not at all. I just think we should listen to their complaints."

"Their complaint that Egypt doesn't have a theocratic dictatorship?"

"Now," I interrupted, "what time do the girls get up in the morning? I want to be sure I'm available to make them breakfast."

* * *

"What's that you're reading, Naqib?" I asked, sitting down beside him on the beach.

"Oh, it's a legal journal. It helps keep me up to date." He set the publication down beside him.

"I understand you have a new job. Congratulations!"

"Yes, I'm very pleased!" He turned a delighted smile on me. "It's more money, but unfortunately, longer working hours."

"Tell me about it!"

"Well, it's a small, prestigious firm located in downtown Cairo. I'm a senior associate."

"A senior associate already?"

"Yes, and they have me doing some traveling."

"Really? Where have you been?"

"I went to Aswan for a couple of days."

"What was the client's case about?"

"It was a bakery with a dispute over the price of flour."

I nodded.

"Come in the water, Papa!" It was Basima, trying to take him by the hand.

"OK, my little cherub. Shall we go swimming together?"

"No, Papa, just in the water!"

I watched them hurry down the beach. My eye fell on the blue and white journal two meters away. I stood and looked down at it. Repression of Freedom of Speech: Recent Cases. On the cover was the emblem of the United Nations: olive branches and a global map.

What does a UN report on repression of freedom of speech have to do with his job? Then I thought about his trip to Aswan:

to see a bakery about a dispute over the price of flour. A bakery in Aswan hires a prestigious Cairo law firm to deal with a dispute over the price of flour? A couple of days of meetings?

* * *

Saturday after dinner, we all left Al Jamiah. Naqib and family departed in their newly-acquired, secondhand Volkswagen. Wahida, Kalifa and I were in my Honda Civic.

"That was interesting," Wahida volunteered.

"What was?" I asked.

"The fact that Naqib tells different stories to me and to Anisa."

"What stories?"

"He tells Anisa that he's making nine thousand (Egyptian = $1500) a month. He told me – when I asked him – he is making fifteen thousand."

"Well," I suggested, "I would guess that Anisa's figure is right, but when his younger sister asks, he wants to look better."

"Papa, I'm only making sixty-four hundred. He could have told the truth and still come out on top."

"I think he has a bit of a problem seeing things the way they really are," Kalifa said. "I know you told us no political discussions, Papa, but this afternoon, we were walking on the beach and he was saying that Sinai will be the next state which is a part of ISIL."

I shrugged. "At the rate things are going, he may be right."

"Oh, come on, Papa! Do you really think that el-Sisi (President of Egypt) as an ex-military man, will cede the Sinai to ISIL, or that Netanyahu (President of Israel) will permit the existence of an anti-Israel, terrorist state on his southern border?"

* * *

That evening, after Kalifa had taken the bus back to the base and Wahida had gone to bed, I sat at my desk thinking. Why does Naqib withhold the truth from his wife and family? Is it just a matter of courage: being afraid of our condemnation if he told us the truth? But Naqib has never lacked courage. It takes courage to join an outlawed organization. It takes courage to marry a divorced woman with two small children. Why would he present such an obviously false client for his trip to Aswan? And why didn't he cover up that UN journal he was reading? It's almost as if he accepts that we know the truth and wants to make it easier for us to pretend that we don't know. And what about his comment about Sinai? He was obviously shocked that his younger brother might be fighting terrorists there. What does he know about the plans of Ansar Bayt al-Maqdis (the name of Al-Gama'a al-Islamiyya under new leadership) in Sinai? The only conclusion I felt I could safely draw was that Naqib cares about us and wants to protect us from the truth and from the consequences of his own actions.

* * *

Adeeba approached me in the cafeteria. "Would you like to join us for lunch next Saturday?"

I'm sure my happy surprise was evident. "Yes, I'm sure I would."

"Nakia and Sagira will be home. Can Wahida and Kalifa join us, too?"

"I don't believe Kalifa has a pass next weekend."

"Oh, Sagira will be disappointed."

We both laughed.

"I can't speak for Wahida, but I think she'd be happy to accept."

There was an amused smile. "That means you'll be outnumbered four to one, Kareem. Based on those odds, do you want to reconsider?"

"Based on those odds, surrender is my only option."

"Excellent! Shall we expect you about noon?"

* * *

After lunch, we were sitting in the small garden at the back of the house. Red trumpet flowers cascaded down the far wall. To the left, a small water lily pond was fed by a tall pewter lady pouring water from her vase. We could hear the animated discussion of the three young women through the open doors of the house. Cups of coffee and not-quite-finished plates of baklava were in front of us.

"How is Naqib, Kareem? You haven't spoken of him lately."

I told Adeeba about the call from Anisa, my seeing him in the meeting at the mosque, my conversation with him later, and the family interactions at Al Jamiah the previous weekend.

"Boys are such a problem!" she said, shaking her head. "I'm glad I have only girls. The worst thing they can do is get pregnant with some idiot. Boys, on the other hand . . ." She let the sentence trail off.

"OK, Adeeba, tell me what you would do if Naqib were your son."

"I think the only thing you can do is to have a kindly, fatherly confrontation with him. Maybe you can get him to admit he's not being honest with you and Anisa and your other kids." She paused. "You know, Kareem, I think Kalifa may have a point when he says that Naqib may not be seeing the situation as it really is."

"I'm not sure he wants to see the situation as it really is."

Adeeba gave a concessionary nod. "All you can do is try. I think I would stay well clear of this family assistance program that the government has started to offer."

"You mean the program which is supposed to turn around would-be jihadis who are reported by their families."

"Yes, that's the one. I think they'll be so heavy-handed in dealing with these kids that the kids will be convinced that the government is corrupt and should be overthrown."

"Except these aren't necessarily kids."

"All the more reason to be concerned. These young adults have pretty clear ideas about how a government should behave. And they tend to have a low level of tolerance for what they perceive to be harassment or punitive actions."

"Thanks for your advice, Adeeba. I'll try having a heart-to-heart talk with him."

For a long moment, she sat considering me. "Is there something else bothering you, Kareem? I mean, apart from Naqib. You don't seem quite yourself."

"Oh, I don't know. Maybe I'm just getting older and more disagreeable."

"You are never disagreeable, Kareem."

"Thanks, but I'm not sure about that. Sometimes I feel that I'm missing something."

She leaned forward. "What could that something be?"

"I don't know. I mean, ever since I've been on the trips that the Saudi lady recommended . . ."

"Oh, that woman!"

"No! No! It's nothing to do with her!" I shook my head.

"What is it, then?"

I tried to identify the feeling. "This may sound odd," I said, "but it's sort of existential."

"Hhmmm." She was searching my face. "Where were you and what were you doing when you last had this existential feeling?"

"I was standing by the tomb of Muhammad."

"And what were you feeling?"

"I felt that I was in the presence of a powerful mystery."

"But you didn't feel a sense of connection, of understanding?"

"Yes, I think that's the point. I mean, I feel very well connected to my children – sometimes – and most of the time to my colleagues. In fact, I feel connected to you."

She smiled. "And I feel connected to you, Kareem."

"So what do you think I should do?"

"Carry on."

"Just carry on?"

"Yes, and if the weather is nice, you might think to invite us to Al Jamiah sometime."

"How about next Saturday?"

"Next Saturday would be fine."

* * *

We were in the Honda on the way home.

Wahida said, "You and Adeeba seem to get on very well."

I glanced over at her, unsure how I should take her comment.

"She's a very nice lady."

"Yes, I know she's a very nice lady."

"But?" I suggested cautiously.

"No 'but'. I'm just glad to see you enjoying the company of a very nice lady."

"Why wouldn't I enjoy the company of a very nice lady?"

"Papa, you have been a hermit, stranded on your own desert island, since Mama died."

"No, I haven't. I've been teaching, talking to students and colleagues, helping you kids out, even doing a little travelling."

"With no interesting female in your life."

"Well . . ."

"Well what?"

"Well, I guess you're right."

"I am right! And Adeeba is a classy, bright, well-educated woman of means and, as you put it: 'she's a very nice lady'."

"And she's coming up to Al Jamiah next weekend."

"Good! Maybe I'll leave you two alone."

"Don't you dare!"

Chapter 6

Arba'een

"Ah, yes, Professor! It's good to see you again. How can I help you?"

"Well, I'd like to ask you, Mahdi, to arrange a trip for Arba'een."

"For Arba'een, Professor? The Shia pilgrimage to Karbala in Iraq?"

"Yes."

Mahdi put on a sad face. "I'm sorry, Professor; we don't do Arba'een."

"Is that because it is a Shia pilgrimage?"

"No, no. We frequently get requests for Arba'een. The problem, Professor, is that we can't guarantee the level of service that our clients normally expect."

"Why is that?" I asked.

"Well, to start with, last year there were reportedly twenty million pilgrims on Arba'een. It is the largest annual pilgrimage in the world. There are only 700 hotels in Karbala. Getting a room is next to impossible. It is absolutely chaotic! And what happens is that local villagers accept the pilgrims, offering them food, drink and a place to rest in tents called mawkebs. There were seven thousand such resting points along the roads. There is no government subsidy. The cost of the mawkebs is borne entirely by the villagers; they save all year to provide for the pilgrims! I've even heard of pilgrims being offered foot massages and having their clothes washed! Quite a large percentage of the pilgrims come from Iran – on foot – can you imagine it? It is about seven hundred kilometers from Basra or the Iranian border to Karbala. Millions of people make the journey on foot over several weeks! The roads are rivers of people."

"It sounds like the Hajj."

"No, Professor. The Hajj is like an American tailgate party compared to Arba'een.

"Tell me, Mahdi," I asked, "is it safe?"

"Well, yes and no. Yes: last year there were no major ISIL attacks, partly because there were 30,000 troops assigned to protection, and that's in addition to the Shia militias that are everywhere. But, one has to recognize that the Shias are the sworn enemy of ISIL, and an attack is always threatened. And no: with that many people on foot in the countryside, you're bound to have accidents, illness and premature deaths."

I asked, "Do you know anybody who has gone on Arba'een?"

"Yes. A neighbor of mine went a couple of years ago. He said it was the experience of a lifetime."

"Did he say why?"

"He said the emotion of so many peaceful pilgrims was breath-taking. Husayn, the grandson of the Prophet, is revered as a perfect imam and near-perfect human being. His death is mourned as a great tragedy."

"I think it sounds really intriguing."

"I'm sorry we can't help you, Professor."

"Is there any agency in Iraq that I might contact?" I asked.

Mahdi shook his head. "There are travel agencies in Iraq, but none of them offers Arba'een packages. The year before last, we tried to put together a joint venture: this company, a Bagdad agency and a dozen mawkebs from one area. We proposed to pay the mawkebs to provide hospitality exclusively to our clients. They weren't interested." Mahdi leaned back in his chair and considered the ceiling for a few moments. "Professor, I think your best bet is to make a connection with a group which is planning their own Arba'een pilgrimage."

"What kind of a group?"

"Well, in your case, it would be a university group – perhaps the University of Bagdad."

* * *

I continued to think about how an Arba'een pilgrimage might be possible. Clearly, any attempt I might make to organize something in Cairo and implement it in Iraq would be certain to fail. I would have to attach myself to something that had been organized in Iraq. Mahdi's suggestion of the University of Bagdad made sense. I knew that it was the second largest Arabic university (after Cairo); some faculty would surely be going on the pilgrimage. And it was located less than one hundred kilometers from Karbala. How to make contact with the interested faculty? Research!

I found that there was no philosophy department. But, there was a College of Islamic Sciences which had been founded in 459 AH (1067 AD). This was promising! I found the name and email address of the dean of the theology department. I sent him the following email:

Esteemed Dean Aziz,

May the blessings of Allah be upon you!

I am Head of the Philosophy Department at American University in Cairo.

I would like to enquire whether any of your colleagues at the College of Islamic Sciences (or, indeed, at University of Bagdad) are planning to make the Arba'een pilgrimage this year, and, if so, whether they would consider the inclusion of an Egyptian Sunni in their party. I desire very much to make the pilgrimage in honor of the noble Husayn.

May Allah reward your kindness!
Professor Kareem al-Busiri

Several days later, I received the following reply:

Esteemed Professor al-Busiri,
Greetings in the name of the Prophet!
We wish to thank you for your email, below, which I have referred to my colleague, Professor Akram Al Basra of the College of Islamic Sciences. Professor Al Basra is organizing an Arba'een pilgrimage for staff of the College departing Bagdad on the fourteenth of Safar and returning on the twentieth. As you know, Arba'een itself falls on the twenty-first of Safar, but the crowds then are so intense that it is nearly impossible to reflect on the loss of Husayn and worship at his mosque or at the Al Abbas Mosque. (Abbas was the brother of Husayn and his flag-bearer at the Battle of Karbala.) If these dates are agreeable to you, may I suggest that you make contact with Professor Al Basra at the above email address?
The blessings of Allah be with you!
Dean Ali Aziz

Well, I suppose it makes sense to avoid the tremendous crowds on the day of Arba'een if one wants to see and to think as well as to feel. I therefore forwarded Dean Aziz' email to Professor Al Basra:

Esteemed Professor Al Basra,
The grace and blessings of Allah be with you.
I write at the suggestion of Dean Aziz.
The timing of your proposed Arba'een pilgrimage on the fourteenth through the twentieth of Safar would be very suitable for me, and fits our half-term break at the American University. I will make reservations for my flight to Bagdad. Would you kindly advise me of any hotel reservations I should make, and any funds I should transfer to your good self to share in the group travel and accommodation expenses?

I pray Allah may reward your great kindness!
Professor Kareem al-Busiri

The same day, I received a reply:

Esteemed Professor al-Busiri
May Allah send you his blessings!
Our group of eight professors and three instructors is pleased that you will
accompany us on our Arba'een pilgrimage. May I suggest that you make
reservations at the Al Rasheed Hotel, which is in the International Zone
and not far from our campus, for the night of the thirteenth of Safar. We
will pick you up at the hotel at seven am on the fourteenth and begin our
trip to Karbala on the College minibus. We can return you to your hotel late
on the afternoon of the twentieth. As to other accommodation, last year we
pre-booked three rooms at the Hotel Caliph Ali in Karbala. This accommodation will be crowded but more comfortable than taking our chances
with the mawkebs. We generally eat whatever is on offer along the way. If
you are able to bring with you one hundred and fifty thousand Iraqi dinar
($130), that will certainly cover your share of expenses. May I suggest that
you bring comfortable walking shoes and pack your clothing in a knapsack?
Should you have any questions, you are welcome to call me on my office
number: +964 1 483 1796.
Extending you all the good will of Husayn!
Professor Akram Al Basra

* * *

One hundred and thirty dollars for room, board and travel
expense for seven days! This is going to be a memorable experience! I didn't know whether to laugh or cry.

I decided to tell Hafez about my plans.

Hafez shook his head with great determination. "Sorry, Professor, there's no way you're going to get me to go into a war
zone with millions of unwashed Shias!"

"I knew you wouldn't mind if I didn't ask you, Hafez."

He continued to shake his head. "Why in the name of . . . of heaven would you want to do something like that?"

"They say it's like the Hajj – all that emotion and mystery – but on a grander scale."

"Grand scale? Twenty-one dollars a day for an all-inclusive pilgrimage! You're going to be living on Unicef dried beans cooked in ditch water!"

"Oh, I don't think it'll be as bad as all that, Hafez."

"Well, don't expect me to fill in your lecture schedule when you come back with dysentery! Besides, you'll probably get lice – or worse – from rubbing up against all those Shia!"

"Hafez, that's a terrible thing to say! Shia are Muslims just as we are; they worship the same Allah and they believe in the same Messenger."

"Yeah, but have you ever seen pictures of Basra and parts of Tehran? They live like animals, and they don't speak proper Arabic."

I gestured toward Cairo. "We've got plenty of desperately poor, uneducated Sunnis living not far from here. Shia living in Iraq speak Arabic, because they're Arabs; Shia living in Iran speak Persian because they're Persian. What's that got to do with anything?"

"Oh, come on now, Kareem! Shia have a different religion!"

"What's so different about it?"

"Well, we Sunnis believe that there is no god but Allah, and Muhammad is the Messenger of God. The Shia add that Husayn is the friend of Allah. So they say they believe in three things."

"Different, but not very important in a cosmic sense."

Hafez was not to be deterred. "We believe that our leadership comes from Muhammad's tribe, while the Shia insist that the imams, the political and religious leaders, must come from the blood lines of Muhammad. And the Shia believe that their imams are selected by Allah and are infallible."

"What's so important about that difference?" I asked.

"Well, it has led to different hadiths (writings which interpret Muhammad's thought and teaching). I mean, for example, they have to say only three prayers instead of five. They have different interpretations of Islamic law."

"For goodness' sake, Hafez, those are details. We both believe in the five pillars of Islam:

There is no God but Allah, and Muhammad is the Messenger of Allah;

We pray five or three times a day;

We give alms;

We fast during Ramadan;

We make the Hajj, if we are able, during our lifetime."

"OK, but how about this: the Shia believe that the twelfth imam, who, by the way, is infallible in all things religious and legal, is still alive and has been in living in The Occultation (a Shia term; literally: an object in the background is blocked by a foreground object) since the year two-fifty eight (872AD). That means he has disappeared and won't reappear until Allah wills it. He will reappear with Jesus to restore justice to the world. Can you imagine believing in that stuff?"

"I have no more difficulty with that than I have with Muhammad flying on a white horse to the seventh heaven and back. Look, Hafez, as I understand it, the cause of the animosity between Sunni and Shia is not religious – it is political, and it dates back to the year nine-o-six (1501 AD), when Shah Ismail founded the Safavid Dynasty, which ruled Iran and some of the surrounding area for two and a half centuries. Ismail was a fanatic: he forced the conversion (or death) of Sunnis to Shia. He did this, in part, to establish a uniform Safavid empire which would compete successfully with the Sunni Ottomans. But Ismail's savage intolerance was matched by Sunni rulers and tit-for-tat intolerance has continued to this day."

Hafez gave a shrug. "Sort of like the Crusades for the Christians and us."

* * *

I felt that I should definitely have an airing of views with Naqib. But how to do it? Having a meeting at his apartment would not work: no privacy and he could take refuge in his family. He would come to the university (or home) to meet me, but he would be suspicious and defensive. How about at his office? He could produce excuses to cut the meeting short. But suppose he thought I am a new client making a first appointment? Yes! But he could still cut the meeting short . . . unless a specific amount of time had been set aside for it. Lunch! That's it! I'll set up a clandestine lunch date with him.

I called Anisa at work and told her my plan; she gave me the name and address of the law firm: Kamal Saleh and Partners; 46 Al Mahrani Street, not far from Tahrir Square. Nearby, on Sabry Abu Alam Street, was the Kazaz Restaurant, which had good reviews.

I called Kamal Saleh and Partners. "Good morning. I would like to make an appointment to see Mr. Naqib al-Busiri."

The receptionist asked, "Who's calling, please?"

"I am Mohammad Shalik al-Yemini."

"Just a moment, sir, I'll put you through to Mr. al-Busiri's PA."

There was a pause. A cheerful female voice said, "Good morning, Mr. al-Yemini, how can I help you?"

"I would like to make an appointment to see Mr. al-Busiri." If this doesn't work out, I'll have to end up with no appointment at all.

"Mr. al-Busiri is in a meeting at the moment, sir. May I ask him to call you?"

"No. That won't be necessary. Can you nominate a date next week when he would be available to meet me for lunch?"

"May I tell Mr. al-Busiri the nature of your business?"

"Yes. You can tell him that I wish to speak about certain relationships. I am a colleague of Sayel al-Qusam (reportedly, a prominent leader of the Brotherhood underground). He asked me to make the appointment."

"Oh, I see." There was a pause. "Would next Tuesday be suitable for you, sir?"

"Yes, Tuesday would be fine. Kindly tell Mr. al-Busiri that I will meet him at one o'clock at the Kazaz Restaurant on Sabry Abu Alam Street."

"Mr. al-Busiri is quite tall, he's about thirty and he usually wears a dark blue suit and white shirt."

"Yes. I have seen pictures of him."

* * *

After I had hung up, I felt a twinge of shame at having used an outright lie to make the appointment. I had never set eyes on Sayel al-Qusam, if, in fact, he existed. But judging by the PA's acceptance of me as an important potential client, perhaps he did exist, and perhaps the Brotherhood was well known to Kamal Saleh and Partners.

* * *

I took an immediate dislike to Kazaz. It was dark and there were lingering odors of garlic and cigarette smoke. The tables were interspersed with leafy potted palms – probably to give each table a false sense of privacy. I had arrived early enough, as Mr. al-Yemini, to select a booth next to the kitchen door, and to advise the staff that I was expecting a Mr. al-Busiri.

Naqib came in three minutes early. He paused to query the owner and made his way to the back of the restaurant. When he saw me, he stopped, shocked. For a moment, I thought he would turn and leave, but overcoming the temptation, he approached me. "Papa, what are you doing here?"

"I am here to have a meeting with my son. Come and sit down."

He was standing at the table. "But why the subterfuge? Why not just call and say you wanted to meet me for lunch?"

"Because subterfuge was the only way to get you to block out an hour and a half to talk to me. Sit down."

He sat, shaking his head. "This is crazy, Papa!"

"Yes, it is."

"I don't understand," he murmured.

"Neither do I." I waited for eye contact. "I don't understand why you couldn't just tell us you went to Riyadh."

He sat back in his seat. "You just went to Saudi."

I frowned. He abandoned the obfuscation. "I went to Saudi on business."

"We knew that."

"How did you know?"

"Well, in the first place, we knew you didn't go to Aswan."

"I might have."

"Naqib, this is exactly why I'm here! It made no sense that an up-and-coming lawyer would spend a couple of days in Aswan working for a bakery client on a pricing dispute. Maybe subconsciously you wanted us to know you were somewhere else." He unfolded his napkin but said nothing. "Besides," I continued, "I got a call from my contact."

"Anisa?"

I looked him straight in the eye and steeled myself. "No. The other one." He picked up a menu and scanned it. "Naqib, why can't you be honest with your family?"

"Some things are better left undiscussed."

"Like what?"

He put down the menu and turned his attention to the far wall. "Papa, I'm not like you or my brother and sister."

"We don't expect you to be like us."

"The three of you and Anisa accept the el-Sisi government. I cannot. It is a fascist dictatorship. What Egypt cries out for with its very soul is an Islamic government, and . . ."

I interrupted: "How are you so in touch with the soul of Egypt? It seems to me that what the Egyptian people want is to live their lives in peace with an honest, supportive government."

"Honest?" he retorted. "We know for a fact that generals are personally raking off at least ten percent of the military hardware budget. Do you know how much that's worth in Egyptian pounds?"

I asked, "Who is the 'we'?"

"The Brotherhood. And you speak about supportive. Do you realize that disabled, unemployed people have had their support cut by twenty-three percent? Begging is rampant!"

"So what is the solution? Another coup?"

He ignored my question. "In Gaza, the Palestinians are literally being crushed by the Israelis."

"So you think we should go to war with Israel again? The last couple of times it didn't work out so well."

He ignored my sarcasm. "Papa, we've got to wake up to what's going on in the world!"

"Wake up," I replied, "to the fact that the last war in Gaza was started by Palestinian militants firing un-guided rockets into Israel?"

"What else could they do? Gaza is literally a prison!"

"Or possibly wake up to the fact that the Morsi government ignored its campaign promises and began to implement the Brotherhood's agenda? Hence the el-Sisi coup."

"Papa, it was the only way to get things done!"

"There is also a democratic way to get things done."

"Egypt has never been a democratic country. It has been ruled by kings and autocrats since the beginning of time. Democracy has never taken hold in the Middle East: it's probably against our tribal culture. Nothing ever gets done in a democracy. In fact, Plato said that democracy is a faulty form of government."

"No. What he said was that an oligarchy – rule by a few good people – is better than a democracy which can degenerate, if it fails, into a tyranny – rule by one tyrant."

"Well, what we've got now is a tyranny under el-Sisi."

"If that's so, why replace one tyranny with another?"

"I'm not arguing for a tyranny, I'm arguing for an oligarchy."

"Oh, come on, Naqib! Where in the world – let alone the tribal Middle East – is there a true oligarchy?"

"I think we ought to order, Papa."

While we were waiting to be served, Naqib asked me off-handedly, "How is Khalifa?"

"He seems to be accumulating quite a few honor points. Near the top of the roster in that respect."

Naqib leaned forward; there was intensity when he asked, "Is he still aiming for the infantry?"

"Yes, I think so."

"He would be so much better off in Signals or Engineers."

"You told him so."

"He might listen better if you told him." (I smiled inwardly at the implied corollary that my older son would also listen to me.)

"What should I tell him?"

"That the infantry isn't particularly safe now, and will be less so in the future."

"You think we'll go to war in Libya or Yemen?"

"I think that the Sinai is a more likely flash point."

"Naqib, what can you tell me about Ansar Bayt al-Maqdis (Supporters of the Holy House)?"

There was a long pause while he considered my question. "They are Islamic socialists who believe strongly in the implementation of Sharia law."

"But they don't believe in democracy."

"I told you: democracy has failed."

"They are affiliated with the Brotherhood and ISIL, correct?"

Naqib considered for a moment. "They have publicly sworn allegiance to ISIL, and ABM has been renamed Wilayat Sinai (Province of Sinai) With the Brotherhood, the relationship is more uncertain. There may be some feeling in ABM that the Brotherhood's methods have failed."

"Failed how?"

"Failed in the sense that protests achieve nothing and only end up getting protesters jailed."

"Who runs ABM?"

"I'm not sure. Some people say it may be Ahmed Refai Taha. He was leader of al-Gama'a al-Islamiyya (the Islamic Group, an Egyptian terror organization which renounced bloodshed in 2003)."

"Have you met him?" There was a brief nod. "What does ABM really believe in?"

"There is a belief that Islam has become too secular, too corrupt, too lax, and that the enemies of the faith must be destroyed."

"Including Christians and Jews." There was a nod. "I suppose you understand that if your mother and your sister were to visit North Sinai today, they would likely be murdered."

Our plates arrived, saving Naqib from the necessity of a direct response. We ate in silence.

As the waiter cleared our plates, I asked, "How does ABM do its recruiting?"

"Most of their members are Bedouins who have historically been very badly treated by the Egyptian government."

"And the other members?"

"They tend to be educated people – many of them disaffected Brotherhood members."

"What is your view, Naqib, on the beliefs of ABM, or WS as it is now called?"

"I think that Islam has become entirely too secular and lax."

"What are the remedies for this?"

He shrugged. "I think there is a need for the rigorous enforcement of Sharia law."

"And what else?"

"Nothing much." A slow, reluctant response.

We both ordered sweet almond cake and coffee. I said, "We ought to talk about how you will discuss your work with family members in the future."

"What do you mean, Papa?"

"What I mean is that obvious fabrications do not lead to trusting relationships."

"If I told them the truth, they wouldn't like it either."

"Maybe not, but they don't like it when someone they love lies to them."

Naqib's lip trembled. "What do you propose, Papa?"

"I suggest that you tell them that you and your law firm work – sometimes – for the Brotherhood."

"But the Brotherhood is effectively an outlawed organization."

"Yes, but it doesn't go around killing people – at present."

He took a sip of his coffee and shook his head. "I can't."

"What can't you do?"

"I can't talk externally about the work we do for the Brotherhood. It's against the law firm's rules."

I shrugged. "Do you think for one minute that I, or Khalifa, or Wahiba, or Anisa would breathe a word outside the family?"

"No, I guess not."

We sat in silence for a few moments. Then I said, "Naqib, you have been pretty honest with me today, and I appreciate that. I really do. I'm going to leave you with one request."

"What is it, Papa?"

"That you continue to be honest with me in the future."

"OK, Papa."

* * *

As I made my way home, I thought about Naqib's 'OK, Papa'. The tone and the lack of eye contact were as before: 'I'm OK, Papa; leave me alone'.

Wahida and Anisa both seemed pessimistic when I told them about the encounter.

Anisa thanked me for my 'good diplomacy'.

Wahida's comment: "Well, it was about as we expected, wasn't it Papa?" Then she added, "Except for the part about Ahmed Refai Taha."

"What do you mean, Wahida?"

"Well, it's pretty unusual for someone who is thought to be the leader of a terrorist organization to meet someone like Naqib who's not even a member. She paused for a moment. "Unless . . ."

* * *

Bagdad airport was not what I expected. There were no piles of rubble or burnt-out aircraft. The black tiled ceilings whose vault ribs were outlined in low-power fluorescent lights made it seem dark inside. But it was clean, with few shops and amenities, and populated with businessmen and armed, watchful soldiers. A yellow taxi took me – without incident – east through the city: a panoply of two- and three-story ochre-colored buildings interspersed with darker high-rises and the occasional skyscraper. Few trees or public gardens, but as we crossed the river, the banks were green with vegetation along the flood plains.

I had looked up the Al Rasheed Hotel on Trip Advisor, and at first, the reviews were awful: terrible food, poor service, high rates, 'but it is one of the safest hotels in the city'. Then there was a recent review which mentioned that the hotel had been taken over by a Dutch hotel group: food, service and amenities 'all excellent'.

I found it to be well short of the Kempinski Nile, but satisfactory.

* * *

Promptly at seven the next morning, I was paged in the lobby, and I met Professor Al Basra. He was robust, of medium height, with only his eyes and upper cheeks showing through a mass of facial hair. He was wearing light tan shalwar trousers, a white business shirt and blue canvas blazer. There was a black skull cap pinned to his mass of hair.

"Professor, you are very welcome!" he announced, steering me through the lobby with an arm around my shoulders. "Our bus is outside, and you will meet my colleagues."

A light green Kia Combi mini bus, somewhat the worse for wear, with 'College of Islamic Science' and a coat of arms painted on one side, stood at the curb. My knapsack was dumped in the back, and I clambered into the bus.

"Now," Al Basra called out, "I am pleased to introduce Professor al-Busiri of the American University, Cairo, who will be accompanying us on Arba'een." He then mentioned the name and title of each of his colleagues, who offered slight bows and words of welcome.

"Professor, you may sit here, if you like," Al Basra said, indicating a window seat in the second row on the right. I sat.

To the bus driver, he said: "All right, Kaleel, we are all aboard. You may go now." And he sat down beside me.

"Now then, Professor . . ." he began.

I interrupted: "Please call me Kareem."

"In that case, may I invite you to call me Akram." He gathered his thoughts for a moment. "Now then, Kareem, we will be leaving Bagdad to the south, down route eight; after about forty kilometers we will go southwest down the main road to Karbala, which we will reach after another forty kilometers. Even now, although we are a full week before Arba'een itself, there will be many people on the highway. For this reason, we don't expect to reach the Karbala junction until late this afternoon, and our plan is to stop at a mawkeb in the town of Alexandria. Tomorrow will be even slower, as more pilgrims converge on Karbala. Somewhere near the town of Musayib on the Euphrates River the pedestrian traffic will be so intense that the bus can offer us no advantage, and we will walk the last fifteen kilometers into Karbala."

I nodded. "I suppose we will reverse the process on the return to Bagdad."

"No. On the return trip, the torrent of pilgrims will have become a flood. No motor vehicle will find space on the highway until the Karbala junction. Therefore, we will walk three days to the junction, where we will find the bus."

"What weather are you expecting, Akram?"

"We are expecting bright sunshine during the day, with a maximum temperature of about eighteen degrees (64°F) and night time temperatures down to about three (37°F)."

"And how many pilgrims are expected this year?"

"About twenty-five to thirty million. The authorities have no way of counting."

I said, "Arba'een means forty, and it falls on a day forty days after Ashura, which, in turn, has something to do with ten. Can you help me understand the significance of the numbers?"

Akram stroked his beard. "Well, Ashura means the tenth in Semitic languages. The Battle of Karbala took place on the tenth of Muharram (the first month in the Islamic calendar) in 61 (680 AD). Therefore, Ashura commemorates the death of Husayn, which is a great tragedy for us Shiites, and a reminder of how good – personified by Husayn – is always in conflict with evil in the person of Yazid, who stole the caliphate from Husayn. As you say, Arba'een means forty, and it occurs forty days after Ashura – forty days being the traditional period of mourning.

So both dates relate to Husayn: one to his death and one to his mourning."

"One might think," I commented, "that Ashura would be the more important event."

"I suppose that history and tradition have established their relative importance. For a Sunni, like yourself, Ashura is known as the Day of Atonement. When Muhammad came to Medina he found that the Jews were fasting on the tenth of Muharram, and he asked, 'What is this?' The reply was, 'This is a good day, this is the day when Allah saved the Children of Israel from their enemy and Moses fasted on this day." Muhammad said, 'We are closer to Moses than you.' So he fasted on the day and told the people to fast. Thus, for Sunnis, Ashura is a day of celebration; for Shia, it is a day of mourning. And, to make matters more complex, in some Shia communities, there has been a tradition of self-flagellation with knives, swords or bladed chains in memory of the suffering of Husayn. But in many jurisdictions, these practices have been declared un-Islamic, and have been replaced with a day of mass blood donations to the Red Crescent."

"If I think back a few years," I observed, "I don't recall there being these huge pilgrimages to Karbala."

"That is because for thirty years when Saddam Hussein was in power, Arba'een was prohibited: he feared that the minority Shia would use the occasion to rise up and overthrow him. The pilgrimages began again in 2004, and have grown in volume every year since. The first pilgrimage to the burial site of Husayn took place in the year after the Battle of Karbala when Jabir ibn Abd-Allah (a companion of Muhammad), the surviving female members of Muhammad's family, and Husayn's son and heir Imam Zain-ul-Abideen, who had all been held captive in Damascus by Yazid, undertook the pilgrimage."

There was much to consider in what Akram told me: the importance of values and tradition in religious practices. Identity was also important as the example of the two different observances of Ashura demonstrated: the minority, persecuted Shia engaging in mourning and self-flagellation; the majority Sunni sharing in a Jewish celebration.

* * *

We had crossed the Tigris River and had turned south onto the four-lane highway. At first, there were only a few pedestrians walking along the shoulder. But at every intersection, a few more people would stream in, mostly dressed in dark clothing, women and children as well as men. By the time we had reached the outskirts of Bagdad, there was a queue, three and four abreast taking up not only the shoulder, but half of the slow lane. Our bus slowed to a jogging pace as it followed its own single queue of vehicles.

All along the eastern side of the highway were collections of small brick houses, haphazardly arranged, amid mounds of earth. Could this be the effect of bombing? But there was no evidence of war. On the western side of the road was a series of walled industrial conclaves: some active, some derelict.

The bus was quiet. Akram stretched his legs out into the aisle, and fell asleep, his shoulder firmly against mine. Most of my fellow pilgrims seemed either to be asleep or reading. Once, the bus pulled into a vacant lot where we could descend and relieve ourselves.

There was a rustling of papers and brief acknowledgements. Falafel, shawarma sandwiches, and mugs of tea were passed around. The shawarma – layers of meat of uncertain origin which had been pressed onto a vertical spit and roasted – was still juicy and delicious.

The afternoon descended into quiet. The windows of the bus were closed to keep out the cloud of tan dust raised by thousands of shoes – not yet a torrent, but certainly a minor river.

There were few buildings, now, on either side. Instead, there was a vast plain checkered with harvested fields and barren fruit orchards. Visible also were dark veins of irrigation ditches.

As daylight was beginning to fade, we reached the town of Alexandria, with its small mud brick houses arranged along narrow roads. Near the center of the town was a large maroon sign; the Arabic script read, "If it rains Daesh (Arabic acronym for ISIL: one who sows discord), we will still go to Husayn."

My goodness! That's real commitment!

The bus pulled over and stopped. "This is the same mawkeb where we stopped last year," Akram announced. "Let's hope it's as good this year."

By the side of the road was an expanse of canvas awning stretched between palm tree trunks. Dozens of dark-clad pilgrims, men and women, were seated at tables or standing nearby. Smoke and aromatic steam rose from the center, where food was being served from huge pots and open grills. The atmosphere was contagiously cheerful: shouted greetings, Arabic kisses and embraces. Akram was embraced by three village men in a kind of huddle. He said to them, "The blessings of Husayn be upon you for your generosity! We have the same devoted pilgrims as last year with one addition: Professor al-Busiri from the American University in Cairo." I found myself embraced irresistibly by the same three villagers, one of whom inquired urgently, "Are you American, then?"

"No, I am Egyptian." As an afterthought, in the general hubbub, I added, "But my wife was American."

"Oh, you did not bring her?"

"No, she is with Allah."

"Ah, she is with Husayn!"

I had understood that everything in the mawkeb was provided gratis, but I found it difficult to understand how poor villagers could provide such hospitality. Surreptitiously, I removed five one-thousand dinar notes ($.90 each)) from my knapsack and put them in my pocket. Just in case they are needed.

Our group was herded to the rear of the tent, where two more tables and assorted chairs were unfolded. We sat in turns and went to get the food. This was the first opportunity I had to talk with my fellow pilgrims from Bagdad. They were all male, from the black-bearded young instructors to a white-bearded Methuselah, an honorary professor emeritus. All most interested in me and the American University. Their curiosity satisfied on those points, they wanted to know my expectations of Arba'een.

"Well, it is a great pilgrimage, steeped in emotion and mystery. How could one not want to be a part of this?"

"You are right about the emotion," one of the young instructors offered. "We have this great love for Husayn, who allowed himself to be sacrificed brutally by a false and wicked caliph for the sake of the religion of his grandfather – a beautiful religion!"

"There is emotion, too, in the hatred we feel for Yazid," the other young instructor added. "He is for us the embodiment of evil."

A Professor Aziz with a long russet beard added, "And there is the loss we feel for Husayn: a perfect man, the grandson of the Prophet, a true caliph."

"For you, then," I summarized, "it is a personal example of the never-ending struggle between good and evil."

"Yes, Professor," the Methuselah interjected, "but it is also a reminder of how we Muslims must emulate the example of Husayn: to be pure in heart, to love Allah, and to treat other humans with justice and respect."

Listening to my Bagdad colleagues and having learned from Elizabeth the story of Christianity, I could not help but be amazed at the parallels between the executions of Christ and Husayn.

While the food may have lacked in sophistication, it was remarkable in the generosity with which it was served: a stew of beans, rice, carrots and chicken; tea, unleavened bread hot from the griddle, sweet lemon cake and weak tea.

For a time, I listened to stories about Arba'een's past. The topic turned inevitably to attacks by Sunni extremists.

"Do you remember back in O-nine," a soft-spoken professor began, "there was that attack on the outskirts of Karbala: two boys in suicide vests and another ten men with automatic weapons?" There were nods around the table. "One of the boys detonated in the middle of a crowd. But the other one raised his hands in the air and started shouting, 'Father Khaliq! Father Khaliq!' until one of the terrorists shot him and he exploded!"

"Why was he shouting for Father Khaliq?" I interrupted.

"We don't know," a sharp-nosed professor responded.

"I think an explanation could be that the boy did not want to commit suicide and was trying to surrender," one of the instructors observed. "Perhaps his father was named Khaliq, and the boy was calling him to be rescued."

I stretched out my hand. "What I can't understand is how people can build up so much hatred that they believe they should kill others who offer them no harm."

"It has always been like this in Iraq."

"But why? It makes no sense!"

"Logic can be bypassed when it comes to religion," Methuselah suggested.

Akram said, "It seems to me that there are several pre-requisites. The terrorist has to feel that there is something in it for him, personally – perhaps greater recognition – or a belief that he will go straight to heaven. And he has to think that what he will do is correct – other people have done it, or my religious leader encourages it, or it is a cultural belief. But at the same time, there is a logical blindness in the terrorist: he is unable to comprehend the actual reality of what he will do. Or, to put it differently, he has zero empathy."

"I have often thought," one of the instructors said, "that the devil selects and prepares people who are vulnerable. He causes vulnerable people to feel excited about their expected reward, and he is able to erase their feelings of empathy."

"How does he do that?"

"I don't know, but I believe that he has every incentive to do so. Religion is about worshiping God – the devil's enemy – surely the devil would like God to weep for the innocent people who have been killed in the process of worshipping Him."

* * *

The sleeping arrangements were not ideal. Behind the main tent, there were two further tents: a large one of men and a smaller one for women and children. Plastic covering had been spread over the earth, and straw had been placed on top. There were piles of old fabric that one could use as coverings or pillows. As the night wore on, the sleeping accommodation became quite crowded as more pilgrims arrived. The warmth of several hundred bodies banished the night chill, but there was a cacophony of snores, grunts, and coughs. The night was only slightly restful. I will sleep on the bus, I consoled myself.

Two latrine trenches, one for men, one for women, had been dug fifty meters from the sleeping tents. A pretext of privacy was provided in the form of fabric partitions in the men's latrine. Hopefully, the women's privacy was more substantial.

* * *

Akram roused us at six the next morning. "Get yourself some breakfast and board the bus. We want to get under way before seven."

Even at seven o'clock the road was crowded, and our bus was limited to walking speed. By late morning, we crossed the Euphrates River: smaller than the Nile, but its banks were green, though far less cultivated.

164

We stopped for the midday meal at another mawkeb a few kilometers south of Musayib. "From here," Akram announced, "we make the rest of the way on foot. The road ahead is closed to vehicles." At that point, from my map, we were about twelve kilometers from Karbala. I was pleased: with only a dozen kilometers to walk, there was the prospect of sleeping in a hotel room rather than another night on straw in a mawkeb.

At about two o'clock we melded into the great stream of people moving down the road. It was impossible not to feel part of an immense living thing with its own heart and voice. It would chant, it would sing:

O self, you are worthless after Husayn.

My life and death are one and the same,

But my love for you is all I claim.

The voice of the living thing would be still for a time, and one could hear only the shuffle of feet ever the dusty road. Then someone would shout out the beginning of another song of grief or praise, and the collective voice would pick up the verses and carry them forward for another kilometer. Sorrowful chests would be struck, a forest of arms raised in loving surrender, a thousand heads bowed in stricken prayer. And the emotion on every face, the language of every body amplified the mighty message: Husayn is who we want to be: perfect, tragic Husayn, destroyed by the embodiment of evil.

The emotion was completely overpowering: one could not walk one hundred meters in the river without being overcome with love and sorrow: absolute commitment. I found myself singing and chanting – not knowing but understanding the words. My arm was raised, my head was bowed, my chest was struck. Husayn was mine!

"Professor, do you want a . . . ?"

I couldn't make out what it was. Amid all the human voices, I tried to focus on who was shouting. It was Professor Aziz, beside me, clutching my arm.

"Professor, do you want a banner?"

"What banner?"

"The yellow or the green." He was pointing to the side of the road. I looked. There were fluttering cloths suspended there: yellow or green with Arabic script. "Do you want to carry one?"

Carry one? Carry a banner to Karbala? "Yes!"

"Come, then, we get you one!" He towed me out of the river. "Yellow or green?"

"Yellow."

"He'll take a yellow," Aziz shouted at a man by the banners. The man unwrapped a yellow banner on a three-meter pole and passed the pole to me. A breeze caught the fabric and opened it. I Love Husayn, the green Arabic script read.

"How much is it?" I asked the man.

The man shook his head.

Aziz looked into my face. "He wants you to have the banner, Professor."

I reached into my pocket, withdrew the Iraqi bank notes, and pressed them into the man's hand. "This is from Father Khaliq for your children."

Aziz took my arm, steering me back to rejoin our group in the human river. "But," he shouted, "who is this Father Khaliq?"

Leaning toward him so as to be heard, I said, "I don't know. It's just a name that sprang to mind. I couldn't say that the money was from me. He wouldn't have taken it."

"Yes, I see."

A cheer of approval went up from the crowd around us as a breeze caught my flag and unfurled it.

We continued our chanting, singing and marching toward Karbala, down the four-lane, divided highway, our river over-flowing the two southbound lanes, onto the shoulder, onto the median and into one of the northbound lanes so that only one lane of traffic could go north. We passed harvested fields and orchards which had given up their leaves and all but a handful of shriveled fruit. There were mud brick houses and compounds from which women in black watched and children ran, keeping pace for a few hundred meters and holding aloft their own small banners before dropping back. Several times, our group left the river to pause at a mawkeb for a drink of water, to relieve ourselves, and to watch the human tide wash by.

As dusk was falling, we reached the outskirts of Karbala; there was, to the left a township of closely-packed houses, and then the highway split: our southbound lanes continued straight on, while the northbound lanes converged from the left.

Akram dropped back beside me and took my elbow. Leaning close to be heard, he said, "We are now less than two kilometers from the holy shrines. But for now, we will go around them, because our hotel is on the other side – on Zaid bin Ali Street. You have not been to Karbala before?"

"No, this is the first time."

"You will notice that this is one of the wealthiest cities in Iraq."

"I suppose that the city benefits from all the pilgrims."

"Yes, but it is not only accommodation, food and religious icons that represent income. There is also a very large funeral business here."

"A funeral business?"

"Yes. It is more than the shrines that we Shia consider holy. It is Karbala itself which is holy because the Battle took place here and because interpretations of the Qur'an and many hadiths identify Karbala as a holy place. For many Shia, Karbala is on the path to paradise. Many old people come here to await death and be buried." I shook my head in wonder. "And," he added, "on the secular side, there are a large number of government offices here, as well as a strong agricultural sector. Dates are a particular specialty."

* * *

The Hotel Caliph Ali was a jumbled assortment of buildings that had been joined by physical addition or acquisition into a maze of some five hundred rooms. In Cairo, it would have been flattered to be awarded two stars; here, in Karbala, it boasted four stars. Our party of twelve academics was to share three double rooms, but none of the rooms was large enough to permit the addition of more than one cot. Methuselah and I were assigned a room with two of the instructors. The room had twin beds with a permanent sag and one narrow canvas cot. Thoughtfully, there was a pile of extra blankets and a pillow on the floor beside the cot. Methuselah swung his knapsack onto one of the twin beds, and announced, "That one is yours, Professor," indicating the other twin bed.

"But," I protested, "I am a late addition to the party, and I'm quite content to sleep on the floor."

"Nonsense!" Methuselah growled. "Professors sleep on a bed; instructors sleep where they can!"

As it turned out, I regretted not having pursued my protests more forcefully: the bed turned out to be more like a hammock, while the cot seemed to offer firmness without rigidity.

* * *

That evening we ate in a noisy, smoky eatery; we were given two adjacent tables for four which were joined to accommodate the twelve of us, shoulder-to-shoulder. As soon as we were seated, we were served: tea, un-leavened bread, rice, beans and a vegetable-mutton stew. This was followed immediately by a sweet cake and pomegranate seeds. Our tariff was collected and we were back on the street within half an hour.

* * *

I found myself walking beside Aziz. "If we sit over here," he said, indicating a low brick wall at the edge of the street, "we can observe the Arba'een pilgrims." He removed a dark cotton shawl which was normally slung over one shoulder and spread it on the wall. "For me," he continued, "the treasure which is Arba'een may be captured as much by observing other pilgrims as in one's own experiences." He looked over at me, and probably noted my puzzlement. "For example," he went on, "I try to identify every emotion I see on the face of these strangers, and I ask myself, 'Have I ever felt that during Arba'een?' If I have, the memory of that feeling is renewed and confirmed within me. If I haven't experienced what I see on a stranger's face, I ask myself, 'Why not?' Two that I haven't experienced are guilt and shame." He glanced at me again, with a smile this time. "Of course, I admit to having felt guilt and shame at other times in my life, but never during Arba'een. So I try to look deeper into the pilgrim with shame or guilt on his face: beyond his heart and into his mind."

It was my turn to smile. "And have you succeeded in reading the mind of the guilty pilgrim, Aziz?"

"I am doubtful. Of course it is easy to conclude that the pilgrim wants to wash away some old sin with his commitment to live a new, upright life like Husayn." He paused. "Have you ever had similar feelings, Professor?"

At first, I did not understand his question. Then I said, "No, when I feel guilty, I try to do something which puts things right with the person I've hurt."

He nodded, "Why did you decide to come on Arba'een, Professor?"

"I was told that it is a more profound experience that the Hajj, and that is true."

"Yes, but your motivation was not religious?"

"Probably the answer is 'no', but I'm not sure what is religion."

"It is what we believe – at a spiritual level – but do not know."

"If that is the case, I am unsure what is my spiritual level."

"Kareem. May I call you Kareem?"

"Yes, of course."

"Well then, Kareem, you have struck at the heart of the matter. I suppose it is the same for philosophers as it is for theologians: what is spirit? We cannot agree on a precise definition. For each of us, the meaning is somewhat different, but on some characteristics we agree: it is not tangible or material; it is associated with a living thing; it is non-trivial and worth our attention."

For a few moments, I observed the toe of my sandal dig a small trench in the dust. "Then, to answer your question, Aziz, I think the motivation for my being on Arba'een is to enhance my spirituality, or to find out if I have any."

Aziz laughed. "Of course you have spirituality, Kareem! Perhaps with many years' emphasis on logic, factuality and knowledge, it has been left to itself." He considered me as my foot filled in the trench and patted it down. "What I tell my students about spirituality is to experiment continuously with an open mind, relying on what feels right for them, as individuals."

I asked: "So you don't believe there is one answer?"

"How could there be one answer for seven billion individuals?"

"But maybe Allah has one answer," I suggested.

He shook his head vigorously. "If one acknowledges that God created seven billion unique creatures, how could one think that He had one answer for all of them?"

* * *

The following morning, Akram led us slowly past the Mosque of Husayn. The crowds were so dense that we could only inch forward as if we were in a forest of close-packed cypresses. One's thoughts were drowned out by the cacophony of singing and shouting in love or grief. One careful step forward, a pause, a lateral move, then half a step ahead, trying to keep Akram's black turban and green shawl in sight. In about an hour and a half, having covered less than one kilometer, we reached the long plaza that connected the mosques of Husayn and Abbas. Here, Akram wrapped an arm around my shoulder, and we slowly progressed as a unit: sometimes facing ahead; more frequently with tiny side steps, crab-wise. "In the Arba'een we like to build up to the adoration of Husayn," he boomed. "We will therefore first visit the Mosque of Abbas. Are you familiar with the history of Al Abbas?"

"I know only that he was Husayn's half-brother."

"That is correct. Both were sired by Ali with different mothers. Abbas was trained as a warrior by his father. He was with Husayn and a small party of family and cohorts when they journeyed to Kufa, here in Iraq. The army of Yazid, who was intent upon stealing the caliphate for himself, blocked the way and forced Husayn to detour to Karbala. At Karbala, Husayn's party ran out of water, and access to the Euphrates River was denied by Yazid's army. But Abbas approached the river on horseback, carrying an empty water bag and the standard of Husayn. His intention was not to fight, but to obtain water for the women and children who were with Husayn. Abbas filled the water bag and was riding back to camp when he was attacked by Yazid's soldiers, who punctured the water bag with an arrow and cut off his arms. He fell from his horse, carrying the standard of Husayn to the ground. Abbas was buried here, where he fell." Akram paused to clear his throat, which had become hoarse with emotion. "So you see, Kareem, Abbas was a man of great loyalty to Husayn: he dropped the banner of Husayn only when he could no longer carry it. He was a great warrior who, in previous years, had killed many men. But in this instance, he came to the river in peace, seeking water for desperately thirsty women and children."

I looked up at the twin minarets and the golden, pear-shaped dome that topped the beige mosque with its many high, pointed archways. I could not help but think, *This is quite a tomb for a man who was killed in a fruitless mission. But the Shia don't see it that way. They see Abbas as a symbolic character in a great Islamic morality play.*

Two more hours were required to squeeze past the thousands exiting the mosque, and make our way inside. It was like two opposing streams of water, each one seeking a way through the other.

Inside, the huge mosque was glittering in the light from millions of mirrors and crystals set in the walls, columns and vaulted ceilings. Chandeliers were ablaze with light refracted through crystals, and one chandelier, in particular, sent an intense burst of gold light from above the tomb of Abbas. The tomb itself, covered in gold, was the size of a huge shipping container. Latticework at the sides held emerald rectangles which were lit from within. Layers of ornate filigree work crowned the tomb, and, on the gold roof, pilgrims had hurled further layers of clothing, so that many were naked to the waist.

I was pressed irresistibly by the crowd behind me toward the tomb, and I realized that every pilgrim was intent on touching the tomb.

Over the loudspeakers came the announcement: "Take your places! Prayers will begin shortly!"

Pressures eased as pilgrims at the tomb retreated to claim a spot on the prayer carpets. Akram propelled me forward until I found myself at the tomb. "Say a prayer!" he boomed. I reached out, touched the gold lattice work and murmured, "I pray for your courage and devotion, Abbas."

Later I thought, *Why did I pray to be like Abbas? Why didn't I pray for my family? I suppose I was a captive of the overpowering emotion that surrounded me.*

Exact rows of pilgrims were forming, aligned to the patterns on the carpet, and we each took a space, kneeling and sitting on our heels.

I don't know how long the prayers lasted: some were familiar, many unfamiliar and a few seemed to be extemporaneous, motivated by the adoration of Abbas. There was an address by the imam, a booming torrent of veneration, the details of which were unclear, but the vast congregation – several hundred thousand strong – responded as one with frequent "Na'am!" (yes) and "Labaha Allah!" (praise God!).

It was late afternoon by the time we returned to the hotel, having reversed the lengthy process of squeezing out of the Mosque of Imam Al Abbas and pressing our way through the hordes of devoted pilgrims.

Chapter 7

Daesh

That evening, Akram told me the story of Husayn's death. "When Abbas had been murdered, the slaughter of the seventy-two members of Husayn's party began. Women and children were not spared in acts of pure evil. These martyrs are buried in a mass grave beside the tomb of Husayn. Husayn and all the men with him were decapitated. Husayn's head was taken to Damascus where it was put on a pole and displayed as a triumphant prize by Yazid, the false caliph. After forty days, Ali, one of Husayn's sons who was not murdered at Karbala, retrieved the head from Damascus, and had it buried with the body of Husayn forty days after the murder. This is one of the reasons why Arba'een falls on a date forty days after Ashura, the anniversary of Husayn's death."

"But Akram," I protested, "we Egyptians believe that the head of Husayn is buried in the Al-Hussein Mosque in Cairo."

"Yes, I know. This is pure Sunni bullshit, and it makes no sense. The impossible story is that Husayn's head remained in Damascus for a couple of hundred years until it was taken to Ashkelon in Israel, and from there, it was moved to Cairo. Pure bullshit."

I gave a concessionary nod. "So Husayn is greatly admired for his resistance to Yazid the false Caliph."

"There is much more to Husayn than that, Kareem. You know that Husayn's brother, Hasan, was selected to be caliph after the death of their father, Ali, but to prevent a civil war between them, Muawiyah was permitted to be caliph. A treaty was agreed between Hasan and Muawiyah, the only conditions of which were that the people would be governed fairly and that on Muawiyah's death the people would select the next caliphate. Muawiyah broke the treaty by declaring his son Yazid caliph. Yazid was a corrupt and evil caliph. He demanded that Husayn swear allegiance to him. This Husayn refused to do; his view was that Yazid's rule was oppressive and religiously misguided. He also believed that Yazid's ascension was an attempt to establish an illegal hereditary dynasty. But he did not raise an army to fight Yazid. Instead he was en route to Kufa, here in Iraq, to take up the invited position of imam, when he was met by Yazid's army. The army asked Husayn for his water, which he gave to them. The final treachery, you know. So you see, Husayn was a man of great wisdom and integrity, a man who always placed the welfare of the people above his own desires. He was upright and honest: for this he was murdered."

* * *

The following day we endured the nearly-irresistible human tide to reach the enormous Mosque of Imam Husayn. This was similar to Abbas' except that the walls and ceiling were burnished in gold rather than crystal and mirrors. Again, my body was moved with the tide until I could touch the splendid tomb, but my prayer was different this time: Husayn, lend your wisdom so that I can be an exemplary father and teacher.

* * *

Back at the hotel that evening, I began to reflect on the pilgrimage we had undertaken. I asked Methuselah, when we had finished evening prayers, "This has been a memorable experience for me, Professor, to better understand the Shia version of Islam, to visit these two splendid shrines, to participate in the adoration of the martyred imams, and to know my colleagues at the University of Bagdad . . ."

He offered a knowing smile. "But you as a Sunni think that we Shia have become obsessed about the succession to Muhammad and the martyrdom of one of his grandsons."

"No, it isn't that. I understand the importance in the culture of Islam of the identity of the caliph and ascension to the position."

"What then?"

Again I hesitated. "My question is: what does all of this have to do with Allah – the One Supreme Being to whom we pray every day?"

"You are thinking, perhaps, that it would be more appropriate if the shrines were dedicated to Allah and that the ceremonies and prayers should focus on Him?"

"Something like that. He just seems to be absent."

"He is not absent, I assure you, Professor."

"How do you know?"

"Because if He were truly absent, there would have been no Husayn or Abbas or Muhammad."

"So, you're suggesting that He lives in them?"

"Yes, and the reverse is also true, Professor: they live in Him."

"All right. But where is the evidence that Allah lives in Husayn?"

"Professor, you must know that there is no proof. I think Allah wants us to live in doubt, but surprisingly, all three of the world's great monotheistic religions have real human figures who stand between Allah and his people. For me, it's as if Allah is saying, 'I cannot give you proof of who I am, but I will let someone who has seen me tell you'. In the case of Judaism, it was Moses and the prophets; for Christians, it is Jesus; for Muslims, it is Muhammad. If we didn't have these figures, we would all be atheists!"

I nodded. "But I guess my question is: how does the adoration of Husayn bring us closer to Allah?"

"It is in the whole context of Arba'een and Husayn – the context of the Shia faith. The experience of Arba'een and the love of Husayn makes the Shia faith more personal and real. That strengthened faith makes Allah more real, so that tomorrow we are more comfortable in offering Him our thanks and praise." He paused. "Tell me, Professor, have you been to the tomb of the Prophet in Medina?"

"Yes."

"And did that visit strengthen your belief that there really was a Muhammad, the Messenger of God?"

"Yes." I thought for a moment. "I guess my problem is that I find it difficult to believe everything that Muhammad said."

"May I make a suggestion, Professor?"

"Yes, of course."

"Make a summary of what you do believe. Let that be a kind of platform. Then argue with Muhammad about the rest of it."

"Argue with Muhammad?"

"Yes. It's a special kind of internal dialogue. You should try it."

* * *

The next day we began our trek back toward Bagdad. It was still three days before Arba'een itself, but the road was like the exit tunnel after a big football match, except on a grander scale. Our party of twelve was forced into a single-file queue on the right hand side, and the queue was constantly being broken by surges from the huge flow on the left. We were barely out of Karbala when I had passed my yellow Husayn banner to a giant bearded man who was shouting, "Long live Husayn!" Then, as we inched along at two or three kilometers per hour, I had to focus on the instructor ahead of me in the queue. But in spite of the shuffle of feet, the bursts of song and shots of prayer, I was able to entertain my own thoughts. What about a dialogue with Muhammad? What scripture in the Qur'an do I not agree with? I thought for a moment. Well, there is that ayah in the Jonah sura that says: "No soul can believe except by God's will, and He brings disgrace on those who do not use their reason." To me, this sounds like an arbitrary God saying: "I decide who my believers are and I'll punish those whom I do not select!"

What do you say to that, Muhammad?

There is another way of looking at it, Kareem.

Which is?

That God is just and loving and that He wants all souls to believe in Him. He is not choosing; He is inclusive.

What about the disgrace part?

Do you not think, Kareem, that people who do not use their reason bring disgrace on themselves?

OK, but it says that God brings the disgrace.

Look at it this way, Kareem; suppose you are a great singing teacher and you teach a man to sing glorious opera but instead, he picks pockets at the opera house. Wouldn't you be annoyed?

I suppose so.

* * *

That night, having covered about half the distance to the Euphrates River along route 9, we stopped at a mawkeb.

The next day, we noticed a change on the road: it was two days until Arba'een and the throngs pressing their way down the highway eased, while the crowds leaving Karbala had increased. "We'll have one more night on the road," Akram opined. "By tomorrow the road should be pretty clear and the minibus will be able to pick us up. Anyone who is thinking of making it to

Karbala by the twenty-first will have to run or ride with Muhammad on his white horse."

* * *

The proprietors at the mawkeb on the second night seemed edgy. I attributed it to several long weeks of being inundated with pilgrims – some without Arabic, some destitute and some quite ill. But Akram had a different opinion. "They're afraid that Daesh is in the area."

I asked, "Why don't they say so?"

"Because they're afraid of frightening off their guests."

"What would make them suspicious?"

Akram shrugged. "Who knows? It could be just rumors, or people dressed the wrong way for Arba'een, or a couple of people carrying AK's. Who knows?"

I must confess that I was particularly observant of people around the mawkeb, and I did not fall asleep until about midnight that night.

I woke to the sound of screams. It was still dark. Several shots. More screams. Terrified. Imperious shouting. Several lights appeared in the men's sleeping tent.

"Get up!"

Several men half rose and turned to see who it was.

"Get up! Or we'll shoot you vermin where you are!"

We all immediately got to or feet.

"Get out your identity papers! Where are the university professors?"

No one made a sound.

"Where are the university professors? If you don't identify yourselves, we'll kill the lot of you!"

"We are here," Akram said.

"Are you the leader?"

"Yes."

"How many?"

"Twelve."

"Identify them!"

Akram began pointing us out. We were herded together at one end of the tent. Men in black baklavas, long kameezes, trousers and tan desert boots snatched at the proffered identity cards of the other pilgrims. The cards were ripped in half and allowed to flutter to the straw.

"You lot: get out!" This to us from the Daesh leader, who brandished an automatic pistol and whose face was barely visible beneath the black turban and the mass of black facial hair.

"Let's go," Akram said reluctantly.

"Wait, where are you taking them?" shouted a boy of about ten.

The Daesh leader turned on the boy and shouted, "Shut your mouth, you little cockroach!" He drew a pistol and fired a single shot directly at the boy's chest. The boy stumbled backwards in shock and collapsed. His father fell on the boy, wailing an agonized scream of protest. The Daesh leader shot the man in the head, silencing him.

We were outside the tent, literally paralyzed with fear: unable to think or speak or decide to move. You are going to die, Kareem. Prepare yourself. . . . Well, I will see Elizabeth. But my children! . . . Great Allah, if it be your will, let me survive this terror.

"You lot, move! Get in that truck over there!"

The Daesh leader and two of his men escorted us with gun-muzzle prodding to the road and the canvas-covered truck. This was probably a US Army truck 'liberated' from an Iraqi military base. We climbed in and sat on the floor. The two escorts closed the tailgate and stood at the rear, their AK's at the ready.

"Take care of the vermin!" the Daesh leader shouted, and climbed into the cab. Loud bursts of automatic weapons fire, punctuated with screams, came from behind the mawkeb. Then silence. The truck started to move. My God, there must have been seventy other men and boys in that tent!

Akram began speaking to his colleagues. Not in Arabic; it must have been Farsi. Perhaps he was trying to console them, to keep their morale up. Anyway, I couldn't understand what he was saying.

"Shut your mouth! No talking!" One of the guards made threatening motions with his AK.

Akram ceased talking. All that could be heard was the roar of the engine and the rattling and squeaking of the truck body.

They could have killed us with the others. Why not? Because they have some use for us. . . . Probably as hostages. . . . But Daesh doesn't have a very good record of releasing hostages. . . . They keep them for a while – make a lot of noise about them and then . . .

We traveled for about an hour. The first part of the trip seemed to be over back roads at cautious speed, bumping through or avoiding potholes. Then the truck accelerated along what must have been a paved road.

We were stopped.

"Get out!" The voice of the Daesh leader.

When our feet were on the ground, we could see that we were on a narrow, unpaved residential street. There were no street lights, but the lights of the truck were still on. The village – if that's what it was – appeared to be deserted. We were prodded unceremoniously into one of the narrow two-story houses: different styles, but abutting each other. I noticed that where a house had shutters, they were closed.

Once inside the house, we were shoved into a back room without furniture. One of the Daesh lit a kerosene lamp and hung it from a nail that had been driven into the dirty wall.

"Search them!" the Daesh leader ordered.

Most of us still had our knapsacks. *Save your phone, Kareem!* flashed suddenly through my mind. I didn't care about the money I had with me: fifty thousand dinars ($45). My passport? No! It doesn't matter. Your phone!

In the confused semi-darkness, I slipped off my knapsack, reached into a side pocket, retrieved the phone, and slid it down the front of my trousers.

The Daesh weren't particularly interested in the small sums that were surrendered. There were, of course, no weapons: just three pocket knives. They were interested in the identity cards. As each card was produced, the Daesh leader scrutinized the card and the face of the pilgrim.

"You are Adel bin Chakroun?" he demanded of Methuselah.

"Yes."

"You are a professor of religion at Bagdad University?"

"I am Professor Emeritus of religion at the university."

The leader snorted derisively. "You are a Shia apostate?"

"I am a Shia Muslim."

"Stand over there!"

As the questioning continued, it became apparent that the leader wanted to be sure that his captives were full professors. I suppose he considers full professors of religion at the prestigious University of Bagdad valuable hostages.

My suspicions were confirmed when the first instructor, the youngest one, was questioned.

"You are too young to be a full professor, boy!"

"I am an instructor."

"Stand over there!" the leader said dismissively, indicating the opposite side of the room from the professors.

"But I am a Sunni!" the young instructor shouted.

The black-bearded Daesh turned immediately on the young man. "So you are a Sunni?" His face was eager with hostility. "Tell me then, Sunni scholar, the name of the author of one book of hadiths (religious doctrines attributed, indirectly, to the Prophet) that Sunnis consider to be completely accurate."

The instructor considered for a moment; he hesitated. then: "al-Kafi."

There was a sneering guffaw. "No! Wrong! Who is al-Kafi? Another one of your inventors of perverted stories! Deal with him, Abdul!"

The terrified instructor shrank toward his colleagues. Two Daesh pinned his arms, dragging him toward a third, who drew a long knife, slashing him across the throat. The young man made a choking sound as an eruption of blood cascaded down his chest. His mouth was moving and his eyes were desperately fastened on me as his life drained away in diminishing pulsations of blood. His body collapsed to the floor. Abdul reached down and severed his head.

To this day, I still have graphic nightmares in which those twenty seconds are repeated, live and in 3D color. I wish I had had the foresight to turn away. What message was in his staring eyes? What did he want of me?

"Now," the Daesh leader asked, "who has more lies to tell?"

The tension was intense; no one said a word.

"You, there!" the leader gestured toward another instructor whose name was Hajji.

He stepped forward. "I am Shia!" he announced. Something about the pride in which he made the confession struck a chord of admiration in me. This guy is something!

"Of course you're a Shia, you scumbag, but are you also an instructor?"

"I am an instructor." Again, there was pride in his voice.

Say what you are thinking, Kareem! "He is indeed an instructor, and he soon will be a full professor. He is as valuable to his university as any of these great men," came out of my mouth. I held my breath in anticipation of the onslaught.

"Who the fuck are you?" the leader demanded.

"I am Professor Kareem al-Bushiri from the American University in Cairo."

"An American? Let me see your papers!"

I handed him my passport. He considered me for some moments. "How do you have an American passport?"

"My wife was an American; I was born Egyptian."

"But you are Shia."

"No, like most Egyptians, I am Sunni."

"Then what the fuck are you doing with this vermin?" He made a sweeping gesture toward my colleagues.

"I came on Arba'een as part of some research I am doing at the university."

"How do you know shit about this cockroach?" he asked, pointing at Hajji.

"He has helped me with my research, and I checked his credentials with the university. He is highly regarded." I glanced toward my Iraqi colleagues for confirmation.

There were nods. "He will be made a full professor when we return to Bagdad," Akram averred.

"If your universities pay your ransom, you mean. Otherwise, you will join the cockroach over there (with a gesture toward the murdered instructor) in hell."

The lamp was extinguished, the Daesh departed, and the door was noisily locked. We were left in the dark with the murdered instructor. We could hear our captors moving about in the front room.

Akram whispered, "I am very sorry to say this, but neither the College of Islamic Science nor the University of Bagdad nor, for that matter, the government of Iraq has any money to pay ransom." He paused. "I suppose that in your case, Kareem, America would refuse to pay ransom."

"I'm sure that's right," I conceded gloomily, "and since I'm not here on university business, they will certainly wash their hands of me."

"So that means," Methuselah put in, "that we either have to escape or be rescued."

"There's nothing we can do about escape tonight; let's think tomorrow. To be rescued, the right people have to know where we are."

"We don't know where we are, and we can't communicate."

Suddenly, I remembered. "I have my phone," I whispered.

"Praise Allah! How did you keep it?"

"Does it still have a charge?"

"I charged it at the hotel the night before last and it's been off since."

"Who can we contact?"

"I think I still have the email address of your Dean."

"Much better to send a message to the university Chancellor," Akram said.

"How about the Americans?" someone asked.

"I don't have any useful contacts in America."

"How about Barack Obama at gov dot US dot com?"

"I don't know if that's right. Besides, he takes forever to make a decision. Anyone in the Iraqi government?"

"Worse."

There was a long moment of pessimism.

"What kind of a phone do you have?" Hajji asked.

"I think it's an iPhone 5. My daughter made me get it. She knows about this sort of thing."

"May I see it?"

I reached into my trousers and withdrew the phone. Moments later the white apple appeared in the darkness.

"What's your password?" I told him. The rows of colored icons appeared. "It's picked up a Zain base station . . . pretty weak though. Ooh! There's a strong Wi-Fi signal – password protected. Somebody nearby left their modem on when they left."

"Never mind all that, Hajji," Akram interrupted, "let's concentrate on getting a message out."

During the next fifteen minutes a message to the Chancellor was composed and sent.

"But he won't know where we are," Methuselah objected.

"We can send him a map," Hajji whispered.

"What map?"

"A Google map. Here let me have the phone again." Hajji's fingers worked on the screen. Then he held it up. "We're here. See the blue dot in the center, and over here is the centre of Ramadi. It looks like we're a couple of kilometers to the west."

"They'll never find us with that map."

"Well, we can send him this one which shows in general where we are, and then we can zoom in so that it almost identifies the house."

Click. Hajji took a screen shot, then another shot. He sat looking at the screen for a moment. "OK. They're on their way."

I took the phone back; it had 47% power remaining. I turned it off and put it in my trousers.

* * *

The following morning, Akram asked for permission to bury the murdered instructor. We were refused permission to wash the body or wrap it in a shroud.

"He was apostate and does not merit janazah (Islamic funeral)," the leader announced. I wanted to ask him if he had an imam's credentials, but I thought better of it.

Akram and I were given access under guard to the small, naked plot of ground behind the house.

"Which way is Mecca?" he asked.

"I think it is south of here," I said.

"Which means?"

"That if he should be facing south, the grave should be dug parallel to the wall of the house."

We found a shovel and took turns chopping into the hard-packed earth. Eventually, we cut a two meter long trench, quite deep and narrow. Akram hoisted the dead man's shoulders, I took his ankles, and we laid him in the trench, right shoulder down. Hajji appeared, carrying the head, which he was about to place in the bottom of the trench near the shoulders.

Akram shook his head. "No, no, Hajji! It must be done like this!" The professor knelt by the grave and made a large ball of earth. This he placed at the bottom of the trench by the shoulders. "Now, you can put his head on that, Hajji. It is customary. He must face Mecca!"

Hajji carefully placed the head. "We have to find a way to keep the dogs from digging," he suggested.

"First, we must say the janazah prayer." Akram bowed his head. "God is great. God is great. God is great. God is great." He took a handful of earth and motioned for us to do the same. "We created you from it, and return you into it, and from it, we will raise you a second time."

We filled the grave with earth, making a mound.

I took a moment to look around. "The shutters on our window have a closure on the outside," I whispered to Akram.

"There is a closure on the inside, as well."

* * *

I thought of parallels – in life, or in death – between Husayn and that young instructor of religion. Both were good men; both were undoubtedly religious. But the instructor had lost his life in trying to save it by denying his religion. Husayn died for his beliefs.

* * *

We were taken to an open area with no visible landmarks and photographed with our captors, who must have looked triumphant with their black flags, broad grins, their military swagger and their AK47's.

When we were alone, I checked my phone. There were no messages. 38% power.

* * *

Meals consisted of rice and beans in a communal pot. We ate with our hands.

There was one lavatory and sink on the ground floor, but we were supervised whenever someone used it. Why? Who knows!

Akram announced the times of the five-daily obligatory prayers, but someone was nearly always prostrate on the cement floor, facing south.

During the day, there were usually two Daesh on guard duty, fully armed and ready. They said nothing, except to forbid any approach to them or any whispering among ourselves.

* * *

On the second day we were taken to the same open area and videoed – perhaps to demonstrate that we were uninjured. Again no messages. 29% power.

* * *

The leader came in on the third day. "Does any of you have a message you would like to send to your family? Perhaps they can be instrumental in persuading your university to make the necessary payment so that you can be released."

No one responded, but tensions were certainly increasing. Methuselah had a fever, and several professors had lapsed into total silence, broken only by the murmuring of their prayers.

* * *

Aziz asked, "Can you get Al Jeezera on your phone?"

I said I didn't think so.

"You probably could if you had their app," Hajji commented.

"Let's do it!" Aziz continued. "I want to see what they're saying about us."

"Don't forget, Aziz, he doesn't have the app now. It's probably at least five megs, which would take half an hour on the connection we've got. Then, if you're going to stream video, he'll be out of battery in no time."

"I was just wondering."

* * *

I woke up restless; it was quiet except that two people were snoring. Turn on your phone, Kareem. I sat up, pressed the button and waited. The white apple appeared. Two-forty-seven am. 21% power remaining. A red number one on the email icon. I pressed it. A single message in my inbox – from a.qureshi@175brigade.iq:

In the name of Husayn, the 175 Brigade has been assigned to your service. Please can you advise more precisely your location, and the number and armaments of Daesh.

Colonel A Qureshi

175 Brigade

I read it again. It must be somebody trying to rescue us. What to do?

Gently, I woke Akram. He sat up immediately. "What is it?"

I pressed a finger to my lips. "There's a message." I pressed the phone into his hands. He looked at the screen, took a deep breath and gave a long sigh. "We have to answer his questions."

"But who is he?" I whispered.

"I assume he's the commanding officer of the 175 Brigade."

"And who are they?"

"One of the best Shia militia units – trained by the Quds Force in Iran. Not quite up to your US Navy Seals, but under the circumstances, I think they'll do."

Together, we composed the following response:

Number of Daesh approximately 8. Pistols and AK's; nothing heavier seen. Eleven of us in back room, ground floor. Some Daesh in front room ground floor. Others may be upstairs. Brought here by truck; there is also a jeep. Recent grave mound behind the house. Can't be more precise about location. Phone is low on power.

I sent the message. 18% power remaining. I switched off and lay awake trying to estimate the odds of a successful rescue. 40%.

Akram nudged me. "Check!"

Another message from Colonel Qureshi: "In the name of Husayn, thank you. Can you send me a Google Earth fix? Don't waste phone battery!"

I told Akram, "We've got to ask Hajji about Google Earth."

Awakened and briefed in whispers, Hajji stared at the phone screen. "Our only chance is to hack that Wi-Fi. Let's try no more than ten passwords."

We took turns suggesting passwords. After seven failures, Hajji reminded us, "Let's not forget: this used to be a Sunni area."

"OK," I said, "in that case I suggest 'Bukhari'."

"Why?"

"Because that's the name your late colleague didn't know."

"Oh, my God, it worked. . . Have we got bandwidth! . . . Google Earth . . . Here's the app – eight megs. It'll take less than a minute. OK, here we are. . . Need the latitude-longitude grid. . .. Got it. . . Screen shot. . . Close the app. . . Send the picture. Done!"

He handed the phone back to me. 13% power remaining.

I tried to estimate the chances of getting out alive: 60%

There was another message from the colonel at four-forty-seven am:

In the name of Husayn, Google Earth no help. Will attack Daesh at 4:30 tomorrow am. When you hear an owl call, lie flat on the ground. Does rear door open into your room?

Shit! That means they don't know exactly which house we're in. If they attack the wrong house, we're dead! Odds are dropping: down to 25%. Five percent power remaining.

Akram, Hajji and I had a brief conference. Hajji said, "I guess the colonel was hoping the Americans let Google have their accurate GPS data on this area." He shrugged. "They'll just have to look for the grave."

"We have to answer his question."

The following reply was composed: "Look for the grave. The rear door by the grave opens into our space. If the outside bolts on the shutters of the rear window are opened, we can escape via the window. We wish you success in the name of Husayn!"

The phone went dead.

The three of us decided not to tell the others of the impending rescue attempt. Akram's comment was, "The mood will change completely, the Daesh will notice and they'll suspect that something's afoot. We can't afford for them to be dreaming up counter-measures!"

The day was interminable: every minute took an hour to pass and every hour a day. I could think of nothing but what was going to happen that night – in what way could I better prepare myself – where in our somewhat cramped space it was best to lie – face down? on my side? in which direction? When I tried to share a tactical concern with Akram or Hajji, they shrugged and turned away.

Maybe I have only hours to live.

By late afternoon, I decided to pray in earnest. Not just the scripted routine prayers, but serious attempts to communicate. I don't remember what I said, but it was about my family, including Elizabeth, hoping that they would know His grace. And I recounted my life, the points of pride as well as regrets, hoping for forgiveness on the latter.

I do recall that, repeatedly, I asked Allah to speak to me: Let me hear your voice, great Allah. I didn't ask Him to spare me, or for the success of our rescuers. I just wanted to know that He was there.

At about midnight, a sense of peacefulness came over me. I don't know why. I don't know what brought it on, but I was grateful, and I fell asleep.

* * *

"What's that?" An urgent whisper. "There's somebody outside!"

"Ssshhh! Quiet!" Akram hissed.

There was a squeak of rusty metal at the window. A louder, longer squeak. A rectangle of moonlight appeared among us.

A hoarse whisper: "Somebody's opened the shutters!"

"Ssshhh! Quiet!"

An owl hooted. "Everybody down!"

Boom! A tremendous explosion in the front room! Whoever had stood up to go to the window was down again. Screams from the front room. Shouts from upstairs and outside.

"Stay down!" A burst of automatic weapons fire shattered the window. More firing from another direction. Plaster and glass raining down on us. Another explosion – this one upstairs. A chunk of ceiling fell on us. Deafening chatter of firing. Screams – shouts – unintelligible commands. I lay face down, protecting my head with my hands. The air was filled with dust and cordite.

Quiet.

There was a groan nearby. I reached out. My hand felt warm wetness. A light blazed through the window. The door swung open. "Come out! No weapons! Hands up!"

No one moved.

"Come out! We are the 175 Brigade!"

I got to my feet. Others did the same. Outside, there were three militia men dressed in camouflage fatigues and wearing baklavas. "Where are the others?" one demanded. "I thought there were eleven."

"They need help; they're inside."

"Let's see."

Four of my Iraqi colleagues were still inside. Aziz and another professor named Saleh had been killed – most likely by shots fired by the Daesh through the floor above. Methuselah, though still alive, had been shot in the abdomen, and Hajji had wounds in both his legs.

The Shia militia led us out through the front of the house. The darkened front room was blackened, the furniture and walls shattered by at least one grenade. Two bloody Daesh corpses lay on the floor, two more on the couches.

Out in the street were eight or ten more militia. They were surrounding two Daesh who were kneeling, frightened and demoralized, on the ground. A deeply-tanned, older soldier was questioning the two. "What was your leader's name, scum?"

"Kadri Al Zahabi."

The man who answered received a stout kick in the ribs from one of the militia men. "When the colonel speaks to you, you say 'Sir!'"

The man clutched his side. "Kadri Al Zahabi, sir."

"Who sent you in this mission?" the colonel demanded.

"Don't know, sir. Someone high up in Raqqa (the ISIL HQ in Syria), sir."

The colonel turned away. "Continue with the questions, Kaddori. Who is Kareem?"

"I am, Colonel."

"Are you the leader of this group?"

"No, sir. That would be Akram," I said.

The colonel eyed the group of ex-hostages.

"I am Akram. We want to thank you and your men very much, Colonel."

There was an almost undetectable nod from the colonel. "I'm sorry about your losses. How many are they?"

"There are two dead, one has leg wounds and a distinguished professor has a serious abdominal wound. Did you have losses, Colonel?"

"No, thanks be to Husayn." He raised his voice. "All right, let's get a move on before they stage a counter-attack. Kaddori, you and Jebali find the keys to the jeep, and take it and the prisoners to brigade HQ. Mahmoudi, you find the keys to the truck; take the wounded, the deceased and two carers from the hostages to Al-Bitar Hospital. Call and tell them that you're coming. The rest of you, come with me in one of the two Humvees; we're going to brigade HQ, Bagdad."

There was a chorus of 'Yes, sir's' and people began hurrying about.

Akram approached the colonel. "Excuse me, sir, but what should be done with the other deceased?"

"Absolutely nothing, Professor! Let the scum rot where they are! It leaves a useful message for any of their asshole buddies who show up: Don't fuck with the Shia!"

* * *

I've seen a few of them around Cairo, and I know they're considered very trendy, but based on my 'test ride' in an armored Humvee from Ramadi to Bagdad, I definitely prefer my little Honda. The Humvee was dusty and drafty inside. Of course, much of this was due to the opening in the roof where an alert gunner swung the heavy machine gun back and forth. Much of the hundred kilometer trip passed through territory where ISIL had a presence, and we had to bypass Falluja entirely. The vehicle jolted rather heavily over the potholed roads. This, I suppose was the result of its additional armor. It was noisy. An oversized engine to push all that armor? And with seven of us, including the gunner, inside, it was uncomfortable. But at the time, my concern wasn't comfort, it was roadside bombs. I held my breath every time the driver swerved around a dubious spot on the road.

* * *

At about seven in the morning, we arrived at 175 Brigade HQ, consisting of several two-story brick barracks and a warehouse in what must have been one of Saddam's military bases along the Army Canal, near the Al-Rasheed Airport. Contradicting the derelict, bullet-scarred appearance of the buildings, there were soldiers in military fatigues everywhere.

Colonel Qureshi showed us to a room, where two young soldiers with laptops were waiting. For the next two hours, every detail of our ordeal was recorded. We were then given a very welcome breakfast of eggs, beans and bread.

"Akram," I said, "I would like to invite you and any of your colleagues who are able to come to my hotel for a farewell dinner this evening. I want to express my thanks to all of you . . . in the name of Husayn."

He smiled. "It is not necessary, Kareem."

"For me, it is essential."

He gave a nod of concession. "I will call you at the hotel to let you know who can come."

* * *

"May I see Colonel Qureshi, please?" I asked the white-helmeted soldier with the carbine beside him. He turned and knocked on the door. Another soldier appeared in the doorway. "Yes?"

"I'd like to see Colonel Qureshi for a moment. I'm Professor Kareem al-Busiri from Ramadi."

"From Ramadi?"

"Yes, he'll know who I am."

The colonel was sitting at a battered steel desk on one side of which was an Iraqi flag stand and on the other side a yellow banner with an Arabic coat of arms. "Yes, Professor."

"Colonel, I'd like your permission to interview the prisoner you spoke with in Ramadi."

He frowned. "Why do you want to speak to that scum, Professor?"

I had decided to deviate somewhat from the truth. "I am working on a project at my university which concerns the motivations of terrorists, and this is a chance to question an actual Daesh. Besides, if I learn anything of interest to you, I will come back to you."

He shrugged, picked up his telephone, issued an order and hung up. "Hamawi will take you, Professor."

* * *

Before going into the bare and rather dirty interrogation room, I asked the guard if he could get me a cup of coffee.

The prisoner's name was Amir Islambouli. He was twenty years old and came from Haditha in northern Iraq. I was unexpected; he was very nervous. I pushed the mug of coffee across table to him. He looked at it longingly and sat back against his chair.

"It's only coffee, Amir. Just coffee." I reached for the mug, took a sip and set it back down. "I got it for you, Amir."

He took a careful sip, evaluated his condition and then another sip.

"Amir, tell me why you joined the Daesh."

"Why do you want to know? Aren't you the American?"

"I am Egyptian. I have an American passport, but the only connection I have to America is my late wife's family. I am a professor at a university in Cairo. I am studying terrorism."

"I am not a terrorist."

"What are you, Amir?"

"I am a soldier."

"As a soldier, have you ever killed a woman or a child?"

He shrugged. "They get in the way."

"Get in the way of what?"

"Killing our enemies."

"Who are your enemies?"

"Those who oppose us."

"That's pretty much everybody, isn't it, Amir? Iraq, Iran, Syria, Turkey, Jordan, Saudi Arabia, Russia, America, all of Europe . . . shall I go on?" He shrugged. "Why did you join the Daesh, Amir?"

"Because I believe in the new Islamic state – the caliphate – for Muslims only, with sharia justice, cleansed of devil worship, and corrupt Western influence."

"Like it used to be a thousand years ago?"

"Exactly."

I thought for a moment. "Have you been to Raqqa, Amir?"

"Yes."

"It's the capital of Islamic State?"

"Yes."

"And as the capital, it must be beautiful, with grand marble buildings, quiet parks with palm trees and sweeping lawns. There must be lots of well-dressed men and women strolling about. Is it like that, Amir?"

"No."

"How is it then, Amir?"

He seemed to withdraw. "I don't know."

"Of course you do, and so do I. It's not beautiful – more like a military prison where residents are thrown out of their homes, beaten or even killed by Daesh foreign fighters. There is no sharia justice. The gun rules. There is hunger, not enough electricity or water. Local girls are forced to marry foreign fighters from Chechnya, Libya, Sudan and Tunisia. And beheadings are the standard form of punishment, with the heads put on public display. There is no music, no smoking and no fun. Is this what you were looking for when you joined Daesh?"

He inclined his head slightly but didn't answer.

I paused for a moment to relieve some of the pressure on Amir. "You remember a few days ago when you took us prisoner back in the mawkeb?" He nodded. "Why did Kadri kill that boy?"

There was a sour expression on Amir's face. "I don't know."

"Kadri is dead now. What you say can't be used against him – or against you."

"I guess he was angry."

"He probably was angry. Don't you think that giving the kid a good slap and shouting, 'Shut your mouth, you little cockroach!' would have expressed the anger and have been more in line with sharia justice?"

"But the kid was an impudent devil-worshipper."

"You mean he was a Shi'ite and he loved Husayn."

"Exactly."

"Why do you think that Husayn is the devil?"

He shrugged. "He just is."

"Do you know who Husayn's grandfather was?"

"No."

"His grandfather was the Prophet – the Messenger of God. Do you really think that God would actually let the grandchild of his Messenger become the devil?"

Amir gave me his sour face and said nothing.

"Amir, how well did you know Abdul?"

"He wasn't my friend."

"Why not?"

"He wasn't very friendly."

"You mean he was kind of a loner?"

"He was like two different people. Sometimes he was OK, but then he would be really hostile."

"How many people did he behead?"

"I don't know. Six or eight."

"Do you think he enjoyed it?"

"Yeah, I think he did. When he did it, it was like he was on a mission."

"A mission from Kadri?"

"No. Kadri and the other officers knew that Abdul was on a mission to behead people. They just had to tell him, 'Do that one!' and he would do it."

"Do you think that Abdul heard voices?"

"Yeah, I do."

"Amir, just one more question, and I promise I will not pass your answer on to anyone who could harm you." I paused for a moment to give him time to react; he gave an acknowledging nod. "Why haven't you left the Daesh and gone home to your family?"

"My family is quite poor."

"OK, but money isn't what's keeping you in the Daesh."

"I still believe in the New Islamic Caliphate."

"Yes. Except the one you believe in isn't the one with its headquarters in Raqqa."

He looked around the room as if searching for answers.

"We're all in this together."

"So there's a lot of peer pressure to carry on: once you've made a commitment, you can't back out." He nodded. "What happens to deserters?"

"When they're caught they're beheaded as apostates."

"If they're not caught?"

"Their family pays the price."

Later, I realized that I had insisted on this opportunity to interview a bottom-of-the-pile terrorist for personal reasons. If Naqib was becoming a terrorist, I had to know what went on a terrorist's head.

* * *

The dinner that evening was somber, but well-attended. All of the remaining pilgrims, including Hajji in a wheelchair, were there. There was a deep sense of loss: Methuselah had died en route to the hospital. I was probably the only one who questioned – in my own mind - value of this Arba'een: we had lost four devout pilgrims who were also very valuable teachers. It was one third of our group. To what end? But this was not the sense of my Shia colleagues: they chose to remember the fulfillment of a much-sought religious experience. They had succeeded in connecting with Husayn, a connection which had profound powers of rejuvenation, and against which they did not weigh the costs. While I fell short of making the connection my colleagues made, I came to understand and value the connection. Perhaps I was like a lonely man who has never fallen in love.

At the end of the evening Akram led us in a prayer of thanksgiving for Arba'een, followed by a prayer that our four colleagues are with Allah, in the name of Husayn.

Chapter 8

Adeeba's Garden

The beach seemed lost and wild. White foam from the surf piled up at the high water mark and trembled in the gusts of wind. Gulls flew low over the breakers, wings tipping precariously, until they turned to the land and settled with satisfaction on the wet sand. The wind had a penetrating chill when the sun was obscured: the mood was pessimistic. But when the sun suddenly lit the sea, the air was light and welcome, smelling of salt and seaweed. There was no sound but the gentle boom and hiss of the surf; sea birds were mute and watchful.

Early Friday morning in December, eight degrees Centigrade, wind northwest at fifteen knots, gusting to thirty, waves two meters, fifty percent cloud cover, not a soul in sight to the east or the west.

I had carried a folding lounge chair down to the dappled edge of dry sand: it had rained Thursday night. My black windproof jacket encased the heavy wool sweater, and the hood was drawn tight around my face. I had carefully wrapped my desert boots and legs, to my waist, in a warm blanket. So, comfortable and cocooned against wind and chill, I could reflect on the wild sea, and the world as I knew it.

That university term, I had no morning class on Friday, and Al Jamiah was, for me, the perfect environment to consider the incongruities of Arba'een. Why was I among our group of twelve pilgrims the only one who was learning what faith is? Not that I object to being a learner, but the others were all teachers. Why did a harmless pilgrimage bring death to four pilgrims? Why did eight Daesh give up their lives in a failed attempt to extort money that would have been of no benefit to them? Why is there so little understanding, or tolerance, on the part of adherents of slightly different strands of the same religion? Arba'een is both an individual experience of faith and a shared demonstration of faith. At how many million people does the shared experience overpower the individual experience? Is it fair that huge numbers of subsistence farmers subsidize the room and board of millions of pilgrims, many of whom would willingly pay? Why did Princess Basheera suggest that I go on Arba'een to seek Father Khaliq? Did she know my life might be threatened? Was it worth it?

The last question was most easily answered: yes, it was worth it. I have lived a quiet, rather drab life: like a painter whose palette has mostly black and white, with traces of light blue and pink. Suddenly, I have blood red, emerald green, gold and sapphire blue! What to make of them? It doesn't matter: I have them!

* * *

When I told Hafez about my Arba'een, he was horrified. "I told you not to go!" (He didn't, actually; he said that he didn't like the idea and that he wasn't going.) "But you went anyway! And you damn near got killed! Not to mention rubbing up against thousands of unwashed Iranian peasants. I can't imagine anything worse!"

"One has to focus on the purpose of it all," I said.

"What purpose?" he demanded, "to mourn an imam who happened to be the Prophet's grandson and who walked into an obvious trap, getting himself and most of his family killed?"

He shook his head. "I've got better things to mourn. Have you heard that class sizes are going up ten percent next year, while our take-home pay is actually going down?"

"Hafez," I asked him patiently, "do you ever think long-term, existentially?"

"Yes! With all due respect, Kareem, I think that, existentially, it is unwise to go into a war zone unless you're well to the rear of the winning army."

"I meant existentially in a religious sense."

He shrugged. "Of course, religion is very important. I went on the Hajj with you, didn't I? As good Muslims we have to do our religious duty. But I never heard that Arba'een was on our list."

"Does an experience have to be on a list to make it worth doing?"

"I suppose not, but then it becomes a matter of personal preference."

"Exactly."

He looked into the distance, thoughtfully. "Perhaps I should propose an experience that I think would be appropriate for the two of us."

"An existential or religious experience?"

"Possibly."

"As long as it's legal and not too expensive, I would consider it."

* * *

I returned to the beach and the incongruities of Arba'een.

As well as painting with an incomplete palette, I probably am naïve! Is that so bad? Well, it may seem charming to some women, but you have to admit, Kareem, that it makes it more difficult to paint the scenes you see, since the scenes are also lacking color! Do I want to give up my naiveté? Even if I wanted to, it is doubtful that I could succeed at my age. What to do? One possibility is to be a better student: to study my acts of naiveté and to learn from them. I have been in teaching mode for over thirty years – not that I didn't learn during that time: of course, to be a good teacher, one has to broaden one's knowledge. But my weakness, my naiveté, results from my identity as a teacher. If I can examine instances when I underestimated the situation, I may be able to build up new neuron paths in my brain, so that in the future I will be more likely to see things as they really are.

A gull landed on the sand three meters away, took a step or two in my direction, and cocked its head to better appraise me. Clearly, it was looking for a handout, but as I had left even my coffee mug back at the house, there was nothing to suggest that I had food to offer. Nonetheless, the gull continued its patient appraisal. I held out a hand, seeming to offer something to the bird. It took a step or two toward my hand, stretching out its neck for a more accurate evaluation. It stepped back, refolded its wings, and scratched its beak with one foot. It seemed to be saying: "You'll have to show me some real food, if you want me to come closer!" That gull is not gullible!

One aspect of my Arba'een experience where I had clearly foundered was in my failure to understand and anticipate what I regarded as the irrational fervor of pilgrims and Daesh, alike. How could they be so determined to behave as they did when a systematic harvesting and threshing of the facts would have persuaded them to pursue a different course? It was obvious in retrospect that the facts to the irrational were unimportant. What could be more important than the facts? There has to be something which is more important than the facts when someone is apparently willing to throw his life away! For a time, no useful insight came to mind. Then: Belief! But it was not any belief that trumped the Facts, it was Belief in an action which reinforced one's most cherished Identity. The pilgrims identified themselves as Shia – not ordinary Shia, but proud, devout Shia.

This Identity made them different and gave real meaning to their lives. Going on Arba'een was an essential part of who they were, and, that being the case, why even consider the dangers of the pilgrimage? For the mawkeb proprietors, the subsistence farmers, their Identity was their annual charity, feeding and housing hundreds of devout pilgrims. What did it matter that they could not afford to buy new shoes; they were who they wanted to be! For the Daesh, their Identity was wrapped up in a vision of medieval, unforgiving, and pinched interpretation of Islam; they saw themselves as Allah's chosen soldiers, ready for martyrdom. Nothing else mattered. If there were voices urging them on, it must be the voice of God or His angel. Since they were on God's side, the voice could not be the devil's!

* * *

I decided to tell Naqib about Arba'een – not so much to inform him of what his father had been doing as to elicit a reaction from him on the Daesh and their terrorist mindset. I could not let him be seduced into that diabolical cult! Why was I worried? I thought, There was nothing in Naqib's upbringing which could lead to that seduction: he was privately educated in secular schools; his mother set an example of concern for others in her work and at her church; I am hardly a radical professor. Perhaps at university . . . but he studied humanities and the law – hardly a radical education. His wife aspires to the middle class good life –nothing there. I had to admit that I didn't know his university-era male friends. When he started at university, he began an independent life, seldom visiting home, much less bringing with him friends of either gender. But then I thought, There is one thing that always distinguished Naqib from his brother and sister: he has always wanted to be different. It was not football for him: it was basketball. Comic books didn't interest him; he liked mechanical puzzles. He liked to argue against what ordinary people tended to take for granted. For example: people should pay their taxes. No!! Taxes just find their way into the pockets of the corrupt politicians! Sometimes, he came across as an argumentative Marxist. Elizabeth once said: "Naqib is very special, and he knows it." At the time, I thought: that's a mother expressing her love for her first born! Now, I began to wonder whether Elizabeth's insight might have meaning beyond her intention.

* * *

Naqib returned my call the following morning at 7:20. Before his workday begins.

"Naqib, I'd like to have lunch with you – sometime in the next week or two."

"I'm very busy, Papa."

"I'm sure you are. We can have a quick lunch. I'd like to fill you in on my trip to Iraq."

"You went to Iraq?"

"Yes."

"And what did you do in Iraq, Papa?"

"Oh, I met with some of the faculty at Bagdad University." That should pique his curiosity. He'll wonder if I have an offer to move to Bagdad.

"Tell me more, Papa."

"I will." Pause. "Over lunch."

I could hear him shuffling some papers on his desk. "I could do Thursday at 1:30. There's a shawarma (sandwich) shop on Mohammad Mahmoud across from the university."

* * *

There were two cooks in the shawarma shop when I arrived at 1:20 on Thursday. Both were overweight, dressed in stained T-shirts, unwashed aprons and sweaty white bandanas. They must be father and son. The older, leathery-faced man let his white hair fall in disorder on his shoulders, while the younger one, muscles bulging through his T-shirt, had half a centimeter of black stubble on his jaw. They were busily filling long, crusty rolls with chicken, turkey or lamb, sesame paste and whatever the customer selected from the array of cooked and fresh vegetables. It actually looked rather good, and the smell was tempting. The only problem was: nowhere to sit; most customers strode off immediately with their shawarma enclosed in newspaper. I looked over toward my old campus, and I recalled that through the archway to the left there was an open courtyard with benches.

Naqib arrived at ten minutes before two, immediately ordered a lamb – really mutton – shawarma with red peppers, cucumbers and diced black olives. I opted for chicken with basil, green peppers and cucumbers. Naqib took a bite and for a moment, we stood on the sidewalk. I turned and walked toward the university archway.

"Where are you going, Papa?"

"Place to sit down."

He followed me to a bench in the courtyard, where we sat in the weak December sunlight.

"So, tell me about Iraq and Bagdad University." There was a hiss as he opened his can of orange soda.

I took a sip from my tea. "I went on Arba'een, Naqib."

He put the can down, held the shawarma with both hands and looked at me. "Did you say you went on Arba'een?"

"Yes. Yes, I did."

"Why did you do that?"

"I've been on the Hajj; I've been to the Prophet's Tomb. I thought I would go on Arba'een – just to see what it's like."

"But . . . ." he gestured hopelessly with one hand. "But it's a Shia thing."

"Not entirely, there were Sunnis and Christians, some Hindus and Buddhists, and probably a few atheists."

"But how many Sunni Egyptian professors were there – apart from you, I mean?"

"Well, Hafez didn't go, but out of thirty million, there were probably at least a couple of thousand Sunni Egyptians who are university graduates."

For some moments, Naqib stared across the courtyard. "Are you thinking of converting?" he asked almost under his breath.

I shook my head. "No."

"What about the University of Bagdad?"

"Oh, I went with eight professors and three instructors from the College of Islamic Sciences. Four of them were killed."

Naqib stared at me. "Four of them were killed? How?"

I made eye contact as I responded. "They were killed by Daesh."

"You mean they were killed by ISIL?"

"No. There was nothing Islamic about the killers, and one of them admitted that the state is a fabrication. No, they were just Daesh: sowers of discord."

Naqib looked away again. "What happened, Papa?"

"As we were on the way back to Bagdad, in the middle of the night they took the twelve of us away at gunpoint to Ramadi. They wanted ransom."

"How much?"

"I have no idea, and whatever it was, they would never have gotten it."

"How did you get away?"

"We were rescued by a Shia militia."

Naqib sipped his soda in silence. "Papa, what I don't understand is why you would risk your life to go on a pilgrimage that has nothing to do with your heritage."

I shrugged. "There is nothing sacred about my heritage, and I thought the probability of me being killed was about the same as my having a heart attack on the beach at Al Jamiah." He continued to look at me blankly, but said nothing. "Let me put it this way, Naqib: what I learned on Arba'een was that a pilgrimage can be an almost overwhelming experience which purifies the heart and mind."

"And how does it do that?" His tone was barely polite.

"One's emotions almost reach the limits of love and sorrow."

He made a hopeless gesture. "For what?"

I knew that he wanted me to say 'for Husayn'. But I said, "The object doesn't matter – in my experience. What matters is being with others whose love and sorrow is epidemic."

He shook his head dismissively. "I prefer the solitary devotion of daily prayers."

It was my turn to pause and consider. "I think . . . I think that daily prayers are one of the reasons for my lack of commitment to the Muslim faith. For me, they are repetitious and without personal substance."

"It doesn't have to be that way," he said. "I find that one can pray for positive change in the world, and that this is uplifting."

"May I ask what sort of positive change you have in mind?"

"Of course. I pray for a world where Islam reigns supreme and where Allah commands."

"How does Allah issue his commands?"

"Through the leaders of his caliphate on earth."

I was going to ask how the leaders of the caliphate were chosen, but I realized that this was a dead end. His response would be 'by Allah', and if I pointed out that the current 'caliph' was self-appointed, his response would be that the caliph was only responding to the appointment of Allah. Instead, I asked, "How is your work going?"

"Very well, thank you."

I frowned. "Naqib, you remember we talked about the need for candor about your work when talking with family members. What I really want to know is: are you working for the rebels in Sinai?" (I chose the word 'rebels' rather than the word 'terrorists' to make the question a little more palatable.)

"I am not working for anyone in Sinai. Most of our funding – as I've told you – comes from the Brotherhood and other sources in the Gulf. But it is fair to say that the Brotherhood has contacts in Sinai."

(He hadn't told me about the 'other sources in the Gulf' but it was common knowledge that funding for radical Islamists was available from rich men with similar theo-political views.) I had to ask the next question, but it took me some moments to phrase it in seemingly innocuous terms. "Naqib, if I were a rebel leader in the Sinai, and I was thinking about the indirect efforts which Kamal Saleh and Partners makes on behalf of my cause, how would I characterize it?"

"Probably as communications and logistics."

"And by logistics, do you mean . . .?"

He interrupted, "That's all I can tell you, Papa!"

"Can I assume, Naqib, that your work is satisfying?"

"Yes, Papa."

"Ideologically, personally and financially satisfying?"

"Yes, Papa." He rose to go. For a moment, we stood facing each other; he took my shoulders and kissed me on either cheek.

"Naqib, do you travel to Sinai?"

"No, Papa."

* * *

As I drove back to the New Cairo campus, my feelings were at war. I was profoundly shocked by his admission of support for the Sinai terrorists – however remote that support may have been. But there were genuine stirrings of pride in a son who, on his own, had carved out an important niche for himself. I never would have visualized this. I would have guessed a political career beginning with a low-level, local appointment, progressing to an elected town council, and perhaps continuing to a district council. But I could sense both his powerful ambition and his successful advancement into authority.

* * *

Wahida was at home when I got there. "How did it go?" she asked.

"Just a normal day. Two classes this morning and a couple of conferences this afternoon."

"No, Papa, I'm asking about your lunch with Naqib."

"Oh, I forgot I told you about that."

"Papa, I was the one who suggested it; don't you remember?"

"Oh, yes. Well, it turns out he's doing something for Wilayat Sinai (the ISIL affiliate in Sinai) but apparently it's being done through the Brotherhood."

"What's being done through the Brotherhood?"

"He was vague. Something about communications and logistics."

"Anisa believes it's a lot more than that."

"How do you know what Anisa thinks, Wahida?"

"Well, we have sort of evolved a first-Tuesday monthly lunch." I nodded. "She's worried about Naqib."

I shrugged. "As any intelligent wife would be."

"Papa, I got the impression – she didn't say this, but she hinted at it – that communications may include intelligence, and logistics may include money and weapons."

Money and weapons! Great Allah!

I had to sit down: there was physical and mental dizziness. "Are you all right, Papa?" I just looked at my daughter. "Shall I get you a glass of water?"

I shook my head. "How did you get the idea, Wahida, that your brother is dealing in money and weapons for the Daesh?"

"What Anisa said was that the law firm had taken on new responsibilities for certain clients. When I asked her about the new responsibilities, she said something about 'funds' and 'supplies', but then she got nervous and changed the subject."

"So you think that the law firm is a conduit for Saudi or Gulf funding to Wilayat Sinai?" I asked. She nodded. "But Wahida," I protested, "there could be a lot of other benign explanations."

"Yes, I know, but why would she get so nervous about benign reasons?"

I was feeling quite unwell, but I had to persevere. "How do you get from 'supplies' to 'weapons'?"

"Well, what kind of 'supplies to a client' would make a normal Egyptian clam up? Certainly not food, clothing or fuel to a bakery in Aswan!"

"But how could a law firm in Cairo arrange for the supply of arms to jihadis in Sinai?"

"I don't know, Papa! But I think there are arms dealers out there somewhere who will deliver whatever you want, wherever you want, if you pay for it. . . Well, maybe not anything you want. . . Let me get you a glass of water, Papa."

This glass of water is clear. My older son is opaque.

"What else did she say, Wahida?"

"She said they've moved to a new apartment with four bedrooms and a view of the Nile. She has a professional mother's helper – full time – and the baby is doing well."

"I wonder why Naqib didn't mention the new apartment to me."

"Because you would have asked him how an up-and-coming lawyer could afford an apartment like that."

Exactly what I would have done. "So, you think he's doing it for the money, Wahida?"

"I think the money is a very convenient way to keep Anisa at his side."

"So it's not the money, then," I mused.

"No."

"What then?"

"Naqib has always wanted to be someone really important."

"And the money can be a measure of importance," I suggested.

"He knows it's important to most people, but not to him."

"The ideology: that could be important," I offered.

"I don't believe that Naqib wants to make the world a better place by ushering in a universal, ancient Muslim culture." She paused to think. "I mean: yes, he probably thinks that would be good idea, but Naqib always wanted to be ahead of the game. He can see that radical Islam is gaining ground, and he thinks: Yes! There is my ticket to greatness!"

"I very much hope that you are wrong, Wahida."

"I hope I am wrong, too, Papa, but it is also essential to understand what may be happening."

"Without making pejorative judgments."

She shrugged. "I agree."

"Sit with me, Wahida."

She sat next to me on the couch.

"There's one other thing, Papa." I looked over at her. "Anisa told me that Naqib is in touch with Kalifa."

"That's good."

"Is it, Papa? Those two didn't get along. Why now?"

"Well, they've both grown up, and they'd probably like to have a mature relationship."

"Papa, Kalifa is an Army officer in a war zone. His enemy is a client of Naqib's. Does it really make sense that they should be having regular friendly chats?" I gave her a puzzled frown. "Papa, Kalifa does not know what you and I know – or suspect – about Naqib."

"OK, I'll talk to Kalifa."

* * *

The meeting at the Tahrir Square campus had finished mercifully early; it was cool and sunny: a day to be savored. I walked the three blocks to the Qasr Al-Nil Bridge, and was leaning against the south-side railing watching the water traffic. Passengers on a large Nile cruiser bound – probably – for Alexandria were waving up at us. I waved back.

"Professor?" A familiar female voice. I turned. A woman in a quilted blue jacket, dark trousers and a black niqab was standing behind me.

"Oh, good afternoon, Princess. I . . . I didn't expect to see you here."

There was a slight nod. "Shall we have a cup of coffee, Professor?"

"Yes, by all means." I looked around. "If we go to the Semiramis Hotel over there, perhaps we can sit on the terrace and enjoy the sunshine."

A waiter escorted us to a table which had an excellent view to the west over the Nile.

"So you had a meeting on the old campus, Professor?"

"Yes, it was an inter-disciplinary meeting – one where I have to represent the philosophy department – a complete waste of time."

"But can I assume that not every attendee considers the meeting a waste of time?"

I considered. "I suppose you're right, Princess. Some people participate with great enthusiasm. But for me . . . well, I have better things to do."

Her voice had a lilting tone. "Such as drinking coffee with a bothersome woman?"

I had to laugh. In a way, she was a bit – I would say 'persistent', but, "Bothersome is entirely the wrong word, Princess. Would we ever say that our conscience is 'bothersome'? Besides, you are always very kind, and I imagine that you are lovely."

"So, you've come to think of me as your conscience, Professor?"

"Not exactly. I mean, you have been forthright and constructive in your suggestions, which have – by and large – been quite beneficial."

"Beneficial?"

"Yes. I have discovered that my life – which I always felt was quite satisfactory, apart from the loss of Elizabeth – was rather two-dimensional and lacking in color."

"Can you tell me something about the third dimension?"

"It is still rather hazy, but it has something to do with faith and spirituality and commitment to something more than life itself."

"So, you see this third dimension as beneficial?"

"Potentially, yes. But as I have not actually experienced it for myself, I tend to rely on the experiences of others. What I observe is a kind of paradox: in the third dimension, the individual seems to become both larger and smaller at the same time. He becomes smaller as he surrenders himself to a larger concept – call it Allah or Islam, or something similar. He becomes larger in identifying himself with that concept, because it gives his life new significance and meaning."

She nodded. "You suggested earlier that my suggestions were not always beneficial. Can you be more specific?"

"Well, when we were returning to Bagdad from Karbala during Arba'een, we were held hostage by the Daesh – or perhaps I should call them ISIL."

"I am perfectly comfortable with Daesh, since that is what they are."

"Four esteemed teachers in our party were murdered by the Daesh."

She nodded.

"Princess, when you suggested that I go on Arba'een, were you aware of the danger that I would be in?"

"Professor, you yourself are aware that while one is alive, one risks ceasing to be alive. It is a certainty that accompanies one's mortality. Perhaps the more essential question is whether there is a positive dimension to the outcome of survival."

"Yes, yes, of course there was! For the first time in my life, I saw evil incarnate. For me, evil has been a kind of abstraction: something you hear about on the news or see in the newspapers, or perhaps you are aware that you, or someone you know, has been touched by it. But in Iraq, I looked into the eyes and faces of men who were pledged to do evil, who would kill a kind and innocent person on a whim, in an instant. There is, I conclude, a living and powerful force for evil in the world. Whether it is embodied in an entity called the devil, I don't know."

"That doesn't sound very positive."

"Actually, it is, Princess. It has stripped me of my naiveté, and I no longer feel blind. I feel that I am able to see the world for what it is – without what the advertising people call 'smoke and mirrors'."

She chuckled. "Any other positives?"

"Yes, I feel a strong sense of connection with the people who have been affected by the evil. It isn't just sympathy. I have a bond with the seven survivors that will last for the rest of my life: I know them and I treasure them."

She looked out across the Nile to the sinking sun. "Professor, you mentioned finding a genuine force for evil. Have you discovered a similar force for good?"

"You mean: do I believe in Allah?"

"Call him what you will."

"In principle, yes, but I fall far short of the understanding and commitment that I have observed from many pilgrims."

"Do you aspire to achieve that higher level of understanding and commitment?"

"Well, I've come to admire the people who have it, so yes, I think so, but I am uncertain how to proceed."

"Is it not the case that your colleague, Hafez, is planning a trip with you?"

"Yes, but how did you know that?"

"Oh, I hear about a lot of things. . . It may be a good occasion to resume your search for Father Khaliq."

* * *

I looked up. The sun was setting behind the jagged cityscape to the west, but it left a fiery red sheen on the river in the near ground. In front of me was a white coffee cup in the bottom of which there was dark brown sandy sediment. To my right there was an identical cup, but the chair beside me was vacant. Where has she gone? I looked back toward the entrance to the terrace. There were three well-dressed women at one table and two businessmen deep in conversation at another. There was no Princess Basheera. Beside my coffee cup, there was a small brown folio. Inside was a bill; it had been paid. I beckoned to the waiter. "Has the lady paid this bill?"

"Sorry, sir, I just came on duty." He picked up the folio. "Yes, sir, the bill has been paid."

"But did you happen to see the lady who paid it?"

"No, sir. As I say, I just came on duty."

She appears and disappears like a morning mist. Is she real? Yes, of course she's real! I remember exactly what we talked about! But how does she know what Hafez is planning, and how does she know to find me on the Qasr Al-Nil Bridge? For that matter, she seemed a little defensive when I accused her of knowing I would be in danger on Arba'een, as if she knew about the danger all along! And why is she always hidden behind that niqab?

* * *

217

"And when you touch this logo next to his mobile number, you'll be making a Facetime call," Wahida explained. The screen was suddenly a reflection of me and there was a large red button at the bottom. "It's trying to connect," she added. The screen changed again: there was Kalifa, head and shoulders in an olive drab tunic, and I was reduced to a small replica.

"Hello, Papa!"

"Hello, Kalifa. Wahida is here with me."

"I could have guessed you might have a technical adviser. Besides, I can make out her shoulder and right ear."

"Turn it this way, Papa, and then he can see both of us."

It worked; the replica was a landscape view of the two of us.

I asked: "Where are you, Kalifa?"

"On the base – in the officer's quarters."

"And where is the base?"

"I'm not supposed to say, but it is near Diqla."

"How far is it to the Israeli border?"

"About ten kilometers."

"And from the sea?"

"Three kilometers, but it's off limits."

"Why is that?"

"This is basically a war zone, Papa. You don't go swimming in a war zone."

"If you can tell me, what do you do during the day?"

"We conduct exercises and go on patrols – day and night."

"Have you encountered the Daesh?"

"Yes."

"Can you tell me about it?"

"Well, there was probably something about one incident in the Cairo papers. The Daesh attacked a military stores facility about twenty kilometers south of here."

I said, "I think the papers said something about twenty-five Egyptian military personnel were casualties."

"There were over thirty killed."

218

"Your people weren't involved, were they?"

"I lost two of my men."

"If the stores facility was twenty kilometers away, why did you get involved?"

"We were called at four o'clock that morning to counter attack."

"And what happened?"

"We saw them off."

"Did you take any prisoners?"

"No. There were sixteen bodies for identification."

Wahida asked, "Why bother with identification – just bury them."

"Because, Wahida, most of these Daesh are Egyptian. We want to know who they are and where they came from, so we can find out who knows them. When we know that, we can prevent more Daesh from coming."

Wahida muttered, "Typical el-Sisi strategy: get rid of the protesters."

Kalifa responded, "You say that, Wahida, but if something serious isn't done, Cairo itself won't be a safe place to live."

I considered for a moment. "Kalifa, do you think your training has prepared you adequately for what you have to do?"

"I feel prepared, but many of my soldiers aren't. I mean: they've been trained, so they know what to do, but they don't do it."

"What are you saying?" Wahifa asked. "Are you saying they're lazy?"

"No, not lazy. They just haven't got it. They don't understand what they're fighting for. The Iraqi army has the same problem."

I said, "The Shia militia in Iraq know what they're fighting for."

"That's right, Papa, they're fighting for their families, their heritage, their religion: they fight! These guys here, they think they're on a two year assignment to protect the government!"

"Kalifa, I haven't told you that I have personal experience of the Iraqi Shia militia."

Then I told him the story.

"Papa, you are absolutely crazy!"

"In retrospect, that's true, but I also learned a lot."

"If that's what it takes to learn, I'd rather have an uneducated father."

"As you know, Kalifa, we each make our own choices, and part of the reason for this call is to tell you about some choices that Naqib has made."

"OK, tell me."

"He is still with the same law firm, but his clients seem to be shifting."

"Shifting to the left or the right?"

Wahida replied, "They're not shifting politically, but ideologically. We think that the Daesh are a surrogate client via the Brotherhood."

"Holy shit! Did he tell you that?"

I shook my head. "Not directly. I had lunch with him and he hinted at it; Wahida got more or less the same impression from Anisa."

"That bastard! What's he doing for the Daesh?"

"We think," Wahida answered, "that there may be funds transfers and possible arms purchases, and you've been talking to him, Kalifa?"

"Yeah, he calls me about once a week. All very brotherly. Wants to know what's going on."

I said, "I suggest you avoid any military discussions, Kalifa."

For a moment, my younger son looked away from the camera. His eyes returned to us. "Two can play his game."

"What do you mean, Kalifa?"

There was just a shrug. "Well, I've got to get ready for night duty."

"Kalifa," I asked hurriedly, "when can you get home on leave?"

"I don't know, Papa. It won't be any time soon."

"Well, maybe I'll drop in and you can give me a tour of the base."

He was suddenly shouting. "Don't even think of it, Papa! You stay in Cairo! Do you hear me?"

"Just kidding, Kalifa. You be careful. We love you."

The screen went black.

I asked Wahida, "What do you think he meant by 'two can play his game'?"

"I think he meant: 'he's been using me; I can use him'." I looked away, frowning. I still don't get it. "Papa, he's probably thinking of giving him wrong information in the future."

I put the phone down. "That can also be dangerous."

"Papa, the law firm has to be reported!" Wahida's jaw was tight and her eyes intent.

I looked away. What would Elizabeth do? "Papa, are you listening to me? We can't let this go on!"

Niqab was Elizabeth's favorite. "If only there is a way to . . ."

"To do what, Papa? To persuade Naqib? You know he won't listen!" She was insistent.

"But if I report the law firm, I'll have to mention Naqib."

"No you don't! You make an anonymous phone call to the Security Service."

* * *

What would you do, Elizabeth? He believes that if he is honest with us, we will not report him. Would you call the Security Service?

Yes.

Is that you, Elizabeth?

Silence.

* * *

"Hello, I would like to speak to someone confidentially about a national security issue."

"May I ask the nature of the issue?"

"It involves a company giving assistance to Wilayat Sinai."

"Just a moment, please."

"Hello, this is Colonel Arafa. May I help you?"

"I would like to report confidentially a company giving assistance to Wilayat Sinai."

"What is the name of the company, please?"

"Kamal Saleh and Partners"

"They are located in Cairo?"

"Yes."

"We are aware of this company. What is the nature of the assistance they are providing?"

"I wish to emphasize that we are not sure of this, but the assistance could include transfer of funds, weapons and military information."

"What is the nature of the military information, please?"

"We have no specific information."

"On what basis do you suspect that Kamal Saleh is engaged in these practices?"

"We are acquainted with an employee who hinted at the practices."

"May I have your name, sir?"

"I wish to withhold it."

"Your occupation?"

"University professor."

"Are you a member of any political parties?"

"No."

"And your age?"

"Late fifties."

"Thank you for your call, Professor. If you have any further information, please call me. I am Colonel Youssef Arafa, and I am on extension 4241."

As I put the phone down, my hand was shaking. Calm yourself, Kareem! Calm yourself! He called me 'Professor'. Could he have known who I am? Perhaps they traced the call. That would just give them the switchboard number of American University – not my extension.

The calm, got-to-do-it resolve I felt before and during the call was shattered. Now, I was queasy with doubt and fear. Fear for my son – for both my sons – for myself, my family – our reputation. What would happen now? A thousand possibilities: all sinister. I knew that the Egyptian intelligence meant business.

* * *

I walked over to the small pond which was half-covered with lily pads. There, under the splash of the falling water, was a lazy flash of gold and white. Koi! In fact, there were three of them: one gold and white, one black and gold and one almost entirely white. I stood watching them as they followed their inquisitive noses in search of interesting items.

"They don't seem to be hungry," I observed.

Adeeba shook her head. "They're too fat! Sagira feeds them too much."

The red trumpets had fallen from the vines on the far wall, and what remained was the muscular brown structure of stems. There were slate paving stones and ribbons of grass under foot. Opposite the pond were several gardenia bushes with bulging buds and three waxy white flowers.

"This garden is balm for the senses, Adeeba."

"Just for the senses, Kareem? I find that it lifts my spirits when I'm down."

I turned to face her, finding her assertion difficult to understand. "You have moments when you feel that the tide runs against you?"

Her face was lit by a smile of kinship. "Of course the tide runs against me sometimes. It seems to rising against you, Kareem." I must have shrugged. "Tell me about it."

I said, "Sometimes I find it difficult to be both mother and father to my boys."

"What I think you mean is that you have no one to share your concerns."

"When Elizabeth was alive, we would discuss a problem, disagree on what the issue was, and how to approach it. Eventually, we would agree on the cause of the trouble, debate how to solve it and negotiate a compromise."

"Exactly!" Her smile brightened. "So tell me about the problem you're wrestling with alone."

"It's about my boys, Adeeba."

She said, "I don't believe they will ever see eye-to-eye. They have entirely different ideas of the purpose of life."

"How could that be? They come from the same blood: Elizabeth's and mine; they have been brought up together in the same environment."

"Blood and environment are not enough, Kareem. There are other dimensions over which you and Elizabeth – or any other parent – could have no control. Call it personality; call it God-given identity. Whatever it is, it is not transmitted by inheritance or formed by nurture."

"How do you know this?"

"By scientific observation of my own daughters, Kareem. Nakia, the married one, is very conservative in every sense: she backs el-Sisi, she goes to church at least three times a week, she manages her husband's finances like a stingy banker, and the thought of cheating on him would never enter her head. Sagira, on the other hand – and by the way, she has quite serious designs on Kalifa – is a totally free spirit. Her guiding principle is the enjoyment of life, conditioned only by causing no collateral pain. She has three hundred and seventeen Facebook friends and no enemies. She has been a C+ student. Being a B+ would have cut into her social time and falling to D+ would have incurred the wrath of her mother. Isaac, their father, was an erratic conservative: he preached conservatism and practiced what he fancied. I am just erratic. Fancying this and that and trying to keep hold of myself."

I was unable to stifle a laugh. "You are not in the least erratic, Adeeba! How could an archaeologist with your reputation possibly call herself erratic?"

"I should take you out on a dig with me sometime. . . But seriously, my students consider me erratic when I supervise a dig, because they don't give me credit for my magical intuition."

I thought about what she had said. "Yes, I suppose you are quite intuitive."

"Like most women."

"Adeeba, I wasn't really aware that there is anything between Kalifa and Sagira. What's the situation?"

"They spend at least half an hour every evening on Facetime."

"You mean Facebook?"

"No, I mean talking in real time, face-to-face."

"OK. I know what you mean.

"I hope, Kareem, that either you or Elizabeth explained to Kalifa about sex."

"I'm pretty sure Elizabeth did. Why?"

"Because I've refused to put Sagira on the pill."

"You don't think they . . ."

"Yes, I do."

"Oh, my heavens! How do you know?"

"Intuition. Actually, it's a combination of my experience and observation of my daughter."

I was stunned. What would Elizabeth do? "Shall I say something to Kalifa?"

"Well, you could say something like you're aware that Sagira is very fond of him, and that you think that Sagira is a nice girl, and . . ."

I interrupted, " I think Sagira is a lovely girl!"

"Thank you, Kareem. Yes, she is. And then you could say you expect him to be prepared and to take proper precautions if a situation should arise."

"OK. Yes, I'll call him. Thanks for telling me! Where do you suppose they . . . ?"

"I haven't any idea, Kareem. It's like trying to track two owls in the forest after midnight: they can see everything and we can see nothing."

"You're probably right."

I sat down on the weatherproof cushion next to her on the wrought-iron two-seater.

She gave me a sideways look. "We haven't attacked the problem between your boys, Kareem."

I took a deep breath, and told her about my lunch with Naqib, Wahida's meeting with Anisa, and our phone call to Kalifa.

She asked, "Have you contacted the General Intelligence Directorate?"

"I mentioned only Naqib's law firm and my suspicions, not my son. They said they were aware of the law firm, and they gave me a contact number."

Adeeba looked toward the darkening buildings beyond the garden wall. "I think you've done all you can do, Kareem."

"But there must be something more I can do. I just don't want . . ."

She interrupted, "You want to control the situation so that a catastrophe is avoided."

"Exactly!"

She shook her head, fastening her eyes on mine. "The only one who can do that is God. If you try, you'll just get in His way."

"I wish I could believe that, Adeeba."

"Did I ever tell you that my husband was a philanderer?"

"I think we knew that."

"So did half of Cairo. Anyway, at one point I was feeling as you are now: wanting to take control to prevent a disaster. I was concerned that one of the cuckolded husbands would take some terrible revenge, and I was considering writing an anonymous letter to the husband of one of his lovers. I woke up in the middle of the night, full of anger, but suddenly a thought came into my head: 'Leave it alone! You've done all you can'. At that point, I had told him I knew, that I had lost all respect for him, and that if he didn't stop, I would apply for divorce."

"What happened?"

"I prayed, 'Lord, please get me out of this mess!' A sort of miracle happened. Isaac's brother, who knew all about Isaac's philandering, approached the head of the financial syndicate for which Isaac worked and which was negotiating a long-term contract with the Saudis. The brother's message was: 'If the Saudis ever find out what an adulterer your man Isaac is, you can kiss their money goodbye'. Thereafter, Isaac terminated all his illicit relationships and made a public show of marital loyalty to me. . . He was still a lousy lover."

I wondered how she knew he was such a lousy lover if she had as little premarital experience as she had previously implied. But I decided on another tack. "I suppose, following your example, I should pray for the intervention of Allah."

"It certainly wouldn't hurt."

Later, I mentioned to Adeeba that Hafez was planning a brief trip for the two of us.

"Where are you going?"

"I'm not sure, but the other day, he mentioned something about Jerusalem."

"Why Jerusalem?"

"Well, he said that it has the Dome of the Rock Mosque from which Muhammad took his night flight to heaven. He says it's the religious center of the world: very important to Jews and Christians, as well as Muslims."

Adeeba considered me for a moment. "When you get back from Jerusalem, if you're still interested in religious centers, I could take you on a tour of Rome."

"Rome?"

"Yes, it's home of Christianity and a very interesting place."

"You would take me to Rome?"

"Yes."

"Aren't you concerned about what people would say?"

"Oh, for goodness' sake, Kareem! We're both single people and we don't have to share a room. We would attract zero notice from the people of Rome, and what the Muslims in Cairo would say, I couldn't care less."

I thought for a moment about her reaction to her husband's reported infidelity. Was there a double standard here? No. Nobody was married in this case.

On my way out, I saw Sagira in the living room. She was holding her mobile phone in front of her face. "Excuse me a second," she said, "your dad's here. Do you want to talk to him?"

I shook my head. "Tell him I'll call him later."

"He says he'll call you later." She put the phone aside for a moment. "Bye, Kareem, we hope to see you again soon."

Who was the 'we'? I had had the distinct impression that the 'we' represented a female conspiracy.

* * *

When I got home it was nine-thirty. Wahida was watching television in the living area. "Have a nice time?" she asked.

"Yes. Do you think it's too late to call Kalifa?"

"No, he's probably still up, but can't it wait until tomorrow?"

"I think I ought to speak to him while this question is fresh on my mind."

Her comfortable slouch became upright with interest. "What's the question, Papa?"

"It's not something that involves you, Wahida," I said gently.

She leaned forward on the sofa. "It's something to do with Sagira."

Damn this female intuition! I tried to ignore her suggestion and turned to go to my office. She rose and followed me. "Papa, I can help you if we talk this through! Is it about marriage?"

"No, it's not about marriage."

"Is Sagira in trouble?"

"No, she's not in trouble," I retorted. "Yet."

"Oh. So Adeeba's worried and wants you to make sure Kalifa takes precautions."

"Wahida, I think you ought to go on one of those quiz shows. You'd make a lot of money!"

She laughed. "Papa, it doesn't take a nuclear scientist to figure this out."

"So you've known about Kalifa and Sagira for some time." She shrugged. "How did you find out? Did he tell you?"

"No!" she replied indignantly.

"Did somebody tell you?"

"No!" Even more indignantly.

"So, you just guessed."

"I didn't guess, Papa. I knew."

Woman's intuition! "OK. What do you suggest I tell him?"

"I don't think you need to tell him anything. He's a knowledgeable guy."

"Are you absolutely sure?"

Her certainty slowly melted. "No."

* * *

"Kalifa, it's Papa. Am I calling too late?"

"It's OK, Papa. Lights out isn't for ten minutes. What's up?"

"I had dinner with Adeeba tonight."

"That's good, Papa. She's a wonderful lady. Carry on!"

I said, "I happened to see Sagira. She's a lovely girl."

"Yes, she is."

"Ah, Adeeba says she's very fond of you."

"That's good. I'm very fond of Sagira."

I shifted the phone from one ear to the other and back. "Ah, umm, Kalifa, I just wanted to mention the importance of being prepared in case something should happen."

"What are you worried about, Papa?"

"Well," I blurted, "I'm not anxious to have unplanned grandchildren!"

Kalifa chortled. "Don't worry, Papa. I'm planning to have three – maybe four – but I don't think I'll start until I get out of the Army."

"Very good, Kalifa. The prevention of accidental fatherhood can be nearly as important as fatherhood itself."

Chapter 9

Jerusalem

I remember my father talking about Jerusalem when I was a small boy. "It's an important place in Islam, Kareem. You should go there when you're older."

"Have you been to Jerusalem, Papa?" I asked.

He shook his head. "Too much trouble there with the Jews, but some day it will be quiet and you should go."

* * *

"Have you got your visa for Israel, Hafez?" I asked.

"Yes, there's a ten-day educational visa for students and teachers who complete the necessary form. You can do the same, Kareem."

With an easy gesture, so as not to appear smug, I said, "You remember: I have an American passport, so I don't need a visa."

"Oh, yes, I forgot."

"Have you an itinerary in mind?"

"Well, I thought we'd take about three days, take in the Dome of the Rock Mosque, and the other one next to it . . ." He paused to think for a moment. "What's the name of it?"

I shook my head. "I don't remember, Hafez."

"Anyway, I thought we would take in the culture of the city. You know: the people, the food, the activities . . ."

"What sort of Israeli activities strike your fancy, Hafez?"

He became uncharacteristically evasive. "Oh, I was just speaking generally; perhaps we can go to a concert, or something. Besides, you have an interest in the religious side of things. And we can keep an eye out for your Father Khaliq."

"Would it be all right with you, if we stop by and see Mahdi? He's the travel agent who arranged our Hajj trip."

* * *

Mahdi's office in Abwal Foreign Travel seemed to be in hibernation. Many of the cubicles were vacant, and the telephone chatter had been replaced with upbeat Latin dance music. Madhi, however, greeted us as favorite uncles. "So good to see you again, Professors. I trust you both are in the best of health! What travels are you contemplating?"

"Mahdi," I asked, "what's going on at your travel agency? Has there been a big layoff?"

"Not so big, Professor. Some people are on holiday and some are still at lunch." I gave him a skeptical look. "But also, business has been affected by the cautious travel advisories issued by several European countries."

"Really?"

"Apparently the Americans and the British have picked up information which suggests terrorist attacks on foreigners in Cairo."

I recalled Kalifa's comment about Cairo itself becoming unsafe.

Hafez shrugged. "Our travel plans do not involve Cairo."

"But," I suggested, "they do involve the use of the International Airport."

"I shouldn't be concerned about the airport, Professors! The Army already has a major presence there. After Tahrir Square, it's the best place for soldiers to see and be seen. But tell me about your destination."

Hafez said, "It's Jerusalem."

"Well, Tel Aviv airport is super secure," Mahdi confirmed.

Hafez explained his idea of the trip. Mahdi glanced at me for verification.

I said, "Well, we may take a little extra time and see more of the country."

Hafez blinked several times. "Really?"

"Yes," I said. "The mid-term break is a week, and if there is something beyond Jerusalem itself which interests us, why not see it?"

Hafez gave a reluctant shrug.

"May I suggest, Professors, that I book you flights with an open return; two rooms in a comfortable four-star hotel in the Old City, and make arrangements for a Muslim guide."

"I assume," Hafez said, "that the guide would be able to advise discreetly on cultural activities."

"Yes, of course."

What does he mean by 'advise discreetly on cultural activities'? I wondered.

* * *

We entered through Bab al-Huttah (the Gate of Remission) on the north side of the Temple Mount, our passports (the Egyptian one in my case) having been scrutinized by the Israeli police. Our guide, Nazim, gave the policeman an OK nod, thereby sparing us from the possibility of having to recite aloud the first sura of the Qur'an to prove that we were Muslim. (Non-Muslims could enter only via a ramp on the west side; Muslims have access by the other ten gates.)

Sunlight reflecting on the gold-plated Dome of the Rock Mosque created a momentary blind spot in my eyes, and I had to look away at the open, white-paved plaza bordered by cypresses. In the center stood the octagonal, grey-sided mosque, imposing in its physical dominance and the reflective power of its dome.

"We should see first the Al-Aqsa Mosque. It is the more important," Nazim announced.

Walking south, down some steps, another plaza opened and at its end there was an unremarkable, old building of sandy stone, with a series of arches across the front. Four minarets and a grey dome rose behind it. Immediately in front of the mosque was a circular ablution fountain where worshipers could perform wudu, the ritual washing of the hands, arms, legs, feet, and face before entry into the mosque.

"It was here," Nazim explained, "where the Prophet flew from Mecca on Buraq, the white horse. It is said that the horse was tied over there along the western wall. The Prophet conducted prayers here, then rode to heaven on Buraq, where he met with many of the prophets and received instructions from Allah."

"Al-Aqsa means 'the farthest mosque'," Hafez added.

"Yes," Nazim agreed, "but there was no mosque, as we know them today, existent here during the Prophet's lifetime."

"So maybe Muhammad went somewhere else." I suggested.

Nazim shook his head. "Islamic scholars say that isn't the case. Masjid, the word we use for mosque, literally means 'place of prostration', and it applies to monotheistic places of worship – not necessarily to a building. Don't forget that Muslims used to pray toward Jerusalem until it was changed to Mecca by Muhammad."

"So was this a place of worship in Muhammad's time?" I asked

Nazim said, "Archaeologists have found evidence of old Christian and Jewish places of worship here."

Hafez announced, "I don't think one should get too technical about it: one either believes the Qur'an or one doesn't."

I was absolutely dumbfounded! I would have expected Hafez to take the position (at least secretly) that scientific facts undermine the Qur'an. I said, "Spoken like a true believer, Hafez!"

"Look," he said, "every important religion has the same problem: they rely on the testimony of people who have been dead for over a thousand years, and who didn't have digital cameras or laptops to record their observations. What do you expect?"

I gave Hafez a momentary pat on the shoulder. "That reminds me of something my late wife used to say: God wants it that way."

"Meaning?" Hafez asked.

"Meaning that God likes to leave us with some uncertainty. Certainty means we would all be angels and that would be very boring."

Hafez gave another shrug.

The inside of the Al-Aqsa Mosque was not the memorable icon I had expected: white pillars and arches, mosaic-tiled ceilings in abstract patterns, carpeting with red ovals to mark the space of each worshiper, and symbolic stained glass windows below the dome.

One could even hear the sound of distant footsteps of the few worshipers in the mosque; we could whisper to each other and still be heard.

"Father Khaliq!" a female voice called out in distress from the far side of the mosque.

I turned to identify her.

"Did you hear that?" Hafez asked in an urgent whisper.

"Yes. I think she must be over there!" I began walking, but I felt a hand on my shoulder.

"What is it?" Nazim demanded.

"He's trying to find a Father Khaliq. He was asked if he could find him by a Saudi princess." The words tumbled out of Hafez. "We've got to speak with that woman!"

"It's best to wait for her outside. Speaking to her inside the mosque will cause trouble!"

We waited on the northern porch of the mosque for ten minutes. "Did you see what she was wearing?" Hafez asked

"I couldn't really tell: I think she was all in black."

Twenty minutes, half an hour. No women came out.

"Is there another exit?" I asked.

"There are two exits on the east side," Nazim answered.

"But we haven't seen any women leaving the area."

"Maybe she's still inside."

We went back into the mosque. The women's prayer space was empty.

* * *

"Shall we look now at the Dome of the Rock Mosque?" Nazim suggested; we retraced our steps toward the north gates of Temple Mount. "It was built in about the year seventy (690 AD) by Caliph Abd al-Malik, the same caliph who had the Al-Aqsa built in its present form. The two mosques were built at about the same time, although both have been damaged by earthquakes and modified since by others."

Hafez asked, "Why would the caliph build two mosques in different styles at the same time in more or less the same place for the same reason?"

"This elevated area," Nazim said with a sweep of his arm, "which we call the Noble Sanctuary (Temple Mount) has been a sacred area for thousands of years, but it was largely barren when the caliph came to power, and he was determined to make it a great place of worship. There were different architects and engineers involved in the two projects; different materials were used. It is said that al-Malik's son, al-Walid, actually completed the Al-Aqsa using labor from Damascus. We don't know what was in the caliph's mind, but we can see that he left us two great mosques."

As we approached the Dome of the Rock, Hafez mused, "I can't think of another mosque that looks like this one: an octagonal shape with a raised dome. Why is it like this?"

"Much of the design and decoration is very similar to Byzantine churches and palaces in the area. In fact, the dome, which is a twenty meter hemisphere, is almost identical to the Christian Church of the Holy Sepulchre."

"Why would you want to copy Christian architecture?" Hafez asked.

"Why not?" was my reply.

Mazim looked from one to the other of us, uncertainly. "The two engineers in charge of the project were both Muslims: one from Jerusalem and the other from an old city in the Jordan River valley. Both locations at the time were dominated by Christian Byzantine architecture. They wanted to build a mosque which was at least the equal of whatever Christianity had to offer."

"I think they should have decided to build one mosque that was bigger and better," Hafez declared.

"But if they had done that, we might have ended up with nothing," I said, and in response to Hafez's puzzled look, I added, "Given the building materials and techniques that were available in the year seventy, it seems doubtful to me that a larger building could have survived the earthquakes that destroyed so many other structures. Besides, what difference does it make?"

We began to debate the effect which the beauty of a mosque may or may not have on the faith of its worshipers. Perhaps recognizing that neither of us was qualified to pursue this argument, Nazim led us to the interior of the gold-domed mosque. I expected to see an expanse of carpet punctuated by columns, a minbar (pulpit) and a qibla (indication of the direction of prayer). Instead, under the dome, there was a jagged opening in the floor which exposed the rock beneath. At first, I thought this must be some sort of renovation. Nazim led us to the waist-high barrier at the edge of the opening in the floor. "This is the Foundation Stone from which the Prophet flew to heaven. There, you see the fingerprints of the Archangel Jibril (Gabriel) where he held back the rock as Muhammad ascended!" Moving to his right and pointing, he added, "And there you see a footprint of the Prophet!" Yes, there it was, set in stone.

"What are these stairs?" Hafez asked, with a nod to the stairs leading down into the stone grotto below.

"They are the stairs to Bir el Arwah (Fountain of the Souls). It is possible to obtain permission to go down into the cave below to pray."

We walked around the center, along the two concentric, carpeted circles, their marble columns and arches set with mosaics. Nazim pointed out the inscription from the Qur'an (19:33) which read:

So peace is upon me the day I was born, and the day I die, and the day I shall be raised alive! Such is Jesus, son of Mary. It is a statement of truth, about which they doubt. It is not befitting to (the majesty of) Allah that He should beget a son. Glory be to Him! When He determines a matter, He only says to it, "Be", and it is.

"Christians would consider that blasphemy," Hafez commented.

"Yes, but at least the Prophet acknowledges that Jesus was a great prophet and the son of Mary," Nazim said. "In fact, over there, it is written: 'O Lord, send your blessings to your Prophet and Servant Jesus son of Mary'. Theologians say that these inscriptions reflect both a rivalry and a desire to get along with the Christian community at the time."

Farther along, we encountered a large flat rock on the floor. "This is the slab which covered Solomon's tomb. The Prophet is said to have driven twelve gold nails into it."

* * *

From the Jewish Quarter of Jerusalem, we descended many flights of steps, but always with the huge, ancient, stone wall looming up from the plaza below. "That," said Nazim, "is the

Western Wall. It is all that remains of the great Jewish temple that the Romans destroyed almost two thousand years ago."

"It is said to be the holiest site for Jews," Hafez added.

I said, "But it's only an old rock wall."

Nazim frowned. "But you see, Professor, for the Jews this temple – the one here that was destroyed – was uniquely a place where one could pray with the assurance that prayers would be answered. That was because they believed that Allah lived in the Tabernacle of the temple, and the Tabernacle was what the Jews call the 'Holy of Holies'. It was where the Ark of the Covenant, which contained the Ten Commandments, was kept. As you know, the Ten Commandments were given to Moses by Allah."

"But is the location of the old Tabernacle known?" I asked.

"There are various opinions about this, and in any case, Jews were never permitted to enter the Tabernacle. As it was the Holy of Holies, only the high priest could enter once a year, during a particular Jewish celebration. There is also doubt of where the foundation stone of the temple is located: some say it is near the top of the wall; others say that it is on the other side of the Temple Mount. As a result of this uncertainty, some Jews do not ascend to Temple Mount for fear of stepping into the Holy of Holies. And in any case, Jews are prohibited from praying on the Temple Mount, as this would be offensive to us Muslims who also venerate the Temple Mount."

I asked, "Why would it be offensive?"

Nazim was taken aback. "Well . . . naturally . . . it would be offensive to Muslims because we consider the Temple Mount to be a holy place."

"But," I rejoined, "Jews also consider it to be a holy place, and yet Muslims pray there every day. Are Jews offended by this?"

Nazim held up his hands in surrender. "I don't know. I suppose so."

Hafez intervened, "I've read that the prohibition on Jews praying on Temple Mount was a political decision, so that Mus-

lims wouldn't feel that the Jews – who actually run Jerusalem
– favor the Jews."

I laughed aloud. "An excellent example of a political decision which entirely misses the point and creates a new problem. The point was that both religions could have been allowed
to pray with the single caveat: don't interfere with one another.
That would have created a sense of harmony. As it is, the Jews
feel slighted and disharmonious."

"The problem is," Nazim replied, "that there are trouble-
makers on both sides who would always be interfering."

"I think one would treat them the same way we treat trouble-
makers at football matches: we don't allow them in the stadium."

As we walked across the plaza toward the area that was
reserved for worshipers, I noticed that male and female worshipers were separated, as they are in a mosque. I remembered
Elizabeth's comment: "Unnatural separation of the sexes is a
symptom of fear of equality."

To which I responded, "I don't fear women as equals."

"I'm not talking about you, Kareem, I'm talking about your
religion. In your case, you feel that men are slightly better than
women."

"Well, aren't they?"

"No! You've got it backwards!"

Sometimes, I think she was right.

We took a few moments at the barrier to the area of prayer
to look at what was going on. Nazim explained that the bits of
white paper that had been crumpled into the crevices of the wall
were actually written prayers. "Jews believe that the wall is the
gateway to heaven and that it is the best place to make one's
prayers."

There were perhaps half a dozen men, dressed in black, their
heads covered, standing at individual lecterns and reading aloud,
their heads bobbing for emphasis as they read. "They can go
on for hours and they take turns at their reading. You see the

small groups behind them? They are the super religious. We have nothing quite like this in Islam. There are men with a wife and perhaps half a dozen children who do not work for a living; instead they are religious zealots – but not rabbis – they read and pray constantly, and they are supported by their religious communities."

"It must be very boring!" Hafez said. "I suppose that every now and then they sneak a look at an old copy of Playboy."

What does Hafez know about Playboy? I remember finding what was probably a fourth-hand copy tucked into a binder of laboratory notes on Kalifa's desk. I allowed myself a brief inspection and I remember that the women were quite attractive, but mostly blonde.

* * *

Over dinner at the hotel, we talked about our experiences of the day.

"It was better than I expected," Hafez volunteered.

"In what way?"

"Well, when you actually see something that the Qur'an talks about, it becomes more real."

"Does that mean that your faith was enhanced today?" I asked.

"It isn't a matter of faith. As you know, I'm not a religious person, but I feel that I can speak more knowledgably about the Temple Mount and the Western Wall."

I didn't want to hurt Hafez' feelings by telling him this, but it occurred to me that he might as well have visited Sydney, Australia, gaining first-hand insights into the Opera House and the Harbor Bridge.

"Do you feel that your faith was enhanced today?" he asked.

"Not immediately and directly."

"What do you mean?"

"I mean it's more of a vicarious experience: by seeing actual evidence on which people base their faith, I can better understand why they believe as they do. At the same time, since the evidence is not conclusive, I understand that the faithful have taken a leap."

Hafez nodded. "Are you taking a leap?"

"For me, it isn't really a leap. I'm a bit like a painter who starts out making sketches of real still life, and gradually learns how to paint a surreal picture which is more satisfying and informative."

"I don't know what you're talking about, but it doesn't matter. We should make a plan for tomorrow."

"What did you have in mind, Hafez?"

"Well, I think we could walk around the Jewish Quarter of the Old City, and I understand that there is a district of Jerusalem which is largely Orthodox Jewish. It would be interesting to see what they're about."

"May I suggest that we hire a Jewish guide?"

"Why?

"Hafez, for goodness' sake! We've invested the time and money to come here. For about four hundred shekels ($100 US) we can hire a good guide who will show us what we want to see, who can answer our questions, and who can keep us out of trouble."

* * *

Mordecai Liebenfeldt joined us for coffee the next morning at the hotel. He looked like an ancient Greek warrior: handsome but battle-scarred, full black beard and matching eyebrows, wearing a maroon shirt, jeans and a wide-brimmed black felt hat, which he rested on his knee. He listened attentively to our proposed itinerary for the day. "I have the impression that you would like to know more about Jewish culture and Judaism."

We nodded. "Culture and some details of the Jewish religion we can cover during the tour, but perhaps I should take a few minutes to describe the main differences between Judaism and Islam." Again, we nodded. "You know, of course, that there is no prophet Muhammad in Judaism. We have a book of the prophets, Nevi'im, which we read in an allegorical more than in a literal sense. Many of our prophets are the same as those in the Qur'an. We do not believe that Jesus was the Messiah; we are still awaiting the Jewish Messiah. Like you, we believe in an all-powerful God, the creator of the universe, and we pray directly to him alone. At the core of Judaism is the concept of Emunah, which means an innate conviction, a perception of truth that transcends reason. Emunah becomes part of a worshiper's identity, so that God, and his unique relationship to God, are intrinsic to who he is."

Is this what I'm looking for: Emunah?

"This conviction," Mordecai continued, "is enhanced by study and understanding of sacred Jewish texts, and by living each day in thankful awareness of God as a personal God and in striving to meet his commandments . . ."

Hafez interjected, "There are the ten commandments."

"Actually, there are six hundred and thirteen commandments, covering a wide range of subjects."

"Are children expected to learn all six hundred and thirteen?"

"A good Jew is expected to know all the commandments and the reasons for them."

I said, "In Islam we have the Qur'an and the hadiths; what are their Jewish equivalents?"

"The 'Jewish Bible' – the Tanakh – consists of the Pentateuch (the five books of Moses), the Nevi'im and the Ketuvim (Writings): twenty-four books in all. And there is the Oral Torah, the instructions of the rabbis."

"Has the Oral Torah been transcribed in a written version?"

"Yes, there are various written versions and interpretations."

243

"Islam is divided into two main sects: Sunni and Shia," I said, "and of course there are numerous subsects. Is there a similar structure in Judaism?"

"Broadly speaking, there are Orthodox Jews who take a historic view of the law and emphasize strict compliance; Conservative Jews take a more open and flexible view of the law; and Reformed Jews place individual autonomy above Jewish law, giving the individual the right to form his own beliefs. In Israel, it is easier to think of a division between dedicated, religious Jews and secular, ambivalent Jews."

Hafez looked doubtful. "It sounds quite different from Islam."

Mordecai shook his head. "If one considers the basic principles, the two religions have a great deal in common. If you place the Ten Commandments alongside the Five Pillars of Islam, there are two principles that stand out: worship God and be kind to your fellow man. The differences are in all the details. So as we travel around today, I encourage you to look for similar values: they're much more important than different practices."

* * *

We ascended and descended the steps of the Old City, hand carts delivering goods to the shops bumping up and down over the worn stone steps. It is much like any other bazaar in the Middle East, except that the merchandise is better quality and the customers more prosperous.

"Tell us about the Palestinian situation," Hafez suggested.

"It is difficult. Hamas is a thorn in our side – without Hamas, a solution might be reached. But as you know, Iran is supporting Hamas, and Iran denies Israel's right to exist. The Iranians are cowards: they do not dare to attack us directly; instead, they send money and rockets to Hamas – money to prop up their corrupt administration and rockets to fire at Israeli civilians."

"Why don't the people of Gaza throw Hamas out?" I asked.

"You are educated Egyptians – you believe in democracy. But democracy does not always work in the Middle East. Votes can be bought, votes can be coerced. The people of Gaza are hostages."

"What about the deal that the US has negotiated with Iran on nuclear weapons?" Hafez asked.

"It is very dangerous! In two ways. First, Iran can still acquire nuclear weapons by stealth or at the end of the treaty. Second, with their funds unfrozen, they have billions to fund Hamas and other terrorist organizations."

"But," I countered, "isn't war the alternative to the treaty?"

"Probably. The view of the Israeli government is that it is better to cripple Iran now than to see the Jewish nation disappear in a nuclear holocaust in a few years' time."

"Mordecai, do you think Israel faces a threat from ISIL?" I asked.

He smiled. "ISIL are also cowards. They don't pick any fight that they aren't pretty sure they can win, and they position themselves to win by terrorizing their opponents. Israel is not afraid of ISIL. They know that if they were to attack us, we would invade Syria and destroy ISIL completely."

Hafez said, "That would leave Assad in power in Syria."

Mordecai shrugged. "The Assads don't bother us; they're also afraid of us. It is Hezbollah – again with Iranian funding – that are the nuisance."

I told Mordecai about Kalifa's army duty in the Sinai.

"My son," he announced, "is in the Israeli air force. Right now, he is on duty. He could be airborne in his F16 in fifteen minutes, and over his target within the hour. You are worried. I am worried. It is the price we pay for our freedom."

I felt my vision misting and I blinked several times. "Listening to you," I began, "I have the impression that Israel and the

Jewish people are determined to deal with the world from a position of strength. But you are only eight million people."

He nodded. "You say it is eight million people, but it is only six million Jews. There are two million Palestinians living in Israel, who have a far higher birth rate than we Jews. At some point we will be out numbered. That is why we encourage Jews from around the world to immigrate to Israel. But to your point: yes, we must deal from a position of strength! There were six million Jews murdered by the Nazis. This afternoon, I can take you to Yad Vashem, the Holocaust History Museum, here in Jerusalem, and you will understand why we have this determination that it will never happen again!"

"Is there an element of this conviction which is religious, as well?" I asked.

"Yes. Most Jews believe that we are a people chosen by God. Not because we are better than others: that's not the point at all. We have been chosen by God to live in a distinctive relationship with God: not a better relationship, a different relationship. You remember I told you about Emunah? That is the relationship, and we believe that since God has chosen that relationship for us, we must preserve it!"

That afternoon, we did go to Vad Vashem. I had read a little about the Holocaust, and I had seen grainy photographs of the concentration camps, but for me and perhaps more particularly for Hafez, it was nauseating. How could human beings treat their fellow creatures – even children – as vermin to be eradicated? The museum itself was dark, with grey cement walls and sparse lighting. The exhibits were immediately and emotionally powerful. The viewer was spared nothing! I had the inescapable impression that the Jews were led meekly and without resistance to their deaths. Hafez agreed.

"Don't you think," I suggested later, "that this meekness and lack of resistance contributes to the aggressive, zero-tolerance attitude in Israel today?"

"Yes, you're probably right, Kareem. But the meekness you mention is not unique to the Jews in the 1940s. Do you remember those video clips on the news showing the Shia soldiers in Iraq being led away to be shot by the Daesh?"

* * *

With Mordecai, we visited an Orthodox residential area in Jerusalem. It had a 'down at the heels' feeling about it; the shops did not look busy. No one lingered on the streets to look in windows or talk: they hurried on their way.

Hafez observed, "All the men seem to have strings hanging down from the waist. What are the strings?"

"They are tzitzit (tassels). It is a requirement in the Torah that men must have a tassel at each of the four corners of a garment – either a shawl or a vest-like undershirt. There are many different traditions on the making of tzitzit."

"But why don't you wear them?"

"I am not an Orthodox Jew."

"All the men seem to be wearing black hats. Is that a requirement?"

"No. Men must have their heads covered when praying or reading scripture. Otherwise, a bare head is acceptable. The black hat has become a Jewish fashion. Married women outside the house must cover their heads, either with a wig or a shawl."

"Speaking of women," Hafez asked, "is it true that many Russian women have immigrated to Israel?"

"Yes. Some have come with their families, but some have come looking for husbands."

"And I have read that they tend to congregate in certain nightclubs."

"I really couldn't say."

* * *

We had to duck our heads to enter the synagogue, and once inside Mordecai placed little white skull caps on our heads. The interior was crowded with dark wooden furniture: benches, a huge chair, a table, a large cabinet and a grand bimah – what we Muslims would call a minbar or pulpit.

"What's this chair for?" Hafez asked.

"That is the Elijah chair. It is used in circumcision ceremonies."

Hafez and I looked at each other and shook our heads.

"And this cabinet?" Hafez persisted.

"That is the Ark, where the scrolls of the Torah are kept."

Hafez frowned. "Wouldn't it be easier to keep them as a book?"

Mordecai sought guidance from the ceiling. "Yes, of course it would be easier, but it wouldn't be the same ceremony. Rabbis have been reading from scrolls for thousands of years. Wouldn't your mosques be more comfortable if you had seats, as we do here, instead of carpets on the floor? Yes, it would be more comfortable, but it wouldn't be the same! You're focusing on the differences! The overriding similarity is that in synagogues and mosques, imams and rabbis have been praying to the same God and reading the same messages for hundreds of years!"

* * *

Over dinner that evening, I thought I would tease Hafez. I said, "Hafez, why the interest in Russian women which you expressed this afternoon?"

He gave a dismissive gesture. "It's just idle curiosity. But I do think that Russian women are attractive."

"What makes you think so?"

"Well, they are quite substantial, and they tend to have pale skin and brown hair."

An image of Hafez's wife, Naamah, flashed through my mind: a tiny woman with dark skin and black hair.

We said our goodnights and took the elevator up to our rooms. It was nine-thirty, there was little of interest on the television, and I was not ready for sleep. I took my book, Socrates in Mediaeval Arabic Literature, and went down to the lobby to find a comfortable sofa.

I looked up. Perhaps the sound of his voice from across the lobby attracted my attention. Hafez was in consultation with the concierge. He went outside, got in a taxi and disappeared. I bet he's going to the nightclub frequented by Russian women.

* * *

Hafez is usually at breakfast at seven-thirty, and he is finishing his coffee when I arrive at eight. Except the next morning. At eight-twenty, I was about to telephone his room, thinking he had overslept, when he dashed into the dining room, quite disorganized. His clothes were those of the previous evening. Hurriedly, he poured himself some coffee.

"Good morning, Hafez," I said. "Did you find her?"

He glanced at me, then away. "What are you talking about?" he demanded.

"I'm just asking if you found your Russian woman."

Setting his coffee cup down, he studied me for several moments. I looked back at him calmly. "Yes," he said, "yes, I did."

"Did she meet your expectations?"

"Kareem!"

"I'm just asking if she was substantial with pale skin and brown hair."

He paused for a moment. "Quite substantial. . . Yes, quite substantial – a slight suntan, and blonde hair – bleached."

I nodded. He looked up at the waiter. "Three scrambled eggs, a plate of toast and more coffee."

That evening, and the three successive evenings we were in Jerusalem, I was left unaccompanied after dinner.

I began to wonder why Hafez had not suggested I accompany him to the nightclub of the Russian women. After all, we were on this trip together. Would I have accepted an invitation to join him? No. He has his faults, but reading people is not one of them. He just saved himself the slight embarrassment.

* * *

"I'd like to find out about these Druze people," Hafez announced.

"What Druze people?" I asked.

"Don't you read the newspaper in the morning, Kareem?"

"I can't read Hebrew; how am I going to read the newspaper?"

"No! The Arabic newspaper, Al Quds!"

"What did it say?"

"It said that the Druze people – many of whom live on the Golan Heights – are protesting that Israel is supporting the Nusra Front opposition fighters in Syria." Hafez lowered his voice and spoke with unaccustomed intensity. "There are quite a few Druze living in Israel. Over a hundred thousand. Israel treats them like citizens, and many serve in the Israeli armed forces – even in high positions – but most of them consider themselves Syrian by origin. They have aligned themselves with Assad, but now the Nusra rebels who are fighting Assad have begun to attack Druze communities in Syria. And," he continued almost breathlessly, "there is evidence that the Israelis – who are also against Assad – are providing arms to Nusra! In fact, last month, as an Israeli army ambulance approached an Israeli military hospital in the Golan Heights, the Druze stopped it. They found two wounded Nusra rebels inside, and they beat them up and killed one of them. Netanyahu called it a 'lynching'."

I could only shake my head. "How can one tell, in this part of the world, who is your friend and who is your enemy? It is all so capricious; there are no solid loyalties."

* * *

We found that renting a car to travel to the Heights was permissible: only one area is restricted to Israeli military personnel, and we passed through two random Israeli checkpoints without difficulty. Hafez wanted to find the town of Majdal al-Shams, a Druze concentration on the Heights. I thought we might be able to see the Syrian civil war in the distance.

Hafez drove east out of Jerusalem, then north past Jericho on route 90 until we reached the Sea of Galilee, then on route 98 until we entered Majdal al-Shams, the eastern boundary of which was perhaps one hundred meters west of the Ceasefire Line.

I had researched the Druze on the Internet, and printed excerpts in the hotel business center. Only in the Middle East could a religion like this arise! The Druze are an Arabic-speaking, monotheistic, ethnoreligious group who trace their origins to Jethro of Midian, the father-in-law of Moses, their spiritual founder and prophet. They are an historical offshoot of Shia Islam, but share so little of the Islamic faith that they are regarded as infidels by some Muslims. Their beliefs arise from Greek philosophy, Judaism, Christianity, and Hinduism. They believe that God both transcends the material world and is manifest in it. In God there are no attributes apart from His existence: He is complete and incomprehensible. Reincarnation is central to the Druze faith, and it takes place only between Druze of the same gender; moreover a Druze cannot be reincarnated into the body of a non-Druze. Since the number of Druze souls in the universe is finite and there is no possibility of proselytism, the faith is closed. There are seven moral principles in the Druze faith, including repudiation of the devil, care of fellow believers, truthfulness, and absolute submission to God's will. I wondered how the Druze gained the knowledge of God's will. How did they know it wasn't the voice of the devil masquerading as God?

Jethro, the ancestor of all Druze, was a shepherd and non-Jewish priest who lived in what is now northwest Saudi Arabia. Moses fled Egypt, having killed an Egyptian who was beating a Jewish slave. He worked for Jethro as a shepherd for forty years and married Jethro's daughter, Zipporah. The Druze believe that Jethro was the 'hidden and true prophet' who communicated directly with God and passed the information on to Moses, the 'recognized and revealed prophet'. The holiest site and most important pilgrimage for the Druze is Nabi Shu'ayb (the tomb of Jethro), which is located in lower Galilee.

* * *

Majdal al-Shams sits on an undulating ridge looking north-east into Syria. The town had little to recommend it: jumbled cubes of houses crowded together along narrow, misdirected streets. Hafez was eager to make contact with an 'uqqal (Druze sheikh). "I want to understand the political situation here."

I thought I knew enough about the political situation that any further information would confuse, rather than enlighten. But there we were on the Golan Heights, at the epicenter of a minor political tremor within sight of the major earthquake in the Middle East. I might as well view the seismograms.

Hafez, having parked the car in what seemed like the center of the town, began to ask passersby where an 'uqqal could be found. His requests were met with blank stares and head shakes. "Hafez," I said, "I think the problem is that you are obviously a foreigner, who has no business asking for an 'uqqal. Maybe if you were wearing a bulletproof vest with 'Al Jazeera News' plastered across your chest, and if I were balancing a video camera on my shoulder, we would have better luck."

"OK, but how are we going to get the inside story?"

"Why don't we find a likely looking café and listen in?"

The café Hafez selected was shrouded in pungent tobacco smoke, but it was crowded with bearded men in animated, noisy discussion. Once inside, we hesitated, looking for places for two. The barman waved us over. "Where you from?" he asked in Hebrew then in Arabic.

"We're from Cairo," Hafez explained. "University professors," I added.

"You want to have what they're having?" he asked. We nodded.

He produced two glass mugs resting on china saucers. There were wisps of steam and a bitter-sweet scent. I took a sip. "This isn't just coffee."

"It's coffee with Sabra. We call it 'Wake Me!'"

"What is Sabra?" Hafez asked.

"It's made from Jaffa oranges, chocolate and thirty percent alcohol."

We put our saucers down on the bar.

I said, "I think we'd rather have a plain coffee."

"You don't like the Wake Me?"

"We are Muslims."

"What a shame!"

The coffee arrived in small china cups. It was molten and bitter, requiring three spoonfuls of sugar.

"What brings you Egyptians to the Golan Heights?"

"We are very interested in the political situation for the Druze," Hafez began. "You are here, safe in Israel; you have families within sight who are being killed by terrorists; and the Israeli army is helping the terrorists who also want to kill Assad."

The barman nodded. He gestured at the noisy room. "That's all this lot talks about. But if you come back late this afternoon, they will be discussing women."

"Do you have family in Syria?" Hafez asked.

"Yes. Who doesn't?"

"And did you serve in the Israeli army?"

"Of course. Most of us have."

Hafez gave him a sympathetic look. "A very difficult situation."

The barman shrugged. "It is difficult for everyone. Even Israel. They are good to us Druze, and we have a lot in common. But Assad has been supporting Hezbollah, which has fought a war with Israel and snipes at Israeli soldiers. So Assad has to go. Too bad; he has been good to the Druze, also."

"How is all this going to end?" I asked.

The barman gripped the granite bar as if it were a podium. "Syria will cease to exist – most of the people will be gone anyway. Assad and his friends will be hiding in Iran – or Russia. They'll be some kind of a strange coalition: something like America, Saudi, Russia and Iran that finally gets pissed off at the Daesh and wipes them out with help from others. When the dust is settled, the coalition will divide Syria up like Germany in 1945. Saudi will get the western oil fields; Iran will get a big chunk next to Iraq; Russia will get the west coast, and America will give what's left to Lebanon and Turkey."

Hafez asked, "What will happen to the Druze?"

The barman gave another of his shrugs. "Maybe America will give us to Israel."

This scenario galvanized Hafez into action: he spent the afternoon engaging any willing table in a debate about the future of the Druze.

As I sat watching and eating a grilled bread roll stuffed with smoked cheese and mutton, I was approached by a bookish young man with long, unwashed hair and steel-rimmed spectacles. "Your friend is very interested in our politics," he said.

"Yes," I said with a touch of irony, "he may write a book about it."

The young man's eyes widened. "Really?" I nodded sagely. "What about you?" he asked.

"You know what I'd like to do? I'd like to have a look at the battlefield."

"You mean you want to go down into Syria?"

"No. No. I'd just like to look down at what's going on in Syria."

"I can take you to a good viewing spot and point out some of the towns."

"OK. Let's go!"

We walked east along a winding residential road. It was washing day: laundry hung from balconies; children and dogs were cavorting in the street. At the end, there was a T-junction with a road that bordered the edge of a steep decline. Ahead was a view that seemed to take in all the earth. The sweep was astonishing: from a mountainous horizon in the north to endless plains in the south, and hundreds of settlements and villages in between.

"You see that smoke there?" the young man asked, pointing left of center. "That's Damascus."

A dark pall of smoke hung over what seemed to be the profile of a remote city.

"How far away is Damascus?"

"About fifty kilometers."

As I studied the distant smudge of city, an ugly eruption of smoke blossomed to the right. "Is that some shelling?" I asked.

"No. I think that's the Americans dropping bombs. There's not so much of that during the day; they must have been called in to hit a specific target. At night it's a free-for-all. You can hear the drones and see the trails from their rockets."

A soft, dull, attenuated 'boom' reached us.

There was a flash of silver between the clouds. "Is that the Americans?" I asked.

The young man studied the rolling aircraft. "No, that's a Tornado. Must be the Emirates."

"No Saudi aircraft?"

"I haven't seen any. They are all tied up in Yemen."

Beyond the green agricultural fields below us, among some mud-walled villages, there were repeated flashes, left and right, followed by distant percussions. "Is that Assad vs. the Daesh?" I asked.

"No. Assad doesn't get that far from home in Damascus. It's probably Hezbollah against the Daesh."

There below me was what could have been – should have been – a pastoral view of the world: green farmland, dark forested mountains, ochre villages, and the outlines of a great city. But this tableau was punctuated by bursts of smoke, flashes and concussions: man was at work destroying his world.

* * *

On the way back to Jerusalem, Hafez gave me a near-verbatim recap of his discussions with the Druze. As I listened, I had a mental picture of a moth caught in the center of a spider web, but as Hafez continued, the web became three dimensional, with different species of spiders having built inter-woven webs. The moth was fluttering in the vortex, responding to the web tremors caused by the attacks of one spider on another at the perimeter.

"So what do you see as the solution, Hafez?"

"I don't think there is a solution. It'll just have to play itself out."

I reminded him of the barman's projected outcome.

"Nah! There's no way those guys could work together. What do you think, Kareem?"

"I think cooperation, setting aside differences and working toward a shared objective is the only solution."

"That's not going to happen, Kareem. You know that."

I gave a brief shrug. "I think it's interesting to focus on the cause of all this turmoil."

"There are plenty of causes to talk about!"

"No. I think there may be just one cause, ultimately."

"Man's stupidity?"

"I would say that man's selfish focus on his own needs is a contributing factor."

"OK, but what do you think is the main factor?"

I thought for a moment. This will be a little bit tricky. "Hafez, do you believe in good and evil?"

"Yes, of course."

"And do you believe there could be an ultimate good and an ultimate evil?"

"You mean like Allah and Satan."

"Yes."

It was Hafez's turn to think. "You know I'm not particularly religious, Kareem, but I think there probably is an Allah somewhere."

"And Satan?"

"I haven't given him much thought."

"Well, would you agree that if there is an Allah, the ultimate good, it makes sense that there is an ultimate evil? If not, things get kind of out of balance. Every other measure I can think of has a name at each end of its spectrum. There's north and south, hot and cold, positive and negative . . ."

Hafez interrupted: "I get it! You think that Satan is ultimately responsible!"

"Well, if he's there and he's not asleep, he's had plenty of opportunity to make a real mess of things."

Hafez glanced at me skeptically. "But how does he go about it?"

"Hafez, how would I know? But consider this: after each instance somebody makes a bad or selfish decision, things get into a real mess. Assad crushes his people's desires for more democracy: they rebel and a civil war starts; the Americans pull out of Iraq too soon – they never should have been there in the first place: ISIL morphs out of Al Qaeda. You want some more examples?"

"No, I get the idea. Have you checked this out with your imam?"

"I don't know his name," I confessed.

* * *

When we returned to Jerusalem, Hafez said: "I think we'll keep the car overnight. Do you mind?"

"No, what do you want to do?"

"I'd like to better understand the Palestinian situation. First, I thought about going to Gaza, but it seems that no tourists are permitted in Gaza. So I asked about Palestinian hot spots, and they said that Ramallah is the de facto capital of the West Bank. The Palestinian Authority's headquartered there."

"So, you want to have a chat with Mahmoud Abbas?"

Hafez gave a slight shrug. "Perhaps we could speak with one of his advisers."

* * *

We found a white, bustling city where we expected a dusty, sleepy town. Ramallah was clearly in evolution.

Hafez was able to find the Muqata'a (headquarters) in Ramallah, an impressive white stone building with blue-uniformed guards. We visited Arafat's nearby tomb, a tall rectangular edifice with a glass portal at its base, and inside we could see wreaths placed against the tomb itself. The inscription above the glass portal announced that this was the temporary tomb of Arafat, and that his final resting place would be in Jerusalem.

Our self-guided tour had exhausted itself. I asked one of the guards if he knew of a professional guide. He gave me the phone number of an agency, and a guide, Salman Farsoun, met us at the Muqata'a half an hour later.

I remember being impressed, as we drove around, with the number of diplomatic missions and NGO's which had their offices in Ramallah.

"All these overseas organizations must contribute substantially to the economy of Ramallah," I suggested.

"Yes, that is what gives us a sense of pride that we are living in what is essentially a national capital," Salman responded. "But the prosperity of Ramallah is due to something else. The taxes are quite low here, and many businesses which used to be in East Jerusalem have moved to Ramallah. These businesses attract the hordes of customers you see here."

Over lunch, Salman talked about the history of Ramallah: originally a Christian agricultural settlement, part of the British Mandate, then under Jordanian rule, and occupied by Israel after the Six Day War. The two intifada (popular uprising), which had some of their roots in Ramallah, had given the city a reputation for radicalism.

"But now," Salman said, "we are seen as a more liberal city – open to discussion and negotiation – perhaps because we are the capital. It is Gaza that is radical."

Hafez asked, "What is the future for a Palestinian nation?"

"It is difficult to say but we on the West Bank, the Palestinian Authority, are moving closer and closer to autonomy. We are engaged at the United Nations, so we have credibility on the world stage and to some extent with the Israelis. They like to complain about us but they much prefer us to the Gazans, and if there is to be a Palestinian Nation, they would much prefer its capital to be in Ramallah rather than Jerusalem."

* * *

Leaving Ramallah, we drove north a few kilometers to the town of Al-Berih.

"It's a little out of your way, but you should see the Martyrs' Cemetery in Al-Berih," Salman suggested. "There are the tombs of many famous Palestinians there."

We walked through the wrought-iron gates of Martyr's Cemetery and there before us lay the enclosed plots and vertical markers at the head and foot of hundreds of graves. The scene, however, was tranquil: the grave enclosures and markers of white or grey marble; trees and shrubs everywhere; and green grass covering each grave.

We began to look for names carved in the marble; many were anonymous; a few had names we did not recognize. But Hafez found the recent grave of Abu Ein, a prominent Palestinian activist and leader.

"Oh, Father Khaliq!" The shrill voice of a woman.

Hafez pointed to a group of people in the distance. "She's over there!"

We hurried toward the group.

"Oh, Father Khaliq!"

As we approached, the single group became two adjacent funerals.

We stood between them, waiting for the lamentation to be repeated. There were several black-glad women in each funeral.

We waited, not knowing what to do.

One of the funerals began to disperse. Hafez approached a male mourner. "Excuse me, sir, but did someone in your party call for Father Khaliq?" The man shook his head, pointing to the other party.

We waited for the second party to disperse.

Hafez asked a mourner, "Did a lady in your party call for Father Khaliq? We are trying to find him."

"Perhaps."

"Can you point out which lady called for him?"

"I think she is in that group up ahead – one of the professional mourners."

We tried to catch up with the group indicated, but they were already passing through another gate.

Hafez shouted after the dispersing women. "Ladies, which of you called for Father Khaliq? We are also looking for him!"

Several of the women turned around to look at Hafez. They seemed to be amused, turned again and continued on their way.

"Damn! Why are they so rude?"

I shrugged. "Leave it, Hafez."

* * *

Before dinner at the hotel, I turned on the Al Jazeera news. The news from Cairo was sickening! A car bomb had been detonated outside the museum. Thirty-seven people had been killed – about half of them tourists. They want to destroy our tourist industry – our lifeblood! There was a video of the aftermath: shattered cars, debris everywhere, confused men in day-glow vests moving here and there, emergency lights flashing. Fortunately, the victims had been removed. There was also a story about 'a major incident in the Sinai'. There was an anonymous mobile phone video of Egyptian army troops carrying rifles and running toward a village. The newsreader said: "The Egyptian army says they have engaged terrorists in northern Sinai, and have cleared the area."

Cleared the area! How can they put out rubbish like that? No mention of casualties.

I called Wahida's mobile. She said, "I spoke with Kalifa. His unit wasn't involved, but he said that there are rumors that there were a lot of casualties in the unit which was attacked at four o'clock this morning in their barracks. Apparently the security wasn't so good. He said not to worry: they have excellent security."

"Not to worry!" I repeated. "How can I not worry?"

"I know, Papa, it's awful! When are you coming home?"

"The day after tomorrow. Please stay out of downtown Cairo, Wahida."

* * *

Over dinner, Hafez reminded me: "Our flight is at ten fifteen tomorrow morning."

"I think I'll reschedule it for a day later."

Hafez regarded me through narrowed eyes. "What are you going to do?"

"The one thing we haven't done: see some of the Christian landmarks."

Hafez considered this for a moment, then shook his head. "I don't think I'm interested."

"I didn't think you would be."

He regarded me thoughtfully. "I suppose it's because of Elizabeth and Wahida."

I gave a concessionary nod. "Wahida would expect that I take at least a slight interest – not that she has the smallest expectation of my conversion."

I asked Hafez if he had heard the latest news from home. He hadn't.

"I don't understand why we can't wipe these bastards out," I said. "We have a huge army!"

"That would involve a lot of casualties."

"Even if it did involve a lot of casualties, wouldn't it be better to be rid of these terrorists, once and for all?"

"Kareem, with all respect, you don't understand how terrorists work. When you try to attack them head-on, they melt away. They look for a weak spot, attack and melt away again. That's why the Americans could never win in Vietnam."

"But," I protested, "the Viet Cong had horrendous losses."

"They didn't care and it didn't matter. There were always three new recruits to replace each fallen hero."

"But Hafez, it's an appalling philosophy: human life is worth nothing; what's important is that we are in power with our form of government."

"Part of the problem, Kareem, is that human life is worth so little in these situations. In Vietnam, peasants wading in rice fields all their meager lives with no chance of betterment are offered a chance to be a hero, creating a communist paradise for their children. In Egypt unemployed, uneducated, impoverished young men with no future sign on to Wilayat Sinai for two or three hundred pounds a month, plus food, comradeship, accommodation and clothing for an opportunity to create a true Islamic state with benefits for all."

* * *

How was I going to have a look at the important Christian sites in one day? When I proposed this question to the concierge at the hotel, his response was, "Professor, there are at least two solutions. One can hire a guide, and he will take you here and there to the various Christian churches. Or, with the same guide, one can follow the Stations of the Cross. The first option gives one a smattering of Christian history and beliefs. The second option concentrates on what Christians believe about the last day in the life of the prophet Jesus."

"What are the Stations of the Cross?" I asked.

"Christians believe that the prophet Jesus followed a certain route through the Old City on his way from being condemned to death until he was placed in a tomb. Along that route, Christians believe that certain things happened. Each of these events is given a number and a location on the route."

"And my guide would explain each of these events?"

"Exactly."

"How long is the route?"
"I'm told that it is six hundred meters."
"I will select this option."

* * *

I would summarize my feelings about the Via Dolorosa (Way of Suffering) on which the Stations of the Cross are located as sadness at a preordained, cataclysmic event which is steeped in improbable folklore and myth. Why do I say 'sadness'? It's not just that my guide, a young priest named Father Simone, took a sorrowful view of Via Dolorosa. He did. Rather, it was that no event on the Via Dolorosa hinted at the ultimate outcome: a resurrected Jesus. Father Simone was clear in his belief that Jesus is alive today, and reigns alongside God, His Father. This is the same belief that Elizabeth and Wahida have. The only omens that there could be a joyous outcome from Via Dolorosa are the sense of preordination and the enormous ceremony in which Via Dolorosa is surrounded: swarms of believing faithful, and a magnificent, mysterious candle-lit cathedral. Why do they call it a 'church'?

The preordination is, it seems to me, part of the mystery and the significance. From the sentencing of Jesus to his burial on the same day, there could be no deviation. How could the Jewish leaders, the Roman authorities, and the people who had adored Jesus, the rabbi, have failed to raise a single voice of dissent against the murder of a guiltless man? When I asked Father Simone about this, he said, "You are right, Professor. His guiltless death was preordained. It was God who sent his Son into the world with a new message of life eternal and living without sin."

I had mixed feelings about the interior of the Church of the Holy Sepulcher: everything is there in close proximity: the Rock of Calvary on which the crucifixion took place, the stone on which Jesus' body was prepared for burial, a prison where he was kept, and his tomb. How could all of this have been within one hundred meters? When I asked Father Simone about this, he said, "Well, there are different theories about the exact locations, but here it is all to be venerated." And this is what I felt when I crawled into Jesus' Tomb: Maybe this isn't the exact tomb where Jesus lay, but this place feels holy, and I believe that Jesus lay in a tomb like this somewhere.

Before we parted company, I asked Father Simone, "What do Christians believe about Muslims like me? Do they consider that we can have eternal life, even though we believe that Jesus was a great prophet, but not the son of God?"

"I cannot speak for all Christians, but I believe that Jesus' promise of eternal life to all who truly love God and who love others as themselves applies to all people in the world."

Chapter 10

Rome

"Papa, I don't know what we can do! He says there are skirmishes with Wilayat Sinai almost every day!"

I asked, "What are these skirmishes, Wahida?"

"He says they're out on patrol or they get called out, and then the shooting starts. Just when they think they've got the terrorists pinned down they disappear into a settlement."

"Are there casualties?"

"He says that occasionally they kill one or two terrorists, who almost never leave their wounded behind."

"How about Army casualties?"

"Kalifa says that they are all under strict orders not to discuss casualties."

I felt suffocated in a blanket of anxiety, dark and confining. How could it have come to this? My little boy – to me he was always the naïve, precocious, handsome one – was in unbearable danger. It had just happened: he wanted some valuable Army experience. OK. But then he chose Sinai. I should have prevented it – told him 'No!' – Choose Cairo! Choose Alexandria! But I didn't know! Oh, Elizabeth! I really didn't know that Sinai would be so dangerous!

I became aware that Wahida was looking at me with great intensity. My lips were trembling. She was shaking her head.

"What?" I asked

"You think you could have sent him somewhere else?"

"Yes!   Maybe. I don't know."

"Not a chance, Papa. It was his choice. If you had said, 'You must take a post in Cairo!' he would have disobeyed you."

She stepped forward and put her arms around me. I clasped her head against my shoulder so that she would not see my brimming eyes. "Papa, I'm sure he'll be OK. He's so clever and resourceful. You know that."

I fumbled quickly for my pocket handkerchief and blew my nose. In the same motion, I wiped my eyes. Wahida was handing me her handkerchief with a look of compassionate familiarity. "It's OK, Papa."

This young woman – my daughter – understands me more than I knew.

"Sit down, Papa, over here. Tell me about Jerusalem. I've never been there and some day, I'd like to go."

"You want to hear about the Christian part?"

"No, tell me everything. How was Hafez? Was he a good companion?"

"You know Hafez. He has his own mind about things."

I told her about the trips to the Golan Heights and to Ramallah, leaving out the visit to the Martyr's Cemetery.

"Still, that must have been quite interesting, and could you really see the fighting in Syria?"

"It was so far away that it seemed almost unreal – as if one were Allah looking down on the distant, angry men on earth."

The analogy made her smile. "And what did you do in the evenings?"

"Most evenings I was on my own."

"Where was Hafez?"

"Well, he was . . . he was otherwise engaged."

Sensing juicy gossip, she leaned forward. "Come on, Papa, tell me!"

"Well, he met a . . ."

"Woman, and?"

"And . . . well, he spent some time with her. This is not to be repeated, Wahida!" I added sternly.

In acknowledgement, she clasped her lips between thumb and forefinger. "Did you meet a woman, Papa?"

"No! Absolutely not!" I slapped the arm of the chair for emphasis.

She frowned. "Why not?"

"Well," I spluttered, "in the first place, she would probably be Jewish in Jerusalem."

"Probably, not necessarily, but what difference does it make if she was nice?"

I was still irritated. "Wahida, I don't go around picking up women!"

"I'm talking about meeting women – nice women."

"I don't see the need for that."

"Well, I do! Papa, you are lonely! You need to be with a woman – a nice woman, like Adeeba!"

"Wahida, I'm not lonely. I have my colleagues at the university – my students – I have my family."

"Papa, you're not friendly with any of your colleagues – not even Hafez – and your students can't be your friends. The only family you have at the moment is me. Papa, you need a nice woman!"

At the time I thought, Typical woman's harangue! But later, I began to count the number of friends I actually had. There was Hafez, there was a colleague in the ancient languages department, but I seldom had much contact with him. There were half a dozen old friends from my student days, but they seemed to have drifted off. There were some neighbors: we didn't seem to have much in common. Was I lonely? I didn't think so. I was pretty much self-sufficient. But what would it be like to have somebody like Elizabeth? The remote prospect was enticing and frightening.

* * *

"So, what did you think about Jerusalem, overall, Papa?"

I considered this for a time. "I think it's the usual story about religious contradictions: does one believe or not; is there proof or not; is it logical or fanciful? In Jerusalem one finds three major religions; they share one principle belief – in one all-powerful God; and they share one important value – be kind to your fellow man. But each, in its committed zeal, belittles and nit-picks at the others: 'You can't pray here! This is my prayer area!'"

A smile of amusement crept across Wahida's face. "And what do you make of these contradictions, Papa?"

"It would be easy enough to blame them on human nature as long as they remained petty," I said, "but they're not petty! Religious people can become savagely indifferent to human life! It's almost as if there were an inhuman force for evil at work."

Wahida gave a nod of confirmation. "Papa, Christians call that force 'the devil'."

"And Muslims call him Satan," I added.

"I never heard you mention Satan before, Papa."

"I haven't thought much about him before."

"So, you think there is a real Satan?"

"I don't know, Wahida. He's a very convenient explanation."

"An explanation for humanity's major shortcomings?"

"Yes, exactly, but perhaps he is a little too convenient."

"If he's not there, one needs to find another explanation."

"Perhaps the explanation is that man – or some men – have a genetic weakness: evil."

"But why would man, alone, of all the creatures on earth, have this genetic weakness?"

"Some wild animals are cruel, Wahida."

"But Papa, 'cruel' implies the conscious infliction of suffering. Lions don't kill an antelope to see it suffer; they kill it to survive!"

"Wahida, do you remember that cat, Petunia, we used to have?"

"Yes, the black and white one."

"You remember how it used to bring half-dead mice into the house and bat them around the kitchen floor?"

"Yes, but I always thought that Petunia was playing hunting games with the mouse. I doubt that Petunia was aware that the mouse was suffering."

* * *

It had become somewhat of a habit: having lunch with Adeeba in the faculty dining room – if she wasn't away on a dig. She certainly was an excellent woman: good looking for someone in her fifties; bright and successful – she had a worldwide reputation as a scholar of the ancient Copts; and she was always cheerful. I couldn't figure out how some-one could always be cheerful. Yes, of course her university position, her economic and family situations were all secure, but, in my experience, that's not enough to assure that one can have a sunny disposition. I mean, it's enough to have an ugly, bad-tempered driver in an old wreck of a car cut you off from your place in a queue, and have the temerity to shake his fist at you to bring revengeful thoughts to mind. But I had come to take Adeeba's sunny disposition for granted. What I really couldn't understand was why she seemed to like me. Of course, I had grown to admire her unashamedly and look forward to her lunch-time company. But it didn't seem to be just polite, reciprocal friendship. Adeeba, if she put her mind to it, could have most any man she wanted: why me? I was not bad looking, but certainly not handsome. Yes, I was depart-ment head of a major university. So what? Was I a witty con-versationalist with an infectious sense of humor? Certainly not! What then? Could it possibly be that I somehow triggered an instinctive feminine response from Adeeba? What was it about me? I didn't know, and I certainly didn't dare to ask.

We had been talking about my trip to Jerusalem. She had enlightened me on some of the ancient linkages between the Druze and Christianity. When I told her that I had followed the Stations of the Cross, she laughed out loud.

"What's so funny?" I asked. "I thought it was rather sad."

"The Via Dolorosa is sad," she said, "What I find amusing is that a Muslim like you, who knows the sanctions on apostasy, would walk the Via Dolorosa with a Christian guide."

"Why not? I have no intention of becoming a Christian – far too late for that – but I wanted to find out for myself what all the fuss was about."

"Good for you, Kareem! I like the 'why not?' spirit!" She paused for a moment. "Does your 'why not?' spirit extend as far as Rome?"

I felt a surge of inexplicable excitement. "Why not?"

"OK, good. I thought between the bank holidays and Muhammad's birthday at the end of the year, when the university is closed, we might go."

"Yes, I look forward to it." I really do! I removed the iPhone from my jacket pocket.

"How about leaving on the twenty-eighth and returning on the second of January?" she asked.

"Yes, that's fine."

"I'll make my reservations through the university travel service and send you an email, so you can get the same flights and hotel."

We then went on to talk about her discovery at a recent archaeology site. "It appears to be a diary, written on papyrus, but it's not in good condition."

"Can you read it?"

"Some of it. I don't recognize some of the characters, and I don't know whether it's the author's handwriting, or something I haven't seen before – like a dialect."

"Is it fair to assume that only an important person would have kept a diary?"

"Yes, I think so, but its historical importance will depend on what he – or she – had to say."

"May I join you?" It was Hafez, tray in hand.

"We've finished lunch, Hafez," I warned him, hoping he would take the hint.

Adeeba said, "It's OK, Hafez, I have to go and prepare for a class." She rose, gave us a smile and left.

Hafez gave me his investigator's look. "What have you two been talking about? Christianity?"

"No," I said, evenly, "we were talking about an ancient diary written on papyrus that she's discovered."

"How interesting. The two of you have become quite an item."

"What are you talking about, Hafez?"

"It's obvious that you are more than just colleagues."

"Oh, for goodness' sake, Hafez. I've known Adeeba for thirty years. She was my wife's best friend."

"And now," he said with a flourish, "she's your best friend!"

"Hafez, we're not in kindergarten; we're colleagues at university."

"I'm not jealous. I would just like to make you aware of the dangers."

"What dangers?"

"People talk."

"You mean people gossip."

"Exactly."

"So?"

"Well, they might say things that you don't like, so be careful."

"Hafez, thank you for your advice. I'm sure you have the best of intentions. I also have to prepare for a class." I gave him a nod and left.

* * *

The next morning I had an email from Adeeba giving me the details of her Egyptair flights and advising me that she had booked a room at the Hotel Campo De' Fiori. The Egyptair flights were non-stop and reasonably priced (there was competition from Alitalia). She said she'd stayed at Hotel Campo De' Fiori previously, and while it was 'a little expensive', she said it was 'lovely'. I checked the room rate: $370 per night! Maybe because it's the holiday season. Other four star hotels were similarly priced, and some of the five stars were twice as much and more! Three hundred and seventy dollars per night was certainly more than I would have spent for myself. I can't very well book myself into a cheaper hotel – even one close by. That would make me look cheap and coordination difficult. Could I ask her to share? No! That would send the wrong signals, entirely! I looked at the photographs of the hotel and the reviews which had been posted. It looks and sounds very good. Kareem, if you like Adeeba, and you want to show your interest in her, you have to go for it. I did.

* * *

My junior class in classical Arabic philosophy was studying Al-Kindi, among others. Al-Kindi, "the philosopher of the Arabs", was born in 185 AH (801 AD). His contribution to philosophy is mainly in his assimilation and appropriation of Greek philosophy and science. But he did not accept all of Greek philosophy: for example, he rejected the eternity of the world, in contradiction with Ibn Rushd and others. I felt it would be a good exercise for my class to write a paper explaining how Al-Kindi reached the conclusion that the world is finite (in time) rather than infinite. I told them, "Don't just parrot what Al-Kindi says. That will not help me conclude whether or not you understand Al-Kindi. Write your paper as a letter to your grandmother, in simple Arabic, using words that she would understand. There are bonus points for those of you who submit a paper with your grandmother's handwritten endorsement." This instruction generated a good deal of tittering among my students.

In fact, Al-Kindi's logic is not easy to follow. It depends on concepts of measuring time. In Rasa' al-Kindi l-falsafiya he says, for instance: "Before every partition in time (for example, a day) there is a partition (such as an earlier day) until one arrives at a partition before which there is no partition, that is to say, a partitioned duration before which there is no partitioned duration." And he goes on from there.

One of my students had written: "Grandma, there has to be a starting point for time, because if there isn't, how can we measure time?"

That's not exactly what Al-Kindi said, but she has the germ of his idea.

I was writing comments in the margin of her paper when Hafez came in, unannounced. He sat down in front of me, waiting for my attention. "Good afternoon, Hafez." I put my pen down.

"Kareem, didn't I tell you to be careful?"

"Yes, I think you did. What recklessness have I committed?"

"You know perfectly well!"

"I'm afraid I don't."

"You are taking a woman who is no relation to you to a foreign city for several days, unchaperoned!"

"I am?"

"Yes! Don't try to deny it! You told me you were going away over the holidays, and I assumed you were going to Al Jamiah, but your secretary said she didn't think so. I found out you're going to Rome and that Adeeba is going to Rome at the same time."

"Probably just a coincidence," I said, trying to hide my amusement.

"Is it a coincidence that you two are going on the same flights and staying in the same hotel?"

"How do you know that?" I was beginning to bristle.

"I happen to have a source in the travel service!"

I sat back and thought for several moments. "Hafez, when you cautioned me before, you mentioned 'gossip'."

"Of course I did!"

"And how far have you spread this gossip?"

Hafez recoiled. "Kareem, how can you say something like that?"

"So you and the travel service are the only ones who know about this travesty?" He nodded. "I don't think there's a problem, Hafez, because I'll have a word with the travel service and I know you would not engage in gossip because you wouldn't want to hear of gossip about a substantial blonde Russian Jewess."

He sat in resentful silence for a moment. "Setting aside the gossip, are you sure, Kareem, that this is a wise thing to do?"

"Yes, I am sure. We are old friends, we are staying in separate rooms and she is going to show me St Peter's and the other sites in Rome."

"So you're thinking of converting."

"No! I have no intention of converting. But I think it's about time I learned something about the religion of my daughter and late wife."

When Hafez left, I picked up the telephone and dialed travel services. "May I speak to Adel, please? It's Professor al-Busiri." (Adel Mansour was a nervous man, and head of travel services.)

"Adel speaking, how can I help you, Professor?"

There was an accusatory tone in my voice. "I thought you ran a professional service, Adel."

"Indeed, we like to think so, Professor."

"Would you consider it professional if one of your employees engaged in gossip about the travel plans of university professors?"

"No, indeed not, Professor. Has something of that nature occurred?"

"Perhaps you could have a word with your employees, Adel. I'm sure they would be very disappointed if the university decided to outsource its travel services."

* * *

Was I too heavy-handed? I didn't think so. Egyptians love gossip, particularly male-female gossip in hierarchical organizations like universities. Was a worst-case scenario likely to be quite grim? No. But I felt it could be an irritation for Adeeba, and if she suspected that I was the source of the gossip, could her view of me continue to be favorable? Was I acting like a moon-struck teenager whose overriding ambition is to grow the affections of a particular female? Not really. But are teenage ambitions to be condemned?

* * *

Kalifa called in the evening – at the time that Wahida usually called him. "I've got a three-day pass and I'm coming home on Friday."

"Kalifa," I said, "that's great news! Where and when can I pick you up?"

He said he would call when his bus was approaching the Fayid military base, which is just east of Cairo.

"What would you like to do during your three days?" I asked.

"Eat, sleep and see Sagira."

Wahida was about to say something until I held up a hand.

"Oh, and I want to see you, Papa, and Wahida."

"Phew!" I said, "I thought you'd disinherited us for a moment!"

"Not a chance, Papa. I definitely want to talk to you both."

* * *

Later, I asked Wahida, "What do you suppose he wants to talk to us about?"

"He wants to get engaged to Sagira."

I knew that Sagira and Kalifa were very good friends, and that perhaps they had talked about getting married some day, but I thought the issue would arise after he left the army.

"Are you sure that's what he wants to talk about? He has almost two years of army service remaining."

"Papa, there are married officers in the army, and yes, I'm pretty sure."

* * *

Wahida was right.

Kalifa was barely in the door when he sat us down, and without introduction said, "I want to do things the right way, Papa. You have to ask Adeeba if I can marry Sagira."

I shook my head dolefully. "What if she says 'No!'?"

Kalifa recoiled in horror. "She won't say 'no', Papa!"

I looked at the ceiling. "I just want to know your backup plan."

"Papa, I . . ." He broke into a smile. "Come on, Papa, this is serious stuff."

"I know it's serious and I'm delighted!"

I had never seen such happiness on my son's face. I wish Elizabeth were here!

Kalifa held his clasped hands to his chest. "We need to work out the mahr (money paid by the groom's family to the bride's family for expenses) and I'll need your advice on the shabka (valuable jewelry given to the bride-to-be)." Breathlessly, he continued, "I need your advice, too, Wahida."

"The mahr doesn't need to be paid on the engagement, but before the wedding," I said.

"Do you know Sagira's taste in jewelry?" Wahida asked.

Kalifa looked from one to the other of us. "Yes, but the amount has to be agreed at the engagement. No, not really. She has simple gold bracelets."

"If she says 'yes', I can talk to Adeeba about the mahr."

"Do you think she would like a necklace?"

"Can you see Adeeba tomorrow, Papa? Maybe she'd rather have a ring."

"I'll call her first thing in the morning."

"Are you thinking of a ring with a stone?"

"Do you think she's home on Friday morning? Maybe a diamond or an emerald."

"OK," I said, with a calming gesture, "I can see Adeeba tomorrow morning. She will probably say 'yes'. After that, we can talk about the mahr. She'll probably need to think about it. Then I can ask her about Sagira's taste in jewelry. OK?" There were nods. "When are you two thinking of getting married?"

"As soon as possible."

"There aren't any other . . . ah . . . circumstances involved?"

"No, Papa!" Kalifa said with exasperation. "We love each other and we want to get married."

Elizabeth would say it. I better say it. "Are you sure you want to get married now and live apart for two years, while you're in Sinai? Isn't it better to marry when your service is over and you can live together?"

"No, Papa, it's not!" Each word was deliberate. "Sagira and I have talked it over and we've made a decision."

OK, Elizabeth. I tried.

* * *

"Adeeba, have you a little time today that I can come to see you?"

She hesitated. "Yes . . . of course." There was an edge of uncertainty in her voice. "What's going on, Kareem?"

"Kalifa is home on a three-day pass, and he asked me to have a chat with you."

"Oh! I see!" The uncertainty was gone. "Yes. Any time. This morning?"

* * *

I was seated at the table in Adeeba's modern kitchen, a cup of coffee, sugar and milk in front of me. Adeeba was wearing jeans and a fluffy white sweater. She was chatty, relaxed and seemingly ignorant of the nervousness I felt on behalf of my son. I had rehearsed a little speech about how proud I was of Kalifa, how certain I was that he had a bright future ahead of him, and how lovely a young woman Sagira was – all leading up to the big question. I even had some points I could make in the event of a 'let me think about it' response. But, what if she says 'no' or 'not now'? The only response I could think of was 'why?', but I knew the response would only cut Kalifa (and me) deeper.

Adeeba sat down opposite me with a smile and stirred her coffee. "What is it you wanted to chat about, Kareem?"

To hell with the speech! "Kalifa would like your permission to marry Sagira."

"Yes, of course."

For a moment, I was dumbstruck. "Thank you, Adeeba!"

She laughed. "Kareem, did you think for a minute that Sagira hasn't been hounding me about getting married? Thank you, Kareem!" She kissed the tips of her fingers and brushed my cheek.

"Well," I said, still trying to get my bearings, "there is the matter of mahr to be settled."

She nodded. "As I understand it, they want to get married soon. That suggests it will be when Kalifa can next get some leave. The situation being what it is in Sinai, granting of leave is likely to be a last-minute decision. So we won't be able to plan months ahead for a big wedding. I don't think Sagira wants a big wedding anyway. If we were to ask for fifteen thousand pounds (£1200 Sterling), would that be all right?"

I had prepared myself for a request of about one hundred thousand. "Yes, that's fine, Adeeba. May I ask your advice about the shabka? What are Sagira's tastes in jewelry?"

Adeeba laughed. "She doesn't have any taste in jewelry because she has only a few bracelets. Don't go overboard, Kareem. A nice ring would be fine."

"Kalifa was thinking of a ring with a good stone."

"That's fine."

"Her eyes are hazel, if I remember. Would an emerald be appropriate?"

"Not too big, Kareem. Don't spoil her!"

I reached across the table, and she shook my hand. Adeeba stood up. "I'm going to call Sagira." Then . . . "Sagira, come down, please!"

My daughter-in-law-to-be appeared in the doorway, wearing a white dress covered with green flowers. God, she is pretty. Sagira is a tall girl, slender and graceful, with long dark hair. Kalifa has chosen well. She looked from me to her mother, gauging the situation.

Adeeba said, "It's all settled – except the date, Sagira."

"Oh, Mama, thank you!" She rushed at her mother and embraced her. Then she turned to face me, her face wet with tears, and she gave me a deep bow. "Thank you, Professor!"

I shook my head. "I am only a happy messenger; please call me Kareem."

"Sagira, sit down," Adeeba suggested. "We should talk about a party. When does Kalifa have to return?"

"Monday."

"Yes, Monday."

"OK, so the party's tomorrow. And we'll have it here," Adeeba announced. "It will just be family and a few close friends.

I don't want to explain the short notice to others. Kareem, how many will you have?"

I thought for a moment. "My family, including Naqib, is five and three children. Probably three or four friends. Say eight adults and three small children."

"Don't you have a brother?"

"Yes, but he wouldn't understand the short notice. He would like to come to the wedding."

"Shall we say six o'clock tomorrow?" Adeeba asked.

* * *

"Well done, Papa!" Kalifa almost shouted in my ear, embracing me on my return.

"Well done, you, Kalifa. She's a lovely girl."

"How much is the mahr?"

"That's not your business."

"And the shabka?"

"A ring with an emerald would be fine."

"Can you come with me to help me, Papa? I don't have much money."

"Can you go with him, Wahida?" I asked.

"Yes, sure."

I fumbled in my billfold. "Here's my credit card; the PIN is 1074. The upper limit is twenty thousand pounds. Off you go."

It was a moment of great happiness for me, watching brother and sister go out the door together. If Elizabeth could see them! Kalifa's feet barely touched the ground, and he was chattering like a five year old at a birthday party. Wahida was caught up in empathy for the groom and bride, but proud also of her status: older sister/wise adviser.

Two hours later they returned with a receipt from Damas Jewelers for nineteen thousand five hundred, and a small gold box with a silver ribbon.

"Sit down, Papa. You have to see!" Kalifa ordered.

Wahida dexterously untied the ribbon, lifted the lid and took out the white cushion. There was a gold band surmounted by an emerald and two small diamonds.

"It's very nice," I said. "How about the size?"

"It fits me and her hands are about the same as mine," Wahida responded, "but if not, Damas will resize it."

Kalifa added, with great satisfaction, "Thank you, Papa. Thank you very much! The emerald is just under a carat and a half." He began reassembling the box. "I'm going to take it to her now!"

* * *

I was half listening to Wahida chattering about the shabka selection process. Then she asked, "How was your meeting with Adeeba?"

"It was fine. She was very pleasant and helpful. When I arrived at her house, she seemed to know why I was there, but at first, when I spoke to her on the phone, she seemed to be a little nervous. Strange."

Wahida shook her head, but she said nothing.

"You don't think it's strange, Wahida?"

"No."

"Why not?"

"Papa, she knew from Sagira that there was the possibility of a marriage proposal, but she was probably hoping for another proposal."

"Another proposal?" I was puzzled.

"Think, Papa."

Another proposal? Another proposal? Not business or financial. Personal? "Oh. Do you really think so?"

* * *

After being harassed by Wahida about my scarcity of friends, I called Hafez and invited him and his wife to the engagement party. I also called Professor Ibrahim Elbadry, my colleague in the Classics Department, and invited him and his wife. To both men, I explained the reason for the short notice: my son's Army service in Sinai. They were both happy to accept. In Ibrahim's case, I thought, *It's probably my fault that we haven't seen much of each other. I've got to make more effort.*

* * *

Adeeba's house was furnished with contemporary Persian carpets and polished antique furniture. It was comfortable and welcoming. The day of the party, it smelled of jasmine: the plants themselves with their copious white, waxy flowers, were placed where they could be seen. Garlands of white bunting were hung from the ceilings, and a piano concerto was playing softly in the background.

Adeeba wore a simple green dress. Perhaps she didn't want to compete with Sagira in her sculptured white silk dress. I noticed that Sagira's right hand, on which the ring appeared, hovered perpetually between her chest and her throat. Kalifa, in his dress Army lieutenant's uniform, was always beside her. This is a couple which could appear on the cover of a celebrity magazine!

"Thank you very much for inviting us to this special occasion, Kareem," Hafez burbled. "This is an important party! Your son and his wife to be – she's lovely – look so happy. And I think the way Adeeba has arranged the alcohol is very clever."

"Oh? I haven't noticed."

"Yes. All the fruit juices and soft drinks are here or in the dining room. But I've seen some people – I guess they're Christians – carrying glasses of champagne, and I found out that the champagne is available in the kitchen."

"Oh, I see." I whispered, "Well, I won't tell anyone if you have a glass of champagne."

Hafez shook his head and frowned. "I couldn't possibly drink champagne in front of Professor Elbadry!"

Elbadry's wife, Sara, was a small, effusive lady, dressed in an elaborate silk pantsuit and too much jewelry. "Kareem, it's very kind of you to invite us to this festive event. I'm so happy for your son and his lovely bride to be. It's wonderful. And it's so good for Ibrahim to get out and socialize! He doesn't see enough of his friends. I will certainly invite you and Adeeba over for dinner sometime soon!"

Later, I puzzled over the potential invitation to me and Adeeba. Is Adeeba going to be asked to reciprocate for the invitation today or because she is seen as my 'special friend'? Does it matter?

Naqib, Anisa, the two little girls, and my infant grandson asleep in a portable baby basket arrived about six-thirty. Anisa and her daughters gravitated to Wahida, the two women speaking in confidential tones.

Naqib shook Kalifa's hand warmly. I moved closer. I want to see how they get along. Naqib was fingering the three service decorations on Kalifa's left breast. "That one's for service in a combat zone," Kalifa was saying.

"And this one in the middle with the silver stars?"

"That's for leadership in combat."

"You got it more than once?"

"Twice."

"How do they decide when to award it?"

"It's supposed to be for something like 'outstanding leadership'. I don't know. The colonel decides."

"And this blue one here?"

"That's for combat-related injuries."

"I didn't know you'd been wounded." (I must confess I didn't know about it either.)

Sagira intervened; her tone was slightly hostile. "Yes, Naqib, he was hit in the leg," she pointed to his left calf, "by a piece of shrapnel from a mortar bomb."

"It's all right now?" Naqib asked. "I keep telling you to get transferred out of Sinai, Kalifa. There are plenty of other places where you can serve."

To no one in particular, Sagira said, "So Sinai – and then Egypt – can be taken over by terrorists."

"Naqib," Kalifa began, with a gesture that included himself, "this is me! Do you understand? I am a combat infantry officer! That's who I am. I am not some smart-looking officer on a parade ground."

Repenting, quietly Naqib said, "I'm just concerned about the danger you are in."

"There would be less danger," Sagira said, "if the terrorists were not supplied with weapons."

Naqib turned away.

That girl, Sagira, may look like a naïve doll, but she's got some fangs!

Professor Elbadry came over to me toward the end of the party. "Kareem," he said, "I want to congratulate you on your family! Your son, Kalifa, the bridegroom-to-be, is exemplary! He is fighting for the survival of his country against sinister subversives. Wahida, your daughter, works for the Red Crescent providing much-needed aid to desperate Egyptians, and your son, Naqib, who works for a law firm, tells me that his firm provides pro bono legal assistance to poor Egyptians."

Are members of the Brotherhood who want to overthrow the government of 'poor Egyptians'"? But I bit my tongue. "That's very kind of you, Ibrahim. I'm very glad that you and Sara were able to join us. We haven't had much chance to socialize lately."

"You are correct, and we will put that right." Then, in a more personal tone: "I understand that you and Hafez have been on the Hajj. Sara and I would like to go, but we are concerned about safety. It seems like every year there's a terrible tragedy where hundreds of people are trampled to death."

"Hafez and I took one of the VIP escorted packages, and we were moved by bus from one location to another, so we did very little walking. Of course, we could see the great streams of people moving about, but we weren't aware of any accidents."

Ibrahim nodded, "Well, as we know, the Saudis are apt to cover up any news which reflects badly on them. But could you send me the details of the agency you and Hafez used?"

* * *

When the new university campus was opened in New Cairo, a new, larger library was built there. It is an impressive building, clad in white marble, six stories high. Most of that height is taken up by the stacks, where several million books are arranged on row after row of shelves, according to an Arabic version of the Dewey Decimal System. Professors, instructors and students who have been assigned a thesis have access to the stacks, where they can not only find a particular book but they can peruse it before borrowing. Those without stack permits must fill out a request form and wait for a library attendant to retrieve it from the stacks.

In the American University Library stacks, there is a precious collection of works by Arabic philosophers – some are actually handwritten. I find this collection to be very useful when I have the need to read what a particular philosopher actually said, when all that is otherwise available is a summary or outline.

Fortunately for users like me, there are a few tables and chairs scattered about each level of the stacks. I can take an ancient, leather-bound book down from the shelves to a table, and there read and take notes. It is very quiet in the stacks: there are few people, and those who are seeking a book, find it, and go to the check-out desk on the ground floor. As you might expect, there is seldom another person in the philosophy section.

* * *

On a Wednesday afternoon, I was sitting at the desk on the fifth floor of the stack, reading a handwritten manuscript of Hayy ibn Yaqzan (Alive Son of Awake), a philosophical novel written by Ibn Tufayl in the fifth century AH (12th century AD). In the book, the protagonist, Son of Awake, suddenly finds himself on a desert island, and explores the natural things around him. The antique writing is sometimes unclear, the exposition is not always captivating, and the stacks were silent as a cave. I found my mind wandering from time to time.

"Good afternoon, Professor."

I looked up in surprise. There, opposite me, stood Princess Basheera, dressed in dark jeans, a loose grey kameez and a midnight blue niqab.

"Oh, good afternoon, Princess. Please sit down. If you had called, I could have met you anywhere."

"That's all right Professor. I was able to obtain a stack permit in connection with my studies, and I decided to drop in on you." She sat down at the table.

"May I ask what you are studying, Princess?"

"My interests tend to be comprehensive. At the moment, I am trying to define the overlap between ethics and morality."

"Al-Farabi touched on the subject of ethics in Directing Attention to the Way to Happiness."

"Yes, I know, but he defines ethics as arising from a knowledge of mathematics. I am seeking a more practical understanding."

"I'm afraid I can't help you there."

"Actually, I think we could jointly arrive at such a practical understanding, but at the moment, I am more interested in hearing about your trip to Jerusalem."

I started by describing the Noble Sanctuary (Temple Mount).

"And do you believe that the Prophet actually flew on a horse named Buraq to Jerusalem and on the heaven?"

"No, I don't think so."

"What do you believe, Professor, about the Night Journey?"

"I believe that the Prophet dreamt of the flight to Jerusalem and on to heaven, and I believe that in the dream he actually spoke to Gabriel, Moses, Elihah, other prophets, and that he spoke to Allah."

She nodded. I continued my description of Jerusalem.

"So you walked the Via Dolorosa," she said. "What do you make of that journey?"

"I think that it really happened: that there was a Jesus who was wrongly condemned to death, walked to his crucifixion, died and was buried."

"What about rising from the dead?"

"I believe in an afterlife."

"But Christians believe his body was resurrected and that He is the Son of God."

"I am not a Christian, Princess."

She sat back in thought for a moment. "Professor, do you see a common purpose in the stories of the Night Journey and the Via Dolorosa?"

That's a good question.

"Yes," I said. "Both journeys promote the protagonists – Muhammad and Jesus – in their special relationship of prophet with God. They are both stories that capture our attention and interest by stretching belief: in Muhammad's case by the inclusion of Buraq, and in Jesus case by his bodily resurrection. It seems to me that the stretching of belief is what makes each story so important, and by its importance demands belief."

"So you're saying that if each story were more ordinary, it would be less worthy of attention and therefore less credible."

"Exactly!"

"For you, Professor, how does Allah figure in all of this?"

I had to think for a moment. "He is the obscured focus of both stories in the sense that He is the reason for both journeys: for Muhammad to converse with Him, and for Jesus to demonstrate His message."

Princess Basheera leaned forward. "In that case, if Allah is the focus, isn't his message, 'believe in Me!'?"

"Yes, I think so."

"Do you believe in Him?"

"Yes, but the quality of my belief is threadbare," I conceded.

"What do you mean, Professor?"

"I accept the logic – the concept – of Allah, but there is no personal connection. He is not in my heart."

She nodded. "Sometimes, it takes desperation to find Him."

"Fortunately – or unfortunately – I am not desperate."

She regarded me for some moments, then: "Professor, I understand that you are planning a trip to Rome."

"How did that come to your attention? I have told almost no one, Princess."

Her eyes took on an additional sparkle, and she shrugged. "As you already know, I take a special interest in your situation, Professor."

She's not going to tell me how she knew. "Yes, I am going to Rome in a few weeks' time with an old friend . . . of my late wife's. She happens to be a Coptic woman." I paused. "Do you think that's all right?"

"Yes, indeed I do!"

"Oh! Thank you! Of course, I'll still look for Father Khaliq."

"You will have difficulty finding him there."

I was surprised. "Because he doesn't go to Rome?"

"No, I understand that he goes there frequently, but under a different name."

"What would his Roman name be?"

"Unfortunately, I am not at liberty to tell you. I wish you a memorable trip, Professor."

Princess Basheera rose, walked down the stack corridor, and disappeared.

Is she real? I mused. Well, at least she approves of my trip with Adeeba.

* * *

I wondered how Adeeba would handle the wedding protocols: her Coptic daughter marrying a Muslim soldier. I don't recall that there were any difficulties when Elizabeth and I married in a Methodist ceremony in Chicago – at least I had no discussions about religion with the priest (actually, I think he was called a 'minister'). Perhaps her parents dealt with my foreign religion, and maybe the minister was quite liberal. But Chicago could not serve as a precedent for Cairo: both the Muslim and Coptic faiths are present in Cairo, and families and friends on each side of the divide would not like to see their faith slighted. I was the lone representative of my family in Chicago, and I was so happy to join Elizabeth that I didn't feel the least religious loneliness.

Kalifa told me that the Coptic Church usually does not permit marriages outside the faith, and it doesn't recognize marriages taking place outside the church. A Muslim ceremony, alone, would not be recognized as valid for a Copt, even though it would be legal under Egyptian law. I asked, "What is the solution for you, then?"

"The priest at Sagira's church has agreed to perform the wedding if I will allow our children to be brought up as Copts and if I support Sagira and the children in the expression of their faith. The priest recognizes that it is practically impossible for me to convert, which would be the normal requirement."

What is the point of these barriers between faiths? It just makes the devil's work easier!

About two weeks after the engagement party, Adeeba explained the arrangements: there would first be a Coptic wedding, followed immediately by a Muslim marriage, and then there would be a 'reception celebration' at a golf club. Would I make arrangements for the Muslim marriage at a mosque somewhere near the Saint Markos Coptic Church in Mansheya El-Bakry, just west of the Cairo Airport? "Yes, of course!"

I consulted a map. The small mosque near the university campus which I attend perhaps one or two Fridays a month was not in Mansheya El-Bakry. Besides, I didn't know the imam well enough to ask his advice. But I found that not far from the Saint Markos Coptic Church there is the Abou Bakr El Seddik Mosque. What is it like?

It was monumental: an imposing façade, wide as a city block and twenty meters high with slender minarets on either side of a grand arched portal. Delicate and all-white, it seemed like an exquisitely carved confection. Inside, there was a vast prayer hall, red-carpeted with individual niches, and open to the sky.

But what if it rains? Extending down either side, I found white-colonnaded, red carpeted prayer halls under the arched roof. Altogether there must be space for at least ten thousand worshipers. A wedding party of a hundred would get lost in here! No way Adeeba would go for it.

But she said, "Take us there; we want to see it."

If she's coming to see it, I better have the imam lined up to answer questions.

I called the mosque and explained the situation to a very polite female secretary. "We do a lot of weddings here, of all sizes, Professor. From ten to two or three thousand. There is a sub-imam, Mr. Malik, who handles the weddings. In the lower floor there is a large hall which can be rented for the celebration. And we can supply the catering and flowers."

I made an appointment with Mr. Malik for that evening, and I found him in his lower floor office. He was a short, broad-shouldered man with a full, black beard. I wonder if he used to be a professional athlete. He took notes while I was outlining the wedding plans. "You know that all brides who are married in Islam are subject to sharia law," he said.

This irritated me. "Are you saying that you will not marry a Christian in an Islamic ceremony?"

"No. A Muslim man may marry a Christian woman. I am only offering a reminder about sharia law."

"That's fine. In this case, the husband would have to apply sharia, and the wife would have to forgo civil law."

"I'm sorry, Professor, I don't mean to be difficult. It's just that sometimes these points of law are not understood. . . May I have an opportunity to meet the bride and groom to be? I'd like to go through the ceremony and the requirements."

"My son is an Army officer serving in Sinai. He is hoping to get married when next he can get leave."

"Perhaps I can speak to him by telephone?"

"I can try to get him on FaceTime right now."

"Oh, that would be splendid."

To my surprise, I connected with Kalifa immediately. I explained the situation and turned the phone over to Mr. Malik. Kalifa is a clever one: he talked as if he had memorized the marriage rules for Sunni Muslims; he left the impression that he was absolutely committed to Islam; and that his bride to be was familiar with the Muslim faith and culture. Some of this was probably true; in any case, Mr. Malik nodded frequently and scribbled notes.

"Your son is an impressive young man, Professor."

"Indeed, Mr. Malik."

"When might I have the opportunity to meet the bride-to-be, Professor?"

"I will give you a call proposing a time for the bride and her mother to meet you."

* * *

"Do you think it's ostentatious?" I asked Adeeba as we stood outside the El Seddik Mosque.

"No, not particularly," she said. "I think the Mormon Temple in Washington, DC is ostentatious. It's twice this size, all white, with six spires and with multi-colored night lighting."

The meeting with Mr. Malik was brief: Sagira was familiar with the Muslim marriage procedure; he showed us an area at the end of one of the long galleries which could be segregated for a wedding party of one hundred and twenty; Adeeba had no interest in the celebration hall or the catering services; but she said she would contact Mr. Malik with a firm commitment as soon as a date had been set.

"It's fine, Kareem," she said when we had left the mosque, "but I'm pretty sure they're not anxious to do many weddings involving a Christian bride."

"It's perfectly legal in Islamic law," I said.

"Yes, but most Christians are drinkers, and alcohol is a no-no in a mosque, therefore they don't get the rental of the celebration hall, or the catering."

* * *

Saint Markos Church is certainly not ostentatious. Set amidst tall apartment buildings, it faced an open area on Cleopatra Street, its walls and twin towers pierced with Arabic-style, narrow windows. But its three gaping portals seemed to draw one inside, where a broad, red carpet extended to an elevated area at the rear. The eye was drawn to the large stained glass windows, partially illuminated by the sunlight and sending shafts of colored light down on the rows of wooden pews on either side of the carpet. On the wedding day, I took my place on the left, in the front, and savored my surroundings. Well-dressed people were talking quietly, but the walls of the church itself seemed to be breathing a welcome. Profusions of white lilies partially hid what I assumed was the altar, and around the altar there were pillars of bright candles. The hush was dismissed by the voices of an acapella choir: sopranos and baritones exchanging good tidings.

A voice from the entrance of the church made an announcement in Coptic. The congregation turned to see the priest standing in front of the couple. He appeared quite young, with a russet beard, dressed in a black robe, round black hat and an elaborate, gold-embroidered shawl. The three of them began the promenade toward the altar: the bride in a sweeping white dress, her face obscured by a white veil; and Kalifa in a midnight blue dress uniform, his serious face suppressing joy without success.

The man in nearly black and the woman in white. More sensible than the Saudi tradition of women in black and men in white: a tradition decreed by ancient rulers. Signifying the purity of males and the fickleness of female serfs?

On reaching the altar, Kalifa sat in front of me and Sagira took the throne to his right. To Sagira's right there were five young women, dressed in white and carrying tall candles. The priest took the two gold rings and tied them together with a red ribbon, signifying a union in the blood of Christ. Prayers were said; there were readings from scripture, and the choir filled the church with their voices. I had no understanding of it all: it was in Coptic.

The priest dipped his fingers into a small silver bowl and anointed the foreheads of the couple. Gold crowns were lifted from the altar and placed on their heads. Kalifa stood, and the priest dressed him in a religious robe. The rings, which had been taken from their right hands, were placed on their left hands, amid prayers and song. Finally, the bride and groom stood at the altar, where the priest gave instructions and blessed them. The couple moved down the aisle, arm-in-arm, smiling, nodding and waving to the happy congregation.

* * *

As a Muslim wedding is not a sacrament but rather a contract, the proceedings at the El Seddik Mosque were bland and unemotional. The imam (whom I had not met before) gave a talk about how the Prophet honored his wives, how to honor women, and how women should treat their husbands, honoring them. Then an illuminated for framing version of the marriage contract (a standard version) was brought out. My older brother, Ahmed, and I signed it on behalf of Kalifa, and an uncle and a cousin of Adeeba – both named Derbala and being her nearest male relatives – signed on behalf of Sagira.

The Mirage City Golf Club just south of the airport was Adeeba's choice. The wedding party had a large room adjacent to the terrace, which overlooked the green, tree-lined fairways. Most of us gathered in the warm, winter sun on the terrace where white jacketed waiters offered drinks and anapés. Kalifa and Sagira stood side-by-side, one arm locked around each other, facing their well-wishers. But when a five-piece band began to play, they hurried inside to the dance floor. I wonder where Kalifa learned how to dance. Perhaps he just makes it up.

Do I dare to dance with Adeeba? Perhaps I should. But I haven't danced for years. When was it? Some wedding that Elizabeth and I were invited to.

I stalled for a while, pretending to be occupied with other guests. As the non-dancing guests thinned out, I felt cornered. I asked her.

"Yes, of course."

"I'm not a very good dancer, Adeeba."

"Oh, it doesn't matter, Kareem." And she began to chatter away about the church ceremony. She seemed oblivious to my unpredictable footwork, and I began to relax. She moved closer as my uncertainty began to melt, and I felt the lovely pressure of her breasts against my abdomen. I began participating in our commentary on the two ceremonies.

The music stopped. We found ourselves surrounded by applauding guests. Adeeba began to laugh and applauded back. I bowed and applauded.

Later, Naqib approached me. "It's a very nice day, Papa."

"Yes, and that's all down to Adeeba and Sagira."

"I suppose there was quite a bit of mahr involved."

"Not so much, actually."

"You know that Anisa never received any mahr when we were married," he said.

"That's because she had been married before, her parents never asked for it, and yours was a small, private wedding."

He gave a slight shrug and looked around the room. "Adeeba's cousin, the older Mr. Derbala, what does he do?"

"I believe he owns a small shipping company."

"Do you know what territory he covers and what products he transports?"

"No, but you can ask him."

I was mystified by Naqib's interest in money. Wahida had the impression that Naqib was suddenly doing well in the law firm. Anisa was likely making more than enough to pay for the child care. Through his childhood years and when he was at university, Naqib had always been able to earn enough to supplement the money we gave him. Could it be that this is just a case of Naqib being jealous of his younger brother marrying so well to such adulation?

I noticed that after our brief conversation, Naqib took Mr. Derbala aside, and that the two of them sat at a small table in earnest conversation. What business could Naqib have with Adeeba's cousin?

Just before I left, my brother, Ahmed, came up beside me. "Excellent party, Kareem."

"Yes. We have Adeeba to thank for that."

"Indeed. Sagira is a lovely girl."

"Yes, Kalifa is very lucky."

Ahmed frowned. "He's not very lucky to have that Sinai assignment."

"He requested it."

"That's what Naqib told me. Why doesn't he ask for a transfer?"

"He doesn't want a transfer, Ahmed."

"That's what Naqib says. Shame. But Naqib's doing very well: three kids, great job and an apartment overlooking the Nile."

"Yes."

"How old is Wahida now, Kareem?"

"She's twenty-two," I said.

"Goodness, she should be getting married."

I shook my head. "She says she's not ready."

"Well, she looks ready to me."

"What the hell do you mean, Ahmed?"

"Sorry, no offense meant, Kareem. I just meant that she's an attractive girl at an age when . . ."

I interrupted, "Speaking of marriage, how is your son, Shakil, doing? Is he engaged? He certainly has the good looks."

Ahmed shook his head. "I can't pin him down, and he finds fault in every girl I suggest. Do you know of anyone, Kareem?"

"Yes. There are some attractive women in my senior classes."

"Do they have money?"

"I haven't spoken with their banks."

"Of course not, but what do you think?"

"Well, I can make some discreet inquiries and let you know."

"Please do."

When my brother is around me, he is a constant fount of irritation, and I haven't been able to pinpoint the cause of the irritation. Our conversations always start out politely, but he will find some fault with me or mine. He's three years older than I; even as children, I was subject to his regular corrections. At the time, I thought, He's older so maybe he has a point. Now, he has retired from a mid-level civil service position. He has two boys: an older son who is married and Shakil, who is thirty, single and lives at home. Ahmed's wife, Salma, is very protective of Shakil, speaks frequently about their friends 'high up in government', and dresses very smartly. Elizabeth used to say, "I'll bet she sleeps in made-to-order, silk pajamas." I wonder if Ahmed has enough to do now that he's retired. I know he plays golf, but I doubt that he could afford a golf club membership. Elizabeth's verdict: "He's just jealous of you, Kareem."

"What's to be jealous of?"

"He thinks you're incredibly lucky, rather than talented."

"Well, maybe that's at least partially true."

She shook her head. "He doesn't understand what is real talent."

I miss Elizabeth. She was a dependable morale booster.

* * *

"You really need to be here to get the idea of Rome," Adeeba was saying.

I looked around. "This looks to me like one of your digs."

"I would love to dig here, but the Italians prefer to save it for the tourists, and perhaps they are right. You are standing where the Forum used to be. It's important because it was the beating heart of Roman civilization. It was here that important public speeches were made, elections and criminal trials took place, important commercial transactions were sealed, and people came to see and be seen."

We walked and walked past crumbling stone walls, great marble pillars, and through triumphal arches. I remember being particularly impressed with the Coliseum with its basement where wild lions, gladiators and Christians waited to be lifted into the arena. They certainly could have heard the blood-thirsty roar of fifty thousand spectators. What would they have felt?

Bowel-loosening terror for some; joyous anticipation of victory for others.

"I suppose civilization has moved forward somewhat," I said, "in the sense that human life seems to have more value now."

"I think that in the case of Rome, the spread of Christianity into the ruling class had a major impact."

"Because of the 'love your neighbor' commandment?"

She smiled. "It's not so easy to feed your neighbor to the lions when you're professing to love him."

"Adeeba," I asked, "do you think the Middle East would be more tranquil if 'love your neighbor' had made it into the Five Pillars of Islam?"

"Probably, but we both know plenty of Muslims who practice 'love your neighbor'."

* * *

For dinner, Adeeba selected a small restaurant around the corner from the hotel. They gave us a table by the window from which we could see and be seen. There was miniature glass vase with a red carnation. The waiter, who spoke a little English, brought us menus with fractured English subtitles. My experience of Italian food has been limited to pizza and spaghetti Bolognese. Here, we had spaghetti with pistachios and prawns, a whole grilled fish, and cannoli with gelato. The dessert still lingers in my memory, a crisp pastry stuffed with creamy chocolate and extraordinary vanilla ice cream.

"Do you mind if I have some wine, Kareem?" Adeeba had asked.

"Of course not. Why would I mind?"

"Some Muslims might be offended."

"Why? Because they can't have it or because they think you shouldn't?"

She laughed. "I don't know. . . . Good Italian wine is practically unavailable in Cairo, and it's only a few Euros here."

She began to tell me about her father, who was killed in the Six Day War in 1967, and her older brother, Rami, who was killed in an automobile accident when she was sixteen. "Rami had become my surrogate father. It was a terrible loss when he was killed." She looked down through brimming eyes. I reached across the table for her hand.

"Thank you, Kareem. It would be so easy for you to say 'I'm sorry to hear that', and change the subject. That's what most men would do. You take a moment to understand and share my feelings. Why are you different?"

"It's just the way I am, Adeeba."

"I like the way you are." She broke into a smile.

"What are you laughing about?" I asked.

"Another thing that makes you different is that you're normally not much of a conversationalist when you're with a group of people. You prefer to listen, and you are a good listener, but with me, you're not exactly chatty, but I can get you going."

"I like talking with you."

She propped her chin on her hand as she looked at me. "What makes my conversation so interesting?"

"You like to discuss important things. Maybe it's because of your education. You don't do trivia."

"That's a good point," she said, smoothing the table cloth. "We're both over-educated specialists in solving problems that the world would prefer to ignore."

"Well, we have to earn a living."

"OK. Besides being PhD's, what else do we have in common?"

"Well, we were both brought up in a conservative, middle-class environment."

"So, we share a social class."

"No, much more than that. Our basic values are very similar."

"For example?"

"Money is not part of who we are. Respect for others is – including the poorest and least educated. Learning and knowledge are important to us. We are comfortable in most social environments. We believe in democracy, freedom of expression and religious beliefs. And we have learned a certain set of manners which we drill into our children."

"Shared values. So that's why I like your company, Kareem."

Say it, Kareem! "I like you a lot, Adeeba."

"Good!"

* * *

I got off the elevator on the fourth floor of the hotel. She followed me. "Adeeba, isn't your room on the fifth floor?"

No answer.

At the door to my room, she asked, "May I come in?"

"Yes, of course."

Once inside, I put the key on the dresser and turned to find her with a smile of anticipation. Oh my goodness! Something's going to happen!

We each took a step forward. The smile never left her face as she slowly put her arms around my neck. Our faces converged until I kissed her . . . again . . . and again. The world disappeared; there was only Adeeba, the source of deep magic.

"Shall we get undressed?" she asked. I nodded and began to take off my jacket, shirt and vest. Don't rush, Kareem! It's not polite. I don't know why I thought that, but I turned slightly to see that Adeeba was already naked. She stood, hands at her sides. There was her dark bush, her breasts, and I saw that she was chewing on her lower lip. Without further thought, I rushed to embrace her. She breathed a deep sigh and pressed me to her.

"Don't you think you should take off your trousers and shoes?"

"Yes, I will," but I didn't release her. I looked down at the swell of her breasts against me. "Your skin feels so good, and you're lovely."

Her hand glided over my chest. "No, I'm not."

"I'm not sure I remember how to do this," I said.

She pushed me to arm's length. "Well, the first thing you do is get undressed. Then I'm sure you'll remember the rest."

She pulled down the bed covers, adjusted the pillows and lay down, having no modesty for her nakedness. I, however, had to resist an urge to cover up as I approached the bed. After all, the only person who had seen me naked as an adult was Elizabeth.

We lay facing each other, kissing and kissing. What a difference between a chaste peck on the lips and adulation of another's mouth! My awareness narrowed to the incendiary body beside me, and to my great joy, I was inflaming her! I kissed her neck, her breasts, her mouth again. I felt her hand on my hard penis. My hand found her bush, and, as her legs parted, my fingers explored her slippery folds.

"Let's do it, Kareem."

I knelt between her knees. She took hold of me and drew me to her. My arms on either side of her supported me as I watched her face. Intense concentration became concern, became satisfaction, became wild abandon. After a few moments, we synchronized our frantic thrusting. I kissed her briefly again, but we were panting with intensity. I felt the warning signs of explosion. "I'm going to come, Adeeba!"

"Yes! Come, Kareem, come!"

The fiery joy of my ejaculation. She cried out her release and crushed me to her.

There was a look of tenderness on her face as her fingers brushed my cheek. I marveled at the soft warmth of her skin as I moved my hand from her waist to her thigh and back. "It was so unexpected, so beautiful," I said.

She laughed. "I was just copying Elizabeth." I gave her a puzzled look. "She said she had to seduce you to cement the friendship."

"I guess that's true," I said, "but you were my friend already."

"Not like now."

"No, not like now." After a moment, I said, "Do you think Elizabeth was watching?"

Another laugh. "Watching: yes, but more importantly: cheering."

* * *

I remember several things about our visits to St. Peter's. We came back to the Vatican Museum and the Sistine Chapel, where I stood looking up at the ceiling until I got a crick in my neck. The value of the art owned by the Catholic Church must be in the trillions. Really! We had a look later inside a couple of minor churches in Rome, and they were filled with precious art. Extrapolate that around the world and the Church has assets larger than nearly any country. But why is there no famous Arabic art? We've had great philosophers, mathematicians, scientists, poets, and architects, but no Michelangelos. The answer occurred to me when we were looking at the Pieta, Michelangelo's statue of Mary grieving over the body of the dead Christ. It's right there, inside St. Peter's, and it's difficult to believe that it is carved from marble: the folds of the fabric, the sorrow on her face are so real. Islam forbids the creation of images of heavenly or earthly beings. So Islamic art is limited to calligraphy and geometric patterns. There is nothing in the Qur'an prohibiting the creation of images. Idolatry is forbidden. This must be the basis for the restrictions on image-making which appear in the hadiths. The Christians who were standing next to me as we looked at the Pieta: were they worshipping the idol of Mary and Jesus? I think not. The image before them brought into their minds their personal images of Mary and Jesus, and if they were worshipping anything as they stood there, it was the heavenly versions of Jesus and Mary. I think it deepens the religious experience to have images – not idols – which connect us with the saint, the prophet, or with God.

Of course, satirical images are wrong. What is their purpose other than to criticize and belittle the beliefs of others? Is their purpose to demonstrate that there is free speech? Does free speech include the right to shout 'Fire!' in a crowded theatre when there is no fire? Should there be a law against satirical images? Probably not: how does one define a satirical image? But thoughtful, educated people know what satire is.

* * *

The few days we had together in Rome passed in a blissful blur, but some images remain: the water spewing from the mouths in the Trevi Fountain; the hole in the centre of the Parthenon's ceiling; the Pope speaking from his window in the Vatican; the finger of God reaching out to man; the view of the city from our restaurant on the Quirinal Hill. But mostly I remember Adeeba: concentrating on a serious point, laughing, joking, and freeing her body to the pleasure of our lovemaking. Only once before have I felt so connected and in harmony with another person.

* * *

As we waited at Fiumicino Airport for our flight back to Cairo, I thanked Adeeba for being a guide and companion far beyond my expectations.

She laughed. "Well, I found you to be an attentive and compliant tourist."

We then got to talking about some of the things we had seen. "What's your impression of the mass at St. Peter's?" she asked.

"It was a fantastic pageant. That long column of black and red cardinals leading the white Pope – the hundreds of candles – the smoke from the incense – the thunder of the organ and the crescendo of voices from the choir. All to focus our attention on God. There's nothing quite like it in Islam."

She shook her head. "Why should there be anything like it? You have the Hajj and Arba'een. Surely, they do more to focus attention on Allah than a hundred masses at St. Peter's."

"Maybe so, but I have learned about the value of pageantry and music – and art – in promoting faith."

"So you feel you've rounded out your knowledge of the last of the three Abrahamic religions: Christianity?"

"Probably enough. There is only one point missing, but I didn't expect to complete it."

"What's that?"

"Oh, you know, there's that Saudi person who wanted me to look for Father Khaliq on my trips."

She nodded. "I've been doing some research on 'Father Khaliq'."

"Really, what did you find?"

"I found that 'Khaliq' is one of the ninety-nine names for Allah, but it's used infrequently."

"So you think that 'Father Khaliq' refers to Allah?"

"Possibly."

"But why would she send me looking for Allah? I know about Allah."

"Perhaps she was hoping that in finding Allah you would come to know Him, rather than just know about Him."

"But how does one find Allah and come to know Him?"

"I think that maybe that's the task she gave you."

"Why didn't she just spell it out?"

"Would the task have captured your imagination if she had spelled it out?"

I shook my head. "Probably not." I thought for a moment. "If she'd spelled it out, I don't think I would have gone on the Hajj . . . or to Medina . . . or . . ."

"So it wasn't really the search for a person that motivated those trips?"

I shrugged. "No."

"What was it then?"

"It was to understand . . . what all the fuss was about."

"Curiosity satisfied?"

I shook my head.

Chapter 11

Sinai Provence

I had to say something to Nane, my housekeeper; I had to cancel our arrangement. It wasn't really prostitution. Well, yes, money did change hands, but that wasn't the point. It was more like an extra service which increased her role and therefore her compensation. I never met her husband, but I knew him to be older, and maybe she liked a little extra male attention. She never failed to respond when I suggested that we 'go to the kitchen'. The question I struggled with was: what was the reason for my terminating the service? There were three possible answers. I was getting too old, or I was no longer enjoying it, or I had a new relationship. The first two alternatives weren't convincing. In fact, last month, we (both of us) had enjoyed a coupling. The advantage of the 'new relationship' answer was that the lack of a relationship was the original reason for the service becoming available. Besides, it was truthful.

So when Nane next arrived on a Monday, I asked her to come sit in the living room. When she was seated, I could see that she was apprehensive. "What is it, Professor?" She is probably worried about her job.

"Nane, you are a very good housekeeper and cook." She seemed to brace herself for countervailing criticism. "There is just one aspect of your role which will no longer be needed."

"What is that, Professor?"

"Well, you know: we go to the kitchen sometimes, and you raise your skirt, and . . ."

"You put your prick in me."

It took me a moment to get past her crude abruptness. "Yes."

"You no longer want me, Professor?"

"It's not that you don't provide a good service, Nane. You see, I have a new lady friend." There! I've said it!

"That's all right, Professor. I would never say anything."

"That's very good of you, Nane."

"It can remain our little secret."

"But we can't continue, Nane. The lady wouldn't like it."

"How is she gonna find out? I'm not telling her. You gonna tell her?"

"No, of course not. But you see . . ." How am I going to explain this to her? "It is my preference."

"You prefer her to me?"

"Yes."

"That's OK. I'm not a lady, but I still take your prick pretty good."

"I was thinking, Nane, that perhaps you have come to depend on the one hundred pounds ($15) a month . . ."

She interrupted: "Last month it was two hundred pounds."

"Yes, and I was thinking that I would raise your pay by fifty pounds a month to make up for the lost income."

She shook her head. "Should be at least a hundred pounds, Professor."

Damn! "OK, one hundred pounds."

"And when you want, I still take your prick for a hundred pounds. I tell nobody."

I thought it was best to nod at that point. After all, I was still in control.

"We go to kitchen now, Professor?"

"No, Nane, not now. Can you make us a lamb stew with potatoes and carrots for dinner?"

* * *

I was sitting in my sophomore Classical Arabic Philosophy classroom. The room was vacant; all the students had left twenty minutes ago, but they had left behind the one-page essays they had prepared on the assignment of: Why did Ar-Razi (b 864; d 932 AD) say 'Philosophy is imitating God to the degree that humans are able'?

I thought I would mark these essays in the solitude of the classroom. The essays were all typewritten, but the students would have to contend with my handwritten comments in blue ink. Most of the essays picked up on the main reason for Ar-Razi's assertion: it is complete knowledge which God has, and if we can imitate that knowledge (or a part of it), we become philosophers. But some of the students became sidetracked with arguments about power, and there are always students who, when they hear 'one-page essay', feel compelled to spew forth six hundred words, of which a good four hundred are rubbish. I was considering what grade to assign to one of these verbose essays when I became aware of movement in the room. I looked up and saw a female figure dressed in grey, loose-fitting trousers, royal blue jacket and a beige niqab. "Good afternoon, Professor."

"Good afternoon, Princess. I'm sorry there's only one chair in this room. Shall we go to my office?"

"No, Professor, we can sit here," she said, gesturing toward the student seats, which were arranged in tiers, ascending toward the rear of the room. We sat in the front row on either side of the main aisle.

I've always wondered how the rulers of two countries manage to talk comfortably with each other when they meet. At the beginning of a meeting, they are photographed in comfortable chairs, facing the photographers, but not each other. Do they turn the chairs around when the photographers leave? Or do they get stiff necks, as each of them strains to see the other? In the classroom, the chairs were fixed, so we turned as much as we could to face each other.

"I understand," she began, "that your trip to Rome was successful."

I hope she doesn't get into personal matters.

She smiled at my discomfort. "I just meant that it was successful in terms of your religious experience."

"Yes. The Catholic Church is interesting. Its use of art, music and pageantry seems to transform the religious experience: there is clearer perception and therefore deeper involvement. But, in my opinion, it is actually a polytheistic religion. I understand that the Church has a concept of 'three in one': God, Jesus, and a Holy Spirit which they consider one god, but they have all these saints, and they pray to them for different needs."

"So the saints remind you of the old tribal gods?"

"Yes, exactly."

"And you've decided to remain a Muslim?"

"Yes." I paused. "I want to ask you about Father Khaliq."

"You have learned that Father Khaliq and Allah are the same."

"Yes. What I don't understand is why you asked me to look for Him."

She gave a brief nod. "Professor, your sophomore class is studying Ar-Razi at the moment?"

"Yes, I was just marking some essays when you came in."

"And do you believe that Ar-Razi was correct when he said, 'Philosophy is imitating God to the degree that humans are able'?"

"Yes, I believe that's true."

"Well then, is the sense of Ar-Razi's statement changed entirely if it were to say: 'A philosopher approaches God to the degree that he is able'?"

I repeated the sentence several times in my mind. At first, I felt that I had been tricked: using a twisted version of a statement by a respected, ancient scholar who wrote more than two hundred books. But then, as I turned the statement over and over in my mind, I began to see that it was true. If we accept that God has complete knowledge, and I, as a philosopher, strive to increase my knowledge, it follows that in some sense I am trying to approach God. That approach could amount to a seeking of God to gain His knowledge. But was there a God with infinite knowledge? By my definition of God, He had infinite knowledge. But did he exist? If He didn't, I began to see that there wasn't much point in being a philosopher. If there was no single repository of knowledge, and therefore no unifying truth, all truth would become subjective. No philosopher believes that truth is subjective.

"Now. Professor, do you understand why I sent you to find Father Khaliq?"

"I think so, but I'm afraid that I have failed in my mission."

"Do you really feel that you have failed? Don't you feel, rather, that you have made great progress but have not reached some sort of nirvana?"

"Yes, I suppose so, Princess." I looked at her thoughtfully. "I seem to recall that you promised a reward for finding Father Khaliq."

"No. You asked if there was some sort of reward attached to the search, and I agreed that there is."

I considered her response for some moments. "I would have to agree that I have acquired a great deal of understanding – valuable understanding." I looked away, still engaged in thought. "But tell me this, Princess: does one ever find Father Khaliq?"

When I turned back to attend her answer, she was gone.

* * *

Adeeba and I did not feel ready to announce our relationship to our children. Actually, I was the one with reservations about an announcement. I felt that Wahida would be pleased, but I was less certain about the boys. Naqib was – at the moment – an enigma to me. I was reluctant to take a step which might add complexity to my relationship with my elder son, who had been Elizabeth's favorite. Kalifa was less of a concern, but being newly married and stationed in a war zone, there was less opportunity for him to build rapport with Adeeba, who was not only his mother-in-law, but his father's lover. So Adeeba and I had to develop a plan for our secret liaisons. She ruled out meeting at her house, because she had advised Sagira against consummation of her relationship with Kalifa until she was married. For Sagira, who lived at home, to find her mother engaged in what she had opposed would raise accusations of a double standard. Although Wahida was single and liberal-minded, Adeeba felt it would set a poor example if we slept together when Wahida was at home, which was most evenings. Neither of us liked the idea of a hotel, and Al Jamiah was too far away. Nane was at my house all day on Monday and Thursday mornings. We compared our respective class schedules and found that Tuesday and Friday midday were free.

Those liaisons during the first months after our return from Rome were fiery and liberating. We were two casual friends who had suddenly discovered addictive, intense physical intimacy which opened whole vistas of trust, shared hopes and fears, and emotional intimacy. When I tried to compare it to my early experience with Elizabeth, I found that this time there was a richness to the relationship which arose from wisdom and experience. We knew how to deepen and accelerate our relationship through what to an outsider would have seemed trivial actions. Whereas as young people, we could only try and observe the result.

Adeeba was very fond of my two younger children, and she was an astute observer. "Don't worry about Wahida getting married, Kareem," she would say. "She is a very special young woman – bright, practical, with lots of energy. She has high standards. That's why she's not engaged. She's been blowing away a lot of chaff. Somewhere out there is a similar young man who's despairing of finding wheat. Their paths will cross and they'll bake some bread together."

Adeeba's analogies always amused me. "Where will they get the yeast, love?"

"They'll invent it." She stroked my naked chest. "And, as you know, I think that Kalifa is one of the finest young men in the world: bright, honorable, handsome, and sweet – particularly sweet."

"I don't find him so sweet," I said.

"Believe me; he is. I don't know Naqib, so I really shouldn't say this, but there's something about him that bothers me."

"He seems very unsettled at the moment."

Adeeba sat up and gazed into the distance. "For me, Naqib is an enigma – intentionally. He seems to hide behind a mask of ordinariness, as if he wants me to believe there is nothing unusual about him. But he forgets that I've known him for most of his life, and he's always impressed me as striving to be unique – to be famous."

Yes. I remember. "I don't suppose you knew about this, Adeeba, but during his last year at school, when he was about seventeen, he wanted desperately to be named the valedictorian of his class. His classmates nominated Naqib and two others. The head teacher, who reserved the right to select, asked each candidate to write an outline of their speech. We never saw Naqib's; if we had, we certainly would have objected. The head teacher selected someone else, and Naqib was furious – so furious that Elizabeth went to ask the head teacher about it. The first question from the head teacher was 'have you seen his outline?' He then went on to describe a radical essay on the autocratic Egyptian government and how the students should make it their mission in life to bring an Islamic government to power."

Adeeba shook her head. "No, I didn't know about that. Did you talk to him about it afterward?"

"Elizabeth did, but her message probably wasn't very critical. Naqib could do no wrong for Elizabeth." She nodded. "And you know, Adeeba, I've often wondered since which aspect of that rejection made him angrier: not being chosen to give that firebrand speech or not being singled out as the most promising person in the class: the valedictorian."

"Probably it was one must-have package. But you've talked to him about his views, Kareem."

"It's like pouring water on a duck; he just shakes his feathers and carries on. For every argument I present against leftist, theocratic governance, he has counter arguments against right-wing, capitalist governance. The one move I haven't made is to emphasize the risks he is taking for his family and himself."

"You haven't been to his new place, have you?"

"No, I haven't." A thought suddenly occurred to me. "Adeeba, what kind of a shipping company does your cousin, the older Mr. Derbala, have?"

"It's a small company, but it must be very profitable. He has half a dozen small ships and they're used to transport goods to and from small ports in Egypt and neighboring countries. It's a sort of marine courier service."

"What kind of goods does he transport?"

"I think it's anything that a customer wants shipped by sea. Why do you ask?"

"I just remembered that at the wedding a couple of months ago, Naqib asked about your cousin and then he spent a good half hour having a confidential chat with him."

"I doubt that Nahman needs the services of a lawyer."

"Why do you say that?"

"Because Derbala Shipping does things its own way — the key principle is: make lots of money."

* * *

314

Shortly after that, I called Naqib, and said that Wahida and I would like to come around to see his new apartment and spend some time with the grandchildren. At first, he told me how busy he was, but that most any weekend I could stop by to see Anisa and the children. (I had the feeling that he wanted to avoid me.) I said, "Don't you go to Friday prayers?"

"Of course I go to Friday prayers."

"And the office is closed after Friday prayers."

"It's closed formally, but some of us have access."

"Naqib, do you think you could make an exception for your father and come home for a couple of hours after Friday prayers?"

"OK, Papa. Next Friday."

* * *

Wahida wanted to come with me, and I thought it best if she did. Her presence would make it seem more of a family get-together, and less of me wanting to lecture Naqib.

The apartment was on the eleventh floor of a new residential high-rise on the east side of the Nile, in Garden City. "Pretty fancy place!" was Wahida's comment as we waited for the elevator in the black marble lobby, two walls of which were green with living gardens. Anisa welcomed us amidst shouts of "Auntie! Auntie!" from Basima and Husna.

"I have a present for each of you!" Wahida announced.

In seconds, Basima tore the ribbons and festive wrapping from her package. Husna stood placidly watching her older sister, her package clasped to her chest. Out of the tissue paper, Basima flourished a dress. She dropped the wrappings and clasped the dress up to herself. "It's funny," she announced, picking at the smocking on the front of the dress.

Anisa prized the garment from her daughter and looked inside the collar. "Oh, how wonderful! A real French dress for a pretty girl! You're so lucky! What do you say to Auntie Wahida? Shall we put it on?"

Husna carried her package to her mother's lap, and carefully unwrapped it, looking up now and then to see what else was going on.

I, meanwhile, had picked up Ra'id, my grandson, from the floor where he had been sitting and observing. "Here is a present for you, Ra'id."

He sat on my lap, as we unwrapped his present until he could reach in and pull out a brightly colored metal object, from which protruded a handle.

"I know what it is!" Basima exclaimed. "Look, Ra'id!" She snatched the top from his hand, and standing it on the floor, pumped the handle several times. The top began to sing as it whirled, a blizzard of color, across the floor.

Ra'id struggled to get down, crawled to the top, and pounced on it, bringing its song and dance to a halt.

"What a view you have!" Wahida was standing at the floor-to-ceiling living room windows, looking down at the Nile, all dark and sinister as it coiled its way to the north.

"The time of day I like best," Anisa said, "is the late afternoon. You can watch the sun set over the western city."

Wahida flopped down on a massive cream couch, pulling Husna up beside her. "This sofa is wonderful!"

"We got all the furniture on a clearance from Eldogo Design." Anisa made little effort to cover her pride.

"Have your parents been to see your new place?" I asked.

"Yes, several times. They were amazed!"

Anisa's comment called up the picture in my mind of the home of Anisa's parents: a dreary, decaying, fourth-floor walk-up: living area, two small bedrooms and a bathroom, all aging into various shades of tan. I'll bet they were amazed, and probably at least a little envious.

"Naqib isn't home yet?" I asked

"No, he called to say he is on his way."

For the next half hour, we drank tea, ate biscuits and entertained the children.

On his arrival, Naqib took us on a guided tour of the four bedrooms, two bathrooms, and large, modern kitchen. He, too, was immensely proud of the furnishings and decorations.

"Were you able to buy this, Naqib?" I asked.

"No. We're renting for the time being. But I'd like to move into a place like this in a year or two."

"So things are going pretty well at your law firm," I said.

"Yes, I've been made a partner."

"I always thought that partners were the old guys who knew all the judges and spent most of their time in court."

"I know what you mean, Papa, but in my case, I bring the contacts."

"Oh." I was surprised, but on reflection, it made sense. Naqib had always made himself known to semi-obscure people who could pull the strings in his favor. When he was about twelve, there was a family-owned grocery store three blocks from us. Naqib had taken it into his mind to deliver groceries to better-off, stay-at-home customers in the area. He approached the store manager with his idea, which involved him packing the customer's order after school, delivering it and collecting a tip from the customer as well as payment for the order, which he would deliver to the store. He also wanted a small commission from the store. The store manager said 'no': he didn't want a twelve-year-old involved in the business cash. Naqib had made the acquaintance of an uncle who owned a share of the business. He explained his plan to the uncle, pointed out that the service would bring in new customers, and mentioned that he was the oldest son of a prominent university professor. He got the job.

"Speaking of contacts, Naqib, did Mr. Derbala turn out to be a good contact for you?"

Naqib looked away and seemed to tense. "Yes, he'll be able to do some work for another client of ours."

"So your particular law firm not only practices law, but it acts as a kind of marriage broker between clients?"

"I suppose you could say that . . . as long as it earns us money."

* * *

Later that afternoon, the females (Wahida, Anisa, Basima, and Husna) were clustered on the sofa while Naqib, with Ra'id in his lap, and I were sitting in adjacent arm chairs at the other end of the living room. We were talking about airport safety after the downing of the Russian passenger jet.

"I think that jet was bombed by enemies of Putin," Naqib declared. "They want him to look bad for intervening in Syria."

"But didn't Sinai Provence claim responsibility for the disaster?" He gave a brief nod. "Well," I continued, "since Sinai Provence is an enemy of Putin – I'm sure they don't like their comrades in Syria being bombed occasionally – maybe they did do it."

"I suppose they would have good reason to," he said mildly.

I said, "It's not only a tragedy for two hundred and twenty Russian families, who did nothing wrong, but for tourism in Egypt, as well."

Naqib was silent for a time; then he said, "You know I fly into Sharm el Sheik now and then."

"No, I didn't know that. Where else do you go?"

"I go to Riyadh and Dubai fairly often."

"That must be to see clients."

"Yes."

"And you go to Sharm to meet with your Sinai clients."

"What do you know about my Sinai clients?" he asked sharply.

"Too much!" I replied hotly. "I know that they are literally a battleground between my two sons."

"And whose fault is that?"

"I don't think it's useful to attribute fault; you both have your reasons." I paused. "Let me ask you this, Naqib, what is the longest running dictatorship in world history?"

"I don't know: Rome, China, North Korea? What's your point, Papa?"

"My point is that no dictatorship lasts as long as it planned to last. For example, the German Third Reich under Hitler was going to last a thousand years. It barely lasted a decade. Why is this the case? It is because human beings are very fond of doing things their own way. I don't call it 'democracy' because you dislike that word, but it is true that people like doing things their own way."

"What does this have to do with me?" Naqib asked.

"Nothing yet. Islamic State – a concept which you admire, I think . . ." I paused, waiting for him to nod. ". . . does not present itself as a dictatorship. It intends, or so it says, to be a government for all Islamic people, under sharia law, in the name of Allah. But you know, or I assume you know, that the people in Raqqa cannot do things their own way. They can't listen to their own music, for example."

"What's your point, Papa?"

"My point is that when a government won't let people do relatively harmless things their own way, its authority tends to erode; and when it restricts people from doing things that they really care about, they fall apart violently."

"So?"

"So you have a choice, Naqib, between tolerating an existing government which is opposed – sometimes violently – to those who oppose it, and a movement which will sweep away the hopes and dreams of millions of people. There will be no tourism, the wealthy and well educated will have left; we will all be equally poor and devout, and unable to do many of the things we really care about. The problem for you, Naqib, is that the current government has the upper hand, and, for all its faults, it has the support of the Western world. As you know, it will not be forgiving of those who are seen trying to bring it down. But more than that, it will bring hurt upon those who are closest to the rebels. We see examples of this every day."

"So you are worried that I could bring shame on the al-Busiri name."

"That is the least of my worries. And I don't worry about any hurt I may suffer. I have lived my life. I worry about Wahida, Anisa, your children, Kalifa and Sagira."

"I've told Kalifa at least a dozen times to transfer out of Sinai."

I stood up. "I'm afraid you haven't really heard me, Naqib."

* * *

Looking back from the vantage point of today over the period of the next three months of my life, it's difficult for me to explain why I didn't ask Adeeba to marry me. We were blissfully alive in each other's company by every measure—emotionally, intellectually, spiritually and physically—and time seemed to evaporate. Most of my life when I was alone – as in the class-room – my mind was working in one dimension. When alone, time was like a handbrake: slowing down my life. It is not that I 'had it all' and didn't want to be bothered with marriage. I am, after all, a gentleman, and would never compromise a lady for the sake of my own convenience. I think it was more that mar-riage had never been on my agenda since the death of Elizabeth. There was nothing – not even vague hints from Adeeba – which would have prompted the thought; at least I don't recall any hints from Adeeba. We both felt such unworldly happiness that we immersed ourselves completely, suspecting unconsciously that it could fade or even vanish.

During that time, I spent several weekends with Adeeba on a dig in the desert east of Al Barsha. There was evidence that the Nile had, over the last fifteen hundred years, retreated west to its present bed. Overlooking one of the wadis that drained the eastern highlands into the Nile, aerial surveillance had found evidence of human occupation: the outlines of habitations and roads. Adeeba had narrowed the attention of her team to what might be the foundations of a temple, market or other shared facility. I wasn't sufficiently qualified to do any actual digging, but I could watch with intent interest as a young archaeology student first removed several layers of sand and silt, and then began to probe gently for what might lie below. In spite of the intense sun and the dry heat, there was eager expectation among the students. It was as if they were at their birthday party and the presents would arrive soon. I was sitting on the sand next to a student who was on high alert. His careful probing had identified something solid below. Out came a paint scraper and what looked like a paint brush but with metal bristles. Millimeter by millimeter, the silt was brushed away, and the outlines of a pottery vase lying on its side began to appear. "Professor," he shouted, "I think I've got some pottery!"

Adeeba, dressed in baggy beige trousers, shirt and broad-brimmed hat, appeared at once. She knelt next to her student, and together they scraped away the silt on either side, revealing graceful handles. "We've got to find out what's under this," she said. "Let's leave this as it is. Don't brush it clean. We want to be able to wash it and see what may be painted on it. Dig down on either side," she instructed, making a V gesture with her hands, "so we can see what's under this."

An hour later the student had revealed broken pottery on either side. He was able to free the vase which, unfortunately had been fragmented on the other side.

"We think it was an ordinary wine jug," Adeeba remarked later. "Probably no more that fifteen hundred years old."

We would usually have dinner at the hotel in Mallawi with the rest of the crew, and retire to our separate but connecting bedrooms.

* * *

Kalifa got two weekend passes during this time. I didn't see much of him, because he was with Sagira at Adeeba's house. Adeeba kept better track of him. She said that he would arrive exhausted and in a low mood, but that with "rest, in Sagira's company, and some good food" he became his usual upbeat self. Wahida said he told her the pressure from Sinai Provence was unremitting.

* * *

I'm not really sure why – it wasn't really a conscious resolution – but I found myself going to the mosque at the university at convenient times: not necessarily at one of the five daily prayer times. I would face Mecca, kneel, bow my head to the carpet, and begin what felt like an attempt at dialogue with Allah. I suppose what motivated me was my unanswered question to Princess Basheera: "Does one ever find Father Khaliq?" I didn't pray for anything for myself. I would ask Him questions like, "May I hear Your voice?" and "What is the one thing You would like to say to me?" and "How can I get to know You better?" and "Should I try to speak to the angel Jibril as Muhammad did?" and "How do you speak with your prophets?" I never heard a voice or got a specific answer, but there was a welcome feeling of comfort which gradually enveloped me, and which I could not attribute solely to the peaceful quiet of the mosque.

* * *

I also made a small effort toward finding a wife for my nephew, Shakil, as I had promised my brother. But I was somewhat less than an enthusiastic go-between: Shakil impressed me as a bright, good-looking, but rather lazy and self-indulgent young man. I considered all the young women in my junior and senior classes. Some I knew to be committed to a boyfriend or actually engaged. I omitted others from consideration, because they were on scholarships and didn't have the family resources to satisfy my brother, or because they didn't have the looks that Shakil would surely require. This left three candidates, including Mairisha, who was working on a thesis proving the Ibn Rushd was wrong. The admissions office had information on her family which suggested that her candidacy would satisfy my brother: her father was a mid-level civil servant in the Foreign Office. I passed the information I had on the three – including my personal evaluations – along to Ahmed with the request that he engage a marriage broker to take matters further with any interesting candidates. Ahmed told me later that Mairisha's family was approached by the broker, and that she accepted a meeting with Shakil, but for undisclosed reasons, no contract was agreed. In fact, nothing came of my efforts. My opinion of Mairsiha was enhanced: she may have been disorganized, but she was certainly bright and perceptive.

* * *

It was about seven in the evening when Adeeba called me at home. She was choking with grief and at first I didn't understand her. "Kalifa's been killed, Kareem. Sagira is devastated! It's so awful!"

I felt paralyzed: unable to breathe or think – as if all my blood had drained out of me. "Did you hear me, Kareem? Your son has been killed!"

"No. No, Adeeba, it must be a mistake! Wahida and I spoke with him just a couple of nights ago."

"Sagira was called by colonel somebody at Army headquarters. He said Kalifa was killed in combat yesterday. Oh God, Kareem, it's so terrible!"

It can't be true! Elizabeth help me! Allah help me! Tell me it's a mistake! My knees turned to jelly and I collapsed to the floor. Wahida took the telephone from my hand. I heard her speaking. "Let me speak to Sagira, Adeeba."

Vaguely, I thought, Maybe I'm going to die, too.

There was more talking.

How can I go on living when my son, my precious son, is dead?

I felt Wahida pulling at my arms. "Get up, Papa. Here. Sit on the couch. I'll get you some water."

I was numb – without sensation. Why am I here? I should be with him!

Wahida was offering me a glass of water. I shook my head. I looked at her and saw that her cheeks were wet with tears, that her shoulders were racked with involuntary sobs.

She put her arms around me and we both sat, weeping.

Gradually, the room began to intrude on my consciousness. "What," I began, "what did Sagira say?"

"She said that a colonel at Army headquarters had called and asked to speak to the wife of Lieutenant al-Busiri, and he told her that he was very sorry, but her husband had been killed on combat operations yesterday."

"Was that all?"

Wahida nodded. The telephone rang. Wahida answered. "Hello. No, Colonel, he is indisposed. Are you calling about my brother? Yes, we know that. Do you have any further details? I see. Thank you." She put the telephone down.

"What did he say?" I asked.

"He said that he hasn't any further details, but that the lieutenant's body will be returned to Cairo tomorrow."

For some time, we sat in dumb silence.

"I think we ought to tell Naqib," she said.

"Will you call him?"

She nodded and picked up the telephone. "May I speak to Mr. al-Busiri, please? Would you tell him that it's very important? Ask him to call home right away." She put the telephone down. "He's in a meeting."

"At seven-thirty in the evening?"

"That's what he said."

She sat down next to me, and I drew her to me fiercely, perhaps out of fear that she, too, could be taken away.

The telephone rang. Wahida got up and answered it. "No, I tried to reach you, Naqib. Kalifa's been killed in combat yesterday. We got a call from a Colonel Fakhoury at Army headquarters. His body will be returned tomorrow." There was something faintly hostile in her tone. She listened for some moments and then hung up.

I asked, "What did he say?"

"He said he wished Kalifa had listened to his advice."

"Is that all?"

"He wants to know when the funeral is going to be." She stood for a moment, thinking. "I have the phone number of one of the guys in Kalifa's unit. I'm going to call him."

Referring to the screen of her mobile phone, she dialed a number. It rang unanswered.

* * *

I barely slept at all that night. There was too much inescapable pain: in my heart, in my mind, in my bones. I blamed myself, I blamed the Daesh, I even blamed Kalifa. I blamed him for being so willful, so confident, so beautiful. I have lost my special son! The one who reflected me! The thought repeated itself over and over. Towards dawn, there was one thought which afforded slight relief. Wherever he is now, he is with Elizabeth. I got out of bed, knelt down, and prayed that it was so: Mighty Allah, I beg you to unite my son Kalifa with my wife Elizabeth. Leave me in pain, Allah, for allowing him to be killed, but please bring Kalifa and Elizabeth together. Gradually, over the next months, I came to believe that it was so, but my sorrow lingered on. I had often heard it said that to have a child die before you is the worst calamity which a parent can experience. I accepted this as 'conventional wisdom', never believing that it would happen to me. Now, I felt the full, tragic force of this terrible natural law.

* * *

Early the next morning, the phone rang. I was prepared to let it ring, but Wahida answered it. She spoke very little and her face was taut with concern. When she hung up, I asked, "Who was that?"

"It was Anisa. She called from home. She said Naqib told her about Kalifa, and that at first he seemed upset, but then he began acting strangely: wandering around the apartment, talking to himself. He didn't go to bed at all last night. Now he's gone out."

"Where did he go?"

"She doesn't know. You know what I think, Papa?" I shook my head. "I think that Naqib blames himself for Kalifa's death."

"Well, we all do some of that. Is that what Anisa said?"

"No. It's what I think. Naqib has been providing weapons to Sinai Provence, and he realizes that one of those weapons has killed his brother."

"Allah in heaven! Let it not be!"

We stood mute, facing each other. She said, "I'm going to have breakfast, and then I'm going to see Sagira. You should have breakfast, Papa."

* * *

Sagira's older sister Nakia and her three small children arrived at Adeeba's house shortly after we did. Sagira's face was grey with fatigue, her eyes were bloodshot, and her hands trembled around the mug of coffee that she held. But she stood tall and there was a determined look in her eye. Murmuring indistinct condolences, she embraced Wahida and me in turn. I sat next to Adeeba on the couch. The pressure of her shoulder against mine and the feeling of her hand in mine were balm more valuable than words: we shared our unspoken grief.

Wahida was urging Sagira to do something – to call someone – several attempts were made, and half an hour later the telephone rang. Sagira was on the phone for some time, and when the call was completed, the three young women went into a huddle.

Nakia came over to Adeeba and me. "Sagira just spoke with the deputy base commander. She called the base commander, but he couldn't take the call and his deputy called her back. He said that there were eight men, including Kalifa, who were killed in an attack by the Daesh. They were in their barracks when what he called a 'heavy missile' hit the barracks at about eight in the evening. They believe the missile was fired from outside the base perimeter. There are twenty-three other men who are in the hospital. There was a counterattack, and one of the Daesh was killed and one was captured. He said he was very sorry: Kalifa was an excellent officer."

"Why was he in the barracks with his men?" I asked. "Don't the officers have separate quarters?"

"Sagira asked him about that. They think that since Kalifa's platoon was going out on patrol the next morning early, he had gone to the non-commissioned barracks to brief his men about the patrol."

"Shit!" I said. "If he hadn't been so conscientious, he might still be alive!" I thought for a moment. "Nakia, what's this about a 'heavy missile'?"

"Sagira asked about that also, Professor. He said they don't know what it was. It was bigger than a rocket propelled grenade. They didn't think the Daesh had anything like that."

I leaned back on the couch, and turned to Adeeba. "We've got to think about funeral arrangements."

"Shall I ask Sagira to join us?"

I nodded. The young widow came over and stood blankly before us.

Adeeba said, "Kareem wants to talk about the funeral arrangements."

Sagira sank to the floor with a moan, bowed her head and began to weep.

"Come up here, sweetheart, and let's listen to what Kareem has to say."

Out of commiseration with Sagira, I felt my own tears start; I pretended not to notice. "If Kalifa had been single," I began.

Sagira shook her head. "Noooooo . . ."

"This is complicated, Sagira," I rested my hand on her shoulder. "Hear me out. If Kalfia had been single, I would have wanted him buried by his mother." Again, Sagira shook her head. "But," I continued, "his mother was cremated. She never liked the look of Coptic cemeteries. They are full of granite family tombs, built like solemn little houses, without windows and hope. Too few trees and flowers. She said, 'Kareem, don't put me there.'" Adeeba gave a nod and a wry, knowing smile. "So, her ashes are in a marble vase on my dresser." I paused to think for a moment. "Kalifa was a good Muslim. A better one than I. He prayed five times a day." Sagira nodded. "And as a good Muslim, he would not want to be cremated; he would want to be buried, facing Mecca." Sagira was looking at me intently; her tears had momentarily stopped. "This leaves us with two choices," I concluded. "Burial in a Coptic or a Muslim cemetery."

Sagira croaked, "I want to be buried with him!"

"I know you do, sweetheart," Adeeba comforted, "but that's far, far away. In the meantime, you have a young life that needs you."

I glanced in surprise at Adeeba; she gave me a brief nod and a smile.

I said, "I suppose it would be difficult to arrange for Kalifa to be buried in a Coptic cemetery – even if he wished it. Unless, of course, there was a vacancy in a family crypt that was orientated to face Mecca, and special permission could be granted."

"I haven't any family plot," Adeeba shrugged. "I tend to agree with Elizabeth."

"But Mama, we could get one for me, and bury Kalifa there," Sagira insisted.

"Sweetheart, you're forgetting several things. First of all, getting a plot and all the permissions – if they can be granted – will take weeks. Muslims prefer to be buried the day they die. And secondly, it's not clear that Kalifa would have wanted to be buried in a Coptic cemetery."

"Well," I said, "Kalifa agreed that his mother should be cremated rather than go into her church's cemetery."

Sagira began to cry softly.

"Sagira," I added, "if Kalifa were here, I'm sure he would tell you how much he loved you, and that he will wait for you. That you shouldn't worry now about being next to him in death, because he'll see you right after that."

Sagira doubled over in sobbing resignation. Adeeba turned her tear-stained face to me and nodded.

* * *

"Papa," Wahida announced, "that Colonel Fakhoury is on the phone. He said that Kalifa's body will be at that Fayid base hospital early this afternoon. He wanted to know about our arrangements."

329

"Get his number and I'll call him back."

I called a funeral home and made arrangements with a Mr. Fereiha to meet him at the base hospital at 2 pm, and I asked him to arrange transportation to the mosque at 3. He said we could have our choice of ten plots he keeps at the cemetery, and he agreed to have transportation available from the mosque to the cemetery. I called the imam at the university mosque and asked him to be available for a Janazah (prayer for the dead) at 3:30. Then, Adeeba and I made telephone calls to family, friends and colleagues informing them of the times of the Janazah and the interment.

Until I had faced up to the burial dilemma and knew when Kalifa's body was being returned, I was shrouded in a fog of inactivity and grief. I immersed myself in the sorrow of others, saying little, doing almost nothing, with my thoughts largely random, fond memories of my son. But now, I had to proceed with the burial, and twenty-four hours had already elapsed during the last night – thanks to the Army and its inept bureaucracy.

Sagira was standing next to me as I finished the call to Colonel Fakhoury. "I'm coming with you," she said.

"Sagira, I don't think . . ."

She interrupted, "I want to say goodbye to my husband."

"But Sagira, it may not be possible. . ."

"I will make it possible, Kareem." Her face was set with determination.

"All right, let's go."

In the car, I explained that before a Muslim burial, the body needs to be washed; that I would need to find out whether Kalifa's body had been washed; and if not, I would have to wash him; that according to Muslim tradition, the body must be washed by a close relative of the same gender. I had hoped this would make it clear it was unlikely that she would be able to see her husband's body.

"Yes," she said, "I know that, Kareem."

At the base, we were directed to the hospital, where the black hearse was already waiting. I shook hands with Mr. Fereiha and his three assistants. "Follow me, Professor, I am all too familiar with this place."

In the basement, Mr. Fereiha asked for Lieutenant al-Busiri and we were directed to a door down the dimly lit corridor.

"I'm afraid the lady will have to wait outside," Fereiha said.

We went into a chilled, darkened room which smelled of formaldehyde. When the fluorescent lights were lit, there was a steel table in the middle of the space, and on the table there was a white cloth covering a long mound.

"I'm afraid the Army doesn't do a proper job of washing, Professor. But they do keep the sponges, towels, et cetera in this closet."

He produced a bucket, some towels and a sponge. He went to the table and folded back the sheet. "Your son was a handsome man, Professor."

I was drawn forward and became completely disoriented as I looked down. Kalifa's face was unharmed but grey and seemed to be made of wax. His eyes were closed and his mouth slightly open; his hair was all awry. I reached out and touched his cheek. It was cool. Oh, Kalifa! I never thought I'd see you like this! How could you leave us? My legs gave way and I collapsed with my head on his chest. There was a hand on my shoulder. Fereiha was gently urging me upright. Eventually, I found the resources to stand, but I was sobbing, and caressing my son through the cloth. I don't know how long I stood like that, with Fereiha's arm around my shoulders, but my sobs diminished and I looked around the room. It was entirely white: ceiling, tiled walls and floor.

"Are you OK now, Professor? I need to go outside for something." I nodded. The door opened and closed. I looked into the bucket. It was half full, smelling of strong detergent; there was a rime of foam around the edges. The door opened and closed again. I looked up. It was Sagira. I was about to say something when she strode to my side and looked down. "Oh God, Kalifa! My beautiful lover, my husband, my life! What have they done to you?" She bent down and kissed his lips. When she stood again, I saw that his face was wet with her tears.

The door opened, and Mr. Fereiha strode in. "I'm afraid you'll have to wait outside, madam!"

"I am here," Sagira said with emphasis, turning to face Fereiha, "to say goodbye to my husband and the father of my unborn child."

"But madam, it is customary," Fereiha said lamely, "that women not be present for the washing of a male body."

"You think I have not seen my husband before? It is not proscribed by the Qur'an!"

"But madam, the haditha says . . ."

Sagira interrupted, "Mr. Fereiha, I am staying! You can report me to the authorities if you wish!"

I touched Mr. Fereiha's sleeve. "Her husband, my son, was a decorated soldier. The authorities will surely make an exception."

He shrugged and drew the cloth away.

I heard Sagira's intake of breath, and I saw immediately what caused it: there was a huge wound in his left side which had been drawn closed by three crude stitches. Kalifa's skin was pale grey, and the black, body hair on his chest, his legs and at his groin stood out. Looking for other wounds, I saw numerous punctures down the outside of his left leg, and there was a large oozing wound just above his left ear. I picked up the sponge and wiped away the pink ooze. "With this wound, he must have died instantly," I said. Mr. Fereiha nodded.

That thought was comforting: at least he did not suffer.

I began to wash his body, dipping the sponge into the bucket now and then. He had a beautiful body. The last time I washed him, he must have been about four. He was beautiful then, too.

I wasn't really conscious of my emotional state until I tasted the tears in my mouth. Washing Kalifa was strangely satisfying. Acceptance of his death was forced upon me, and as I washed him slowly, lovingly, I felt his spirit hovering nearby: "Thank you, Papa." Sagira must have felt something similar. She floated opposite me, whispering inaudibly and reaching out to touch Kalifa now and then.

We turned him over and I washed his back. Then I rubbed him dry with a towel. Mr. Fereiha produced three long pieces of kafan (plain white cloth) with which we wrapped my son. The funeral assistants transferred him to a trolley, and covered him with a green shroud. He was then placed in the hearse to be transported to the mosque.

* * *

At the mosque, I was startled by the number of people. At first, I looked at my watch, thinking it must be prayer time. But I recognized faculty colleagues – dozens of them, and students – there must have been several hundred – their faces were familiar though I didn't know their names, and there were friends of Kalifa. When I saw Hafez, I said to him, "This is a very large turnout."

He shook his head. "Everyone at this university respects Professor al-Busiri, even if they haven't taken a class with you."

"They respect me even though they don't know me?"

"It's your reputation, Kareem: a great teacher who is wise, but humble."

I was touched. "Thank you, Hafez, that's very kind."

Perhaps my 'reputation' is why I have so many students who are singularly ill suited to study philosophy, yet who fill my classes.

There was a hush as the bier with Kalifa's green-shrouded body was moved into the center of the rotunda. The imam began the Janazah with the call recognizing the greatness of Allah, and shifted into the supplication for the soul of Kalifa, and for humanity in general. He spoke of his personal knowledge of Kalifa: "I knew him well. He prayed here regularly, and we discussed many of the mysteries of Islam. He was a young man of great integrity and faith. He will be much missed by many."

At the conclusion of the short service, many of those present paid their respects to my son by a gentle nod or a brief touch of the green brocade.

The prayer hall was almost empty. Adeeba, Sagira, Wahida, Nakai and I had been waiting in the background. Naqib appeared. He stood next to his brother, his back to me. Perhaps he was saying something to Kalifa. Suddenly, he threw himself onto the shroud and shook with muffled lamentations. After some moments he stood, and without a word to anyone, left the mosque.

* * *

I think Sagira was particularly pleased with the cemetery. After we passed through the gates, she stood, slowly turning and gazing to take it all in. There are no monuments, only grave markers and the occasional low marble headstone. There are trees, and shrubs, and since each grave is covered in grass, the effect was of peaceful green, dotted with flowers, some growing naturally, many placed in vases.

Mr. Fereiha led us to the open grave – only the family and a few close friends. The attendants brought Kalifa's body on a litter. "Professor," Mr. Fereiha asked, "will you place the body in the grave?" Startled at first by this question, I realized that it was obvious. I looked around. There, ten meters away, stood Naqib, alone. I beckoned to him; he shook his head. I was disappointed; I climbed down into the grave with the assistance of Mr. Fereiha. The attendants carefully lowered Kalifa's shrouded body, right side down. I reached up and took the sphere of packed earth that was handed to me, and put it under my son's head. He was lying on his side, in a comfortable position, facing Mecca.

I climbed out and reached for the marble vase I had brought with me. Removing the stopper, I poured the gritty grey dust into the grave. There. Rest in peace, Elizabeth and Kalifa.

I took a handful of the earth that Mr. Fereiha offered me. The others did the same, and each of us sprinkled three handfuls into the grave. Mr. Fereiha led us in the repetition of the verse from the Qur'an (20:55): "From the earth We created you, into it We shall return you, and from it We shall raise you a second time."

I said that each of us sprinkled the earth, but then I noticed that Naqib didn't participate. When I turned to look for him, he was gone.

The grave diggers were filling in the grave. Mr. Fereiha asked, "Shall we plant it with grass, Professor?"

Sagira responded, "Yes, please, Mr. Fereiha, and can you also plant some flowers like those over there?"

"Yes, madam, that's white myrtle."

"And I would like a headstone as well."

"It can't be higher than thirty centimeters, madam."

"That's all right. White marble, with his name, his birth date, his date of death with 'killed in combat defending Egypt' and 'son of Professor Kareem al-Busiri' and 'husband of Sagira'."

Mr. Fereiha was nodding. He had taken out a memo book and was writing in it.

Later, I thought, I should have saved some of Elizabeth's ashes with instructions that they be poured over my body in the grave. But I dismissed the thought. It's done now.

Chapter 12

Ibn Sina

"I don't understand Naqib's behavior," I said when we had returned home, "it's almost as if he feels we banished him from the family."

"No, Papa," was Wahida's answer, "it is he who has banished us."

"Because he feels we have some responsibility for Kalifa's death?"

"No, Papa, because he feels he has some responsibility for Kalifa's death."

"Oh Allah, I pray it isn't true!"

* * *

In the days that followed my son's death and burial, I felt disconnected and lost. Wahida spent most of her free time with Sagira – as did Adeeba. I understood this: Sagira had her dreams for the future utterly shattered. She needed to feel that if the future was uncertain, at least she had love and security in the present. At the university, everyone seemed to treat me with great care, as if it were common knowledge that I had terminal cancer and no one wanted to talk about it. People were kind – too kind, but they were neither spontaneous nor cheerful. I would have welcomed a cup of coffee and some chatter about the Premier

Football League, about which I know next to nothing except who the teams are. But I could have asked some questions about who was leading the league, and what the prospects were. What I missed was the friendly, extemporaneous chat, some purposeless distraction. Instead, my head was inside a grey cloud of grief which was with me at all hours, night and day.

I had come to depend on Adeeba as someone who could somehow bring out a better Kareem: a more spontaneous, self-confident, and outgoing. As it was, I missed both Adeeba and the better Kareem. What was I to do?

I'm sure that Wahida sensed my grey cloud, and one morning, before she left for work, she asked, "When are you and Adeeba going to get together?"

"Well," I said, "she's pretty well tied up with Sagira."

Wahida gave me one of her 'you've missed the point' frowns. "Don't you think she would like to have some distraction? In fact, you could use some distraction, Papa."

"Well, I could invite her out to dinner."

Over her shoulder, on the way out the door, she said, "You could invite her for more than dinner, Papa."

What did she mean by that?

Anyway, I invited Adeeba to one of the five star hotels for dinner. In my experience, the restaurants at the better hotels offer good food and service, but, equally important, the atmosphere is a good thirty decibels lower than in the crowded, trendy restaurants.

Over the first course we commiserated over the loss of Kalifa, and how hard it was on those left behind. When the main course arrived, our discussion moved slightly into the future: Sagira's child (due in five months), and what names had been proposed. When dessert arrived (crepe suzettes in Adeeba's case), she asked, "What about us, Kareem?"

"It's so good to be with you, Adeeba, and I looked forward to this evening so much, and . . ."

"Why don't we get married, Kareem?"

The question startled me, but almost immediately, I thought, Yes! That's it! That's the answer! How can I do this?

"Will you marry me, Adeeba?"

She leaned back in her chair. "Do you think it's a good idea, Kareem?"

"I think it's an absolutely splendid idea!"

"In that case, I accept!"

I reached across the table and took both of her hands in mine. "This is such a good idea!"

A smiling Adeeba beckoned the waiter over. "What champagne do you have in split sizes?"

He mentioned several names. "We'll have one of the Moet, please." She turned to me. "Now, Kareem, I'm going to have a little champagne to celebrate our engagement, and you're going to have at least a sip to participate in the celebration."

I looked around the restaurant to see if there was anyone I knew. There wasn't.

The waiter brought two special glasses and poured the champagne.

Adeeba lifted her glass; I did likewise. "To us," she said, "to a long and happy marriage."

I repeated her words and prepared to drink. As my lips touched the glass, my nose was showered with the bursting of tiny bubbles. The liquid reminded me of very good sparkling water; the flavor was like grape juice but much better. "Very good," I said.

"You've never had champagne before?"

"I've never had any alcohol before."

"Well, one thing I can promise you, Kareem: Allah is not going to send you to hell for one glass of champagne."

I hope she was right, because I finished it. That was my first and only taste of alcohol. Adeeba served it after our wedding, but I didn't want to drink it in front of so many people I knew. Of course. Adeeba has a glass of wine at home sometimes, but I'm afraid to join her. I think: What if I start liking it? What then? It's just better to leave it alone.

* * *

Our wedding(s) followed the pattern of Kalifa and Sagira, with some significant exceptions. There was no mahr. "We're just going to split the expenses," Adeeba announced.

For the shabka, I bought Adeeba a very good two carat diamond with which she could do as she wished. After a long consultation with Wahida and Sagira, she had it mounted on a pink gold band.

There was no wasteful white wedding dress; instead, Adeeba bought a green silk dress. "I can't possibly get married in one of my old dresses." I wore one of my better suits, with a new green tie.

"Why do we have to spend all that money on flowers?" I protested. "They'll be gone in three days and nobody is going remember them." Adeeba's florist was in despair: there were only two arrangements for the altar in church, nothing for the mosque, and half a dozen live stephanotis plants which filled Adeeba's home with their strong, sweet scent.

Apart from our families, there were no young people in attendance, but we enlarged the circle of colleagues who were invited. "I want everybody to know," Adeeba insisted, "that our relationship is not something to be gossiped about. We are actually married!"

I hadn't planned on what people in the West call a 'honeymoon'. The idea is becoming popular among well-to-do young people in Cairo, but we were in the midst of the university term, and colleagues who would have to fill in for us would not take our departure kindly.

"Kareem," Adeeba asked, "why don't we plan to go somewhere this summer?"

"OK." If I had thought my acquiescence would push the subject onto the back burner, I was mistaken.

"Where shall we go?"

"Rome?" It wasn't exotic, but I thought it was acceptable.

"Good idea! We can go back to the Hotel Campo De' Fiori. That will be wonderful!" She reined in her enthusiasm to think for a moment. "And then we can go on to Paris and London!"

Oh, Allah, this is going to be really expensive. "Adeeba," I countered, "I may have a lofty sounding title, but I'm toward the bottom of the university's pay scale."

"No, you're not!" She considered me for a moment. "All right, I'll pick up the Paris and London portion."

There was also the question of where we would live as a married couple. My apartment was closer to the university and was therefore more convenient to both of us, but Adeeba was reluctant to leave Sagira on her own. I suggested that Wahida might welcome a chance to be with Sagira, and Adeeba's house was closer to the Red Crescent where Wahida worked.

"I think it's too early to make a permanent decision, Kareem. Why don't we see how things unfold? If Wahida wants to stay with me, that's fine; when she does, I'll stay with you. We might make a decision to sell one, or both houses, and buy something new."

As it turned out, Wahida decided to stay with Sagira during the week, when there was the added convenience of a shorter commute to the Red Crescent. And, during the week, Adeeba stayed with me, and was therefore closer to the university. Weekends were unpredictable: but usually all four of us were at one place or the other.

* * *

I answered the phone before leaving my apartment on a Thursday morning. Anisa was very distraught. "Professor, Naqib has been arrested!"

340

"Why? What happened?"

"The police woke us up at five fifteen this morning." She was sobbing now. "They took Naqib away in handcuffs."

"What did the police say?"

"They said that he was wanted for questioning, and they wouldn't say what it was about."

"Do you have a lawyer, Anisa?"

"I don't know, Professor. Naqib would have handled anything like that."

"I'll call my lawyer right away and ask him to look into it. Think back, Anisa. Has Naqib mentioned anything that could be a reason for his arrest?"

"As you know, Professor, he is a member of the Brotherhood, but that is secret."

"Well, perhaps the authorities found out and have had him arrested just to scare him."

"Do you think that could be it, Professor?"

"I don't know, but perhaps. Is there anything else, Anisa?"

"Yes. There were three men in plain clothes who searched the apartment after Naqib was taken away. They searched everywhere and made an awful mess. The children were very frightened."

"Oh, I'm sorry, Anisa. I'll let you know as soon as I hear anything from the lawyer."

* * *

I called my lawyer, Mr. Aboul-Nour, who did my will and handles my contracts with the university and my publisher. He said he would look into it right away.

Adeeba had already left when Anisa called; I wouldn't be able to discuss it with her until midday.

I reached Wahida on her mobile. She listened to my report. "You know what I think, Papa."

341

"No. What is it?"

"I think this has to do with Kalifa's death."

"That's a pretty wild theory, Wahida. Why would Naqib want to kill his brother?"

"Why indeed."

My daughter is very stubborn. When she gets an idea, it stays fixed in her mind, and when she is proven wrong, she finds excuses, such as: "Well, if such-and-such had happened, I would have been right!"

* * *

I checked my mobile phone after my eleven o'clock class. There was a message from Mr. Aboul-Nour asking me to call him. "Your son is being held in Tora Prison for questioning," he reported.

"Questioning about what?"

"They won't say, but when they are secretive like this, it is almost certainly a national security issue."

"Was anyone else picked up with him?"

"Yes, they apparently picked up the other three partners of the law firm, Kamal Saleh and Partners."

"They are involved in the same issue?"

"Yes, apparently."

"Mr. Aboul-Nour, is there a possibility I could see my son?"

"Professor, I very much doubt it. You know the reputation of Tora: very tough, and under the circumstances . . . I doubt that they would let him see a lawyer."

I passed this information on to Anisa at work, but it only made her more anxious. I tried (unsuccessfully) to relieve her concern. "We have to be patient, Anisa. This is probably just a big misunderstanding."

Was it just a misunderstanding?

I was feeling very uneasy about Naqib's arrest. I doubted any connection with Kalifa's death, but maybe he had done something that the authorities didn't like. This was easy to do in Egypt.

* * *

What can I do? He's being held on a national security issue. That means the GID are involved. Suddenly, I remembered Colonel Arafa. He was GID, wasn't he? I managed to find his phone number and left a message. When he returned the call, I reminded him that we had spoken months ago. "Yes, I recall, Professor. What can I do for you?"

"My son, Naqib al-Busiri, has been taken in for questioning, and he is currently in Tora Prison. I was wondering if you could tell me what this is about."

"Let me do some checking and I'll call you back, Professor."

Two hours later, he called me back. "Professor, do you mind if I stop by and see you tonight?"

"No, of course not."

I gave him the address and he said he would be there at about six-thirty.

I called Wahida to inform her of the little I knew. She said, "Six-thirty? I'll be there."

* * *

Colonel Arafa was not a full 'aqid (colonel); he was a moqa-ddim (lieutenant colonel), but he was handsome young man – perhaps thirty, in khaki uniform, with a colorful array of ribbons on his left breast.

He stirred his coffee thoughtfully. "Professor, your son has been arrested as what we would call an investigative measure."

"What does that mean, Colonel?"

"Well, there have been several mobile phone calls from the north Sinai area to the law firm where your son works." He took a sip of his coffee. "And the mobile telephone from which the calls were made is believed to be used by the leaders of the Daesh in Sinai." I felt the blood draining out of my brain, like a child who is caught in an indiscretion. "Since we don't know who received the calls," he continued, "or what was said during the calls, we have decided to call in the senior members of the law firm for questioning. That includes your son."

"I see," I said, numbly. Wahida sat mute but attentive at the table next to me.

"Once the employees had been removed from the office, we conducted a search of the office and removed several files. From the files, we learned that your son has made a number of trips during the past year." I felt a chill in my upper spine.

"Yes?"

"In particular, there were several trips to Sharm el Sheikh. Do you know the purpose of those trips, Professor?"

"He told me they involved meetings with clients."

"Do you know the identity of the clients, Professor?"

"No, I don't, Colonel." I sensed an uneasy movement of Wahida next to me.

"And there were a number of trips to Riyadh. Do you know anything about them?"

"He said he had a client in Riyadh, but I don't know who he is."

Colonel Arafa nodded. "There are also two trips to Dubai within the last two months. Was that for a holiday?"

"No, I think that was also for business, also."

"But, you don't know what the business was?"

"No, Colonel, I don't. My son didn't keep me well informed."

He pushed his coffee cup aside. "Professor, are you aware of any other contacts that Naqib may have had?"

"Business contacts?" I paused to think.

"Yes," Wahida put in, "there was Mr. Derbala."

"Ah, yes," I said.

"Who is Mr. Derbala?"

"He is a cousin of my stepmother's," Wahida replied, "and he runs a shipping business."

"What kind of a shipping business?"

Wahida shook her head, "We don't know the nature of his business, but it's called Derbala Shipping."

Colonel Arafa removed a small memo book from his breast pocket and made a note. "Do you know what sort of business Naqib discussed with Mr. Derbala?"

We both shook our heads. "No."

"Is there anything else you can tell us?" Colonel Arafa asked.

"Well," I said, "Naqib has always been a good boy, a bit of an idealist with a bias toward the left, but I'm sure he wouldn't do anything very wrong."

The colonel nodded.

"When can I see my son, Colonel?"

"I'm afraid that won't be possible until we have finished questioning him. I understand he is married."

"Yes," I said, "with three small children."

"What can you tell me about his wife? We will want to interview her."

"She's from a poor background, but she has a responsible job with a bank," Wahida said, "She's a good mother and a very thoughtful person."

"And," I added, "she's very concerned about her husband."

"Concerned that he might have done something wrong?"

Damn! I said the wrong thing!

"No," Wahida said, "I think it's more that she admires him and depends on him to help with the children."

Colonel Arafa rose to leave. "I'll leave you my card in case something else comes to mind."

* * *

The door had barely closed behind the colonel when Wahida said, "We better call Anisa!"

"Why don't you call her," I said.

Wahida spent almost an hour on the phone with Anisa.

"She's very upset," Wahida told me. "She's afraid that Naqib is going to be tortured in the prison and confess to things he didn't do."

"But that's Anisa putting herself in Naqib's position," I said, "She seems to be a worrier, whereas Naqib has an iron determination."

"She's also terrified about being questioned by Colonel Arafa. She's sure she'll say something that gets Naqib convicted and locked up indefinitely."

"A suggestion, Wahida: why don't you coach Anisa on how to respond to Colonel Arafa? You could do a role play, and show her how to answer the questions truthfully without telling the whole story."

Wahida spent most of the following evening with Anisa.

* * *

When Adeeba came to my house later that evening, I gave her a summary of the meeting with Colonel Arafa – including the mention of Mr. Derbala. "I'm concerned now that they're going to arrest your cousin," I said.

"Don't worry about it, Kareem. You didn't accuse him of anything. You just said that he had a business meeting with your son."

"That's true, but don't you think you ought to warn him that the police may be around?"

"No. It'll just give him something to hold against me. If he does get arrested, he certainly isn't going to suspect you."

"He may suspect Naqib."

"That's a risk they decided to take. Look, Nahman's a very dodgy character. Stop worrying about him; he can take care of himself."

* * *

There's that old saying: 'Just because I'm paranoid doesn't mean they aren't out to get me!' In Egypt then, everybody was at least a little paranoid, and in many cases, the government was out to get us, particularly if one opposed it.

* * *

I learned from Wahida later that Anisa survived her meeting with Colonel Arafa reasonably well. "When I met with her," Wahida said, "she was particularly concerned about identifying Naqib as a member of the Brotherhood. I asked her if Naqib had told her he was a member, or if she had ever seen a document that listed him as a member. She said 'no'. So, I said what you should do if Colonel Arafa asks you about membership in the Brotherhood is to say, 'He never mentioned the Brotherhood to me; I've never seen anything to indicate he is a member. Besides, Colonel, I am completely opposed to the Brotherhood'."

"And that's how the conversation went?" I asked.

"Apparently, yes. But she used the same semi-evasive response on other questions he asked."

"Anisa is a bright girl," I said, "and when you first meet her, she gives the impression of being timid, but underneath, there is some of the same metal that Naqib is made of."

Wahida nodded. "I don't think that Youssef was very hard on her. He realizes that Anisa is not Naqib's accomplice."

"Who is Youssef?" I asked.

"His name is Moqaddim Youssef Arafa."

"You're on a first name basis?"

There was a flush in Wahida's cheeks. "No, I just noticed that his first name is Youssef."

* * *

I hadn't attached any significance to Wahida's comment about 'Youssef'. I should have paid better attention. Wahida has always been secretive (and dismissive) about her male friends, but I have learned that she gives unconscious hints of her attraction when she mentions a new friend. I should not have been surprised when I got a telephone call from Colonel Arafa a few days later.

"Professor, I am calling you on a personal matter. My parents have both passed away, so I am pretty much on my own in these matters." He paused. "I have never married; my career seems to have taken priority." Another pause. "May I ask you if Wahida is engaged?"

"No, Colonel, she is not."

"Well, I wonder if I might have your permission, sir, to get to know your daughter better. Of course, she will be chaperoned at all times," he added hastily. "I don't believe there is any conflict of interest with your son's case, as I am no longer involved in any official way. But you should, of course, feel free to say 'no' for any reason."

I was pleasantly stunned! I had not thought of Colonel Arafa as an eligible bachelor, but he was an impressive young man. "Yes, Colonel, you may spend some time with Wahida. Our family is in some turmoil at the moment, as you will understand. My wife and I are recently married, and we haven't yet consolidated the household. So Wahida is sometimes here with me, and sometimes at my wife's house."

"I understand, Professor."

"Colonel, let me call Wahida, and explain the situation to her. If she is in agreement, I will call and give you her phone number."

"That's excellent, Professor."

* * *

Wahida pretended that she was doing me a favor, but I could tell from her follow-up questions that she was pleased to have the colonel's attention. During the weeks that followed, I didn't know how often Colonel Arafa called on Wahida, because during much of that time she was staying at Adeeba's house, but Adeeba gave me her opinion. "He is handsome and a gentleman. Apart from this, I think that there are several characteristics which Wahida seems to like: he has a sense of humor, and when he gets on a likely subject, he can keep us all laughing. This is a trait I don't expect in a military man. He also seems to be very open and honest; I don't have the impression that he lives behind a mask. Also, he has very kindly taken the three of us out to dinner several times."

It was not long after this appraisal that the colonel took Wahida and me out to dinner. We laughed at his made-up stories about life in the bachelor officer's quarters, which included an element of self-effacement. I had the impression that he and Wahida had become good friends.

* * *

Adeeba learned of the arrest of Nahman Derbala about a week after the fact. Arrests by the security services are rarely reported by the media. "He's being held in Tora Prison for questioning," Adeeba reported. "The family knows nothing."

"Oh dear. I was afraid this was going to happen!"

She said, "It sounds to me as if there may be a linkage to Naqib's case. Do you suppose that Nahman transported something for Naqib that he shouldn't have?"

"I certainly hope not," I said.

* * *

When Wahida came home on a Friday night a few days later, she said, "Sit down, Papa, I have some things to show you."

From her shoulder bag, she took two small cards and passed them across the table to me. They were business cards. One was for a Mr. Jabbar El-Hashim, Principal, with the Global Trading Company in Dubai, and the other for a Sheik Sheddad Najim, President, Saudi Imperial Bank in Riyadh.

"Who are these people?" I asked.

Wahida said nothing. Instead, she passed me two more items. One was a color leaflet on a piece of military hardware. The second was a folded file in Arabic. I looked up at Wahida and saw that she was expecting me to examine them. The color leaflet was written in Cyrillic script. This is Russian. There was a photo of a yellow and grey rocket, about a meter long, and a tube on a tripod. I picked up the Arabic file. It was titled: Instructions to the Operator: 9M133 Kornet (comet). I briefly scanned the text. "Anti-tank . . . solid fuel propellant . . . maximum range 5.5 kilometers . . . guidance: laser beam . . . warhead: 10 kg TNT equivalent . . . impact fuse."

"Where did you get this?" I asked.

"From a hiding place in Naqib's home office."

I was dumbfounded. "You went into his apartment when he wasn't there and searched for these things?"

"I suspected he was providing arms to the Daesh, but I had to find out. If I had found nothing, I would have changed my mind."

"So you spent hours ransacking his apartment?"

"No. I went there, and the au pair let me in. I said I wanted to retrieve a book of mine that Naqib had. I went straight to his office, found the book I wanted and found these inside the cover."

"What book was it?"

"An old leather-bound copy of the Qur'an. I think Grand Papa gave it to him when he was about ten."

"How did you know to look there?"

"When he was about fourteen and I was twelve. I knew he had some dirty pictures, because he showed them to his friends. I searched his room and found them in the Qur'an. After that, I would go and check what was in the Qur'an. There was always something there. One time it was a police caution he got for riding his bike down the wrong side of the street."

"But this doesn't prove anything, Wahida," I said with a gesture at her findings.

"It shows that he had an interest in the same kind of weapon that killed Kalifa, and it shows who he probably met on his trips to Riyadh and Dubai."

"What are you going to do with these, Wahida?"

"I'm going to give them to Youssef when he comes here this evening."

That childhood fear of being caught swept over me. "Is that really necessary? Why don't you just destroy them?"

"Papa, I knew you were going to say that. But I decided you have to know what I found. If Naqib has an explanation for these things, he's not guilty. But it is wrong – and you know it – to destroy evidence!"

I thought about Wahida as a child – the middle child – caught between two brothers. The brothers had been close. Four years younger, Kalifa looked up to Naqib, who coached him at football and tennis. Wahida was just a girl – a nuisance who could get in the way of doing boy things.

"You hate your brother, Wahida?" I asked.

"No, Papa, I don't hate him. I respect him for what he has accomplished: a university degree, a law degree, passing the bar exam, marrying Anisa, loving her children, and finding a good job. But I despise his politics, and his attitude that he knows what's best for everyone else."

* * *

Colonel Arafa arrived soon after this unfortunate disclosure. He looked briefly at the business cards. "We know these two guys. They're not exactly friends of Egypt. Sheik Najim is a very wealthy, radical Wahhabi, and he has been identified as a financial supporter of ISIL, which follows his religious ideology. El-Hashim is a freelance arms dealer." He put the cards to one side, and scanned the leaflet and the file in Arabic. He looked at me. "Professor, this is probably the weapon that killed your son. We found fragments of the rocket motor with Cyrillic writing. The Egyptian Army does not use the Kornet, we use the American version. The Russians say they had absolutely nothing to do with arming Sinai Provence. They have their own concerns about blow-back into Russia. Unfortunately, there were nearly forty thousand of these damn things made, and the Middle East is awash with them."

I put my head down on the table and wept.

Wahida brought me a cup of tea. "Sorry," I said.

"Please don't apologize, Professor. This is a terrible situation for you."

"Will these be enough to convict my son?"

"It's just circumstantial evidence, Professor, but it may contribute to the overall picture."

I wanted to ask more, but I was afraid to hear the answers I might receive. When Colonel Arafa suggested that we go out to dinner, I acquiesced, though I was not very good company. Wahida and the colonel chattered amiably about I don't know what. Suddenly, I thought: Did Wahida seek that evidence as a way of pleasing a future husband? When he turns it in, it might help his career! Stop it, Kareem! Eat your baklava!

* * *

A week later, a very distraught Anisa called me before I left for the university. "Professor, I don't know what to do! The rent on the apartment is two months overdue. They've given me two weeks to pay or leave! I found out yesterday that Naqib isn't being paid any more!"

"Oh dear! Have you spoken to his office?"

"Yes, they said that he isn't employed there anymore."

Oh shit! The office manager has probably decided to stop the paychecks of the four principals, so there's money to pay the office staff, who are still at work, but doing nothing! She could take the firm to court, but it will be months before a decision is reached. Probably unfavorable. Her family certainly isn't in a position to help. "Anisa, why don't you and the children come here?"

"Oh, Professor, I couldn't do that!"

"Nonsense, Anisa, of course you can! There's Kalifa's bedroom vacant, and I don't really need my office, which used to be Naqib's bedroom.

"Professor, I don't like to inconvenience you!"

"Anisa, do you have an alternative?"

The line was silent for a long moment. "No, Professor," said the small voice, "no, I don't."

"Why don't you come here this evening? You can look at the situation, and decide what furniture you want to bring with you. Do you have some friends who could help you move?"

"Yes, Professor, that's very, very kind of you. I'll be there this evening."

* * *

I called Wahida and told her of Anisa's dilemma. She said, "I might as well move completely to Adeeba's. I'm there most of the time anyway. So Anisa can have my room, Basima and Husna can stay in Kalifa's room, and Ra'id can sleep in your office."

I giggled inside. The ever-practical Wahida!

353

And that's what we did. I can't say that I liked the situation very much. Grandchildren are lovely when one can select their presence. But they're somewhat less enjoyable when they demand your attention when you're trying to relax and read the newspaper. I will say that Anisa tried to minimize the disruptions from her children. She kept the house in order, hired a new au pair to look after the children when she was at work, and she was able to arrange a transfer for herself to a New Cairo branch of her bank.

We didn't speak much about Naqib, but I'm sure she was as anxious as I was.

* * *

There was a brief announcement in the Egypt Daily News: "Muslim Brotherhood members to face trial for crimes against the Republic." It listed the five names, but it didn't specify the trial date. Anisa and I read and re-read it with a growing sense of foreboding. She asked: "How did they find out that Naqib is a member of the Brotherhood?"

"The GID probably has a more accurate membership list than the Brotherhood itself," I said, yet I also had questions. I called Colonel Arafa: "Colonel, can you tell me, without doing any research, when the trial will take place?"

"Professor, I would guess it will start in a week or two."

"And what do you suppose the charges will be?"

"You understand, sir, that I don't know, but I suspect it will be something like treason."

Treason! Dear Allah! Could there be anything worse? My brain felt as if it had turned to mush.

"And in a trial like this, Colonel . . . I mean . . . in a trial like this, there is no possibility of an independent lawyer?"

"That's correct, Professor. The attorney would have to hold a current top secret clearance, and if you found one, the government would try to disqualify him."

"One final question, Colonel, or rather it's a request: Can arrangements be made that I can speak with my son? Even if it's a monitored telephone call?"

"I will see what I can do, Professor."

* * *

Ten days later the arrangements were made. I had to call a specified number at a certain time; the call was to last no longer than ten minutes. Anisa came to my office; Wahida declined the invitation.

"Hello, is that Professor al-Busiri?"

"Yes, we are calling from my office at the American University. We have you on the speaker phone. My son's wife, Anisa, is here with me."

"Here is the prisoner. You have ten minutes maximum."

"Hello, Papa?"

"Yes, Anisa is here with me."

"How are you, sweetheart?"

"I'm all right. I'm staying with your father now."

"That's good. I guess they stopped paying me."

"Yes. How are you?"

"I'm . . . I'm kind of scared. The trial has started and they're asking for the death penalty."

Oh Allah, this must be a nightmare! Why can't I wake up?

"But you're innocent, aren't you, Naqib?" Anisa suggested.

"The trouble is: the other guys have turned against me."

"What do you mean, Naqib?" I asked.

"I mean: they threaten us with a maximum sentence unless we implicate the others."

"But don't you have a lawyer?"

"There is a lawyer, but he's not much help." He paused. "That's something you could do, Papa: is to get us a celebrity lawyer. Like that Cherrie, the UK politician's wife, or Amal, the actor's wife. I'm sure the other guys would contribute to the cost."

"But Naqib, I've talked to Mr. Aboul-Nour about getting you a lawyer. He says it's virtually impossible."

"But Papa, I'm not talking about an Egyptian lawyer who'd represent us in court. I'm talking about a famous human rights lawyer who would speak to the media on our behalf and bring pressure on the government to give us a lighter sentence."

"I'll see what I can do. But the lawyer would have to believe that you are not guilty."

"OK, Papa, I may have done some things I shouldn't have done, but I didn't mean to kill Kalifa. I promise I didn't!" He broke down into sobs.

"I'll see what I can do, Naqib."

Anisa picked up the conversation. "How are you being treated in prison, Naqib?"

"They treat us kind of rough, but there's no torture. They feed us; we have a place to sleep; there's no exercise."

"Basima and Husna miss you, Naqib."

There was another sob. "I miss them, Anisa. How is Ra'id?"

"He's fine. He'll be walking soon. Your father is very good with him."

"I miss you, Anisa, and I love you a lot."

"I love you, Naqib. We're praying for you!"

* * *

I didn't mean to kill Kalifa reverberated over and over in my mind. Who did you mean to kill? Some other father's son? The doubts had disappeared, but the sorrow and the anguish seemed to intensify. This is so unnecessary! If you had only listened to the many warnings you had! And a Human Rights Lawyer! Naqib believed that human rights were an obstacle to strict sharia governance, but he believed in human rights when he was in trouble!

Anisa seemed strangely calm. I had expected her to be depressed and tearful, but she went about her duties placidly. Perhaps she prays a lot, and she finds comfort in her prayers.

I spoke again to Mr. Aboul-Nour. He said, "The Egyptian government is one of Cherri's clients, and she would not take on a client with whom the government has an issue. In Amal's case, she would want to see convincing proof of your son's innocence. Is such proof available?"

"No, I'm afraid it isn't."

* * *

The children were asleep and Anisa had said good night and gone to her room. The house was very quiet. I could not sleep, though I felt tired. Perhaps I should pray a little. There's no harm in it and it may untie my tangled thoughts.

I knelt on the carpet, and, facing southeast, spoke softly the first ayah (verse) of the Quran: "In the name of God, the Lord of Mercy, the Giver of Mercy!

"I pray to You, Mighty Allah, that You would see fit to relieve the torment I am in. You know that my younger son has been killed. I pray that he rests with You. I fear that the death of my younger son was brought about by my older son, though not intentionally. Now, my older son is threatened with death under the laws of my country. I pray that Naqib may fully repent his errors, may be granted Your forgiveness, and may be spared death. If my late wife, Elizabeth, were still alive, I know she would join me in this prayer. As she is with You, You have already heard her prayers."

My prayer continued for some time, largely repetitiously in this vein, but with additional points about Naqib's family and his accomplishments in which we took pride.

I stood and reflected for a moment. I felt more positive about my situation. Why is that? And there was something else: there were the words, 'You've done all you can, Kareem.' Did I think them? No, I don't think so. I keep wondering what more I can do. But the words are there: 'You've done all you can, Kareem.' And they have given me a lingering sense of comfort.

I asked Adeeba, who for me was an expert in religious matters, about my experience: "When you're praying do you get seem to get an answer which isn't an answer?"

"Can you give me an example, Kareem?"

I told her about my prayer.

"Yes, but not often, sometimes, and I usually wonder: Did I think that?

"Yes, exactly! Do you think it's actually the voice of Allah?"

"My theory is that it's a little more complicated than that. I believe that when each of us is born, there is a tiny spark of God in us. It's as if He left his fingerprints on our DNA in an undetectable way. As we mature, and if we begin to trust and to love God the spark becomes larger and can take over some of our personality. Jesus is the extreme case: his personality was God. The rest of us have a more recognizable human personality with, for example, a large helping of selfishness."

"But if it's part of our personality, why don't we recognize the words as our own?"

"Probably because it is a new dimension of our personality, and we don't yet recognize it as part of us."

"Adeeba, do you believe that this same phenomenon could apply to Satan?"

"What do you mean, Kareem?"

"I'm not saying that Satan puts his fingerprints on our DNA at birth, but do you suppose that when one inclines oneself to him, Satan may begin to affect our personality?"

"I hadn't thought about it, but yes, it's the kind of thing that happens to serial killers."

Later I began to wonder whether it may have happened to Naqib. But he goes to the mosque more frequently than I. Where was the room for Satan?

It occurred to me that I had no notion of the quality of Naqib's religious experience. Was he a devout Muslim, a perfunctory Muslim, or a skewed Muslim? I had no idea.

* * *

I should have been prepared for it, but I was not. When I turned to page five of the Egypt Daily News, the announcement read: "Five Muslim Brotherhood members sentenced to death." It went on to say that they had been tried by the highest military court, had been found guilty of "treasonable acts against the Republic", and had been sentenced to death by hanging. A terrible sense of loss and finality came over me. It was as if I had been told: "You are guilty! And we will hang you tomorrow at dawn!"

But then I thought, I would gladly exchange places with Naqib, if it were possible. An unconditional exchange. I have lived most of my life. He has lived less than half of his. He has children and he will repent.

But will he? Will he really repent? I began to realize it wasn't so unconditional.

I called Mr. Aboul-Nour and asked about appeals.

"Professor, in cases like this there normally is no appeal. In theory the Muslim Brotherhood could bring an appeal, but as an outlawed organization, they have no legal standing."

"Could I bring an appeal?"

"Professor, an appeal would have to be based on a legal argument that, for example, the court did not give proper consideration to certain facts. But since the trial was held in secret, we have no knowledge of how the trial was conducted. We therefore do not have the information we would need to mount a challenge.

I think your only recourse, Professor, is to appeal for clemency to the President. I can help you draft such an appeal if you wish."

* * *

Adeeba, who had heard about the sentencing, took me home from the university. We talked for at least two hours, and I descended into self-pitying weeping three or four times. "I don't know how I can bear this!" I lamented.

"You are strong, Kareem."

"I don't feel very strong."

We undressed and got into bed. The touch of her warm, supple skin was a luxurious balm. Her breasts against my chest. The gentle washboard of her spine. The smooth curvature of her bottom. The pliable stiffness of her shoulders. Her soft cheek against mine. Her warm livingness lifted me out of my cold assurance of death. I fell asleep and woke alive. We made love, slowly, tenderly.

* * *

The letter to the President appealing for clemency was written and sent. I had really done all that could be done.

A week later a letter with the presidential seal arrived at my office. My secretary brought it to me in her hand unopened. She backed away respectfully while I opened it.

"Dear Professor al-Busiri,

The President thanks you for your letter appealing for clemency in the case of your son, Naqib al-Busiri. The President assures me that he will take the mitigation suggested by yourself into full consideration when deciding whether clemency can be granted.

He wishes to remind you that the very life of the Republic is under threat by those who wish to destroy the fabric of our democratic society. The President has sworn to uphold liberty and democracy for the Egyptian people.

The President wishes me to extend to you his best wishes, and his thanks for your support.

Yours Sincerely,

Mohammed B Karzai

Executive Assistant to the President

Republic of Egypt"

I tossed the letter away. My secretary watched it fall to the floor. "I'm sorry, Professor."

* * *

Days later, when I returned to my office, my secretary was busy typing. She did not look up. On my desk was a buff window envelope. Across the front it said "T TELEGRAM" in green. There was a circle around the first T. I slit it open. Inside was a yellow telegram:

"Department of Justice, Prison Service, Tora Prison.

Professor Kareem al-Busiri, American University, New Cairo

Professor,

This is to inform you that the body of your son, Naqib al-Busiri, is available for collection. Please come to the southwest gate of Tora Prison between the hours of 8 am and 5 pm. Please bring this telegram and your photographic identity.

If you do not respond within 24 hours, the body will be consigned to a common grave.

Abdul Nizwaq

Head, External Services

Tora Prison"

I felt as if someone had struck me across the face with a cold, wet fish. How insensitive can they be? No phone call. No condolences. No recognition of human sentiment. Do they think

I intentionally raised a mass murderer? My hurt turned to anger. I sat down and continued to re-read the telegram.

Why not call instead of sending a telegram? Because they don't have your phone number immediately available and they don't want to discuss the message with you.

Couldn't they at least express some sympathy? Because expressing sympathy would imply that perhaps they could have done something different than executing Naqib. But they are absolutely convinced that they did the right thing.

Why is it necessary to respond within 24 hours? Because they are trying to keep within the Muslim rule that a body should be buried within 24 hours. Probably also because the families of lots of common criminals want nothing to do with the deceased.

I began to wonder how this kind of notice would be handled in America, where plenty of people are executed. Then I realized that the whole process is transparent: The family knows exactly what's going on at each stage. The condemned has been given an open trial by jury, with opportunities for appeal, and it isn't the government that makes the decision. It's a truly independent judiciary. The government can be polite and sympathetic.

Well, this is what el-Sisi believes is Democracy in Egypt.

I called Mr. Fereiha. He said, "I have another burial within the next hour, Professor, but I can meet you at the southwest gate at, say, one-thirty? I'm afraid we'll have to go to my business to prepare the body. I don't believe the government does that."

* * *

Tora Prison had a yellow stone façade, topped by a watch tower at each end. The rectangular main entrance was blocked by concrete barricades and several armored vehicles. On the western side of the massive block, I found Mr. Fereiha waiting with his hearse. We approached double steel doors at the southern end and were admitted to an office, where three guards scrutinized my documents. Without a word, but with a sweeping motion of his arm, a guard directed Mr. Fereiha to drive in. The doors swung open, the hearse was admitted, and the doors closed again, with a rifle-carrying guard standing at the point of closure. A trolley was wheeled out into the bright, sandy courtyard. Mr. Fereiha whispered, "Professor, I think it's best if you check that this is your son."

I felt an urge to object, but the surly composure of the two uniformed guards at the trolley quelled that impulse. I walked to the trolley and looked down at the long, black plastic bag. It had an oversized zipper down its length. Gingerly, I gripped the zipper tab and pulled it down. A nose appeared and then a waxy face. It was Naqib. I pulled the zipper tab back up and nodded. Mr. Fereiha and the guards manhandled the bag from the trolley to the hearse.

* * *

I remember two things about washing Naqib's body: the similarity of his physique – though smaller – to that of his brother: the muscled shoulders, the bony knees, and the smooth, broad feet seemed identical. Then, there was the extensive purple bruising around the neck.

"Let me help you, Professor," Mr. Fereiha offered when I was about to turn the body over. "You mind the head." I found that his head was loosely connected to his body.

I had steeled myself to this duty, pretending that I, myself, was absent and that only a surrogate, robotic Mr. al-Busiri was performing the rite of washing and wrapping the body. I allowed no recognition and no feelings to creep in.

* * *

Anisa was waiting for us at the cemetery. It was the same cemetery in which Kalifa was buried, but I had asked Mr. Fereiha to arrange a plot on the perimeter; Kalifa's grave was near the center. As we approached the grave, I regretted, momentarily, having poured all of Elizabeth's ashes on Kalifa. You should have saved half for Naqib. But I didn't know at the time. Does he deserve half? Perhaps it's better as it is, and perhaps someday, they will pour Adeeba's ashes on me.

Anisa was wearing her customary navy blue trouser suit and a dark head scarf. No one else was waiting. She stood, dry-eyed, a respectful distance from the grave, holding a single red carnation, as we lowered the body. Mr. Fereiha pulled me up and out, held a shovel-full of earth for me. Anisa stepped forward and dropped the carnation onto the body. She took a handful of earth and sprinkled it into the grave. As the grave diggers filled in the grave, Anisa stood attentively, an expression of faint sorrow on her face.

"Professor, do you wish me to put in a headstone?" Mr. Fereiha asked.

I turned to Anisa.

She shook her head. "I know where he is."

* * *

I could not go straight home after the burial. I felt the pressure of loneliness and culpability. I wanted to sense the reassurance of family or even friends, but neither Adeeba nor Wahiba would be home: only the au pair, who treated me with reverent civility. I went to my mosque at the university, seeking a surrogate refuge. It was deserted and silent, grey walls and red carpet. I chose my prayer spot under a window and beside a pillar. I began in a low voice: "In the name of God, the Lord of Mercy, the Giver of Mercy . . ," but my words seemed to echo around the space. Continuing in a whisper, "Mighty Allah, help me! I have lost both my sons. My life has lost its meaning. Am I to die also? If that be Your will, let it be. I can be of no further use to You. My life is finished. . . ."

My prayer continued like this for some minutes. I fell silent. I had said what I needed to say. There was merciful, peaceful silence.

'Stand up, Kareem! It is over now. Move on!'

"But Allah, I don't know how to move on!"

There was no response, but the words: "Stand up, Kareem! It is over now. Move on!" echoed in my mind. The command was abrupt; heartless. How can He offer so little sympathy?

I sat on a bench along the wall. In front of me a dusty ray of sunlight lit a crimson parallelogram on the carpet.

But what does it mean?

Stand up? Not literally. Do not lie down! Don't let it get you down!

It is over now. It is finished. It no longer deserves your attention.

Move on! That I understood.

But how? But how?

There was this lingering uncertainty. Strangely, in the face of that uncertainty, I felt at peace with myself. It was as if the How? had been answered and I would find the easy response jotted on a note on my desk at home. I was all right. I had some future. He had assured me.

* * *

Adeeba was waiting for me at home. Her embrace had seldom felt so soothing. She held my shoulders and looked searchingly into my face. "How are you, Kareem? Was it very difficult?"

"I'm OK. I pretended it was someone I didn't know."

"Still very difficult. Are you angry that I didn't attend?"

"No. It was better with just Anisa and Mr. Fereiha."

Adeeba gave a tilt to her head. "She's in the kitchen feeding the children."

"She's amazing," I said. "She seems to have put it all behind her."

Adeeba took my arm. "Sit down, Kareem. Let me get you a cup of tea."

When she returned with the tea, she sat opposite me. I felt her gaze of appraisal.

"Kareem, you have been through hell."

I nodded and sipped the tea.

She was sitting erect, looking at me with intensity. "And when someone has been through hell, they need to re-invent themselves . . . to shake off the slime that's been thrown at them."

The slime I understand, but 're-invent themselves'? "Adeeba, what do you mean by 're-invent themselves'?"

"Well, you used to be the father of two young men. It was an important part of who you were – your identity." I nodded. "Now, you're no longer the father of two young men. In fact, you're surrounded by women now. Five of us: Wahida, Anisa, Sagira, Nakia and me!"

I felt the truth of what she said bite into me: I was a lesser man.

"So," she continued, "I think you should re-invent yourself with a new identity – an identity in which you can have pride."

I shrugged. "But what new identity? How?"

"There are questions to be answered in ways that feel completely right for you."

"What questions?"

"For example: what is to be your relationship to Anisa?"

"Well, she is my daughter-in-law, and . . ."

"Don't answer now!" she interrupted. "Think about it, and think about the implications for you of your answer. Coming back to Anisa, if you establish a father-daughter – almost a blood – relationship that will have an entirely different meaning and set of values than if you view her remotely as the ex-wife of a convicted murderer."

There was an audible intake of my breath. "But, but," I protested, "Anisa may have a preference in the matter."

"Of course, but don't underestimate your ability to create the relationship you want."

"What other questions?"

"The same questions apply to Sagira and Nakia. Don't forget that they have no father."

"Well, Sagira . . ."

She held up her hand, silencing me. "Not now! Think about it carefully, and try to ignore what you think may be my preferences."

"So you're suggesting that the answers will define how I see myself in a family context."

"Not entirely. There's also the question of who lives where and why. I will offer only one of my preferences."

"Which is?"

"I would like to see us sell the house in Al Jamiah . . ." She waited for me to wince. "And buy a much bigger beach house with space for us all – maybe a little cramped for the kids – on weekends and holidays."

This is starting to make sense! "What else?"

"Then there's the whole question of your work."

I frowned. "What about it?"

"Are you going to write another book – or two? Is it going to be a textbook, or some of your personal philosophy? What about a new course in Asian philosophy? Are you going to press for it? How do you want to be remembered as a philosopher? As a great teacher? As a learned professor? As the creator of a new branch of philosophy?"

"I'm starting to get the idea."

"Good."

* * *

My sophomore class in Classical Arabic Philosophy had left the classroom – noisily, as usual. It was quiet now. The ideal time to prepare instructions for their next essay question. My secretary would post it on the website. I looked up at the tiered rows of wooden seats, all but a few having a flat, right-hand writing surface.

I began to write:

"Ibn Sina (980-1037 AD, Uzbekistan) concluded in *The Salvation, Metaphysics* that "Whatever is not necessary does not exist."

(a) What logic did he use to come to this conclusion?

(b) Is the opposite of this conclusion, namely, "Whatever is necessary exists" true?

(c) What logic proves or disproves (b)?

In your opinion, what are some ordinary exceptions to each conclusion?"

I looked up again. There was someone sitting in the first row. She was wearing jeans, an Egyptian Pharaohs football shirt and a grey niqab. I rose from the instructor's desk. "Good morning, Princess."

"Good morning, Professor. Sorry to interrupt your train of thought."

"That's all right. May I suggest we go to my office, where we can have some tea?"

She held up a hand. "I just stopped in briefly on my way to my next appointment."

I sat in the seat next to her.

"You have had a difficult time, Professor."

"Yes, but I am starting to look into the future."

She nodded. "Tell me, Professor, what is your view of Ibn Sina's conclusions?"

"Would you like me to run through his logic sequence?"

"No, Professor, your personal views."

I paused to consider. "Well, after the death of Elizabeth, I felt that what was necessary – my wife – did not exist. A few years later, I began to feel that a wife did not exist and was therefore not necessary. Now, I feel that my wife exists and is absolutely necessary."

"Any other related conclusions?"

Another pause. "I used to think," I began, "that God might not exist and was therefore not really necessary."

"And now?"

"Now, I feel that I need God – that for me, He is necessary, and therefore He exists."

"Perhaps it is the other way around. You have found that He exists, and that He is necessary for you to be what you want to be."

"Yes, perhaps that's the way it is."

She stood up. "I have to go to my next appointment, Professor."

I gave her a bow. "Thank you, Princess."

"Goodbye, Professor."

When I looked up again, she was gone.

Review Requested:

If you loved this book, would you please provide
a review at Amazon.com?

Lightning Source UK Ltd.
Milton Keynes UK
UKOW01f2011291016

286372UK00001B/29/P